Andrea Bolter has always [...] matters of the heart. In fact [...] girlfriends turn to for advic[...] A city mouse, she lives in Los Angeles with her husband and daughter. She loves travel, rock 'n' roll, sitting in cafés and watching romantic comedies she's already seen a hundred times. Say hi at andreabolter.com.

Hana Sheik falls in love every day, reading her favourite romances and writing her own happily-ever-afters. She's worked in various jobs— but never for very long, because she's always wanted to be a romance author. Now, happily, she gets to live that dream. Born in Somalia, she moved to Ottawa, Canada, at a very young age, and still resides there with her family.

Also by Andrea Bolter

Captivated by Her Parisian Billionaire
Wedding Date with the Billionaire
Adventure with a Secret Prince

Billion-Dollar Matches collection

Caribbean Nights with the Tycoon

Also by Hana Sheik

Second Chance to Wear His Ring
Temptation in Istanbul
Forbidden Kisses with Her Millionaire Boss

Discover more at millsandboon.co.uk.

PRETEND HONEYMOON WITH THE BEST MAN

ANDREA BOLTER

THE BABY SWAP THAT BOUND THEM

HANA SHEIK

MILLS & BOON

All rights reserved including the right of reproduction in whole or in part in any form. This edition is published by arrangement with Harlequin Enterprises ULC.

This is a work of fiction. Names, characters, places, locations and incidents are purely fictional and bear no relationship to any real life individuals, living or dead, or to any actual places, business establishments, locations, events or incidents. Any resemblance is entirely coincidental.

This book is sold subject to the condition that it shall not, by way of trade or otherwise, be lent, resold, hired out or otherwise circulated without the prior consent of the publisher in any form of binding or cover other than that in which it is published and without a similar condition including this condition being imposed on the subsequent purchaser.

® and TM are trademarks owned and used by the trademark owner and/or its licensee. Trademarks marked with ® are registered with the United Kingdom Patent Office and/or the Office for Harmonisation in the Internal Market and in other countries.

First published in Great Britain 2023
by Mills & Boon, an imprint of HarperCollins*Publishers* Ltd,
1 London Bridge Street, London, SE1 9GF

www.harpercollins.co.uk

HarperCollins*Publishers*, Macken House, 39/40 Mayor Street Upper,
Dublin 1, D01 C9W8, Ireland

Pretend Honeymoon with the Best Man © 2023 Andrea Bolter

The Baby Swap That Bound Them © 2023 Muna Sheik

ISBN: 978-0-263-30647-7

06/23

MIX
Paper | Supporting
responsible forestry
FSC™ C007454

This book is produced from independently certified FSC™ paper to ensure responsible forest management.
For more information visit: www.harpercollins.co.uk/green.

Printed and Bound in the UK using 100% Renewable Electricity at CPI Group (UK) Ltd, Croydon, CR0 4YY

PRETEND HONEYMOON WITH THE BEST MAN

ANDREA BOLTER

MILLS & BOON

For STAY

CHAPTER ONE

"THAT FLOWER ARRANGEMENT is blocking Melissa's face a little bit."

"It's fine."

"It's not. Help me move it," urged Laney Sullivan, the maid of honor that best man Ian Luss had just met yesterday.

They were watching the bride and groom prepare for rehearsal dinner photos to be taken next to a mammoth display of orange gladiolas.

"Come on, Ian."

Really not agreeing that they should be the ones to make any adjustment, he hesitated. "Wait for the photographer," he said, reiterating his opinion.

"You're not going to get your nice suit dirty, if that's what you're worried about." That wasn't his concern, although it was a valid one. They weren't in wedding attire, as the big event was tomorrow, but were dressed for the dinner and the photo shoot that had been scheduled. In his bespoke navy suit, he needed to stay preened and tucked into photogenic readiness. However, his true objection to Laney's request was that they were at the Fletcher Club, Boston's most austere and opulent private establishment. The premiere wedding destination in town no doubt had staff assigned for every task under the sun. He and the maid of honor did not need to be touching the flowers.

After a run-through of the ceremony on the twenty-seventh harbor-view floor where Melissa Kraft and Clayton Trescott would marry, they'd adjourned and traveled one floor down to the cocktail lounge, which offered a panoramic vista of downtown. At twilight the sky was a glinting blue, the city beginning to twinkle into evening. An area near the windows had been stanchioned off with velvet ropes for the photo session, where the Custom House Tower, Faneuil Hall and more city landmarks would serve as the backdrop.

Melissa wore a tight dress in emerald-green, the wedding party color, as she hung on Clayton's arm while they chatted with guests. Ian knew Clayton from university days and they'd stayed close over the years. His friend was clearly head-over-heels smitten with his bride, his sparkling eyes telling the tale. Ian had no wife or girlfriend but couldn't imagine being married to a woman like Melissa, who never walked past a mirror without looking in it. Who shortly after getting engaged to Clayton made a point of telling Ian, as well as posting on social media, the carat count of her diamond engagement ring.

Truthfully, Ian didn't know what type of woman he'd marry, other than one who understood the basic tenet that a Luss such as himself, of Luss Global Holdings, considered marriage as a strategic merger, just as his family's acquisitions of land were. Marriage was a big thing to the Lusses, although not in the way most people would think of it. Position and thorough breeding were everything.

Love and passion were not factors. At thirty, he was expected to make one of those fortuitous marriages soon.

To the matter at hand, in addition to not moving the flowers Laney was worried about, another way Ian didn't think he should get involved with things would be in mentioning to the maid of honor that her hair was a mess and needed attention. It had probably been carefully styled earlier, and now, for whatever reason, several golden locks had escaped the twisty roll they'd been sculpted into. The errant strands looked less like they were well thought out to frame her face or give a sexy allure and were, instead, more like she was a kid who had been out playing in the yard wearing her fancy clothes after she was told not to. It was actually kind of cute, like she didn't really care about her appearance. Although it wouldn't do, and hopefully, a female member of the wedding party would take her aside and smooth everything back into place.

A couple of guests milling around took out their phones and began snapping candid shots of the bride and groom, the prephoto photos. Next, would some other group take photos of the group taking photos of the prephotos for the prewedding?

He knew that he'd be going through some wedding traditions himself before long. In fact, his grandfather Hugo had begun speaking with some of his old cronies, the wealthiest men in New England, to check on the marital status of their granddaughters. That's how the Luss family did things, nothing left to chance after a couple of slipups had almost brought their fortunes to the ground. He glanced over to Clayton and his big smile, admiring his happiness. Ian's own wedding surely wouldn't be the best day of his life like it might be for an enchanted groom. That was all right, he told himself. Everyone had their roles in life.

"Just help me for a minute."

Ian heard the words enter his ears while he stared at Clayton, wondering what this moment was like for him. Pure, unadulterated joy and certainty about his life ahead of him? What did expressions of love feel like, Ian wondered, as the groom kissed his bride's cheek? What really was romance? He'd seen examples of it, watched other couples in action, but he didn't know what it did to someone on the inside?

Ian's grandfather, and all the way back to his grandfather's grandfather, were probably right that emotional distractions could be costly, and an amicable business-type partnership was best. Love, but without the intensity of being *in love*. After all, it took steely determination to amass an empire such as theirs. Still, as Ian watched Clayton's hand slide around Melissa's waist, he mused on the trade-off, on what he might miss out on. What he'd always read about in books and seen in movies. Courtship! Heart song! Passion!

"Ian, Earth is calling. Just help me out for a minute," Laney repeated, snapping him out of his trance.

The maid of honor was still adamant that the flowers needed some sort of tweak, so she wrapped her fingers around his forearm and gave him a little tug toward the staging area. A strange shock ran through him at her touch, like an electrical current. It was a wholly unfamiliar sensation, and he eyed her disapprovingly for causing it.

She enlisted him to help her rotate the tall glass cylinder of flowers so that the offending bloom was no longer obscuring her cousin Melissa's face.

"Edge it that way," she gestured.

As they did so, the official photographer arrived with cameras around her neck. All of the amateur cell phone snappers respectfully took a step backward.

"Satisfied?" he asked Laney, regarding the flowers, although the difference was minuscule. The bride's larger-than-life orange-lipped grin faded the colors of everything else around them. Yet again, he watched the radiance that took over Clayton's face at his bride's every move. A lurch gripped Ian's stomach. Still, he wondered what love might feel like, literally how it might inhabit the cells of someone's body. How it could influence thought. Maybe even have an involuntary effect on breathing. All things he had never experienced and probably never would. Well, there was that one talk he had with his late grandmother Rosalie, but that was years ago. His friend's wedding was prompting a lot of questions Ian had never asked before.

"It seemed easier to do it than wait around," Laney said beside him.

"Fine. Whatever," Ian said. The photographer brought her meters to Melissa's face and then to Clayton's. "Are you due in makeup before the shoot?"

Whereas the bride and the bridesmaids who were filing into the room were wearing the world's current supply of makeup, they hadn't seemed to have left any for Laney, because she didn't appear to have a drop of it on. Her skin was pale and untouched, and her lips their given shade of dusty pink. Truth be told, she was absolutely lovely, natural and real, even with that messy hair. Yet he was curious if she'd forgotten that one of her duties as maid of honor was to tolerate what was sure to be a barrage of photos in various settings. She was on the shorter side and was dressed for tonight's festivities in a slinky silver dress that showed off major curves he attempted not to pay too much attention to.

"No, I don't wear makeup," Laney answered defiantly, as if she'd been accused of something. "I've tried it, and it's so itchy it makes my skin crawl."

She looked down to her fingernails and rubbed them as if she was making sure they were clean. She didn't have nail polish on either, another convention he was used to seeing on women wearing dressy clothes. Clayton had told him that Laney was moving back to Boston after a failed attempt at running a café in Pittsfield, in the scenic Berkshires region of Western Massachusetts. She surely had the look of someone who spent more time doing something with her hands than she did with them in a manicurist's shop. Clayton had also mentioned something about an ex.

In any case, based on her sharp response he might have insulted her in asking about the lack of makeup. "Forgive me," he said, bringing his palm flat to his chest, "it's just that… I think if you check yourself in the mirror, you'll find that your hair is…a little out of sorts."

She looked him straight in the eyes as her cheeks puffed out as round as they could go, and she exhaled in a slow, steady stream until they deflated. "Thanks for the tip," she said, then pivoted and walked away.

"I was only trying to be helpful," he called after her.

"We're best man and maid of honor. Isn't it our job to try to make everything flawless?"

Argh! Saying that she was anything other than flawless was another wrong statement. He was strangely flustered around her, whereas generally, he was in steely control. Not that his words had any effect because Laney and her curves continued sashaying away from him, out of the bar area completely and blasting through the double doors that led to the wedding party's dressing rooms. His eyes stayed on her until a staff member wheeling a cart obstructed his view.

"Okay, fine." Laney surrendered to the makeup artist's third plea to allow a little lip gloss for the photos. She had not been the first choice for maid of honor, and it showed. As the bride's cousin, she was to be a bridesmaid until Melissa's best friend pulled out at the last minute because of a difficult pregnancy. Laney and Melissa could hardly be more unalike and didn't see a lot of each other as children. Laney grew up with a single mom on the wrong side of Boston, whereas Melissa hailed from the wealthy suburb of Wellesley. Laney's mother was never close with her brother, the father of the bride.

"Thank you for filling in," Melissa said as Laney allowed the makeup artist to glob the goop onto her lips.

Laney figured she'd only need to leave it on for the shoot, then they'd go right to dinner, and it would be perfectly legitimate for her to wipe it off. Likewise tomorrow, glop for the ceremony and more photos, slime wiped off for cocktails and hors d'oeuvres. She could manage this.

"You're welcome," said Laney.

The makeup artist finally moved on, and the two returned from the dressing room to the cocktail lounge.

"You were saying on the phone that you've had a hard time of it lately?" the bride asked.

"Yeah, it turned out I was unlucky in both love and business."

This modern fairy-tale wedding of lipstick and party salons high in the sky was what Laney thought she was heading toward when she met Enrique Sanz. He'd come into the Cambridge café near Harvard University where she'd been working and changed her life. Handsome and cultured, he was in Boston after just finishing a master's degree in business. She thought they were in love. He even consented to buying the café in Pittsfield that they ran together. Although he was always reminding her that she was "not the type he could have on his arm forever." Apparently, owning a café was okay for a short time, but it wasn't a lofty enough goal for a man whose family supplied half of Spain with lumber.

"I hope things get better for you," Melissa muttered sympathetically. "Clayton says I could sell my shop, but I'm going to keep it, at least for now."

"Right."

In addition to being a glamazonian piece of eye candy and marrying a high-ranking bank executive, Melissa had a handbag shop in Beacon Hill that attracted the Boston elite. "Of course, we're hoping to get preggers as soon as possible!"

"I wish you the best."

"Hey, you know, there are some really great single men

coming this weekend. Don't people say weddings are a great place to meet?"

Sure, as if any man in Melissa's social circle would be interested in her. A wave of irritation swept over Laney as she recalled her own misfortune. The café attempt was a disaster and Enrique broke her heart. Having wedding duties just as she'd returned to town wasn't ideal. However, it was time to put all of that aside and get through this weekend. Then she could start over. That first task might be easier without Ian Luss, the best man, who was now striding toward her. She'd only met him enough to say hello yesterday, but an hour or so ago, when she asked him for help moving the flowers, he seemed lost in space, and she could hardly get his attention.

Then he'd rubbed her the wrong way with telling her that she needed to fix her hair, just like some criticism Enrique might have had. As he approached, he looked straight to her lips, which were now no doubt so shiny he could see himself in their reflection. He was probably gloating about having asked her if she was due in the makeup chair and her defensively proclaiming that she didn't paint her face. Although he might be annoying, she had to admit that he was good-looking, with his big brown eyes and black hair that almost reached his shoulders. He stood tall in his finely tailored suit that fit slim along his broad shoulders and long legs. Not that she found him *attractive* attractive. She was just admiring him as one does a piece of art, for example. Attraction to men could only lead to more trouble. She needed a major life do-over and that would start with steering clear of the male species.

"All right, wedding party, let's gather," the photographer called out. "We'll start with the bride and groom, best man and maid of honor."

"That's us," Melissa bubbled as she left Laney's side to take Clayton's hand.

Ian gestured for Laney to go ahead of him toward the photo spot, which was now set with reflectors to produce the best possible lighting. The photographer had some fun poses, such as one where Clayton held out a single orange rose to Melissa as they stood above a seated maid of honor and best man, Ian gifting Laney a rose as well. Laney's heart thumped a beat at Ian's eyes locking onto hers during the motion, making it an unexpected exchange between them. The wedding party was then brought into the shots, followed by various configurations of family holding flowers of their own.

Afterward, the staging area was quickly dismantled, and waiters dressed in black with gold aprons passed Bellinis from silver trays. Laney made sure to grab a napkin with hers, as her lip goo time was officially over, and she happily wiped it off. Ian, talking to a couple of the groomsmen just a few feet away, caught the move, and the tip of his mouth curled up. She really wasn't sure whether he was cute or aggravating, although it really didn't matter, because she was off men. Plus, she'd never see him again after this wedding. Or until Melissa and Clayton's first baby had a birthday party, or something like that.

Appetizer stations were set out. At the mozzarella sampling bar, Laney was trying a burrata with roasted pistachio when Ian came up beside her. "Are you giving a speech?"

She finished chewing before answering, "I don't know if I'd call it a speech, but they asked me to say a few words tonight and leave the traditional speech to you tomorrow."

He grabbed his throat like he was being choked. "The pressure. The pressure."

"Just say something romantic. That's what brides like," Laney said.

He took in her words as if he'd never heard anything like them before.

He helped himself to a piece of the *fior di latte* cheese on a square of focaccia. "So, what, you don't want to paint your nails and gussy up, but you still want the princess tiara and the happily-ever-after thing? You'll make it tough for a guy to figure out, or are you already spoken for?"

"No one is speaking for me." She grabbed a hunk of that milky *fior* with her fingers and popped it in her mouth.

Ian reached over and flicked a speck of cheese from the front of her dress where it had landed.

She rolled her eyes. "Again? First it was my hair. Then my lack of makeup. Now you're cleaning food off me?"

"You're welcome."

"I'm sure a crumb has never dared touch a piece of your fine woolens, but could you just keep your business to yourself, and I'll do the same with mine?"

"I was only trying to help."

"Don't."

He lifted his palms up in surrender and walked away.

Laney fisted her hands in frustration. She knew he only meant well, but the criticism was hard for her to take. She'd had enough to last a lifetime. Of course, Ian and his comments didn't mean anything to her. He didn't have the ability to wound her as Enrique had with his constant disapproval. Whom she should have known from the beginning wasn't a gentleman, but she was fooled. He'd whispered things into her ear that made her think they were truly together. That he'd take her to live in Madrid with him. It was all so exciting. Until he started picking on her. Where she went, how she looked, what she wore. How drab it was that all she wanted was her own café. In retrospect, she didn't know what she saw in him, except that his European glamour was nothing like the small-minded sons born of the rough streets in Dorchester.

When it was speech time, Laney stood holding a mic in front of the guests seated for the rehearsal dinner. "I know people like to share a famous quote about marriage," she said, continuing her toast. A plate clinked at one table, then another as the waitstaff delivered the salads. Voices here and there were in conversation. She lifted her Bellini. "To Melissa and Clayton. Writer H. L. Mencken said, 'Love is the triumph of imagination over intelligence.'"

What she'd meant as a funny bit of cynicism flopped royally. The room fell silent. The bride's big tangerine smile drooped like a sad clown. Laney looked to Ian at her table. He winced at her failure.

This is going to be a long weekend, Ian thought to himself as he finished the pasta flight that had been set in front of him and each guest at the rehearsal dinner. A wooden board with four carved out grooves had contained corn spaghetti carbonara, pesto potato gnocchi, rigatoni with Bolognese and fusilli with raw tomatoes and basil. He'd made short work of the presentation, as he was hungry, and concentration on his food meant less time blathering about nothing with the groomsman and his wife who sat to his right. They were the only ones to talk to because to his left, Clayton was continuously occupied with well-wishers who approached in an endless parade.

The groomsman and his wife beside Ian were from Albany, New York. She pulled out her phone to show Ian their three children, who hadn't come along to the wedding because they were at summer camp. The woman elaborated excitedly on every activity the kids would be involved in while there, from learning computer coding to performing in musical theater. Ian feigned interest.

Politely excusing himself from the table, he wandered from the dining salon back into the cocktail lounge. It wasn't that kids and summer camp were of no matter. After all, Ian planned on having his own offspring and hoped he'd take pride in their accomplishments. It was only that with the Luss methods for maintaining their fortune, which had already been mapped out for the next century, marriage and family were, first and foremost, matters of practicality and logic. Indeed, that's how his parents treated him and his sister, as coworkers, partners and friends. With regard but without warmth. So he wasn't sure how much exuberance there would be over cell phone photos of science experiments.

Ian never saw his parents engage in the gestures of romance that he noticed with other people and in the arts. He worried that having the sense there was a larger emotional life out there, one he couldn't do without, would prevent him from being able to fit into the box his family was saving for him. He strode to the bar and asked the bartender for a maple whiskey rocks. He took a tight sip and glanced around the mostly empty lounge, as the majority of rehearsal dinner guests were in the main room about to enjoy dessert.

"Was that the worst quote in the world?" Laney headed toward him, her satiny dress giving a little swish with every step. Once again, Ian tried not to get caught eyeing her from top to bottom. She surely filled that dress out nicely with her ample bosom and hips. He looked to her pretty face. "I thought it was going to get a laugh, but I think I bombed."

"You did." He had to chuckle. He didn't want to offend her once more, something he seemed to have a knack for, but he wasn't going to lie. Fortunately, she snickered a little bit herself. "Can I get you a drink?"

"What are you having?"

"Maple whiskey on the rocks."

"I'll have the same."

Ian gestured to the bartender.

"Thanks."

Drink delivered, they both gazed out at the skyline.

"Are you from Boston?"

"Dorchester, born and raised."

"Dorchester?"

"Don't sound so shocked. Melissa and I are related, but we didn't have the same kind of childhood."

"What kind of childhood was that?" So, Laney was a scrapper. Who had survived living in one of the most crime-infested parts of Boston, and it didn't seem to have swallowed her up.

"It was just me and my mom pooling our resources. Not these kinds of resources," she gestured around the posh Fletcher Club.

"Is your mom here?"

"No, she's living in Arizona now. She recently had an operation and couldn't make the journey."

"What about your dad?"

Laney took a sip of her drink. "I never knew him. They weren't really together. He took off once she got pregnant."

Ian gulped at that lack of duty. That was why he'd never do anything to defy his family and would fit whatever mold he had to. The Lusses were unflinchingly loyal. For better or for worse, they took care of each other, ran as a pack. Didn't impregnate women they weren't married to. "Clayton told me you'd left Boston for a while."

"I was in the Berkshires for two years. I only returned this week. I'm still adjusting back to city life."

"Where were you?"

"Pittsfield."

"What were you doing there?"

"Operating a café."

"Hmm." He sipped his drink. "How specific."

"Specific? You mean how small-time and limited."

Uh-oh. Had he replied wrong again? He'd only been trying to make chitchat. As people did when they were getting to know each other. "That's not what I meant."

"What did you mean, then?" She cast her eyes down to her drink and swirled the amber liquid in the glass.

"You were running a café. I'm sure the duties were very clear." He shrugged. "Whereas I have no idea what I actually do all day."

Her eyes shot up to meet his. "How do you figure that?"

"I work with my family. We consider purchases."

"Of what?"

"Land."

"That you buy and build on?"

"No. We buy it and hold it. Sometimes we sell it."

"Land?"

"Yes. Mountain ranges and private deserts, things like that."

"How many 'things like that' does your family own?"

"About three hundred worldwide."

"Hmm. That sounds like you're doing *a lot* of things in a day. What's your part?"

"I consult with appraisers."

"Weren't you named in some list of the city's most eligible bachelors?"

"Embarrassing."

"Mountain ranges," she repeated.

He took another pull on his whiskey. One of the city's eligible bachelors implied that he was some kind of prey. To be snatched up. As much as he nodded his head in acquiesce when his grandfather told him it was time to let him choose a bride for him, in reality, Ian didn't want him to. Sure, he might hit it off with one of the highbrow women chosen for her family's name and history. It was possible that would be the woman he was destined to be with. Although he doubted it.

He knew that marriage could be more than what his family outlined. That with the right person, there could be the state of being in love. And that could be what made life truly worthwhile. A union built when two minds, two hearts and two souls melded together and moved through the world as one. Worse still, he sometimes thought that without that, he might never be completely fulfilled and would die empty. He even had the notion that the someone he was meant to be with really was actually out there for him.

Nonsense. He tried to admonish himself. Everyone had their lot, and his was to continue family traditions that hundreds of Luss employees were counting on. Why fix something that wasn't broken? The Luss family didn't have time for romance. That could be left to others. And the more he let himself dwell on silly fantasies, such as one true love, the harder it was going to be to step into the role expected of him.

"Weddings bring up strange thoughts, don't they?" he asked aloud.

"That's for sure."

"So, why aren't you still running that café?"

"It burned down."

He let out a throat-clearing cough. "It what?"

"An electrical line toppled over and started a fire. By time it was extinguished, the damage was beyond repair."

"Oh, gosh. Was anyone hurt?"

"Thankfully, no. But the insurance wasn't enough to rebuild."

"And it left you out of a job. That's why you're back in Boston."

"Yes, and I was in partnership with someone, and that didn't work out, either."

"Oh, sorry to hear that. What are you planning to do now?"

"It's been a heck of a couple of years. I need to regroup. Restart."

"So, you'll get another job?" He sensed she wasn't telling him everything that was going on with her. That she was hurting. Not that it was any of his concern. "What is it that you really want?"

"I've always wanted my own café, so I had that for a minute. I'll have to start from the bottom again and build back up."

"I'm sure there are lots of stories of the humble barista who rises to the top of the café world."

"The humble barista?"

"I've offended you yet again." He shook his head. "I don't talk to many people outside of work. I'm terrible at small talk." Even if he was to marry solely for the family merger, he was going to have to learn to be pleasant company. Something he wasn't doing very well at with Laney so far.

"Oh, right. You have nothing to talk about with the humble barista."

She started to walk away. Without a thought, his hand reached for her arm. Her skin was so silky it startled him. "Laney, don't go. I'd like to hear about owning a café."

She shook off his hold. "It's late. See you tomorrow."

CHAPTER TWO

"BY THE POWERS vested in me by the state of Massachusetts, I now pronounce you husband and wife. You may kiss the bride."

As the officiant concluded the ceremony, Laney stood beside Melissa, holding her bouquet. Like they had rehearsed, Laney handed her own bouquet to the bridesmaid on her right, thereby freeing her hands to hold the bride's formidable array of both pale and vivid orange blooms. As Ian had fulfilled his role of taking care of the wedding rings, the maid of honor and best man executed their duties. They both watched, Ian from his side and Laney from hers, as Clayton took his wife in his arms and kissed her to the cheers of the two hundred in attendance.

The string quartet began the wedding recessional, and Melissa and Clayton turned to glide past the guests down the aisle. It struck Laney how profound the past twenty minutes had been. Melissa and Clayton had walked to the altar single and returned as a married couple, their lives forever changed and defined by what had happened there. With family and friends to witness the ceremony and help launch them forward. What was before was nevermore. They strode forward as one.

It was what Laney had thought she was going to have.

What her mother never had but Laney wanted. And was expecting. What she had begun to plan for in her mind. A future where Enrique was solid and committed to her. Even though she'd been fooling herself, and the signs were there all along. Then, indeed, everything was taken from her. She felt the loss down into her bones.

Laney swallowed hard. This was not the time for self-pity. It was time to move her feet toward the head of the aisle, where she met up with the best man. She hoped they could get through the evening without grating on each other's nerves like they had yesterday. She liked how he looked born to wear his well-tailored tux, even with hair a little longer than was conventional. At last night's rehearsal and dinner, he didn't seem to have a date with him. So she assumed he was alone tonight as well. Did he have a girlfriend, though? Or a boyfriend? Someone stashed away in another city who didn't come to the wedding with him for whatever reason? She wasn't sure, but instinct told her no.

Linking her arm into his, her hand settled on the warmth of his sturdy muscle. He was so...formidable. Substantial. The kind of man a person could wade through the waters with. Her eyes blinked a couple of times as they took their first steps together while she tried not to feel defeated. Things had not gone her way.

"Ceremony went well," Ian whispered into her ear, which prickled from the sensation of his breath. "What did you think of the poem Clayton recited?"

"It rhymed. Need I say more?" She bit her lip to squelch a laugh as the photographer snapped continuously during their march. "The flower girl was adorable."

"She was. Especially when she started picking up all the petals after she'd scattered them."

"A hard worker."

Like her. Laney would make it through this wedding weekend, get a job, and move off her friend Shanice's couch. It wasn't Madrid, where she'd concocted all sorts of scenarios about some perfect life she was going to have there. Boston wasn't the worst place to begin again. Although, the truth was that she was tired. She'd barely caught her breath dealing with the café burning down, then Enrique leaving her a week later. She wished she could get a break. Just for a little while. To rest, relax and plan. Although nothing like that was in her current budget, which was about zero, save for her old roommate Shanice's generosity.

At the end of the aisle, Laney let go of her link to the crook of Ian's arm. And missed the feel of it instantly. *Huh.*

"Best man and maid of honor, please hurry to the mezzanine for first toasts," an attendant called to them.

"Let's go." She gave him a tug and maneuvered them quickly through the crowded area where the guests were assembling. The wedding manager waved them into a side entrance, where they climbed a half flight of stairs onto a raised glass platform that jutted out above the cocktail lounge like a stage in the sky so that all the guests could see them. This was where Melissa and Clayton would make their first appearance.

"Now?" Ian asked, verifying with the manager who handed him a microphone. Melissa had wanted the best man's speech to be before dinner. Laney didn't really have anything to do, but she stood beside him with two flutes of champagne, urging him to take one with his free hand.

He hit all the proper notes. Thanking the guests who came from near and far. Saying how lovely and sweet Melissa was. Congratulating his old friend Clayton on finding his mate. Wishing them a long and happy life together. Whereas Laney had bombed last night with her quote that fell flat, Ian's toast was tasteful and reserved and, well, kind of dull. She'd wished he'd gone out on more of a limb. He ended with a quote by Mignon McLaughlin: "A successful marriage requires falling in love many times, always with the same person."

Laney swallowed hard at that. That was a much more romantic closer than she was expecting from him. Falling in love over and over again. Yes, that did indeed sound like a real marriage. Something Enrique wasn't capable of, or not with her anyway.

Then it was time for the *big wow*. The overheads in the room dimmed so that the fairy lights strung everywhere created a magical glow. Laney and Ian stepped down from the elevated platform, her wobbly on her high heels and grabbing his reliable arm for balance. A spotlight was poised, waiting for the stars of the evening. A voice boomed, "Without further ado, I introduce to you for the first time as husband and wife, Mr. and Mrs. Clayton Trescott."

Melissa and Clayton appeared from within the darkened area and stepped onto the platform and into the spotlight to cheers and applause. Melissa had changed into a mermaid-style gown that glistened like a mirror ball, and her face looked like it was going to crack open from smiling so wide.

Laney and Ian watched from the sideline. She tugged the side of her emerald-green maid of honor gown made of a silk shantung, which was actually scratchy and uncomfortable. They still had a long evening ahead of them.

Laney coached herself again. *Just make it through the weekend.*

The band's horn section jammed as the wedding party bounded through the doors into the reception hall in a gaggle just as the photographer had instructed them to. Then, like a blooming flower, the petals that made up the groomsmen and the bridesmaids opened away from the center. Next, the maid of honor and best man stepped away to reveal the bride and groom who, were met by guests clanging knives against water glasses. In response, they kissed. Melissa had changed into another wedding gown, a custom Ian didn't quite understand yet had witnessed at a few of the upscale weddings he'd been to lately.

He supposed it was simply that women loved to dress up, so why have one wedding dress when you could have six? Yes, six, as the bride at a wedding he'd been to a few months ago had worn. He hoped their marriage was going to last long enough to pay the bill on that wardrobe. Melissa's second dress was a tight-fitting number with a weird extra bottom part that swished like a fish's fin.

Once he and Laney circled the happy couple with the choreography that seemed to him like a square dance's do-si-do and he reunited with Laney, he asked her, "What is a dress that style called?"

They smiled for the photographer, now having mastered bringing their cheeks close to each other for the cute close-up. Ian was determined not to give heed to the delightful feeling of Laney's face near his or the empty sensation every time she pulled it away.

"Mermaid," she answered.

Aha! He was right in his marine reference.

"Do you like it?"

"No. The way it comes in tight over her...behind...and then flares out the size of a lace tablecloth."

A waiter presented a tray of purplish cocktails in stemmed tulip glasses. "This is the bride and groom's signature cocktail, the Mel-Clay. Lemon vodka, blueberry cordial and ginger ale."

They each took a purple potion from the waiter's tray. Bespoke cocktails were another part of the careful attention that went into grand weddings these days. Because his friends were around thirty like him, marrying age, Ian had attended a lot of weddings lately. If the wife he'd take someday wanted to look like a strange creature from the sea, what would he care?

"Have you ever been married?" Laney asked.

"Heavens, no," said Ian. "If I had, I'd still be. One and done. You?"

"Never. Like I was telling you, I co-owned that café with Mr. Almost. When it burned down, so did we."

"Why? The disappointment?"

"Something like that. He blamed me for the fire."

"How so?"

"You name it. Accusing me of not having it inspected thoroughly enough before he bought it. That I didn't have the professional know-how or education to run the operation. That I wasn't on top of the upkeep. In reality, he was ready to break up with me, so he used it as an excuse."

"What a jerk."

Between that and a father that skipped out, she hadn't had much of an example of what a decent man was.

"Do you picture having a big wedding?" Laney asked, moving on from the subject.

"I suppose. My family will want it to be as much a PR event as anything else. It's time for my grandfather to retire, but not until he sees me settled and ready to breed the next in succession for Luss Global Holdings."

"Sounds dreamy." She smirked.

"Anything but. That's kind of the point. The Luss family doesn't spend time or resources on emotions." Why did that sound so awful coming out of his mouth? It was true, but it was so cold-blooded. He'd had limited dealings with women thus far, his imagination far more active than he was. The young women who he'd dated during his Oxford years made it their business to find out about his family's wealth and tried to snare him. Their efforts were so insincere they fell into their own traps, making sure he was wary and distrustful of them. His grandfather's plan was at least safer, two families going into partnership for mutual benefit with both parties vetted.

So far, even dating casually, he'd never gotten close to a woman, so he hadn't had to worry about feelings being ignited. He couldn't take any chances at not keeping love at bay and then ruining everything generations of his family had worked so hard for. His great-great-uncle Phillip had almost destroyed the company in its formative years because of a woman. And when Ian was a child, his father's brother Harley had lost them tens of millions of dollars by acting on impulse. Ian's grandfather would see to it that nothing like that ever happened again.

"Did you just say your family doesn't waste resources on emotions?"

"Right. Marriages are trade alliances."

The music quieted and the band leader took the mic. "Ladies and gentlemen, let's welcome the bride and groom for their first dance."

As Ian watched the mermaid and her fisherman take to the center of the dance floor, he felt that little lurch in his stomach as he had earlier. Because it wasn't as cut and dry as he'd just explained to Laney. In his secret heart of hearts, he'd always wanted to experience a little bit of emotional love, just to know what it felt like. To let himself be seduced into a whirlwind romance with a woman, to know that. Even once. Sure, there'd be a risk that it could be like getting lost and not being able to find the way home. Yet, he was a level-headed grown man. He could see his way back from the journey. He was not going to fall into any snares and let his grandfather or the Luss Global employees down. Of course, he had no idea how he'd ever go about something like that. Women had their own ideas and would have no interest in playing his game. Therefore, he smiled wistfully at the man and the fish, and that was that.

"What, you're an anti-romantic?"

He looked around the reception hall and wondered, if maybe for the first time, what conceptions each and every person here had about love. Old and young, rich and poor, single, married, widowed or divorced. "Anti-romantic? I guess you could say that."

That was his official position and he was sticking to it, even if it wasn't what he really harbored inside. And Laney's sable eyes, the sparkling lights, the passionate purple cocktail and the bride's fish fin of a dress were making him question everything even more.

He watched Clayton again. Why was the expression on his face so difficult for Ian? He'd known his friend's face for a long time. Yet he looked changed tonight. Finished. Anchored. It rocked Ian to the core.

The band leader said, "May we be joined on the dance floor by the maid of honor and the best man?"

"By the way, I don't know how to dance." Laney put her drink down at a side table, and Ian followed.

"I don't know how to do anything elaborate. It's just that one-two-three, one-two-three bit."

"That you learned at cotillion?"

"Yup. From when I was twelve." More formalities from his youth. Step-two-three, with snobby rich girls, step-two-three. No sex or soul in it, even though his body told him that dancing could have been both a sensual and profound act.

"Heaven help you."

"What I want is right there." The band leader began to sing a popular love song. "We were meant as a pair."

For some unexplainable reason, Ian felt giddy as he and Laney took to the dance floor beside Melissa and Clayton, the eyes of all of the guests on them. Was there something so unusual about Laney that it threw his usual steady equilibrium off? Because when he put his arm at her waist, he felt that something he suspected was out there. Not nothing but something. A serious something.

"Ready?" he asked once they were in position. "And one, two, three, one…"

He continued counting, hoping Laney would find the beat and they could sync into a rhythm.

"I would walk without fear," the band leader crooned, "every moment we share."

"Ouch," he couldn't help but snap his foot back as she stepped hard on his toes.

"Sorry, yeah, yeah." She tried to follow his movements. It wasn't going well. "Stop pulling on me!"

"I'm not pulling on you. It's called leading. You're supposed to follow me."

"How am I supposed to know what you're doing so I can follow? I can't see your feet."

"You're supposed to move with me."

"Where?"

"Move with my movements. Ow."

Another stab to the top of his foot. He knew Laney didn't mean to be so bad at this, but he couldn't wait for it to be over. This wasn't how it went in the movies.

As she looked at herself in the Ladies Room mirror, Laney was coming unglued. The armpits of her dress had stretched out and were showing under-boob and sweat stains. The circles under her eyes were dark. Unglued mentally and emotionally, too. Everything about this wedding was harder than she had anticipated it was going to be. Being back in Boston. Knowing that the café in Pittsfield was gone. Enrique out of her life, but not without leaving a figurative scar on her psyche. Here in spirit to remind her that fairy tale weddings weren't for her.

Ian wasn't helping matters any. What a disaster dancing, or attempting to dance, with him had been. She didn't know how to dance with a partner and hadn't thought to learn, hadn't considered that would be one of her last-minute maid of honor responsibilities. Instead, she stumbled all over his feet, feeling like a klutz. Plus, he'd spoken of meeting the right sort of woman to marry and all of that, driving it home for the thousandth time that Laney would be no one at this party's consideration. Ian was just like Enrique. Except he wasn't. She couldn't exactly put her finger on it yet, but there was something inside his eyes. A longing that was lingering under the surface, something caught and unable to make itself known yet. It was none of her concern, even though she kept thinking about it. That secret within him haunted her.

"Here. I think our drinks disappeared while we were dancing," Ian said, standing on the sidelines of the reception hall when Laney returned. He handed her a fresh purple Mel-Clay, the silly unimaginative cocktail name for the bride and groom's brew.

As Laney accepted the drink from him, their fingers brushed along the glass's stem during the handoff. An unexpected current sizzled up her finger. She took a grateful sip, thirsty from their dancing fiasco. "If we could call what we did dancing. I'm sorry I stepped on your foot that once."

"It was four times, but who's counting? I'm beginning to get some feeling back in my feet now." They stood watching older people boogie to an upbeat tune. "I take it you haven't done much dancing with a partner?"

"Yeah, that would be none."

"Crackled cauliflower with a sriracha glaze?" A server thrust her tray at them.

"Oh, yes," Laney said while grabbing a crunchy-looking morsel speared on a pick. "I don't know what 'crackled' means, but I'm starving."

Ian picked a spear also. "Me too."

"Yummy. The sauce is spicy, but it's cut with the sweetness in the glaze."

Another server approached. "Melon cubes wrapped in prosciutto?"

"You bet." Ian answered for them both as he grabbed two and two napkins, which were the same emerald green as Laney's dress and Ian's tie and cummerbund.

The corner of the napkin was decorated with a heart that had *M&C* inside of it. Laney wondered what hors d'oeuvres she might have served at the L&E wedding that was never to happen.

"Nice," she said, voting on her bite. "A little balsamic on the melon to contrast the flavors."

"This isn't the city's most renowned wedding venue for no reason."

"Would you like to get married in a swanky place like this? Or are you more the orchard and barn type? Or the tropical island destination wedding?"

Ian laughed. "I haven't got the slightest idea. I don't even know who I'm marrying. She can choose what she wants, no matter to me."

Right after he said that, his eyes clicked to Clayton,

who was dancing with Melissa. Laney wondered what Ian was thinking. That all this wedding folderol was nonsense?

"Melissa and Clayton are going to Bermuda tomorrow for their honeymoon. But just the two of them, no wedding party on the beach thing."

The bandleader announced, "Ladies and gentlemen, please return to the tables for dinner."

"We have to be host-y and make sure Melissa and Clayton have everything they need."

Laney rushed to help Melissa and that extra piece of dress, as Ian called it, get properly seated at the sweetheart table, which was placed in the center of the room so that all of the guests could see the bride and groom while they ate, an option Laney thought was a horrible fate. Guaranteeing that if a piece of bread went awkwardly into her mouth, the entire room would see it. But Melissa and Clayton chose to sit on an old-timey orange settee, surrounded by floral displays as if they were in the center of a Victorian garden.

After stepping back once the bride and groom were situated, she said to Ian, "It's sweet. Kind of."

"Clayton told me they were adding some special foods to their menu to make things extra unique. A private label wine. Some kind of elite oysters that come from a small-scale farm. They're supposed to be the finest in the world and cost something like a hundred dollars each."

"I hope they're worth it." They took places next to each other at the wedding party's table. With great formality, he pulled the chair out for her to sit.

She looked at him quizzically.

"What?" he asked.

"Nothing."

"Is there something wrong with pulling a chair out for a lady?"

"It's just so… I'm not used to it."

"Your ex didn't pull a chair out for you?"

"I'm surprised he didn't make me pull his out for him."

Ian frowned. "It sounds like you're better off without him." He made a big gesture of sweeping his hand across the chair. "Mademoiselle."

She giggled.

They ate beef tenderloin with chimichurri sauce and red new potatoes while Laney watched Melissa and Clayton feed each other the hundred-dollar oysters. Laney tried not to be sad. It was a challenge. She'd loved Enrique, or at least loved the idea of him. Why wouldn't she have wanted to move to Madrid with an exciting man and open a café there? They might have had a sweet life, might have had children.

She really didn't want to think about Enrique anymore tonight. So she asked Ian some trivial questions. Favorite food, things about Boston and so on. His mind seemed a million miles away, and he barely answered her questions out of the side of his mouth. She'd be glad when she was done being coupled off with him. He was too hard to read. She spent the rest of the meal listening to the bridesmaid seated on her other side blather about her own recent breakup. Laney couldn't wait to get out of her dress, into a pair of jeans and on with her life.

By the time the grapefruit sorbet course arrived, she needed to get some fresh air, so excused herself and made her way through the cocktail lounge to the outdoor terrace. Slipping through the doors, she took a breath of the warm evening air. She sighed at the night-lights, contemplating what was to be her fate. Would she end up alone, like her mother? Then, surely, being a single parent would be her only option for motherhood. With maybe an accidental pregnancy, or adoption or by using a sperm donor. Maybe that would be okay, like it was for her and her mom. *Relax*, she told herself. Everything didn't have to be figured out this weekend. She'd fall back into her place in the city.

On her fifth deep breath, she heard the terrace door open behind her.

It was Ian. "Oh, you're here, too," he said.

She shook her head. There was no getting away from him.

CHAPTER THREE

"Hi."

One of the bridesmaids sidled up to Ian at the bar, where he was having a quiet cordial. Carolyn, Caroline, Carolina... What was her name?

"Hi," he managed to say.

"Do you live in Boston, Ian?"

"Yes. In Back Bay."

"Oh, that's nice." Back Bay was one of the city's most expensive and desirable neighborhoods, with its European flair and great shopping and restaurants. "I'm thinking of moving to town. I'm in West Roxbury with my parents."

"What would be prompting the move?" he asked to continue the conversation. That's what people did, right? Asked questions. Looked for connection points. He needed to start practicing so that he could discern if he liked one woman more than the other. In order for him to choose one, or that they could choose each other and settle down into coupledom. That sounded so bloodless he wanted to scream, but it was his truth. No point fighting it.

The bridesmaid used her pinkie finger to touch one corner of her mouth and then the other. Presumably, she was concerned about her lipstick. "I read you were named one of the city's most eligible bachelors." Based on his family's prominence. "Are you really single, Ian, or are you secretly with someone?" Hmm, that was straightforward. There was certainly nothing immediately apparent that was wrong with Carolyn/Caroline/Carolina. Other than that it felt like pulling teeth to prolong the chitchat. He knew he wasn't out for fireworks, but he at least wanted easy companionship, someone he could be authentic with. That wasn't too outlandish to hope for, was it?

He thought about Laney and a smile came to his face. She was so honest and forthcoming. The way her hair was an utter disaster at the photo shoot before the rehearsal dinner. The way she defiantly didn't want to wear makeup even with the stylist chasing after her. There was something funny and charming about that. Although an impeccable appearance would be required for whoever someone of Ian's standing married. The Luss women managed brains and beauty. His mother was a tall, cool blonde who never stepped out of the house unless she was flawless from head to toe.

"You guessed it. I actually am spoken for," he lied. There was no reason to hurt her feelings, especially after she'd made herself vulnerable. "She is…out of town this weekend."

Carolyn/Caroline/Carolina was a stunning woman, polished and primped. She didn't smack of desperation, just practicality, asking if he was truly single. Then he thought of Laney again, bombing in her wedding speech. She kept popping into his mind. Where was she now? After they'd accidentally both tried unsuccessfully to find solitude on the terrace, he'd come back inside. Had she?

He supposed it was about time to cut the cake, and he'd probably be expected to pose for yet more photos. "I think we're due back inside."

"I'll be there in a minute," Carolyn/Caroline/Carolina said. She'd noticed a couple of men leaning on the far side of the bar sipping drinks, so she sauntered over.

Inside the reception hall, the party was still in full swing. Half the guests were on the dance floor, and others huddled at the tables attempting to talk over the volume of the music. Melissa and Clayton stood in the center of it all receiving well wishes, their smiles maybe a little strained as the event wore on.

He moved farther into the room and watched an older lady dancing with a teenage boy who looked miserable. Every time he stepped away, the elderly lady yanked him back. When they swung apart again, Ian spotted Laney. She was dancing with a short dark-haired man. Ian had no idea who he was. They weren't touching, however they did seem to be looking into each other's eyes. He couldn't think of a reason to, but he felt jealous. Ian and Laney meant nothing to each other. He had no plans to see her after the wedding. They hadn't even established a cordial best man and maid of honor rapport; it had been prickly. Yet he wanted that man away from Laney—immediately. Which was crazy.

As if possessed by a spirit outside of himself, he moved into the thick of the dance floor to find them. He shimmied his shoulders a little bit as if he were into the groove.

"May I cut in?" he asked when he got close enough.

That was how it was done, wasn't it? It was an accepted

social convention to ask her to excuse herself from dancing with the man and switch to dancing with him.

Maybe it should have been, except that Laney furrowed her brows and said, "Uh, no. I'm dancing with... what was your name?"

"Quincy," the man answered, squirming left and right in his too-tight pants.

"Quincy," Laney repeated to Ian as if he hadn't just heard it.

It was ridiculous that any of this bothered him. Why did he want to swoop Laney into his arms and waltz with her like a prince at a ball? They'd already proven they couldn't dance like that together. Plus, that was the lovey-dovey stuff he was supposedly having no part of. Jealousy and sweeping a woman into his embrace! She'd declined his request to whisk her away, so he had to respect that. Which meant he stood on the dance floor alone, not knowing what to do with himself.

He caught sight of the flower girl, probably all of six-years-old in her matching emerald-green dress. He got her attention and followed the butterfly wing arms she was swirling around with. Ian enjoyed the pure impulsiveness and had a genuinely carefree few minutes sharing a giggle with the little girl but he did notice Laney studying him from the corner of her eye.

It was the wee hours before the last of the guests left. Some of the relatives who had traveled great distances were departing in the morning, so Melissa and Clayton pressed on, devoting time to each of them.

"Help me get the gifts onto these carts, and we'll bring

them to the bridal suite for the night," Laney said, still ready to pitch in.

Too tired to argue that the wedding manager could call in some staff to do the task, Ian set to it. They stacked the gifts on the cart, larger ones on the bottom. Many were wrapped by the upscale store where Melissa and Clayton had done their registry, so he knew he was attending to thousands upon thousands of dollars' worth of merchandise.

"Home and kitchen goods, of course," Ian said. "That's what couples are given as gifts."

"It makes sense," Laney said. "In older times, when a bride and groom would be moving in together and had never lived alone out of their parents' house, they would need these things."

Ian had been mentally reviewing wedding customs all night. Making notes for his own. His apartment had a kitchen full of barely used state-of-the-art equipment and appliances. Would he need all new things when he married?

Clayton chatted with some relatives. He'd now switched from ecstatic to something else. Perspiration was beading on his upper lip; in fact, sweat from his brow was running down his face. He must have been exhausted after hours and hours of being *onstage*, as it were. Ian hoped that when he and Melissa got on the plane to Bermuda, they could let their hair down and soak in some much-needed relaxation.

"So, what, you liked dancing with that Quincy guy?" he asked Laney behind the pyramid of gifts.

"What does it matter to you?"

"Not a stitch. Just curious. I thought you were off men."

"I am. It was just something to do. Especially since I was a disaster at dancing with you, the evening got long."

"You just don't know how to dance. You could learn." That image of whirling her around the dance floor popped into his head again.

"Look at Melissa over there." Laney pointed at the bride, who was pale as a ghost as she bid someone farewell. "Her coloring is kind of gray at this point."

"Green, actually," said Ian.

They stood bearing witness as Melissa suddenly put her hand over her stomach.

"Yeah, she doesn't seem right."

"Neither does Clayton." Clayton's face had become red, and sweat had soaked the front of his tuxedo shirt. They turned back to Melissa, whose head rotated in a circle like she was in a daze.

"They can't take much more of this. Should we do something?" said Laney.

Ian and Laney watched Melissa mouth *Excuse me* to her guests and then dash across the reception hall toward the Ladies Room.

"Food poisoning. And judging from the fact that they both have fevers, a bad case of it." The club's on-duty physician was quickly able to piece together a diagnosis.

As the last of the out-of-town relatives had said their goodbyes long after the clock had struck midnight, Melissa and Clayton simultaneously began vomiting in the deserted bathrooms.

"The oysters," Ian said to Laney.

"In August. A month that doesn't have an R in it." The age-old advice not to eat oysters in warm weather should have been heeded.

"The special menu that only the bride and groom ate."

"Clayton told me they were some kind of rare breed of oysters and cost a hundred dollars each!"

"Money well spent. Not."

"Can we sue the caterer?"

The service lamps were on. No longer were the party lights casting a flattering glow on the guests. The staff had cleared away everything from the last plate to spoon to linen, uncovering the tabletops made from plastic and metal. Ian and Laney sat side by side at one of the long-vacated tables. One of the waiters had been kind enough to provide them with a carafe of coffee and a couple of cups. The doctor promised to check back in a little while.

The bride and groom were now slumped on the settee of their long-planned sweetheart table where they had eaten the offending oysters. Melissa's third dress of the evening, a slinky retro movie-star-type gown that clung to her body, was wet and off-kilter from its many trips to the Ladies Room. Clayton didn't look much better in his untucked and soiled shirt, the tie and jacket long since tossed off. They dabbed their faces with cold washcloths. The sequence that had now repeated itself several times began with one of them making a groaning sound. That was followed with a stomach cramp, quickly followed by a mad dash to the bathroom. After a few minutes, one or the other would return with less of a cry than a whimper as they staggered back to the settee. Then a plop down next to the other.

"I love you Mel," Clayton would manage.

"I love you, too, Clay." Then a groan would come and the steps would be repeated.

"We're supposed to be on the way to our honeymoon in a couple of hours," Melissa said in a labored, scratchy voice.

"The resort in Bermuda is expecting us."

"I can't get on a plane."

"I guess we'll have to postpone." Clayton scrunched his face in distress at the realization.

"The doctor said we probably wouldn't be eating normally again for a week."

"Don't mention food."

"I don't think I've ever felt sicker."

"Ian," Clayton called over to him in a feeble voice. "Can you look up the cancellation procedure for the resort?"

"Of course." He reached for his phone in his tuxedo pants pocket and began.

Laney felt so bad for them. Any bride and groom were probably so looking forward to their honeymoon. To recuperate from all the planning and decisions and details that had gone into their wedding day. Even though it was for different reasons, Laney could relate. How much she'd love to be heading to a resort in Bermuda with its pink sand beaches, clear waters and a luxury resort.

It would surely be nice. Oh, to walk with her toes in the water, taking in the ocean breezes and allowing her mind to clear. She could let go of the past, and physically, mentally and spiritually prepare to start over. Of course, she didn't have the money for an exotic island destination. Nothing like that was in her future. Maybe a walk along the city's Charles River next week.

"Not great news," Ian announced, reading from his phone. "There are no cancellations within forty-eight hours of scheduled arrival. I texted the concierge on twenty-four-hour call, and she apologized but restated their policy."

"Oh, great," Melissa said, sulking. "Not only are we not able to go, we'll lose all of the money we spent. We'd booked a first-class flight, the resort's most lavish villa, private beach, private garden, the whole thing."

Laney figured they could afford to rebook sometime later, but still, it was a terrible shame that such a glorious escapade would go unclaimed.

"Private golf cart," Clayton added.

"Gourmet meals," Melissa threw in.

At the word *gourmet*, Clayton lurched and then made his next dash to the Men's Room.

"Unless anybody needs anything," Ian announced after finishing his coffee, "I'm going to check on Clayton and then head to my room."

Some of the wedding party were staying in the exclusive hotel that occupied the lower five floors of the Fletcher Club, compliments of the groom.

Melissa pouted, "Thank you for everything, Ian. It was a beautiful wedding until...it wasn't."

Laney piped up, trying to be helpful. "It will all make for a memory you'll laugh over with your grandchildren someday."

Ian tilted his head and looked at Laney with a wry smile that somehow shot right into her heart. He lifted his shoulders. "Grandchildren. There's a thought. Goodnight. Or should I say, good morning."

"See you in a few hours," said Laney.

They'd agreed to reconvene and help the newlyweds get packed up and get everything out of the club.

Melissa's head lolled back, so she didn't witness Laney eyeing Ian walk across the reception hall as he left. He confused her. Why did his stare pierce through her at the mention of grandkids? As he'd explained, marriage and breeding for him was just part of an overall corporate strategy. In turn, grandchildren extended the family's master scheme for another generation. The Lusses were a strange breed from what he had told her.

Although, perhaps they had a mentality shared with the uber-rich of the world. Mate with your head, not with your heart. Sound thinking, really. That wasn't her, though. She was all or nothing. Madly in love or totally alone, thank you very much. Yet, there was something so adorable about the way Ian had fluttered butterfly arms with the flower girl while Laney was dancing with Quincy. She couldn't imagine him as a dry and distant father.

Laney had found things complicated when he had tried to cut in on her with Quincy. On principle, she wasn't going to let him decide who she was and wasn't going to dance with. Enrique would have objected, which he did most unsubtly, if he didn't like her interactions with other men. Ian had no right and no cause.

Yet, Laney had to admit how much she liked it when he had tried to take her from Quincy. She'd never let him know, but that made her feel coveted. It wasn't something she'd felt very often, and it tickled her from the roots of her hair to the tippy tops of her toes. She was glad she said no, but she thought she might remember the interaction forever.

And what Ian didn't see later was that Quincy kept trying to hold her by the hips even though they weren't partner dancing. She ended up slipping out of his clutches at the earliest opportunity.

"Laney." Melissa bobbled her head up and spoke in a drunken-sounding voice, no doubt loopy from being sick and awake all night. "I have an idea. Why don't you go to Bermuda and enjoy my honeymoon?" The bride giggled at herself.

"What?" Laney sat down near her.

"The nonrefundable villa in Bermuda. The first-class plane tickets. You should go instead."

"Like I'd just go by myself? To your private villa."

"Yeah, why not? I know that you've been through a lot lately. Couldn't you use the vacation and relaxation?"

Melissa had no idea! She was offering a place where Laney could walk on the beach? To think and sort herself out. To send the hurts of the past ebbing away with the tide. To let sunrises fill her with energy and enthusiasm for starting anew. What an extraordinary offer.

"Are you sure?"

"Why not? What's the point of letting my beautiful honeymoon go to waste?" She frowned.

"You'll reschedule when you're better. You have your whole lives together."

"I know, right? I'm a married lady now."

"You sure are."

"You'll meet your man soon, too. I'm certain of it."

Laney doubted that. "Sure."

"Hey, what time is it?" the disheveled bride asked. "We had an early flight. You'd better hurry. We have a car booked to take us—uh, you, to the airport."

"Are you sure about this?"

"Yeah. It's not like we're going to be able to go."

With the snap of a finger, Laney was headed to a vacation in paradise. She couldn't think of a reason in the world not to say yes to the lovely offer. Well, maybe one. She and Ian were supposed to help Melissa and Clayton get packed up this morning. If she had a plane to catch, she wouldn't be able to complete her maid of honor duties. Obviously, Melissa wouldn't mind. Although it did bother Laney that she wouldn't be seeing Ian again this weekend. Which was absurd and didn't matter in the slightest. Not a bit.

"Again?"

"I can't believe…"

"Yup." Ian scratched his chin as he watched Clayton make another beeline to the bathroom, this time in the honeymoon suite. When Ian had found him lying on towels in the Men's Room in the reception hall, he helped him to the suite and texted Melissa that he'd done so. The groom plunked down on the gold satin linens of the king-size bed where wedding nights continued. Long after the band had finished, the ballroom lights had been dimmed and the aunties had gone home, private celebrations would start. Where a bride and groom, whether it was for the first time or whether they'd been sharing a bed for years, would lay down together as husband and wife. Ian found something ancient and sacred in that, the couple commemorating their legal union with a physical act.

"Some wedding night," Clayton lifted his head. "I'm dizzy, but not in a favorable way. Where's my bride?"

"Last I saw her, she was availing herself of the bathroom in the reception hall. Laney was with her."

Ambling around the suite, Ian stopped to finger the petals of a white long-stemmed rose that stood with eleven others in a beveled vase. The petal felt like velvet, an amazing achievement by Mother Nature. Along with, for example, Laney's luminous light brown eyes. *Wait, what?* He was comparing the wonders of a rose to the eyes of a woman he barely knew and who was no part of his life. He was definitely going cuckoo. He needed a vacation.

"Oh, my wife," Clayton blubbered dramatically into the air, knowing she couldn't hear him, then wiped his face with a wet towel.

Still fingering the flower, Ian asked, "How did you know Melissa was the right woman for you?"

Ian and Clayton had met at Oxford University and found they both hailed from Boston. They were sons and grandsons of giants, the American elite of the elite. They never heard the word *no*. Even so, they were taught to be honorable people, and they didn't lord their power over women. They didn't have to. Women flocked to them. They posed and paraded around them like display items for sale. That was when Ian realized that finding someone to trust, someone who liked him for him and not only for his family name, wasn't going to be easy. And on the other hand, the life of a Luss wife was what he had to offer, and he did want someone who understood what would and wouldn't be the arrangement.

"I knew Melissa was the one because when I wasn't around her, I wanted to be." Clayton let out a growl at his predicament. "My stomach is killing me!"

"Do you want some water?"

"Definitely not," he answered with a small heave.

"Anyway..." Perhaps it would help to keep Clayton distracted from his discomfort.

"Anyway, when I'm with her, I feel I'm at my best. Like our hearts are connected. Hopeful. Safe. And what makes it even better is to know I make her feel those things, too."

"When you know, you know?"

"Yeah."

Clayton's family didn't have quite the hard and fast rules about mating that Ian's did. That was okay. Family was family. He was proud that Luss Global Holdings employed hundreds of people who counted on the company's leadership to make smart decisions. "I'm very happy for you, Clayton. Other than the vomiting and all."

At that, he got a comic sneer from his friend. "I know Melissa is going to be disappointed—tomorrow, this morning or whatever the heck time it is—that we're not going to Bermuda."

"You'll reschedule."

"Hey, do you want to go?"

"To Bermuda?"

"Yeah. Use the reservation. Might as well. Otherwise, I'll lose the money."

"Go to the resort?"

"For that matter, you could invite someone if you wanted to. Any female prospects you've encountered lately?"

"No." Ian snickered.

Nothing could be further from the truth. His grandfather Hugo had been pressuring him to find someone. He wouldn't retire until Ian was settled so that the succession was secured. His son, Rupert, Ian's father, was in Zurich running the international arm of the company. And since Ian's uncle Harley proved himself unable to take over the domestic arm from Hugo, Ian would do it, stepping up from his current position directing appraisals and risk management. Ian would produce children and Luss Global Holdings would continue to grow. All of it outlined and scheduled. In fact, Hugo had already set Ian up on a couple of dates with appropriate women, none to his liking.

Ingrid was a chilly neuroscience researcher at Massachusetts General Hospital. During the two dates they went on, she spoke of nothing but her work, using terms like *basolateral amygdala* and *temporal lobe structure*. He was impressed with her distinguished career, but he thought she'd be better suited with someone in a similar field. He had to have *something* he could talk about with his mate.

Thea was part of a family like Ian's, whose domination in their field, of manufacturing plastic goods, made them a massive fortune. With dark hair and thick, busy eyebrows, she was a numbers cruncher, and there were three guests at their dinner together. Ian, Thea and her the calculator app on her phone. She showed Ian one financial scenario after the next, if they were to expand into India. This set of numbers if they forged into Africa. By the time dessert arrived, Ian's eyes were rolling back in his head. He didn't need a wife who exhausted him. The search wasn't going to be easy.

"So go on your own," Clayton suggested. "You could probably use a vacation. When was the last time you traveled when it wasn't for work?"

Clayton had him there. Why shouldn't he take a little time off and just walk on a beach alone? He could think about how he was going to know what woman was right for him. Someone who could really go the distance under their family's rules but who he could live contentedly with.

Ian's mother and father did. Vera was involved in her charities, in her case raising money for women's groups in war-torn areas of the world. His mother also had her female friends who met for lunch and cocktails and shopping all over Europe. She and Ian's dad had that cordial, serviceable and supportive relationship that the Luss family required. Everyone understood what was expected of them, and it all fit together like a puzzle.

His grandmother told him something else, words that spoke to him in the dark of night, but that was beside the point.

Warm sand under his feet and the notifications on his phone set to Off sounded pretty nice.

"Okay," he tilted his head so it was in line with Clayton's. "Thanks. I'll go."

"Great. We booked an early flight, so you'll need to head out soon."

"You know, the maid of honor and I were supposed to supervise getting your gifts and clothes and whatnot rounded up and out. I'll be leaving that all to Laney." That stuck in his craw. He'd not only renege on his duty but miss the chance to spend a little more time with her. She somehow exasperated and intrigued him at the same time with her sincerity and frankness. *Oh, well.* It couldn't be helped.

"Don't worry about it. My mom or Melissa's mom will deal with it. They live for that sort of thing."

"Well then, I guess I'm on my way to your honeymoon."

CHAPTER FOUR

IT WAS ALL happening so fast. A chauffer in full uniform held open the door of a shiny black stretch limo in front of the Fletcher Club. Laney had never been in a limo and slid into the soft leather of the back seat, swinging her legs in after her as glamorous as a movie star. After making sure she was comfortably situated, the driver gently closed the door.

Take that, Enrique. As she had told Ian, Enrique never held a door open for her, always leaving her standing in the cold as he first let himself into a car, sometimes putting on sunglasses or taking off a scarf before he bothered to click the button that opened the passenger door. She never knew whether he was like that with all women, himself the golden child whose mother thought he walked on water, or whether he didn't deem Laney worthy of the chivalrous treatment. He thought he was *slumming it* with her; he made that clear. Why she was dumb enough to think he'd fall in love with her and none of that would matter, she had no idea. Wishful thinking. Lesson learned.

As the limo pulled away, the driver informed her, "Ma'am, in the tray in front of you, you'll find coffee, freshly squeezed orange juice and a bucket of champagne on ice. There's also fruit and warm croissants. Is there anything else you'll need?"

"No," she choked out, trying to keep from laughing. "That ought to do it, thank you."

Of course, she didn't need more than that just to make it the short distance to the airport. She'd had coffee to keep herself awake while she hastily gathered up her belongings in order to catch the flight. She left the formal bridal party clothes behind. Melissa assured her that the resort in Bermuda had shops where she could pick up beach and casual clothes and whatever she needed. In fact, the honeymoon reservation included a generous shopping allowance.

At the airport, the driver pointed out to her where to go in the terminal, and from there, she was ushered straight into the first-class lounge, where a pink-suited attendant welcomed her. Melissa had been able to text her travel agent and get the name changed on the reservation. "I'm Serena from Pink Shores Resort. Will your significant other be joining you shortly?" Laney's mouth opened wide as if to answer, but no words came out. Significant other? She didn't know what this woman was talking about. "While you're waiting, perhaps you'd like a light breakfast. Coffee, freshly squeezed orange juice, champagne, fruit and warm croissants."

"Thank you."

The exact same menu the limo driver had offered. Hmm, that wasn't a half bad way to live! After all, there could never be too many buttery pastries in the world. Although she politely declined, having already gobbled two in the limo. Her rest and reset was getting off to a delicious start.

Boarding began. The first-class cabin was appointed with huge reclining chairs. Laney's was by the window, the one beside it vacant, no doubt the two seats that had been assigned to Melissa and Clayton. Laney began exploring the amenities for the two-hour flight. The headrest behind her was so plush she could sink right into it. A partition offered privacy. She had her own extra-large touch screen to watch whatever she wanted on the personal entertainment center. She flipped through the channels, ranging from first-run movies to hit television shows to live sporting events to dozens of types of music. Padded headphones were provided as well as the latest technology in earbuds. There was an e-reader loaded with hundreds of books. A pull-out tray was positioned for comfortable laptop use or for eating. There was a lighting panel with many options. The flight attendant offered never-used blankets and pillows for her comfort.

"We'll be departing shortly," Serena popped her head in. "Has your companion encountered a delay?"

Laney didn't know what to say or do. Since Melissa hadn't brought it up, she figured she'd just board the plane without any questions. She noticed that Serena was careful to use the words *companion* and *significant other*, not saying any names out loud for privacy and not making any gender assumptions.

"I'll try to reach him, but he'll take another flight if need be," she said, quickly fudging.

"As you know, Pink Shores Resort is a couples-only retreat."

Wait, what?

"We maintain our reputation as a five-star, world-renowned romantic destination by enforcing our protocol. We ask our couples to arrive and depart together."

"I'll call him right now." After Serena moved on, Laney called Melissa in a panic.

"Oh no!" Melissa shrieked in a still-woozy voice. "I didn't know the resort had that exclusivity."

"What should I do now? I lied and said my significant other was on his way. And then I said he was taking another flight."

"I'm so sorry. Maybe if you can just get to Bermuda, I'll call them and explain."

"Didn't Ian do that last night?" He'd relayed to the group the inflexibility of the booking restrictions.

"I'm sorry, Ms. Sullivan," Serena poked around the partition again. "The captain would like to prepare for take-off. As I mentioned, we only allow our resort's couples on the flights. We'll have to ask you to deplane along with me, and then we'll gladly get you onto the next flight once your significant other has arrived. Perhaps you'd enjoy a croissant while you wait. Kindly follow me."

There went her ritzy vacation. That was Laney's luck. Nothing had gone right for her. Not Enrique. Not the café. Not even her interactions with the best man, Ian, this weekend. Now this.

With a resigned exhale, Laney rose. Embarrassed, she looked around at her fellow passengers in the first-class section, which seemed to be filled with Pink Shores Resort guests, based on an identifying tag clipped on the side of their seats. They were, indeed, all couples. Newlyweds and those who looked like they were commemorating milestone anniversaries. Maybe a twenty-fifth. Maybe even a fiftieth. Couples of mixed races, same-sex pairs, all whispering to each other or holding hands or leaning over to give one another a kiss. United in one solitary purpose. Excitedly on their way to celebrate their love. Laney felt horribly out of place.

As she reached down to grab her bag and then get off the plane, she heard a familiar male voice. "There was an accident on the highway that delayed my arrival to the airport."

Where did she know that voice from? She'd heard it recently. Whose was it?

"We're glad you made it," came Serena's voice. "Have a pleasant flight."

Bag in hand, Laney stood and turned to see who was rushing down the aisle.

No, no, no, no!

It was Ian! She sat back down.

The pilot announced over the sound system, "Flight crew, lock the doors for departure."

Ian slipped into the seat that the flight attendant had gestured to and swiveled his chair to face front. He observed that the occupant of the seat next to him had a shapely pair of legs. When he followed the legs up, he did a double take. It couldn't be.

"Laney?"

"What are *you* doing here?" she retorted.

"What are *you* doing here?"

"Melissa invited me."

"Clayton insisted I use the vacation so it didn't go to waste. Everything was prepaid and nonrefundable."

"Please fasten your seat belts for takeoff," a flight attendant instructed Ian, who pulled the strap to comply.

"I know, I was in the room when you called to try to explain the situation. Melissa wanted *me* to use the reservation."

"Without telling Clayton?"

"When you're lying down on the bathroom floor, perhaps you don't do your best thinking."

"Clayton was in about the same shape."

"Apparently, they didn't tell either of us that Pink Shores Resort is for couples only. The resort's representative was about to make me leave because I was onboard without my significant other."

Ian quickly called Clayton before he needed to turn off his cell phone. "Hey, thanks for the invite, but did you know that the resort is couples only? And did you know that Laney is on the plane? That Melissa told her to use the reservation."

"What? No. Melissa, did you...? Let me put you on speakerphone, she's right here."

"Melissa?" Laney brought her mouth close to the phone.

"Yeah." Ian switched the speaker on, and Melissa's voice came through. "Clay and I are lying in bed together, still in half of our wedding clothes. Honey, you texted the travel agent and put Ian on the reservation?"

"I forgot to tell you."

"Can we make some other arrangement with the resort?" Laney piped in. "The rep here told me we have the honeymooners' villa."

Ian asked, "Do you think we could swap it for two smaller rooms?"

"Just go and have a nice time," Clayton said. "I'm sure the villa is big enough that you won't even see each other."

There was nothing to be done. Ian knew he had about one minute to make his objection known, disrupt the flight and force his way off the plane. If he didn't, he'd be spending the week with Laney. She of the café au lait eyes and the bum luck of late.

"I guess we're on our way, then."

"I guess so." She pursed her lips, maybe as unsure about this as he was.

"I've got to get in one more call before the captain insists we shut our electronics down." He tapped his speed dial for a number he used frequently, although he turned off the speaker. "Grandfather."

"Where are you, Ian? It sounds like you're on an airplane."

"Yes, I'm on a commercial flight." Luss Global had its own jet and, if it was occupied, Ian would generally hire a private plane. "I just wanted to let you know that I'm taking a quick holiday to Bermuda."

"All right. But I want you to know that I've been speaking with colleagues, and I'm going to be gathering the names of some more women I want you to have dinner with as soon as you get back. And I need you to give each your serious consideration."

Ian glanced over to Laney, who was thumbing through a magazine. He was glad she wasn't hearing Hugo. The matchmaking was so old-school, it was a little humiliating, if efficient. He didn't like the frailty he heard in his grandfather's voice. After a long and prosperous career, and having lost his wife a couple of years ago, it really was time for him to step down. Ian knew he would stick to his word and not do so until his grandson found a bride. It was all on him.

"I will, grandfather."

The Luss marriage rulebook dated back to Hugo's grandfather, Frederick. He would be Ian's great-great-grandfather. Frederick was to partner with his brother Phillip to buy land using the inheritance that their father had left them, plus money they'd earned. Then Phillip met a wily woman who he fell madly in love with. He worshipped the ground she walked on. She told him that her family had forged south to Georgia, and that was where he should purchase the land. Phillip was too blinded by his love for the persuasive woman to cross his t's and dot his i's, and before he knew it, the land had been bought in the woman's name only, a result of her dishonest relatives brokering the sale. Phillip's half of the investment in the new venture with his brother was gone, and the woman disappeared.

After that, Frederick decided that unions between men and women would become trade agreements, mutually beneficial to all parties, with both families thoroughly scrutinized. The process worked well for several generations until Ian's Uncle Harley fell for a party girl, Nicole, a baroness of all things, who should have fit the bill. That was a disaster, and Harley's globe-trotting and reckless spending cost the company tens of millions of dollars. He knew his grandfather wouldn't loosen the reins after that.

"Ladies and gentlemen," the pilot instructed, "we're pulling out of the gate. Please turn off all of your devices or set them to Airplane Mode."

As Ian did, he gazed over at Laney again. He'd spent more time with her at the wedding than he probably had with any woman in ages, if ever. Now he'd be at a faraway resort with her.

"So, what, we have to pretend to be a couple?"

"Not only that, but because we have the honeymoon villa, we have to pretend to be newlyweds. In public, that is."

He'd never been part of a couple. Even with a cold contract sort of marriage, he'd still have to have some husbandly skills that a woman would want. This could be practice for him. Sure, Laney wasn't the pedigreed type he was expected to marry, but that didn't mean he couldn't masquerade at it with her.

"Is that okay with you? We'll act like we're together when we're out and about at the resort?"

"It sounds kind of wacky, but sure. It seems to mean a lot to Clayton and Melissa that the trip doesn't go to waste."

"Maybe if they feel better, they'll actually decide to come in a few days. And then we'll leave."

They were not going to become fixtures in each other's lives. It was only for a week at most. There was no reason for this not to work out. Perhaps it was fortuitous. It was a chance for Ian to prepare for the next phase of his life. When he accepted Clayton's offer to use the reservation, one of his first thoughts had been that in leaving, he wouldn't get to say goodbye to Laney. In a way, a best man and maid of honor are almost thrown together as a couple. There had already been cheek-to-cheek photos, pulling out chairs, commiserating about speeches and calamitous dancing.

Once the plane was in the air and had reached cruising altitude, the flight attendant approached with a tray. "Can I offer you a cup of fish chowder, a Bermudian favorite, or perhaps you'd like an omelet?"

"I'd love to try the chowder," said Laney. "I love eating like a local."

Ian smiled. "I'll have the same."

He liked that Laney was open to trying interesting food. That was something they could do together on this trip. Plus, as Clayton said, the honeymoon villa was likely to be large. They could each claim their own space and spend the whole week apart if they wanted to. Which he didn't. He wanted to act like he was on his honeymoon. Still, that there were options was a comfort.

The attendant laid cream-colored linen place mats onto their dining trays. She then added a matching napkin and silver utensils. Placing the soup tureens carefully, she presented them with a bread basket filled with warm rolls and a pot of butter.

"What else can I get you to drink?" she asked after also serving glasses of water with ice.

"I'll have a coke," Laney ordered.

"Sparkling water with lime," said Ian.

After a sip, Ian peered across the aisle to study an older couple. They were both holding stemmed glasses that looked to contain red wine. First, they clinked glasses as in a basic toast. Then, without either of them saying anything, they intertwined their arms to feed each other a sip from their own glass. That was followed by a knowing smile, and then the woman leaned closely toward the man and affectionately rubbed her cheek on his shoulder. Ian would bet that they had been together a long time, that there was so much between them that didn't need saying aloud.

"Mrs. Luss."

"What?" Laney looked up from her soup.

"Excellent. I was practicing to see if you'd answer to your new name."

"I don't have to take your name just because we're 'married.'" She made air quotes with her fingers.

"Why don't we just keep it simple and traditional? Less explaining."

"Okay, Mr. Luss. Have you tried the soup, husband? It's delicious."

She helped herself to another spoonful of the chowder, chunky with fish and aromatic vegetables. Then she broke off a piece of the warm roll and swirled it into the soup. Ian expected her to eat it. Instead, she surprised him by popping the bite into his mouth. He fumbled in surprise and then had to lick his lips to make sure all of it made it in.

"That's something couples would do, don't you think?" she said.

A shiver ran down his spine, which was a surprise, ignited by her supple fingers touching his lips with the food morsel. He bunched his forehead, almost annoyed that a couple of fingertips could have such an effect on him. And that wasn't the first time her touch had aroused him. That was the only hitch about spending a week with Laney. She stirred him up. Magic fingers creating involuntary muscle tingles was precisely what he wasn't going to marry, so he surely didn't need to train at it. Or maybe it was that he did need to. To get those longings out of his system, once and for all, so that he could turn his back on them and get on with the future he'd planned.

Hmm. "We should agree on a common story about how we met. Things people might ask."

"Three years ago at a wedding. How about that?"

"You were a bridesmaid and I asked everyone if they knew you. And whether you were seeing anyone."

"Aw, that's cute."

It was at that. He continued, "I noticed you up at the altar in a godawful yellow poofy dress. During the ceremony, you sensed me looking at you, and our eyes met. It wasn't just your beauty, it was your essence, the way you had about you."

"I wanted to stare into your eyes until eternity."

"You hit me like a thunderbolt. I knew you were the one for me. That you'd be the woman I'd marry."

Was he reciting lines from a movie he'd seen or a book he'd read? How else would all of that have come spilling out? Truthfully, he liked the story, liked the notion of love at first sight. Of souls igniting. Knowing in an instant that two people had been put on Earth for each other.

He glanced over to the older couple again. The man brought his wife's hand to his lips so that he could kiss the top of it. His blue eyes crinkled with gratitude.

A lump formed in Ian's throat.

"Welcome, honeymooners." A concierge in a pink jacket met Laney and Ian as soon as they arrived to the Pink

Shores Resort. "I am Adalson, and the staff and I are at your service. On behalf of all of us, may we say congratulations on your nuptials, and we wish you a long and happy life together."

Very nice well-wishes after such a momentous milestone of getting married. Had she actually gotten married, that was. In fact, she was never going to get married. At twenty-eight and after Enrique, that was settled. And certainly not to the devastatingly handsome man next to her, who she barely knew.

"Yes, I'm a lucky man," Ian fake-boasted as he tried to lope his long arm around her so they could co-acknowledge Adalson's words. Except that Laney spontaneously jumped back and away from the swerve of his reach. Which left him hugging air. He stuttered, out of context, "We're the Lusses."

Adalson gave them both a confused look. "Perhaps it was a trying flight? Please look forward to relaxing Bermy style."

"Oh yeah, right," she mumbled and corrected herself by stepping into Ian's wingspan.

He gripped her by the shoulder and pulled her in. She managed an inane grin, like her man was just so cute. Then she immediately had to *not* concentrate on how firm his hand on her was. She also had to *not* concentrate on the sturdy side of his body that was meeting hers. *Not* concentrate on how amazing he felt, holding her warm and tight, and how she melted against him. *Not* replay in her mind bringing that bite of chowder-soaked bread to his mouth when they were on the plane. She shouldn't have made such an intimate move in the first place, but he didn't have to turn it into something so sensual. Then the way she could only gawk as he licked his lips. This masquerade was already a challenge. And they'd just arrived.

"We'll bring your bags to your villa. Would you like to walk there on the beach or take a golf cart?"

"Beach," Laney answered.

"Golf cart," Ian blurted in unison, his voice on top of hers.

"I'm sorry, I meant golf cart," she said, trying again.

Right as Ian corrected with "Beach."

They looked at each other and fake-laughed. "Ha ha, ha ha."

Adalson again averted his eyes for discretion, clearly not knowing what to make of them.

Neither did Laney, other than that her head was starting to spin. Maybe this trip wasn't going to be as easy as it seemed.

"I think you may be a bit tired," Adalson interjected. "Why don't I take you in the cart, and you'll have plenty of occasions to walk on the beach later? That is, if you choose to leave the villa at all."

All three of them knew what he meant. If Laney was the blushing bride type, now would be the time. She wasn't, so she looked lovingly up to her husband, as any happy new wife would.

Adalson drove them along a path that cut through the vibrant green lawn.

"Oh my gosh!" Laney exclaimed when they rounded the corner that allowed them to face the shoreline.

"What?" Ian asked.

"The water is truly turquoise." Exactly like it was in

the photos she researched online before she boarded the flight. She didn't know anything about Bermuda, and suddenly she was here. "And the sand. It really is pink."

It seemed like a minute ago that she could only stand idly by while firefighters tried in vain to salvage the café that was blazing away right before her very eyes. Now she was on an island in the middle of the Atlantic Ocean trying to fathom how sand could actually be pink.

"I'm amazed by it every time I come."

Oh, of course the rich guy had been here before. His family probably owned the island. Which didn't stop her jaw from hanging open at the stunning colors of the water and sand. She'd never seen anything like it in her life. It was incredible. She couldn't wait to take her first walk. She'd bet the sand was soft and would feel magical between her toes. And unlike what Adalson was insinuating, it wasn't as if she was going to be inside the whole time with her groom. She was going to be out on the beach and in the water.

"We're getting farther and farther away from the central buildings of the resort," she said to Ian as they rode through a grove of trees and into a secluded area.

"We've entered your private grounds. You have this entire beach to yourself. There's no access other than for you and staff," Adalson explained, "who will text you before entering your villa compound. So please consider this clothing optional."

"Uh-uh," Ian made a noise she couldn't interpret.

What she did understand, however, is the way the low timbre of his voice sent a hum right through her body. Clothing was going to be mandatory, not optional, around him. This little charade could become dangerous if she didn't protect herself. She couldn't withstand any more hurt. That wasn't what happened on *fake* honeymoons, anyway.

"This is your personal patio and garden." Adalson gestured.

A wooden deck with a white table and chairs, as well as two loungers, were positioned to enjoy a garden. Trees both short and tall swayed in the gentle breeze. A rainbow of flowers grew along a path. Which gave way to the entrance to the villa.

"Our finest and most luxurious accommodations at the resort."

"Wow," said Laney.

It was a house on a beach right at the shore, elevated from the water. The one-story building was painted pastel pink with white trim and a white roof, as was typical Bermudian style. Once Laney and Ian got out of the cart and approached the entrance, she could see that there was a wraparound balcony with a railing made of wooden slats.

"Three hundred and sixty degrees of balcony," Adalson confirmed. "Is that to your liking, ma'am?"

"It certainly is."

"So that you can take in sunrises and sunsets from whatever angle you choose." Ah, as if she might have to settle for only one panoramic view of the sea and sky. "May I show you inside?"

Ian thought quickly to grab her hand as people romantically involved might do. She liked his big palm with its thick fingers. Enrique had slender hands that, to be honest, she never enjoyed holding. He went for frequent manicures, and his hands were always powdery. She liked Ian's; they were strong and manly.

The kind of hand she might like to hold for the rest of her life.

Not Ian's, specifically. Of course.

She'd hold no man's hand until eternity.

Anyway, she was getting flustered in her own thoughts. The point being that his hand felt good.

"Melissa and Clayton pulled out all the stops for this." Ian squeezed her palm as a reminder. "I mean, our travel agents did well for us, honey. Didn't they?"

"They did, my beloved."

The beach-facing section of the balcony was a stunner. From French doors that opened into the house, there was a wide white staircase with white bannisters that led straight down into the water. A staircase into the ocean! All they had to do was descend the steps.

"This will do," Ian declared. Then he winked at Laney. How could a wink feel like a kiss?

CHAPTER FIVE

ENTERING THE VILLA, Ian first thought the aisle of bright red on the floor between the two white sofas was an odd strip of carpeting. Once he got closer, he saw that it was rose petals. Thousands upon thousands of red rose petals created a pathway across the spacious living room.

"There are so many." Laney bent down and scooped up a handful. Bringing them to her nose, she took an exaggerated inhale and exhale. "Mmm."

"If you'll follow the roses—" Adalson gestured "—they'll take you to the newlywed master suite."

Ian managed a close-lipped smile while his stomach hopped. He hadn't had a chance to figure out what they were going to do for sleeping arrangements. Not knowing the other had invited a replacement, neither Melissa nor Clayton had any suggestions. Ian would work something out on how to split up the use of the villa later.

He followed Laney along the rose-petal trail through the next set of French doors, which were symmetrically in line with the set that led to the balcony and staircase into the ocean, all in a row to create a private aisle to the water. His eyes beheld the end of the rose petal trail at the foot of the king-size bed with its four-poster frame and gauzy curtains strung from every side. On top of the bed, many more thousands of red petals formed a gigantic heart atop the lavender-colored bedding. He looked at Laney. She looked at him. In each other's eyes, they almost panicked at the prospect of this giant bed.

Laney covered nicely with a phony yawn. "It's been a long day. I think I'd like to take a little nap before exploring the resort."

Adalson responded, "Ah, yes. Of course. Let me bring in your bags. A member of the housekeeping staff will be by to go over your needs. All of the concierges are available to help you plan activities or sightseeing."

He took his leave and returned with each of their small suitcases, as they'd come with only what they'd brought to the wedding. There hadn't been time for either of them to go home to pack additional bags.

Adalson put the two cases down. "Mr. Luss, I'm so sorry, there must have been a mix up. I will track down the rest of your luggage and have it brought to you immediately. I'm so terribly sorry."

"No, that's okay. That's all we brought."

Adalson tried to hide his surprise.

"We pack light. Like you said, Adalson," Laney said, jumping in. "We won't need many clothes. It's our honeymoon, after all!"

Ian's eyes popped wide and he mashed his lips together.

"Ah," Adalson nodded his head knowingly, although still doing a double-take at the two small wheelies he'd delivered. "I'll... Congratulations again."

He finally departed, and both Ian and Laney stuck out their tongues in relief.

The layout of the villa was clear. There was one enormous master bedroom with en suite showers, bathtubs and every amenity. There was a living room, sun room, dining room and kitchen, everything done in the finest materials with great detail. There were all of the private outdoor areas. What there wasn't was a second bed of any kind. Of course not. This was a honeymoon villa.

This wasn't a problem. All Ian wanted was to enjoy some time away to become mentally prepared to find a wife. So he could sleep on the floor, on the sofa, out on the balcony—it didn't matter. He and Laney would masquerade as husband and wife in front of other people. Which he still didn't mind the idea of, because it would give him some rehearsal at being a couple, the way he would present himself to the world as a married man.

Although when he saw Laney kicking off her shoes and floating from one open window to the next to take in the views, a longing washed through him. Maybe he wanted more than to playact at love for a week on an island far from his family. Maybe he wanted that connection that true lovers had. That way the older man on the plane cherished his white-haired love. They had something bottomless and profound between them. Something that would last forever, even into eternity. Maybe he wanted to experience those feelings, just once. Despite all of his party-line speak.

"Come see this bathroom," Laney called out, having made her way into the en suite. "I mean, look at this. The glassed-in shower is big enough for two elephants!"

"Interesting image."

"It has not one, not two, but eight water jets. Imagine how that would feel spraying onto your body."

No sirree, eight water jets spraying him was not going to be a smart thing for him to imagine. That sounded far too sensual. And he was definitely not going to imagine being in the shower with *her*, seeing what those curves he hadn't stopped admiring would look like wearing nothing but eight sprays of water. Much safer to picture two elephants getting extremely clean.

"What do you want to do?" Laney asked as she sauntered around the villa.

"Do?" Ian raised an eyebrow.

"Yeah, do you want to go into the ocean or check out some of the activities in the main buildings? There are lots of ways we could spend our time."

"I think newlyweds usually find something to do on their honeymoon, don't you?"

"Okay. Let's go in the water." She could cool off from the overheated feeling she got thinking about things she wasn't going to do with him.

"That sounds marvelous."

"Except I don't have a bathing suit," said Laney.

There was obviously not any swimming intended during Melissa and Clayton's city wedding weekend, so she'd had no reason to pack one.

"I don't, either."

Laney wasn't going to repeat what Adalson had said about the privacy of their lodgings making clothing optional. She was already sensing the weirdness of being in this villa with him separated from Boston by a lot of ocean. Pretending to be a couple. Clothes were staying on. She'd bet Ian would look incredible with optional clothing off, but nothing like that was going to be happening.

"Let's walk up to the resort shops to buy some, and we can check out the property while we're at it," Ian said.

"I could use some casual clothes, too," Laney said. She didn't have shorts or sandals or a cover-up.

"We'll have to make it a little bit of a spree then."

Shopping spree with Ian Luss. *Hmm*. That was a turn of events she would have never expected. Why not, though? They both knew the real score.

"Melissa said there was some kind of shopping allowance."

"Or I can buy you a bikini, for heaven's sake."

Suddenly, it occurred to her how self-conscious she'd be in a bathing suit around Ian. At the wedding, he'd commented on her hair, her lack of makeup, a spot on her dress. Although she could tell he'd only meant well, that was a trigger for her, made her feel like it was Enrique all over again, her short curvy body being measured against the tall skinny goddesses of the world. Maybe Ian would have the class to only think insulting thoughts about her body, not need to say them out loud like Enrique did.

She could still hear his voice. *That dress does nothing for your lumps.* Lumps. Not curves. Unattractive lumps.

The center of the resort was comprised of five buildings painted the signature pink and white, and grouped around a mosaic fountain. Guests, indeed in couples, not a single person alone or with children, passed to and fro.

The shopping plaza had a row of establishments. One with mannequins in the window modeling several types of swimsuits from practical styles for water sports to high-fashion bikinis.

Laney decided she would love one of those suits that had a matching cover-up. That would make her feel like a chic bride indeed. Oh, wait, she wasn't that. But, hey, she could have some fun.

As they browsed the store, Ian quickly grabbed a couple of selections, the men's swimsuits much more basic than the women's. Laney picked out a couple of the ensembles like she had in mind and proceeded to the fitting room to try them on. The first one was a modest top and bottom with plenty of coverage, the fabric a sort of ocean motif that had a dark blue, a lighter blue and a white pattern. The cover-up that went with it was styled akin to a man's shirt, buttons all the way down to the hem below knee length. She wasn't sure if she liked it or not. Ian was going to have to see her in these bathing suits at one point or another, so she decided to bite the bullet and poked out of the fitting room to summon his opinion.

"That's…" he stopped himself and she watched his Adam's apple bob as he looked her over from head to toe "…very nice."

She loved that he stumbled over his words. She could tell from his hooded eyelids and the lift to the corners of his mouth that he liked what he saw, that she wasn't getting the Enrique disapproval. She prickled under his observation, shoulders arching closer together. It was a strange turn-on the way he eyed her with a sort of appreciation, as if he were enjoying a leisurely and satisfying scrutiny.

"I don't need to put on makeup or have my hair done?" Her retort was snappy and defensive, harkening back to his comments at the wedding. Here, he didn't have any idea what she was referring to. Flustered, she covered with, "What do you think?"

"You look gorgeous. But shall we compare it to something else before you decide?"

Gorgeous. "Sure."

The next ensemble was far bolder. Solid black, the cut of the top covered much less skin than the first one. The bottoms were certainly more revealing than any she'd ever worn before, basically two triangles tied together on the sides. The sheer crepe kimono that flowed over it made her feel womanly and, well, just plain sexy. She strode toward Ian, whose face froze except for his mouth, which literally dropped open.

She would remember the moment until her dying day. Here she was with Ian Luss, who could have any woman in the world, and he was beaming at her like she was the most enticing creature he'd ever seen. In his gaze she, indeed, felt gorgeous.

It had been cumulative, the way Enrique made her feel not up to par, not attractive enough to keep him from ogling other women. Ian made her feel desirable, which had been hurtful to go so long without. She knew he'd go on to choose one of those classic beauties that billionaires married. But she'd always have today.

Unless…maybe he was just pretending at this, too.

Playing the role of the lovestruck husband. He'd be too polite to let her know.

"Please get that," he said, stuttering in a way that made her giggle. He did, too.

Suddenly insecure, she wrapped the kimono tightly around her and cinched the belt. "I'll just buy a couple of these athletic suits," she said and pointed to a rack of high-neck one-piece suits in black and navy. "Maybe I'll be doing some water sports this week."

"Oh, okay, but you're buying the two you just tried on, as well."

"Why?"

He gave her another one of those crooked half-smiles that might make her faint if he kept them up. "Why, wifey, because you look so hot in them."

Now it was her turn to swallow hard. She wasn't sure if he'd just called her wifey because he wanted to remind her that this was phony talk. Since *Ian* should not say things to *Laney* like Mr. Luss would say to Mrs. Luss. In any case, he could have gotten away with not saying anything. He chose to, making her think that he wasn't just playacting. Picking out expensive items at a resort shop and having a handsome, refined man pay her compliments. Yes, this could be an excellent bridge from where she came from to where she was going. It was also the most fun shopping she'd ever had.

After they bought a few more things, Ian had the bags sent to the villa, and they walked past the shopping gallery to a glass atrium filled with tropical plants. In an open area at the center, couples were dancing to a quartet that played a classic love song.

"They're doing lessons," Laney said, observing an older man walking around the couples making corrections.

He lifted a man's arm just so, adjusted the distance another couple were standing from each other. Laney reflected on the awkward and uncomfortable dancing the two of them did as best man and maid of honor.

"That's what I could have used before the wedding."

The teacher spotted them spying on the ten or so couples who were involved in the class. He approached. "Don't tell me. Your first dance as husband and wife wasn't all you had hoped?"

Close enough to the truth, they both nodded.

"I am Hans. Please join us. This class is for couples who want to know the pleasures of partner dancing."

Ian and Laney looked at each other. She shrugged, "I know you already know how."

"But not with my wife." He held out his arm for her to take it. "May I have this dance?"

"Remember, partners," Hans called out, "in ballroom dancing, one of you is the leader."

"That didn't go well for me last time," Laney said to Ian as the dance instructor guided them into the center of the atrium.

"Here's your chance to learn."

"Leaders," Hans addressed the couples, "hold your partner at the waist. You do not push or pull. When the leader moves, the partner will naturally respond so that you keep your hold. One hand on the leader's shoulder. Join your other hands. And it's one, two, three…one, two, three…one, two, three…" Hans demonstrated with an invisible partner.

How nimble the elder gentleman was. Ian imagined he'd had a lifetime of dancing, and it was what kept him healthy and young at heart. Hans waltzed himself around to check on the other students. One younger couple were already sashaying all over the dance floor. Two middle-aged men were not so lucky, as they kept looking at their feet and couldn't get a rhythm going.

Ian and Laney made an attempt to get started.

"You're not supposed to come that close," she said, objecting when Ian put his arm around her waist and brought her toward him.

"You're right. We're supposed to keep the frame."

He backed away and tried again. He knew the basics of ballroom dancing, as his parents did, in fact, enroll him in lessons. Right now, though, he was having trouble maintaining his distance for this formal style. He wanted to bring Laney close, to feel her silky hair against his cheek, which he'd had a hint of in between her stepping on his toes at the wedding. To feel her luscious curves against his body again. The hills and valleys that had just been on glorious display when she was trying on those bathing suits.

The mere thought of that gave his body a jolt and he fumbled over his own feet. *Goodness!* That was taking the charade a little too far. All of this with Laney didn't feel completely fake, and that was terrifying. She brought up something from the very depths of him. Something lethal because of its power.

As she began to find it easier to follow his steps, an almost visible energy passed back and forth between them. A spark. His pulse sped up as he worried it was the very force that he needed to avoid. He imagined all sorts of green lights when he knew there were only red flags.

Like if Laney was really his bride, the first thing he would have done upon arrival to the villa would have been to pick her up in his arms and lay her down on that heart full of rose petals atop the bed. He'd brush his lips against hers, ever so lightly, leaving the tiniest space for air to pass between them. At first.

Then he'd caress the side of her face with his palms, learning the creaminess of her skin. He'd probably dot more wispy kisses all over her face. Until his lips returned to hers. This time his kisses would be more urgent. He'd let them tell her what was brewing inside of him. The passion that was going to erupt, that would blow those rose petals off the bed and leave them scattered all over the room. Because once he got his tongue...

He chuckled at himself in disbelief of where his mind and, judging from the sudden change in comfort of his trousers, lower down on his body had traveled to.

Get ahold of yourself, Mr. Luss!

He concentrated only on dancing. As he and Laney got more and more comfortable, he was swept into it, as if together they transcended space and time. As if they glided until their feet didn't even touch ground anymore. He loved the possibility. There was something so beautiful and timeless about it, two people's movements becoming a dance as one. The melding of bodies with music was such a lovely manifestation of their union. He was on cloud nine as he waltzed Laney all around the dance floor. Like another scene from a movie. Dancing around the room as if the two of them were the only people there.

Romance.

There it was. That forbidden word. The word his family thought was silly nonsense at best and a destructive force at worst. Yet something he'd always dreamed of feeling with every cell in his body. Was that something he could safely encounter this week, too?

Not safe at all, a fact not to be forgotten. Laney was what was firing him up in the first place, making him think about things like soulmates and joy and passion. There were a list of reasons Laney could never be the woman for him. He couldn't call his grandfather to tell him the search was over.

First of all, she'd made a vow to remain single, so she wasn't even available. Second, he knew that his family expected him to partner with someone from their exclusive and privileged world. Not with a woman from Dorchester raised by a single mom. The Lusses didn't even divorce, let alone give birth out of wedlock. It had simply never happened and never would. Most importantly, most dangerously, was that he could never have a calculated and loveless agreement with her. No, around her, his blood ran hot. Boiling hot. The only possibility with her was an impossibility. The real deal.

By the second song, Hans commended them. "That's right. Now pivot just enough for her to sense you turning her a little bit. You don't want to make her dizzy, but you can add movement."

"We're getting better," Laney said with a melting smile.

"Next," Hans addressed the room, "should you want to dance more intimately, the same rules apply. You create a frame and stay locked in it. Partners, you will feel where the leader is moving. From that, you can dance closely, you can tango, you can do any dance."

After the lesson, they decided to take the long way back to their villa. There was a dirt trail through groves of trees that provided a breezy shade from the midday sun. They exchanged hellos with another couple who crossed their path, the woman wearing a wedding veil on her wet hair, though she was in a wetsuit, as was her groom, as if they'd just engaged in a water sport. While they walked, they talked animatedly about something.

Laney smiled at the sight. "How did she keep the veil on if they went scuba diving or something like that?"

But Ian's mood had changed. A tone of cynicism flew out of his mouth. "Love conquers all."

She wasn't fazed by his sarcasm. "You really don't believe in love?"

"It's not what my family concerns itself with."

"As you've explained. You're supposed to marry for a business merger, and that's that?"

"It sounds cut and dry but it's what we've been doing for generations."

"Your parents, too?"

"Yes, I grew up in town in a house that was run like a corporation. My mother and father kept mainly separate lives. They had morning and evening check-in meetings with agendas their assistants prepared. Even spending time with my sister and me as children was scheduled."

"That sure sounds cold."

"And on Sunday afternoon, there was family time—a contrived picnic or movie date followed by dinner at my grandfather's, where he and my grandmother lived the same routine."

"Did you feel loved?"

Hmm. He'd never really thought of it like that. "I can't say I didn't. My family cares for each other. Looks out for each other. One would take a bullet for the other. I think my parents love each other, rooted in friendship and loyalty. There's just no room in our family for grand expressions and gratuitous emotions. Their position is that there's no logical purpose for romance."

"That's a strange way to grow up."

"It was. But you see, my family has only one agenda. What best serves Luss Global Holdings and protects our employees. My grandfather said it time and time again that success takes total dedication without distraction."

There was never a reason for waltzing around in the afternoon just for the heck of it. From when he was a young boy, Ian knew he was different. He observed other people, couples, and devoured dramatic books and movies. There was something that fascinated him about *feelings* even though they were frowned upon, in fact, maybe because they were frowned upon. They were what made people know they were alive, a vital nutrient. They didn't scare him or hold him back or derail him. But he had to learn to hide them. Although, as his grandfather began to push him into finding a mate, he was no longer sure he could keep everything under the lid forever.

They strolled through a particularly dense grove of low-lying plants that created a wonderful mist. It was almost like they were in another mythical world. The sun streaming in thin rays between the palm trees above made Laney's golden hair absolutely glisten. He so wanted to touch it. Run his fingers through it. Just because. On a whim. Something they might both enjoy the sensation of. If he were another person. And if they were a real couple, of course.

She mused as if she were trying to fathom him. "No one else in your family feels like they're missing out?"

His grandmother found her private way. But his sister was already carrying on the Luss tradition. She married an investment banker, and they settled outside of Boston in exclusive Weston, where they had three young children. They came into the city to have ice cream with Grandfather on Sundays. No deviation from the program.

"How well has love worked out for you?" Oh, he didn't like how that sounded coming out of his mouth. He didn't intend to lack compassion or criticize the love for Enrique that Laney spoke of, but it sounded like it ended poorly.

Nonetheless, her face fell.

"I'm sorry, that didn't come out the way I meant it."

She looked down as they continued on their path. "No. You're right. Perhaps if I hadn't fallen for someone who didn't love me back, I wouldn't be in the situation I am now. Maybe you and your family's singleness of purpose is the better way to live."

Which couldn't be less appropriate given their surroundings. The elderly couple that Ian had seen being lovey-dovey on the plane to Bermuda were ahead. They held hands and shot bright smiles to Ian and Laney as they passed by, the woman saying, "We're celebrating our sixtieth wedding anniversary."

"How lovely," Laney said enthusiastically.

"You keep falling in love with each other, as we have."

Sixty years of falling in love.

Ian wanted to cry.

CHAPTER SIX

WHEN THEY GOT back to the villa, Ian emptied the bag of newly purchased items onto one of the big white sofas in the living room. Laney hadn't forgotten that comment he'd made about how love hadn't been working out that well for her and was still smarting a bit from it. It was true, but it really wasn't his place to say it. Fortunately, the rest of the walk through the peaceful grove and interacting with that charming elderly couple had diffused the situation.

Grabbing a pair of trunks and veering toward the small second bathroom off the living room, he said, "I'm going to change into a swimsuit, and then let's get in the water."

"Right. Sounds perfect." She took her suit into the master en suite.

She emerged a few minutes later with a tube of sunscreen. "Can you get my back?"

He cleared his throat. "Oh, yes, of course."

He seemed distant and she wondered what was on his mind. Perhaps he hadn't told a lot of people in detail about his family like he'd shared with her. Gift cards for his birthday instead of presents, regimented family togetherness times. Laney's mom had to scrimp and save to care for her daughter. Still, she always managed a little bit of spontaneity here and there, even if it was just to go out for a walk on a summer night. A life of ice cream on the third Sunday of the month from two o'clock until two thirty didn't sound healthy.

Still it was quite something that after being thrown together, Laney and Ian told each other a lot about their lives. Far beyond what she'd have figured as a maid of honor with her best man. More than she'd expect with anyone, really. Despite his fortune-focused upbringing, his family couldn't have been too terrible. He was raised to be an honorable man who had sympathy and who listened. Somehow an openness had formed between them. Like nothing she'd ever felt before.

"No one can ever get their own back, can they?" said Ian.

They walked toward each other, and she handed him the tube, then turned around.

"I wonder how people do it if they're alone." Might that be her someday?

Her vow to not put her heart on the line was unlike Ian's. For her, it was the issue of loving too much having done her in as opposed to not loving. What would being alone really be like, especially as the years rolled on? What if she was on a solo vacation and had no one to protect her middle back from harmful overexposure to the rays of the sun? Life was to be lived with others.

However, all musings were halted and siphoned out of her mind and body as soon as Ian's palm laid flat on her back. She was only human, after all, and his hand felt so lovely. She froze and was a little bit embarrassed at her automatic reaction to his touch.

"Is the cream too cold?" he asked, alarmed by her body's sudden stiffness.

"Oh, no, it's fine. Carry on." She couldn't tell him to stop.

No, she needed his ministrations. There was nothing to worry about. By the next time they did this, she'd be immune to the feel of his wide hand that pressed flat between her shoulder blades. He began swirling his hand outward in a slow spiral. That made her eyelids blink rapidly. She shouldn't let him provoke so much physical response. This was billionaire Ian Luss, who she was thrown onto this trip with by no choice of her own and who she would have no future relationship with regardless of what transpired between them. Yet, his hand on her back was intoxicating. Worse still, he seemed to be enjoying it, too, as he circled slowly over and over and over, making sure to rub in the cream, using his fingertips as needed to be sure it penetrated every inch.

A swirl with his palm, swirl with his palm, a rub in with the heel of his hand, rub in with the heel of his hand, finger in the contours, finger in the contours! The rhythm he established was completely unfair. Rendering her defenseless. Her eyes decided to fully close when his movements became overwhelming, dizzying. Fortunately, with her back to him, he didn't know that she could no longer keep her eyes open. Besides, she wanted him to finish soon. And she wanted more than anything in the world for him to not finish anytime soon.

She was sure she could feel the stream of his every exhale causing goose bumps to break out all over her skin. Was it necessary for him to stand so close that she could feel his lungs function? His hands slid down beyond the strap of her bikini top in order to apply the cream to her lower back. She made an involuntary *whoop* sound and her eyes popped open.

"Am I getting everywhere you want me to?"

Somehow those words poured out of him in a slow ooze like honey from a jar. *Am I getting everywhere you want me to?* It was an innocent question but sounded like sin with his cadence. Delectable sin that probably tasted like honey. She was glad she'd at least chosen the slightly more modest blue patterned bathing suit as opposed to the tiny triangles that comprised the black one. Still, she started imagining his hand traveling farther south than the small of her back, perhaps slipping under the fabric and squeezing and lifting and…

"Okay, I think we're good."

She inhaled and although it took all she had, she managed to take one step forward away from those hands that seemed like they were chasing her. And in fact, his hands did catch her to grab her by the sides and smooth the remaining sunscreen in his hands there.

"Wait, you don't want to burn anywhere, do you?"

She was glad that she'd put enough sunscreen on the front of her body while changing that he'd have absolutely no work there. Which isn't to say that her breasts didn't perk up at the idea of his hands getting near them. What if they had taken advantage of the beach being clothing optional and she wasn't wearing anything at all? Maybe he'd want to handle her sunscreen duties from head to toe.

Perhaps one of his hands might slip between her legs. At the thought, that very area contracted. Then released.

Then contracted again. *Wow.* She ordered her body and mind to stop all of this. This had no place in the fake newlywed game.

Finally, after all of that, she turned around. He looked shocked. Blood had drained from his cheeks and his jaw was ticking. His discomfort was obvious.

"Ian, what's wrong?"

Ian wasn't doing a sufficient job at hiding his reaction after applying lucky glugs of sunscreen to Laney's supple skin. He realized the look on his face was probably a combination of unbridled arousal and utter horror. He couldn't even begin to contend with the response inside his bathing trunks. How dare she have skin like that all over! How dare her curves make a man want to keep exploring the swerves and planes until the sun went down and then rose again in the morning!

It had not occurred to him that sharing space with her was going to present this sort of a challenge. He hadn't imagined her modeling sexy bikinis in a resort shop. Or gliding around a dance floor like they were waltzing on clouds. Not to mention that he'd shared with her all sorts of personal things about himself. With a frankness he'd never spoken out loud. Her thoughts did bring him further confusion about the way his family was at odds with his soul's desire. Making him fear he might not be able to keep stuffing down his truth, which left him feeling not only exposed but like a bit of a freak.

To the matter at hand, literally, he'd have to get through this week alongside Laney's luscious flesh. Because his blood vessels told him that his reaction to her wasn't just about her alluring beauty but that she was knocking on what was buried down low. In fact, the very thing he wanted to play at here in Bermuda, like an itch he could scratch. Though he was beginning to doubt that was possible, if he'd ever be able to purge the yearning out of his system. This week could become a disaster he'd carry for life if he wasn't careful.

He lotioned himself. He'd take a chance on his back being burned sooner than he'd let her hands glide all over him the way his just had on her. He willed the inside of his trunks to settle down. The cool Atlantic would help.

"Let's go."

He threw wide the doors that opened to the balcony with its staircase leading down into the ocean. The water glistened as the sun was cresting over into late afternoon. The trade winds created a sultry breeze. Laney took the railing and descended like a Venus born of a pearl in the sea she was returning to. He quickly ran down a few stairs to get ahead of her in case she needed a hand to help her down. Husband behavior, check.

"You're so beautiful." Those words fell out of his mouth. Okay, that wasn't too much, was it? Even a woman he wouldn't be in love with but would marry might still like to hear flattery. Like flowers and chocolates, all the contrived things still had their place.

"Not if you'd heard Enrique's opinions," Laney said. "Which he had a lot of."

"About your beauty."

"About my imperfections."

"Laney, believe me, you have no imperfections."

She tilted her head in contemplation.

"What were these supposed imperfections?"

"He told me I was too lumpy."

"Aren't women supposed to be lumpy?"

"Well, my lumps weren't *elegant*—I think that was his word."

Ian's breath caught. "That's disgusting. Your lumps are everything they should be. You fell for the wrong man." No question, her lumps were quite right just as they were. Every cell in his body was in agreement with that.

"The wrong man. I thought you didn't believe in the *meant to be* mate."

"Not for me. I have hopes for you." He chuckled.

"No way."

With that, they stepped off the last stair and into the ocean, which at that point was only ankle deep. They proceeded to walk farther and farther straight into the water as if they were promenading down the wedding aisle to be married. He wanted to take her arm in his, but of course, didn't, as a weird underwater wedding ceremony was probably the last thing on her mind.

When the water reached their waists, they both dove in, immersing themselves in the cool, clear water. After a few swim strokes, they bobbed their heads up. The water brushed back all of Laney's hair, leaving her shining face exposed, so exquisite it stole Ian's breath.

By the end of the day, Laney and Ian were tired. They decided to make do with the many gourmet snacks and big bowl of fresh fruit that had been left for them in the villa and to call for a proper dinner the next day. A countertop held raised platters with a variety of nuts, cheeses, salads, breads and the gooiest chocolate brownies ever made. There was more than enough to munch on, and they washed it all down with refreshing fruit drinks. Neither cared to open the champagne on ice.

They sat outside on lounge chairs facing the ocean's horizon as the sun set, watching the sky turn almost every color of the rainbow from red to orange to pink to the dark of night. They spoke of trivial matters, childhood things that weren't heavy like they had before—about Laney's poverty and lack of a father and Ian's family with their strange customs. They counted the stars in the sky.

When they decided to go inside, there *it* was, just as they'd left it before they went out. The master bedroom. Still easy to locate by the trail of rose petals that remained on the rich wooden floorboards. And the bed decorated with the gigantic rose petal heart. Where couples immersed in passion, the enticing scent of the flowers reminding them with every breath that tonight was one of the most significant nights of their lives.

Laney thought she might have had a honeymoon night like this with the man she thought loved her. A night to remember with every tiny detail as special as it could be. One she'd treasure not only through photos and videos but in her soul and heart as a commemoration of the beginning of the rest of their lives.

Instead, she was acting in this strange and almost tragic play, one that to Ian was emancipating. Whereas he was clearly fantasizing about a romantic love he wouldn't have, it could turn painful for her if she let herself get sucked into any of it. She was here to recreate, and there was nothing wrong with doing so in the company of a soulful man as long as she kept reality front and center in her mind.

Ian said it first. "We haven't discussed the sleeping arrangements."

Right. Exactly.

"It's kind of funny, all of this elaborate honeymoon stuff just for us. No one knowing that we're just bunking together."

"I'll have to remember to definitely *not* book a place like this for my own honeymoon when the time comes."

"What do you mean?"

He leaned over to the bed to run his hand through the velvety rose petals. "This. Champagne and petals. The romance checklist."

"You don't even want that on your honeymoon?"

"I suppose if my bride wanted it. As long as she understood that it's just for show. That our purpose is to produce the heir and the spare."

"Do you have that etched on a plaque in the office conference room?"

His face shot sharply toward hers, and for a moment, she was worried she had insulted him. His family was clearly suffocating, but she had no right to pass judgment on it.

"I do know one thing," he said after whatever bothered him had passed. "One of us could surely sleep on a sofa or one of the loungers on the balcony."

Sleeping outside alone. That didn't sound too good. "What if creatures from the sea with gigantic tentacles swept up to the mainland, encircled me and pulled me into the ocean? I wouldn't want that to be your fate, either."

"Glad to hear, thank you."

She glanced into the living room at the two sofas as if they would have gone anywhere since she last looked at them. And then she eyed the ginormous bed again.

"That's not a standard size, is it? It has to be custom-made. It's so big." There was fear in her voice.

Surely she wasn't worried that Ian was going to morph into one of those woman-eating invertebrates with tentacles and capture her, turning her into a sea creature who existed only for his pleasure.

Oh, Lordy. What was she thinking, and why did that sound not half bad? A crazy little wave splashed through her insides. Him capturing her with his tentacles.

"Yes, that bed looks as if it were custom-made." His jaw jutted forward. He was having some thoughts of his own.

"I'd imagine we can put a row of pillows down the center as a barrier and do okay."

"A barrier to what?" His eyebrows rose.

"I just… I just…maybe seems a little inappropriate to be sharing a bed with…"

"Don't worry, I think I'll be able to make it through the evening without throwing myself on you." It might not have been him that she was worried about. Reminiscing about his hand thoroughly rubbing that sunscreen into her back was enough to make her grow a couple of tentacles herself.

"I'm sorry, I didn't mean to imply anything. It's only—well, come on, this is unusual, isn't it?"

He turned his head away from her, but she followed it until she could get him to look into her eyes again. She hadn't meant to accuse him of anything untoward. And she was probably silly to think for even a minute that he might have been contemplating the activities that could transpire in that bed meant for lovers. He certainly wasn't thinking of said activities with *her*. Even though he professed to like her lumps, they both knew what he was after in a woman. And what she wasn't.

Although he was hard to second-guess. His eyes were so mesmerizing, dark and big. Like someone could just jump into them and be immersed, whole and surrounded. They locked stares for far too long. With all the strength she had, she was the one to finally pull away. His face twitched a little bit. She didn't dare imagine it was disappointment.

Finally, he said, "I do tend to toss around in my sleep, so let's use many pillows for your barricade."

He gestured at the dozen or so along the headboard. Turquoise, silver and blue cases covered pillows of varying sizes. Together, they built a sort of fortress going down a straight line from top to bottom, quite evenly dividing the bed in half, scattering some of the rose petals in the process. They backed off at the foot and checked their handiwork.

"This is like summer camp," she remarked.

"I didn't go to summer camp."

"Neither did I." She shrugged.

"In any case, it'll do."

He dug into his bag for a T-shirt, and headed over to the extra bathroom. While he was away, she slipped into the master bath to wash up and change as well. A peach-colored tank top with matching pajama shorts was what she'd brought to sleep in after the wedding. She claimed one side of the bed as hers and brought a bottle of water, a tablet and a book to the nightstand. She couldn't think of anything else she'd need for the night.

It was no big deal, she told herself. She was just going to spend the night—oh, wait, the week—with Ian, sharing the same bed. Once they stepped out the villa doors, they were Mr. and Mrs. Luss, but in here, they were just acquaintances taking advantage of an unused ritzy vacation.

It's no big deal, she chanted to herself. They should be able to just kick back and relax. No big deal. Her heart was beating faster than normal, but it was no big deal...

She climbed into bed and watched Ian reenter the room. He tucked himself into his side, and when both of them were lying on their backs, they couldn't see each other over the pillow wall they'd built.

"Goodnight then," he said, somewhat abruptly.

"The fragrance of these rose petals is really strong."

"G'night." He was done talking.

Hours later, she was still awake, willing morning to come. She listened to Ian breathing in rhythmic slumber. A thought circled around her, indeed like a tentacled beast, except this one was yelling at her to hold on and brace herself. Because the tide was rising.

CHAPTER SEVEN

IAN WONDERED WHAT a honeymoon night for a regular couple was supposed to be like as he tried not to toss and turn too much in the bed. He supposed it would surround the betrothed in a celestial cocoon. Whether it was filled with tender affection or driving passion, it would be the couple's own. It was a snapshot of their marriage they'd hold forever. He guessed that's what it would have been like if Melissa and Clayton were in this bed as intended. They'd have already had a wedding night in the presidential suite of the Fletcher Club, probably been excited and elated and punch-drunk from the wedding and reception. Plus, they already lived together, so it wasn't like in older times when the wedding night was the first time they'd have sex.

By tonight, here at the villa, they would have been able to finally exhale into the hope and calm that they believed matrimony was to bring them. Ian figured that even sick and gray in Boston from the food poisoning, they were managing moments of both positive memories and plans for the future. He was sure their good humor would incorporate the offending oysters into their personal folklore.

As for Ian, he was as restless as a slippery eel. He

couldn't see over the pillow wall to gauge whether or not Laney was sleeping. The bed was so big that her movements didn't even register on his side. All he knew was that he was sleepy but wide awake at the same time, and this was turning into a nightmare of a honeymoon night.

He was ruminating over and over again on two points. One was what a genuine night on a honeymoon would be like for him. The other was on the pretend bride he found himself in bed with. He couldn't get off the idea that a lot of realness had actually passed between them and that, in her company, he experienced himself in a way he never had before. Which was absurd, because in reality, it was just the situation that was getting to him.

Still, that authenticity with her nagged at him. It was so unexpected. He thought about that creep Enrique making her feel unwanted and how he'd like to give him a piece of his mind. Not treating her right in the first place and then leaving when her café burned down. Unconscionable. Not that there was anything to be done about it.

He tried to clear his head and meditate until the morning finally broke.

He finally heard Laney's voice after he'd watched the slow turn of sunrise over the ocean through the master bedroom windows. Feeling it was okay to do so, he yanked a few of the pillows separating them and tossed them to the floor.

"How did you sleep?" Laney asked.

"Great," he lied. "How about you?"

She rolled over onto her side toward him, and he followed suit to face her, but he was careful not to get too close physically. "Slept like a baby."

"Where does that expression come from? Babies wake up all night screaming for bottles or to be held, don't they?"

"Yeah, I guess so. How about I slept like a rock?"

"That makes more sense." Now he was engaging in pillow talk while Laney's hair splayed across the sheets, absolutely shimmering in the glow of morning. It was like every moment shared with her was a special one. As if he wasn't waking to the world alone. Just like a couple in love.

He needed to put a stop to all of those thoughts. It was one thing to go through all the actions and even feelings a newly married man might have. But it was another entirely to start thinking of Laney as his real wife. He needed to figure out a way to balance immersing himself in the encounter while not forgetting what it wasn't. That would have to be enough. They should get out of bed immediately. As a matter of fact, out of the villa.

"Shall we get some breakfast? Let's go to one of the restaurants."

"Good morning, and congratulations." The restaurant hostess identified them as honeymooners as soon as Ian mentioned which villa they were in.

With him in a pair of khakis and an untucked white shirt plus a pair of sneakers and Laney in a pretty white dress with orange-and-green-flower detail that she must have brought to wear to one of the wedding events, they appeared as a newly married couple enjoying the paradise they were surrounded by. The outdoor restaurant was under a canopy of shade plants. Every table set a bit apart from the next, with foliage hedges to make each one private.

"Look around," Laney half whispered, "there are only tables for two."

"Yes, remember, this is a couples-only resort."

"What if we made friends while we were here?"

"Let's don't. We already have enough to do convincing the staff that we're a couple."

A waiter arrived with two odd white mugs filled with coffee. Each was shaped into a curvy heart. Ian wasn't exactly sure where he was supposed to sip from, so he took an awkward slurp.

The waiter asked, "Lovers' breakfast for two?"

Ian didn't have a clue as to what lovers ate for breakfast that was different than what ordinary mortals did, but he wanted to find out.

"Well, that's a…presentation." Laney chose her words carefully when the meal was served.

A carafe of mimosas was brought to the table in an ice bucket shaped and painted like a top hat. The waiter poured the drink into two champagne flutes, which were made of glass but also curiously heart-shaped.

Once he left Laney asked, "How do they manufacture mugs and champagne glasses shaped into hearts?"

"I've never seen them before. I'd guess it's just a question of making the molds."

All the tables that Ian could see had the same setup. A couple of women laughed heartily. A young couple sat in silence. Perhaps something had gone wrong the night before in the lovemaking department. Or there had been an argument about something petty. A couples' resort could

be fraught with potential peril, there was so much expe-
catation. Once again, keeping emotions out of partnering
made so much sense. The right woman for Ian would be
the one who didn't make him feel.

Ian wouldn't put his Luss wife, when he found her,
through having to deal with things like heart-shaped
mugs and big smiles if she didn't want them. That was
a relief.

Laney brought her mug close to his. "See, they fit together."

She slid the open curve side of her mug into the
rounded side of his until they formed a whole. Like the
yin and yang symbol. Representing togetherness. One
bending to accommodate the other. In flow, in fullness.

As she locked her mug into place, her finger ran along
his, which gave his body another one of those tingles.
This was the spell lovers cast over each other. A mere
touch could change the other's physiology. He was sure
that if he and Laney had a legitimate honeymoon night,
nothing would have gone wrong in their lovemaking.
In fact, he would have seen to it that what transpired in
their bed would have been something to remember for
the rest of their lives.

Next, a tray was brought to the table. On top of it was
a dome formed of white lace.

"It's a wedding veil!" Laney exclaimed, showing Ian
the way the fabric gathered to a point that was attached to
a clear plastic comb. "See, that's what goes in your hair."

"My hair?"

She laughed. "It could. Traditionally, it would be for
my hair. You know, Melissa wore one."

"Yes, I know what a wedding veil is, I just don't know why it's on top of my eggs."

"Romance." They both sniggered.

"Well, thank you for clearing that up. I had no idea how unromantic my breakfasts had been in the past."

They dug into their eggs, breakfast meats and the basket of hot toast.

"Yes, the toast is heart-shaped," Laney said.

"Couldn't they think of some other shape to make the toast?"

"Like what?"

"What about round with a little protruding triangle like a diamond ring?"

"I love it! I'm going to suggest that to the chef."

"No, let's keep it a secret, and you can use it for your café when you open one."

Laney's head dropped sideways, looking both at him and past him. "You're so sure I'm going to?"

"Well, of course. Why not?"

"Nothing. I just appreciate the vote of confidence."

"Right. What that idiot you were with didn't give you."

She studied him in a silence that said more than a thousand words could. This funny, smart, lovely woman had not been valued. In a parallel world, he might like to spend the rest of his life showing Laney just how wonderful and appreciated she was.

"We should go before they give us a cake shaped like a wedding dress," she joked with a childlike enthusiasm.

"Do you think they might?"

As they strolled back to the villa, an idea hit Ian. "Unless you had something in mind for today, I'd like to take you somewhere."

"Okay."

He punched numbers into his phone.

Seemingly minutes after his call, he heard a car pull up alongside the villa. Adalson from the staff exited the high-end sports car convertible as Ian opened the front door. "For your leisure, Mr. Luss."

Laney, apparently hearing that they had a visitor, came to the door as well.

"How are you this morning, Mrs. Luss?"

"Great, thanks."

They were becoming less and less shocked every time they heard themselves referred to as husband and wife. In fact, it was becoming natural. That was the plan. Ian continued the conversation with himself as they sped up the highway. He wanted all of these married couple situations. For example, it would be okay if he thought his wife was pretty and intelligent and interesting, wouldn't it? As long as he didn't fall in love with her. Okay, that was tricky. In the meantime, Laney would have achieved her goal of relaxing and gearing up to start again in Boston. Then they would go their separate ways.

Of course, as much as he told himself all of that, his mind was a confused jumble, and his heart was sending messages that were becoming impossible to ignore.

"Where are we going?" Laney asked as Ian took the turns of the highway, wind blowing their hair.

"We'll be there in a few minutes," he answered and reached across the car's center console to squeeze to her forearm.

He didn't mean to do that. Which made him again question attraction and desire and how he was going to keep that all straight. Because the minute his fingers made contact with Laney's lithe arm, he wanted to leave it there and cursed the road for needing both of his hands on the steering wheel to navigate the twists as he steered inland from the coastal highway. They reached the salt-water pond surrounded by marshland that he'd read about.

"I thought it might be nice to be in still water today before we go back into the ocean."

As can only happen when one is staying at a top-notch resort where the answer is never *no*, the rowboat he requested was at shore. Alongside it were blankets and a basket no doubt filled with goodies.

"We're rowing?"

"I'm rowing. Your job is to take in the atmosphere." A charge ran through him at his own words. He was about to embark on something scary to him. And it wasn't using oars.

He helped her into the boat, where she sat on one of the two benches. With feet still on dry ground, he pushed the boat into the water and then quickly climbed in. He sat on the opposite bench facing her. He took the oars and began rowing away from shore.

It was happening. They were in a rowboat, the only ones in the pond. The sky was blue. There was enough breeze in the air to keep it from being hot. The over-growth of the marshes swayed gently. He was reenacting a scene from a movie he remembered first seeing when he was a young teen, just at puberty.

In the movie he'd since watched many times, an impossibly handsome strapping man in a white shirt with the sleeves rolled up was rowing a boat like this. Across from him sat a beautiful redheaded woman with pale skin and freckles. She wore a wide-brimmed straw hat with a black ribbon. All of which made them appear like they were in a period piece, although, actually, it was present day when the film was made.

The sort of classicism of the way the couple looked made an impression on young hormonal Ian. Like a painting come to life. The woman was ethereal in her beauty and pure in her grace. As the man rowed, he was solely responsible for her safety, and reveling in that honor and responsibility, their eyes told each other how in love they were.

Ian was so moved by the gesture of manhood in his rowing, something he'd never felt so distinctly before. It wasn't a question of the woman being dependent or fragile. It was simply that in taking charge of the rowboat, he was able to directly display his own masculinity and chivalry in a way that felt so natural, not confusing like the rest of puberty was.

Someday, he told himself back then, someday he would take a woman rowing, and she'd smile a pretty smile, and the thing that passed between couples would pass between them, giving him stature, giving him pride, giving him his place.

Of course, that was all before he understood about family codes and the Luss way of doing things. Secretly, though, he always hoped he'd get a once-in-a-lifetime chance to live out that scene from the movie that meant so much to him.

With his pulse jumping, lower parts in total chaos and all of his will, he embarked on the next part of the scene, when the man stands up in the boat and sings to his beloved. When he was teen, Ian had rehearsed it in front of the mirror using a variety of popular love songs. This time, he was going to sing the song that he and Laney had danced disastrously to at the wedding: "Meant as a Pair." That was going to be *their* song.

He took a wide stance to balance himself in the boat. "What I want is right there. We were meant as a pair. I would walk without fear," he crooned at the top of his lungs, a smiling Laney looking up at him with sparkling eyes. "Every moment we share."

Almost in disbelief that this moment was finally coming true, Ian stretched his arms out as wide as they would open, feeling the freest he'd ever been...

And with that the rowboat toppled over, submerging him and Laney down into the pond.

Oh, cripes! That wasn't part of the scene. He quickly brought his head above water and saw Laney's bobbing as well. "Are you okay?"

"Yes," she called out.

He swam the few strokes to her. The water wasn't deep, and they were able to get their footing. Holding her, he brushed her now wet and weedy hair back from her face.

"I'm so sorry."

"I'll bet," she said with a grin.

Without remembering not to, or deciding to ignore remembering not to, he took her face in his hands and brought his lips to hers. At first, he just brushed his against hers, taking in their pillowy coolness. But the second—yes, second—kiss lasted longer.

Ian didn't pull away. Didn't want to. He pressed his lips into hers with urgency. Which she met. And then he did it again. And again. The more he kissed her, the more he wanted to. His hands caressed her cheeks, finding her bones, getting to know them with his fingers while his lips still pressed into her plush mouth.

His lips parted so that his tongue could meet hers. Warm, almost hot, his throat let out a little moan he couldn't prevent. His hands moved to the back of her head so that he could bring her closer. Her hair was soaked and heavy. His mouth roamed from her forehead to her nose to her chin to her jaw.

This wasn't how the scene ended in that movie from his childhood. It simply cut to the next where the couple continued to flirt. The reenacting was over. This was real life.

Laney picked some leaves from his hair.

"Do you know anything about the Bermuda Triangle?" he asked in between kisses after it popped into his mind. "Why does this place have that name and reputation?"

"I read about it on the plane. It's also called the Devil's Triangle. A geographical region of the Atlantic Ocean where strange disappearances have supposedly taken place."

Disappear with me, Laney.

He kissed her again. "Strange how?"

"People say there's some kind of supernatural vortex."

"What has disappeared?"

"Supposedly, aircraft and ships, although there's no

scientific proof. Mostly around the mid-twentieth century. There was a famous case of five navy torpedo bombers that went missing. But when the investigations were complete, they had just run out of fuel."

He kissed her yet again. Maybe there *was* something supernatural about Bermuda. He was definitely being absorbed into a vortex. The Laney Triangle.

Lifeguard! Rescue ship! SOS! Someone please pull Laney away from Ian's insistent lips! Talk about the Bermuda Triangle.

She had those thoughts, yet it was like a dream in which somebody was mouthing words but no sounds were coming out. Maybe because her mouth was completely preoccupied. Her hair was sopping wet, she was mucky, her clothed body still immersed in water, yet none of that mattered. Not when Ian's seductive lips mashed against her mouth, hungry and demanding. She'd never been kissed like this and knew immediately that every kiss she'd receive for the rest of her life, if there were any, would be dull in comparison.

He tilted his head one way and then the other as he took from her with his mouth. In return, he tasted like the sweet and tart lemonade they had sipped in the boat before it capsized. Nothing had ever tasted so good. His kisses were telling her something. A mystery about him. Or a piece of wisdom about what two people could share. For someone who professed to have no future that included romance, his lips told another story. One of passion. One of bond. One of naked truth.

"What are you doing to me, Laney?" he whispered

against her mouth, unwilling to pull himself away to even ask the question. The vibration of his lips as he spoke each word confirmed she was in the earthly world and not hallucinating. "I can't get enough of kissing you."

"This isn't supposed to be happening." There. As if saying that out loud excused the predicament. Yet they kept kissing. "There's no one around. We don't have to pretend to be a couple."

"I don't know what's come over me."

"We should stop."

They should have. They didn't. She wrapped her arms around his neck, feeling the wetness of his shirt collar under his hair.

"Laney."

Ian's loveless mission made no sense. Enrique's rejection of her—and he never kissed her like that anyway—made no sense. The only thing that made sense was Ian and Laney in the middle of a mucky pond in the middle of an island in the middle of an ocean. That was all there was and all that mattered.

Wait a minute! "Ian, stop. Stop."

He respected her sudden exclamation and pulled back.

"We can't do this. We're not together. Nor will we ever be."

He raked his fingers back through his long hair that, while wet, almost brushed his shoulders. Impossibly sexy. "Of course, you're right. It must have been those stupid heart-shaped mugs at breakfast that made my mental circuits cross-fire. Or your devastatingly beautiful face."

"It's weird when you call me beautiful." Weird and sort of painful, like a wound reopening.

"But you are."

She smiled with a nod, "Enrique wanted me to have cosmetic surgery on my nose."

Ian stretched out his middle finger, which he used to stroke from the top of her nose all the way down to where it met her lips. "What on earth is wrong with your nose?"

"He thought it would look better if it tipped up at the end."

Ian gritted his teeth in disapproval. "That's repulsive, don't you think? I mean, I don't begrudge someone wanting to correct something they don't like about their appearance. But to have that come from someone else? That's just sick."

"Thank you for saying that, Ian," she sighed with a slow exhale. "I didn't think I would ever get close to a man after everything with him. But spending this time with you is making me realize that maybe I could someday, far in the future. With a better man. When everything doesn't conjure up bad memories anymore."

"If you were mine... I'm sure you'll meet the right person someday."

If you were mine.

He stopped himself after that, knowing she could never be his, and it seemed like he sensed it was best not to finish his thought and have it in the atmosphere. She, too, knew that outcome wasn't possible so there had to be a limit on how far this fantasy enactment that they were together went.

"What about you? Ian, those kisses just then didn't feel like they came from a man who has no interest in passion."

"It's your fault. You bring it out in me."

"My fault? Nah, you don't get to tag me with that one," she said with a nervous giggle.

"The secluded pond, your pretty dress, the rowboat, the song. I...lost my reserve."

"Probably something that doesn't happen to you much."

"Never again, if I can help it. You're dangerous, miss."

They smiled at each other for a bit too long. Okay, a lot too long. She had a responsibility here. He could potentially become out of control with this pretend honeymoon, and for her own safety, she needed to make sure that didn't happen. His effusive compliments. That passion directed at her. He was living out the person he truly was inside, maybe for the first and last time. It was like a dream. Too much to ask for her to play along without forgetting the temporary nature of it all.

She was only human, and being treated so nicely was something she was unfortunately not accustomed to. She wasn't immune to romance, either. It was all on her to keep it from going too far, as much fun as it was. To remember that she was on a magical adventure where the sand was pink, the man kissed like his life depended on it, and in a week's time, she'd be in Boston looking for a job and a place to live. Ian would return to buying mountain ranges, and they'd have some unforgettable memories to file away in a locked mental shoebox.

"We should get out of the water."

When they returned to the villa, after they finished picking marsh weeds from each other's hair and clothes, they retreated to separate showers.

His cheeks were flushed as he entered the bedroom afterward, dressed in a thick white robe and drying his hair with a towel. He regarded the bed, which had been cleaned and made up by the resort staff. Tonight's extra touch after the cascade of rose petals from the night before was a single chocolate rose and a scattering of individually wrapped other chocolates on the pillows.

Laney brushed the chocolates into her hand and put them on the nightstand. "We'll have to rebuild our pillow fort. I wonder what the housekeeper thought."

"On second thought, why don't I just grab a few pillows, and I'll sleep on one of the sofas," he said and gestured into the living room.

"Oh." She felt a sting of rejection. "Okay. Or I could."

"No, no, I insist. You enjoy the bed."

She didn't want to ask the reason for his decision. Although she knew fully well what it was. After those kisses that shouldn't have happened, he didn't want to share a bed with her. She could understand. The attraction to each other at the pond was not diminished now that they were back at the resort. Quite the opposite.

The villa was Mr. and Mrs. Luss's home away from home and felt as such. It was only too easy to imagine the next logical course of action. After a day together that included a lengthy interlude of kissing, they would fall into bed to continue. In fact, it might take making love all night long to satisfy the fervor for each other that had built up under the warm sunny skies. It was hard to even think of anything else.

She managed to say, "I'll order dinner."

CHAPTER EIGHT

WHEN SUNLIGHT STREAMED into the villa's living room, Ian was glad he was lying on his back on the sofa. He looked up to the whirl of the ceiling fan that had kept him cool all night. And cooling off was what he had needed following the events of yesterday. He was supposed to be practicing so that he'd have advanced knowledge of how to behave when he met the woman he was to marry. Husband training. The island, the resort, eggs under a wedding veil.

If only he'd stopped there. He'd had that adolescent memory of the movie where the man was rowing a boat with a pretty redhead on a tranquil pond. And he got to live that out. It really did fill his heart to indulge in the romantic notions he'd thought so much about. Even if he had to leave it at that, at just the once. Then, like an idiot, he accidentally tipped the boat over, which led to wet hair and a whole bunch of kisses. A whole bunch. An amount and quality he would not easily forget.

So the lesson learned was that he should not marry someone he wanted to kiss that much.

"Good morning." Laney made her way into the living room from the master suite, rubbing her eyes to get the sleep dust out of them. "I'm hungry. Are we ready for eggs under the wedding veil again?"

"I was reading that a Bermuda breakfast is a *thing*. Let's skip the bridal brekkie ball and go into town. I found a place that's well rated for serving an authentic Sunday codfish breakfast."

"It's not Sunday."

"That's what it's called, and the restaurant prefers to make money every day."

"Ha ha. Okay, I'll throw some clothes on."

She retreated to get dressed.

He tried to shut down the vision, but failed, that she'd be removing clothes in order to put others on.

As they tooled off the resort grounds in the sports car that now had become theirs for use, Laney adjusted herself in the car seat. She'd put on a white blouse that had a little ruffling at the V neckline, a tan skirt and a pair of beige sandals, all of which she'd picked up at the resort shops. He glanced over to her bare legs. She caught him doing so and adjusted her skirt again. He sensed she was feeling awkward about the kiss fest. He wasn't sure whether there was anything left to discuss about it, though. They'd agreed quite matter-of-factly on the drive back that it was a mistake and wouldn't happen again.

His body had told him otherwise in the shower when they'd returned to the villa. While she went to the en suite rainforest shower that had become hers, he again took the smaller bathroom. It was a more than adequate shower, and once in, he soaped up to wash off the pond water that had saturated through his clothes. Using the thick bar of sea-breeze-scented soap directly against his tight skin, he circled everywhere, hoping the suds would relax all of the tension that had built by his and Laney's torrent of kisses.

Unfortunately, all the ocean fragrance and running water served to do was arouse him further, making his groin surge for relief. He pulsed at the thought of her soaping herself up in the other shower. Then he indulged in an even more dangerous thought. If he was the one lathering her. Wasn't he supposed to be picturing elephants in the shower to keep those thoughts at bay? It wasn't working.

Then he was throbbing and turned the shower faucet to a cooler temperature in hopes that would calm his inflamed body. Yet, all he could concentrate on was running his palms down her arms in the pond, skimming along the swell of her breasts, noting in that instant how firm yet pliable they were. As the water cascaded down on him, he succumbed to a mental replay of the swirl of their tongues. He stroked his erection. At first, slowly, like the kisses. Until his whole body began to rollick and he became desperate for release. With long pulls he massaged into his need, bringing himself powerfully closer, closer, closer and then finally into an explosion that left him shaking under the water tap until his heart rate returned to normal. Once he recovered, he toweled off.

"There it is." When they got into the capital city of Hamilton, Ian pointed to the homey-looking shack.

Now that he'd spent most of the car ride reliving his urgent needs from last night, he implored himself to at least be present and enjoy breakfast with Laney, who should *not* be in his shower in any form and with whom he would *not* engage in any further activity that would make it appear otherwise. What he could do was quell his ravenous hunger with a huge breakfast.

He'd found the restaurant online, and they chose a table under the shade awning. About half of the tables were taken.

A tall slim man in a floral printed shirt greeted them. "Welcome. You ready for a big greeze?"

"We're tourists, what does that mean?" Laney asked.

"A great big meal. You're gonna let this old onion feed you a Bermy breakfast?"

"Yes, thanks. Onion?"

"Born and bred. We get that nickname because Bermuda onions are known all over the world. Call me Dack."

"Yes, feed us, please."

"You're staying at Pink Shores."

"How could you tell?"

"The glow of love. You can spot it a mile away."

Although what had passed between Ian and Laney was *not* love, he liked that it showed.

Dack quickly brought glasses of icy water, and they both took sips. "The codfish breakfast, right?"

"Yeah, we're here to try it."

As their food was being prepared, Ian asked, "So tell me about this café you want to open. Why a café in the first place?"

"I like café culture. I like to read and look out a window and sip something warm in the winter and cold in the summer. Of course, coffee and tea cost more than they used to, but you don't have to be a millionaire to buy a place to sit and unwind and daydream for an hour."

"Did you go to a lot of cafés when you were younger?"

"Oh yeah. There weren't many in Dorchester, but when I was a teenager, on the weekend, I'd take the T and find them all over the city."

"Because you liked looking out the window with a cup of coffee?"

"My mom worked all the time. So sure, it was nice to be around other people and just hang out. I didn't really like school."

A teenager with a working mom and a dad who'd skipped out. What lousy examples of men she'd had in her life. That knotted in Ian's gut. His family took care of their own.

"With all the brand-name coffee houses, is running your own café a viable business?" He couldn't help but put his professional hat on. Maybe he could help her.

"Well, I doubt anyone is going to get rich that way, but my business plan shows me making a living for myself after the first year when the expenses of opening are paid off."

"The codfish breakfast." Dack returned, each hand holding both an enormous plate and a smaller one. Once he laid everything down, he said, "Eat well."

"Oh my," Laney said as she surveyed what looked like enough food for a party. "What do we have here?"

"That's salted codfish." Dack pointed to the piles of shredded white fish. "Then boiled potatoes. Boiled eggs. Bananas. Avocado. Those are the traditional foods."

She gestured to the smaller plate that contained pancakes. "Corn cakes?"

"We call them johnny cakes. All right now, you dig in."

Ian forked up one of the potato slices and piled a bit of the codfish on top. The salt of the fish was nicely cut by the bland potato.

"Oh, I like the banana with the fish." Laney chimed in as they tried various combinations from their plate. "Such simple foods but so delicious together."

"I want to hear more about the café." Ian loved that Laney had something so well thought out that she wanted for herself and that even though the Pittsfield place burned down, she was planning to start again.

"I'd like it to have a cozy feel. A small library on bookshelves where people could either donate a book or take one they wanted to read. Big comfortable furniture. Although, of course, all new and gleaming equipment behind the counter."

"That sounds like Café Emilia in New York. Have you ever been there?"

"No. That's the most famous Greenwich Village café. It's been there for, what, a hundred years?"

"You have to see it. It sounds like what you have in mind."

"I'm not glad Melissa and Clayton got sick, but I have to admit, it's nice being on this unexpected trip. It's getting my mind going about the future."

Ian was worried that his mind was going in a direction he couldn't let it. He dug into his food again.

While they were taking a walk afterward, his phone buzzed. The sound of crashing waves made it a challenge to hear.

"Grandfather, I'm at the beach."

"That's all right, Ian, I won't keep you. I'm just calling

to let you know that I have the contact information for some women I'd like you to have dinner with."

Ian looked over at Laney beside him as they strolled barefoot in the sand, shoes in hand, the wind tousling her hair, a fun retro-type pair of sunglasses on her face. He didn't want to meet the women his grandfather had selected.

No one was going to compare to the woman he was with. The lines between practicing at being a husband and real feelings for Laney had become thoroughly blurred.

After exploring Hamilton, they toured the Crystal Cave and its magnificent mineral formations, thousands of powdery stalactites growing downward from the roof. Then it was back into the convertible, and Ian drove them toward the villa.

"If we can ever eat again after that breakfast, we have a booking for dinner at the resort's formal dining room," Ian said.

"Oh. I didn't notice that on the reservations. Melissa and Clayton booked it?" Laney asked.

"If you'd like to go, that is. Otherwise, I can cancel it."

"What would we do instead?" Laney turned her head toward Ian, whose eyes faced forward on the road ahead.

"Huh" escaped his lips.

What would we do instead? She was crazy to ask that aloud.

Surely what they should not do is be alone together. Not when memories of his kisses played over and over again on the sense memory of her skin. When her soul ached for more and her body tingled at the thought.

And if all of that wasn't bad enough, he had to go and say supportive things about her aspirations. As if her goal wasn't totally *basic*, as Enrique had criticized when he begrudgingly bought the café in Pittsfield. Ian heard her ideas as valid and interesting.

"Well, I've got a problem," she said.

"I'll try to have a solution."

That's how he thought. In solutions. She loved that about him. *Oops*. She *liked* that about him. She would never have any reason to *love* anything about Ian Luss. Enrique had all the right answers in the beginning, and look how that turned out.

"I don't have anything to wear. Everything I have with me is too casual," said Laney.

"I have a couple of suits with me, so I'm set. Book a personal shopper at the formal wear boutique at the resort. We'll buy you something as soon as we get back."

Again, Ian Luss was living on another planet than she was. Just book a shopper, buy a dress—that seemed obvious to him.

"If we've used up the shopping allowance, I'm paying for it, so there's no discussion about that."

Another matter of fact for him. Money, or lack thereof, was never an obstacle. Her life had been totally different on that score. Always budgeting, always compromising. Adding to the surrealness of this week were sports cars and rowboats and now, apparently, clothes.

When they got back to the central compound of the resort, Hans was leading one of his ballroom dancing lessons. Since they were trying to get to the shop, they didn't have time for a full lesson, but Ian waltzed Laney across the atrium to get to the other end.

"Well done," Hans yelled out to them. "You have the basics."

Laney was pleased by his comment.

They exchanged hellos with the older couple who had wished them the same sixty years of happiness they had shared. Laney adored how they took turns sipping from a paper cup of coffee while sitting on a bench by the fountain.

"Mr. and Mrs. Luss, I'm Solene." The austere, stiff-backed personal shopper introduced herself when they arrived at the dress shop.

Mannequins here and there were draped in high-fashion clothes, from a beaded gown to a little black dress worn with a strand of pearls to an architectural dress sculpted with a diagonal sash of fabric flowers. Laney was sure they'd be able to find something suitable for the evening.

Ian explained that they were dining in the formal room.

Solene asked, "What type of dress do you prefer?"

Laney didn't know. She thought of a time she had gotten dressed for a family function of Enrique's, and he didn't like what she was wearing. She understood *change into something else* in an entirely new way that night. That was the night she realized she'd never be who he wanted her to be. In fact, if she was honest with herself, that was the night she knew he would leave her. Her biggest regret was that she didn't leave him first.

She blurted, "Something simple."

"You looked great in green at the wedding," Ian explained to Solene, "She was the maid of honor."

Oops.

"At the wedding of some friends of ours last month," Laney said, jumping in, covering for Ian's foible.

He bit his lip in the most adorable way, like a five-year-old with his hand caught in the cookie jar.

"I like blue, too."

"I think you'd look best in a belted dress with a full skirt," Solene suggested. "That would flatter your figure."

Why did she make *flatter* sound like an insult? Thank heavens Laney had been able to shop on her own for those swimsuits in the casual shop the other day. Otherwise, the saleswomen there would have had a field day!

Ian must have seen the reaction in her face, because he chimed in. "Solene, you don't have to worry about that. Laney looks fantastic in everything."

A grin broke out on Laney's face that she couldn't contain. He was a special man, even if his future entailed squelching the best of himself. The pride and old-fashioned charm he had while rowing them on that boat, serenading her—wow. Before the tip-over, of course.

"Would you like to follow me to the dressing room?" Solene asked.

Laney couldn't lie. The shimmery navy-colored dress with a belt made of the same fabric did look great on her. The scooped neckline revealed plenty of cleavage but remained utterly tasteful. The full skirt wasn't too much, and it fell to midcalf. Laney thought that was called tea length.

"I like it."

"Would you like to show your husband?"

Husband lingered in the air for a few seconds, sounding like far too lovely a word. As for the dress, she knew she didn't need his approval, but she wanted it nonetheless. So she nodded and came out from the dressing room.

He raised his eyebrows at her. "My wife, you look stunning as usual."

"You like it, husband?"

"I do."

"*I do.* You've been saying those two words a lot lately, haven't you?"

"They will never get old."

Solene ducked into a storage area and reappeared with boxes. She opened them and removed two pairs of shoes. One pair were the highest, thinnest, heels Laney had ever seen, the vamp crusted in jewels that would go with the color of the dress. The second pair also had sky-high heels and a bunch of ribbons she didn't understand.

"Do you have any flats?" It was her honeymoon, after all. She deserved to be comfortable.

"Of course. But I think you'll find that a high heel gives a long and lean look that won't be achieved with flats."

There we go again. There was always something not perfect about her. She wasn't *long* enough. She wasn't *lean* enough.

"Let's see." Solene came up behind her. She lifted Laney's hair into a twist atop her head. "Perhaps an updo. You can visit the resort's salon, or I can have hair, makeup and nail services sent to your villa."

"I'll wear my hair down, thank you."

"She doesn't wear makeup," Ian interjected, like this was a tedious conversation they'd had a hundred times.

Solene's eyes sprang wide. "Certainly, Mr. Luss. I was only concerned that Mrs. Luss might feel uncomfortable if she was underdressed in comparison to the other ladies who will be guests in the dining room tonight."

"Why don't we let my wife decide for herself? She isn't concerned with comparing herself to others." It wasn't a question. "Darling, would you like to change out of that dress for now? I'm sure Solene will have it sent to the villa."

Gussied up for dinner, Ian and Laney entered the resort's fine-dining restaurant. Located on the second story of one of the buildings, three of its walls were made of glass, so there was an unobstructed view of the waves under the setting sun.

Ian gestured to the bar, "Let's have a drink."

"Good evening. What can I get you?" The bartender welcomed them, wearing a white shirt with a colorful print bow tie.

"Shall we try something local?" Ian asked Laney.

She nodded.

The bartender said, "One of Bermuda's signature cocktails is the Rum Swizzle. May I prepare two of them for you?"

"Sounds yummy."

"Here at Pink Shores, we use two kinds of rum, light and dark, for the subtle difference in taste and depth." The bartender narrated as he made the drinks, beginning by adding ice to a stainless-steel mixing pitcher. "Orange juice and pineapple juice. Grenadine. A few dashes of bitters. You can imagine how the bitters will contrast the sweet juices and grenadine in a most refreshing way."

"I can't wait to try it," Laney said excitedly.

"The most important thing," the bartender said, "is the tradition of churning the drink. This makes it airy and frosty. We use a mixing spoon, but traditionally swizzles were used, which are thin stems from a tree grown in the Caribbean." He poured the drinks into tall glasses, garnishing each with a slice of pineapple, a slice of orange and a cherry.

"Ooh, it is frosty to the touch," Laney said as she took hers. After a small tasting sip, she smiled at the bartender. "This is delicious."

"I'm so glad you like it. I'd recommend having a seat." He pointed to groupings of tables that lined the front-facing glass wall. "We should have a beautiful sunset in about twenty minutes. Very romantic."

"Great," Ian said. "After all, that's what we're here for."

He put his arm around Laney's shoulder, as a beau might do, and in turn, she put hers around his waist. They were very easygoing by now. He moved, then she moved in response, just like dancing with a partner. He led her to a prime table with a 180-degree view of the water. He pulled out a chair for her and slid it closer to the table as she sat. So much like a dance that he didn't want the music to stop. He felt almost drunk before even taking a sip of his Rum Swizzle. Everything with Laney felt not only authentic but enthusiastic and alive and thrilling.

"This is truly paradise," Laney said as she took it all in.

Indeed.

She sipped her Rum Swizzle. "Where did you vacation as a child?"

"Oh, you know, rich people places. Summer on a yacht in the Greek islands, winter on the slopes of Aspen or the Alps. Made for great photos for the media."

"You didn't have a nice time?"

"It was fine. But I would sometimes look at other families who were being affectionate with each other and laughing all the time, sharing food from each other's forks in restaurants, and—I don't know, there's just a closeness between people that I've never felt."

Until her.

"You don't feel close to any of your family?"

"I love them dearly. I was closest to my grandmother. But we're like a monarchy—formal. There weren't private moments that were just ours away from our image. No being curled around each other in front of the fireplace at Christmas, that sort of thing."

"That could be lonely."

Although no one in his family would have left a woman they'd impregnated to her own devices. "Were you happy as a child, Laney? It must have been difficult without a father."

"It was fine. I love my mom. That was what I knew. I didn't do well in school, although I think that was more the fault of the school than it was mine."

"What did your mother do for work?"

"She was a packer at a factory. It was hard on her back. Our world was small. That was why there was something for me about hanging out in cafés. They were places to stare into the middle distance. I would like sitting there imagining the lives of poets and astronauts and shipbuilders and grocery clerks, too. Thinking of the world as big."

They both reached for their drink at the same time, so Ian clinked her glass. Laney was endlessly interesting. He was used to the practicality of landowners and financiers in his orbit, not someone who talked of poets and daydreams.

Drink in one hand and fingers interlocking with the other, they looked out to one more of Bermuda's spectacular sunsets, just as the bartender had predicted it would be. The colors layered over the waves were truly awe-inspiring.

Finally, Ian said, "Too bad Melissa and Clayton missed out on this. It's a bang-up place for a honeymoon."

"Hey, we should call them, see how they're doing."

"Great idea."

Laney made a video call with her phone. Conveniently, both Melissa and Clayton were together. They were recuperating, and had managed to progress from their fare of plain toast and tea to applesauce and eggs. They'd decided not to come to Bermuda for the few days left on the trip, and would reschedule their honeymoon another time.

Laney tapped her phone, switching the camera lens to facing outward at the dazzling view. "Bermuda sure is nice!"

"Are you kidding me?" Melissa called out. "Showing me that is mean." But she giggled.

"We hate you," Clayton said, chiming in.

"Don't worry, it only looks like this when the sun goes down," Ian teased.

"In the morning," Laney added, "when the sun is coming up and the sky turns from a pale pink to white to the milkiest of blue, it's no big thing."

"You two are evil!" Clayton said.

"We have to go now. We're having dinner in the formal dining room where the walls are made of glass overlooking the ocean."

"Enjoy your applesauce," Laney said mischievously before ending the call.

"Your table is ready." The maître d' came to summon them as Laney was putting her phone in her purse.

"Ian Luss?" A booming voice from behind called his name.

"If you'll follow me." The maître d' gestured.

"Ian Luss!" The sound was so thunderous it echoed through the dining room. "What are you doing here?"

"Oh no," he whispered to Laney as he turned and recognized the barrel of a man as big as his voice, his jacket button straining to contain the whole of him. "Connery Whitaker."

"Who's that?" Laney hissed back as the man approached with a snaky slip of a woman next to him.

"He's a fat-cat landowner from Maine," Ian said of the older man. "Luss Global has done business with him. A real blowhard."

"Ian Luss, Ian Luss." Connery stuck out his hand for a shake three feet ahead of reaching them. "Fancy meeting you here."

Ian met his hand with its corpulent pink fingers and accepted a comically robust handshake. "A surprise indeed."

"What are you doing at a couple's resort? I figured

you for sewing wild oats in Beantown, taking all the hot young moneymakers in Boston for a ride."

He guided Laney closer to the conversation. "This is my...wife, Laney."

"Your wife, huh?" Connery regarded Laney with a leer from her cleavage to her toes. Then he spoke into Ian's ear but did a terrible job if he was intending for her not to hear. "You'll want to keep your options open with all the good-looking females at this resort. Nothing like a little honeymoon fling with another adventurous newlywed you get to say goodbye to afterward, if you know what I mean."

Ian mashed his lips, speechless.

Only then did Connery yank his companion into the fold. She was decades younger than him. Adorned with jewelry that looked like it could topple her over, she stuck out a hand as if for a shake and then decided not to bother and put her arm down.

"This is my new wife, Christie."

New wife? That sounded so off. Clearly the one that replaces the *old* wife. He wondered how many new models Connery had gone through.

"Nice to meet you." Ian forced a smile. He wasn't masking his discomfort with this chance encounter. He didn't need word getting back to the Boston finance community, or to anyone in his family, that he was spotted at a couples' resort in Bermuda.

Ian's eye caught the maître d', and he silently pleaded for help. Fortunately, he got the message. "Are you ready to be seated now, Mr. Luss?"

"Let's sit together," Connery announced rather than asked.

Ian whispered to the maître d', "Mr. Whitaker seems to be a bit tipsy."

"Understood, sir. Would you and Mrs. Luss like to follow me to your table? I'm sorry, Mr. Whitaker, but we only have tables for two available tonight."

"It was nice to run into you, Connery," Ian said as he took Laney's hand and quickly pulled her away.

Connery husked to Ian again, not quietly enough to miss being heard. "Funny, Luss. I would have figured you for a beauty queen wife. Must be love?" He guffawed and shrugged his shoulders, which made the jacket button at his belly lift up as if it was ready to pop. "Ya just never know, huh?" His shrill laugh swirled in a circle.

Ian shut his eyes for a moment, as he knew how insulting and obnoxious that intrusion was.

They were seated at a window table near one of the modern chandeliers made of glass blown into the shape of a wave, which fit perfectly with the ocean-blue upholstery of the high-back dining chairs and island wood tables. He could tell Laney was still reeling from that awful Connery. The fun of teasing Melissa and Clayton over the phone seemed like it happened hours ago.

Nonetheless, Ian ordered a bottle of the best champagne, the sommelier poured a small taste for his approval, glasses were filled, and Ian proposed a toast. "To the loveliest woman in the room." He tipped his glass toward her for a clink.

"As long as you don't care what work colleagues and

personal shoppers think." She sniggered as she tapped her glass to his.

"I still say to the loveliest woman in the room."

She sighed at Ian's toast. "Can I order for us?"

"By all means. I eat everything under the sun."

"We'll start with the lobster and mango salad," Laney said when the waiter came. "Then we'll have the grilled wahoo. With that, we'll have jasmine rice and asparagus. And for dessert the Grand Mariner and dark chocolate soufflé."

"You don't fool around," Ian said.

She smiled.

As the first course of lobster was served, Ian asked, "At that café you're going to open, are you going to serve hearty food, or are you thinking of just the typical pastries and breakfast items?"

"I hope nothing I serve will be *typical*."

"Touché."

"I had the idea that I'd like to serve sandwiches and toasts with an international flavor. Most cultures put something yummy on top of bread. For example, an open-faced tartine or a pressed sandwich with appetizing grill marks on the bread. Yet uncomplicated. I wouldn't have a restaurant kitchen."

"I was telling you about Café Emilia in New York. They made clever use of their limited space by transforming an old wraparound bar in the back of the room for their food stations. Same idea as what you're talking about, just soups and pastries."

"I'll have to go see that someday."

"How about tonight?"

"What?"

"When we finish dinner. It will still be early."

"It's in New York."

"It is." Ian pulled his phone out from his pants pocket. After a few swipes and taps, he announced, "A private plane will meet us in an hour. We'll spend the night at the Hotel Le Luxe. I booked a penthouse suite."

"Just like that?"

"Yes, just like that. Although perhaps we'll cancel the soufflé and have dessert there."

CHAPTER NINE

"WELCOME TO NEW YORK," an attendant met Ian and Laney as they made their way down the boarding stairs after their small plane landed.

On cue, a limousine pulled right up on the tarmac, and a driver in a black suit and chauffeur's cap opened the passenger door for them to slide into the black butter-soft leather seat.

"I've taken the liberty of pouring some champagne," the driver said.

"Exactly where we left off in Bermuda." Ian noted that, per his instruction, the same champagne they were having with dinner was served to them in the limo.

"I still can't comprehend this," Laney said as she took the flute he offered. "The flight was like a blink, and now we're in New York. I didn't even change my clothes."

She was still in that attractive navy dress they'd bought earlier from the resort shop. Before they left for the flight, Ian suggested they quickly throw some things in a bag for the evening and morning, and then they'd take a flight to arrive back in Bermuda by lunch tomorrow. After all, they'd be eager to get back to their honeymoon.

He sensed Laney's breathlessness over the impromptu plans and was glad for it. Between that snooty saleswoman at the boutique and that awful Connery Whitaker they'd run into, he wanted her to have nothing but pleasure for the rest of the night. He really disliked that windbag, who was probably on his umpteenth wife and didn't have a clue how to treat a woman. That creature draped on his arm seemed uninterested in anything.

After just a bit of driving, Manhattan came into view, the glittering skyline with its skyscrapers and landmark buildings.

"The city never disappoints with its wow factor, does it?" said Ian.

"I've only ever approached it from a train, so I've never even seen it like this," said Laney.

When the driver parked in front of Café Emilia, he came around to open the door. "Here we are, sir."

"Just as I remembered it," Ian said and helped Laney out of the car.

She read the white cursive on the blue awning, "Café Emilia, Est. 1924." Then she looked up at the narrow red brick building, the second and third floors part of the café, window boxes displaying multicolored flowers.

"So here you are."

In between the two small outdoor patios was a heavy wood door, which he opened for Laney. They stepped inside.

She took a brisk inhale. "Smells so good. They roast their own coffee here."

"Freshly ground coffee, so aromatic."

The walls were covered with historic photographs in

mismatched frames, the owner's family, celebrities and politicians, patrons over the years.

Laney moved toward some of the photos to get a better look. "I love it. Café life. Same as now." She swept her arm to gesture around at the room.

People sat on black metal parlor chairs around creaky wood tables, drinking, eating and talking. Larger groups sat on timeworn benches at long tables. The main room was huge and was divided into three seating sections.

"Between the din and the smell, it's like stepping into history," said Laney. "What a scale this is on. So much management."

"I think later generations of the original family still run it."

"Let's see those." She moved toward a wood case that housed antique espresso machines and other equipment, some chrome and some bronze. "Look at the detailed metal work that went into making those urns. Some have the café's name on them."

"And this collection of coffee cups and saucers spanning the years."

"It's so loud and alive in here."

"How would you like to work in a place like this every day?"

"Nothing wrong with that! But I'd imagined my own place to be a wee bit smaller," she said jokingly.

"Here's what I wanted to show you." Ian cupped her elbow to lead her into the back of the crowded room.

A curved bar top, the counter made of marble with brass fittings on top of a solid wood foundation was probably where customers in the early days would be served a quick espresso.

"See how they use this as their sandwich bar," Ian said.

Laney pulled him backward so as not to be in the way of the staff, who were filling orders at breakneck speed.

"Yes, I see." She pointed to one area where a few cooks in chef's jackets were preparing deli sandwiches. "They have everything well laid out to make the assembly as efficient as possible."

"And over there."

"Old panini presses. Ooey gooey sandwiches with a nice crisp on the outside, lovely with a hot cup of coffee."

"And over there—" he pointed to another station with cooks hard at work "—they're making toast."

"It's all perfect." Along another area was a pastry case filled with selections. "This is great. I've always wanted to come here."

Laney smiled so genuinely it turned Ian's belly to mush. Elation sparkled over him like glitter. Making her happy was profoundly satisfying. Wasn't that what made life worth living? Creating and sharing joyous and meaningful moments, and recognizing them as such.

Ian wondered if his parents had those small flashes of light that added up to a profound contentment. If they did, it didn't show. He never saw enthusiasm or exuberance. Nothing unpleasant, either, only that the day-to-day was all they made room for. They didn't seem *un*happy. Perhaps they had everything they needed. They were able to play by the rules and live within the lines. Still, Ian couldn't help thinking that they only lived half-lives without knowing passionate love.

After Laney had her fill of looking around, he said, "Let's go upstairs."

He followed her as she climbed up the wrought iron spiral staircase.

"Oh, just as it looks in all of the photos I've seen!" she exclaimed when they reached the second floor. "Like someone's living room. Someone who collects old books, that is."

"Yes."

Wall-to-wall bookshelves held thousands of volumes. Dusty hardcovers and paperbacks with cracked spines. More books than the shelves could handle. They were crammed in vertically, horizontally and even diagonally as needed. Some of the shelves buckled from the weight. Stacks of more books with heavy glass slabs atop them created makeshift tables, surrounded by a hodgepodge of chairs and sofas, leather, wood, metal.

Most of the tables were filled with small groupings of patrons involved in conversations as they bit into delectables from small plates and drank coffee. Cups with saucers and tiny espresso demitasse bore the current iteration of the café's name and logo, and tall glasses held milky recipes and frozen drinks.

"The vibe here is so excellent," Laney said, marveling. "Exactly how I thought it would be."

"Photos can only tell you so much. There's nothing quite like being here in person."

"I want to see the top floor."

Another go-round on the spiral staircase led them to a much smaller third-floor room furnished with larger tables and straight-backed chairs. This was the student haven.

In a sotto voice, she said, "I think customers respect that if you sit up here, it's meant as a quieter space."

"For people to read and write and study. It's lower key up here, but you can still hear all the city sounds coming in from the open windows."

"Well, we *are* in New York, after all."

Laney went to one of the open windows and peered down to the Greenwich Village streets. People of every kind bustled to and fro, young and old, local and tourist, student, career person, downtrodden, everyone.

"After this, can we go for a walk?" Laney asked.

"Your wish is my command." Ian Luss didn't generally talk like a lord from the Regency era. Laney had the oddest effect on him.

He was ready to break into a poem but managed to hold himself back. Crooning from the rowboat was enough. The point of this week was to get his longings out of his system. Instead, he was letting them *in*, and *out* was not going to happen without a fight. He'd better start now. He'd better start fighting right now...

He really was having that thought, to gain control and put the week in perspective, but once they stepped out of the café to the breezy, leafy evening, he kissed her. Another unscheduled kiss! That he promised both her and himself they weren't going to have more of. Yet he kissed her, a long passionate press that could not be misunderstood. And there was no denying that she kissed him back with equal zeal.

"Oh, no, again? We're supposed to stay away from

each other." She giggled as she backed away from his mouth, making him lunge forward when she moved her head to the side to avoid the contact.

They both laughed.

"Walk, we were going to walk," Ian said.

They did, about twenty steps to a traffic intersection, where they had to wait for a green crossing light. And kiss. They had to kiss. As if it were the law.

"I have an idea," said Ian.

"What's that?" She slid her fingertips up and down along his arm, a sensation that was sent from heaven.

"I'll show you at the hotel." He tapped into his phone for the limo that came so quickly it was as if the driver was just around the corner.

They whirled uptown to reach the Hotel Le Luxe. With access activated from his phone, they rode a private elevator to the penthouse. The view from the suite of Central Park, its ground-level greenery and the tall buildings that bordered it was spectacular. The lavish layout, far more than they could utilize in one night, was furnished with fine black-and-white furniture, sage green accents and several fresh flower arrangements.

As soon as the door clicked shut, she toed off one shoe and then the other. Then she wrapped her arms around him and initiated another kiss, another five. She hushed into his ear, her mere tone making him twitch.

"What's your idea?"

"I was thinking," he answered in an otherworldly sing-song, "and you don't have to agree. I was thinking that maybe the only hope for us is to take this honeymoon charade to its logical conclusion. We'll make love. Once and just once. That will put to rest the curiosity and temptation that we obviously feel. And then we'll have seen the fake honeymoon all the way through and be done with it. What do you think?"

It was as ludicrous as it sounded once he said it out loud.

But she slid her hands down to his waist and brought him closer to her. So close, in fact, that there was no space between them.

"Excellent idea."

What was Laney doing on the plushest mattress ever made in a penthouse suite at the Hotel Le Luxe in New York? She wasn't going to be able to reason out an answer to that. Because a gorgeous six-foot-plus Ian Luss, with lips that ought to be illegal, was laying on top of her, planting his mouth into the crook of her neck and making mental capabilities impossible.

"Ian," she managed to say.

"Yes?" His breath was hot against her skin.

"Don't stop doing what you're doing."

"I can't promise that."

"Why?"

"Because I might need to do this instead." He threaded his fingers into her hair and with his thumb lifted up her chin so that he could focus his slow kisses down the front of her throat, making her moan repeatedly.

"Ian," she cried, all but begging.

"I'm still here."

"It's that I don't want you to stop doing."

"This?" he teased with the tiniest bite at the base of her

throat. And then he returned to the swerve of her neck, where his bite was bigger and more forceful. "Or that?"

"Yes."

"Yes, which?"

"Yes."

"Yes?"

"Yes."

And with that, he silenced the conversation, at least for the moment, by covering her lips with his, enveloping her with his arms and legs. His hands traveled from her face to her hips. Tugging up the skirt of the evening dress she still wore so that he could slide one hand between her bare legs, eliciting another desperate moan from somewhere far inside of her.

Meanwhile, her own hands wound around him on top of her to pull his shirt out from being tucked in his pants, needing similarly to feel his taut flesh in her palms.

"I think it's about time we get these clothes off. This is their second country in one day. They're tired."

He climbed off her, her whole being screaming at the loss, but knowing it was necessary. He unfastened the belt of her dress, satisfied to separate the two ends. Sliding his hands under her, he unzipped the back. From there, he was able to slip the dress over her shoulders and pull it down to reveal the silvery blue bra she'd worn underneath. Continuing his effort, he pulled the dress all the way down past the gray undies, along her legs and then off, tossing it to the bench beside the bed.

He cupped her breasts atop the smooth fabric covering them and deftly found the front clasp, which he was easily able to click open. He let out a gasp of pleasure that thrilled her to the bone as he held her bare breasts in his hands. He circled their contours, learning them, squeezing, buoying, pressing them together. He buried his face between them, tantalizing her with the slight scratch of stubble from his end-of-the-night facial hair. When his tongue flicked across one tight nipple, her head threw back on its own volition as current after current of yearning ran through her body.

"Oh," she piped, "I need to slow down."

"Of course."

"I want to savor every minute. Because we're only going to do this once."

"Yes. We want to get it right."

"Right," she repeated as she rolled on top of him, straddling his hips with one knee on either side of him and enjoying a slow unbuttoning of his shirt. Delighting in palming a few more inches of his solid chest with each button's release. Reveling in his arousal between her legs. She finally glided the shirt off him.

His hands went to her shoulders, and he flipped them so that he was on top of her again, where she was grateful that more of their naked flesh touched each other than before. Back to that path he was forging down the column of her throat, and this time going farther, between her breasts, down her ribcage to the elastic band of her undies. Where he stopped to deliver a million and a half tiny kisses, making her desperate for his mouth to go farther, to know more. At long last his tongue slid under the fabric, where he kissed across one hipbone and then to the other, intoxicating her with his patterns, sending her into an elated state she'd never been in before.

Just when she thought she couldn't stay still a moment longer, he bit into the gray silk of the underwear and used his teeth to drag them off her. With her sex uncovered for him to see, he used both of his hands to part her legs and then began another of his trails of kisses up the inside of one leg to her very center. Using the tip of his tongue to coax her open, she relaxed her legs and welcomed his attention. He made her bloom, opening and welcoming him more with his slow circles up one side and down the other. He varied the pressure of his tongue from barely making contact to long deliberate licks, occasionally rearing his head back to monitor the pleasure on her face as her eyelashes fluttered.

Her core clenched, contracting and releasing, contracting and releasing as his able tongue measured her responses. When the squeezing became more frequent, he slowed down, helping her prolong the inevitable. Finally, she couldn't hold on and went over the edge, freefalling as her body trembled and quaked while he kept his tongue in her. Then he held her and patiently waited until she stilled.

When she did, her hands appreciatively slid down his sides and then inward to the fly of his pants, where she quivered at the hardness inside. She unhooked the tab, released the zipper and, a bit to one side and then the other, inched them off him, along with the boxer briefs he wore underneath. His hips thrust forward, begging her hands to explore, and they eagerly obliged. His sex throbbed, and she knew the next thing she needed was to have him inside of her. He leaned away long enough to grab a condom from his bag, and she watched as he fit it onto himself.

He crawled back on top of her. His mouth took hers greedily. "I have to have you."

"Be inside me," she said, concurring.

She'd been through so much with him already. The kinship they'd developed. The open conversation, the confiding in each other, the frankness about their lives and their positions and their goals. This was the obvious next step, to learn each other this way, to know each other from the inside. She wanted this, too. Once.

Years from now, tonight would remain one of the defining moments of her life. This gorgeous, brilliant, distinguished man had shared this interlude with her, the week in Bermuda, the pretend honeymoon, this spontaneous overnight to New York, and now this carnal joining. He wasn't Ian Luss of Luss Global Holdings and the constrictions that implied. And she wasn't Lumpy Laney from Dorchester. They were something much higher, much more elemental. They were man and woman. Light and dark. Hot and cold. Heart and soul. Sun and moon. Husband and wife.

It wasn't her fate to have him forevermore even if she was able to. He was only a moment in space and time that she hadn't known she needed. To make her feel hungered for, to put distance between her and the past. Most unexpectedly, they were thrown together to help each other get to where they were going next. Sent from providence for that purpose alone. And that was okay.

He needed to process his genuine torment about romantic love that he wasn't going to carry with him into his family-approved future. For her, he was a gift from the heavens, the recharge that came in a surprise package and would only stay a short while. Although a hunch within her knew it wasn't going to be so easy to say goodbye.

With an even greater level of need, he positioned his body on top of her. In one thrust he entered her sex, which was wet and waiting for him. It didn't surprise her body that he was a perfect fit, shifting into place, to where he belonged.

They rocked together as one being, coming almost apart but then pushing back together, as if their bodies couldn't withstand a full separation. With hips swirling and undulating, they danced a waltz they needed no lesson for, as their bodies somehow knew it already. The music their ears heard intuited how to dance toward the crescendo, the full articulation, the culmination, as the cymbals crashed together into ecstasy.

It was still the deepest black of the New York sky that reflected from the tall buildings when Ian looked out the windows. He'd already sat up, swiped open his phone and was putting the plan he'd devised during the night into play. Once done, he studied Laney beside him on the bed, asleep, resting her head on the palatial hotel pillows. A tug pulled at him from the sight of her like that, almost childlike in her peace, each breath filling her with slumber. She was almost too captivating to wake up. However, he had somewhere to take her.

Leaning over, his fingers couldn't resist threading through her hair and smoothing back the strands that had fallen forward. Her eyelashes flickered a bit. The back of his hand caressed her cheek until she woke enough to smile in acknowledgement of his contact.

"Why are you awake?" she cooed.

"We're going out."

"Wonderful idea. In a couple of hours."

She started to roll as if she were going to turn her back to him. Kisses to the top of her shoulder stopped her.

"No. Now."

"No." She laughed. "Later."

"It's urgent."

"Nothing could be that urgent."

"Okay." He buried his face into her hair and could see her point in refusing to leave the comfort of the bed. "You're going to miss the big surprise."

"Surprises are appreciated during daylight, too." He began administering little suction kisses up and down her neck that he knew would be annoying. He was successful.

She giggled and said, "Stop that!"

"Only if you get up." He pushed the blankets to the side, revealing her glorious nudity.

"Grar!" She made a funny grunt that sounded like it was coming from an old man, but she did get out of bed. "How am I supposed to dress for this surprise?"

"What you're wearing is fine."

All she had on was a little bit of perfume lingering from the night before. Which she didn't even need, because he adored the fragrance of her skin. Of her hair. The taste of her mouth. And of every part of her. Which he'd explored thoroughly and could have been ready to start again from the top and work his way down.

"Very funny."

"We brought jeans and jackets. It might be cold out right now."

"Where are we going before dawn, anyway?"

"You'll find out soon enough."

They rode the private elevator down to the hotel lobby, which was almost empty except for a couple of groups with luggage beside them, perhaps leaving for an early flight. The driver he'd booked was waiting outside as arranged, and Ian and Laney got into the back seat of the town car.

After a quick ride to the border of Central Park, the driver pulled over, and they exited.

"We're going to the park?"

"In a way." He held out the crook of his arm for her to take as he walked her away from the sidewalk and into the grassy dampness.

"What's happening?"

"Over there."

Illuminated by the milky glow of an old-fashioned lantern as morning mist began to lighten the sky, a man dressed in a top hat, black tailcoat and a plaid scarf sat in an open-air carriage led by a white horse. Ian couldn't manage any internal cool at all as they approached. A horse-drawn carriage at dawn was such a silly and cliché symbolism of romance. He was already loving every damn minute and was so glad he'd thought of it.

"What is this?" Laney tilted her head quizzically as he led her toward the carriage, the horse in its magnificence draped with a red satin cloth.

"Milady." The driver hopped down from his seat, crossed his hand around his midsection to bow forward at the waist, extending one foot into a pointed toe that would have been at home on a Broadway stage. "I am Farrell, and my horse's name is Sonny. We are at your service."

"We're going on a carriage ride?" Laney was flabbergasted, which brought a satisfied smile to Ian's lips. He wanted to dazzle her, and he seemed to have succeeded.

"Milady, would you like to get to know Sonny? Perhaps give him a snack?" Farrell pulled a carrot out of a sack and handed it to her.

She didn't hesitate and went right to the horse, with his pristine white coat, and fed him the carrot. Giving a gentle pet down the length of his face, she said, "Hello, Sonny. It's nice to meet you."

After a few minutes with him, Farrell suggested they get going. He brought Laney to the side of the carriage and saw to it that she hoisted herself safely up the step and into the carriage seat. Then Ian joined her. He made a fuss of unfolding a plaid flannel blanket over their laps. Farrell pointed to a picnic hamper on the floor beneath them. "Everything you ordered, sir."

Then they were on their way, *clippetty-clopping* into the almost-silence of the park. Ian opened the hamper to find a large thermos, which he opened. He poured steaming liquid into the two heavy black ceramic mugs, which bore drawings of the carriage on them.

"Hot chocolate." He handed her one.

Off they went through the paths between trees, the sky opening more with every trot the horse took. Daylight was starting to grace the sky with a pale blue glow. The air smelled fresh and woodsy.

"Ian, I can't believe you thought of doing this."

"Honestly, I can't, either."

He reached into the hamper to pull out a crystal bowl filled with bright red strawberries. He wasted no time in feeding her a berry, enjoying in great detail her comely lips opening to accommodate the fruit.

"My turn," she teased and dipped her finger into the bowl to take one.

As she brought it to his lips, the veins in his body coursed with awareness. She put him through an exquisite pace by running the end of the strawberry slowly across his top lip and then around to his lower, making a full circle before feeding it to him. He bit in. It was as sweet and juicy as he knew it would be.

"This is fun."

"I'm glad you think so."

As the carriage passed the park's carousel, wordless without children in the sunlight of day, he dug into the hamper again to pull out a box of the tiny cupcakes he'd ordered. He chose a lemon one and brought it to her mouth, letting her think he was going to feed her the bite-size confection. But instead, he swiped his finger to get the frosting, which he painted across her lips, just as she'd done with the strawberry. Only he took it further and licked the sugary cream straight from her, thinking that was possibly the most delicious thing he had ever tasted. A little sigh of approval escaped her lips. He could imagine listening to both her laughter and her sounds of pleasure for the rest of his life.

Which brought up an interesting point, he thought to himself. The more he lived out these acts of romance, the more he wanted them. Her. It wasn't simply the idea of romance he was enchanted with. It was Laney. He didn't know why or how, but he knew he wanted her beside him and to be beside her. He didn't know how he was going to keep to their nonsensical pact to make love only once to rid themselves of the curiosity and then be done with it. This whole getaway had been so magical, so divine, he knew something absolute had happened. That he wanted to be only with her and for the rest of his life. It wasn't going to be merely hard to part when the honeymoon was over. It was going to be next to impossible, like having to leave his soul behind.

While his arm wrapped around Laney's shoulder, Farrell guided the carriage toward the Sheep Meadow section of the park, so named because actual sheep roamed the vast lawn a century ago. Sonny trotted through the paths that were populated only by a few early morning joggers. Ian felt as if they were galloping away from something and toward something new. As Sonny brought them closer to the Bethesda Terrace and Fountain, Ian heard the sound he was expecting as it seeped through the thick of the sunrise.

Laney turned her head for her ears to chase the sound she couldn't exactly make out. She asked, "What am I hearing?" When they got a little closer the sound came into focus. "Is that a violin?"

"Can you make out the song?"

She sang out the notes as she put it together. "What I want is right there. We were meant as a pair. Oh, it's 'Meant as a Pair.' From the wedding. And you sang it on the rowboat. How can that be?"

When they got to the terrace, she could see that a violinist stood in the shadows of dawn wearing a coat and tie, coaxing the melody from his strings.

"How could he be playing that song?"

"You mean *our* song?" He sang, "I would walk without fear. Every moment we share."

"Did you arrange this?"

"Of course."

"Oh, Ian." She brought her hand over her mouth. Tears welled in her eyes.

Farrell slowed the carriage to a stop.

Ian hopped out and then helped Laney down. He brought her closer to the music, each note resonant, almost weeping from the lone instrument. Then he placed his arm around her waist and began to lead them in a dance.

The violinist played on, accompanied by the morning hush.

"We know how to do this now," he murmured into her ear. "All of it."

Indeed they did, had learned how each other's bodies moved and reacted. In the penthouse bed as well as now. Inside the intimacy of the moment. In New York at dawn. They danced. Just them.

"Ian, for an anti-romantic, you sure know how to woo a girl."

CHAPTER TEN

"THAT WAS THE most incredible experience of my life." Laney gushed from her plane seat. She was holding the bouquet of purple asters that the carriage driver Farrell presented to her when the ride was over. That, of course, Ian had arranged.

He pointed out the window as the plane ascended into the skies. "The Empire State Building."

She watched until the landmark building was obscured from view by the clouds. Ian squeezed her hand in a gesture she could only interpret as togetherness.

"Really, Ian, I want to acknowledge everything you did to make this overnight to New York so special. It's the nicest thing anyone has ever done for me."

A wide smile cracked across his mouth. His grin, coupled with the sparkle in his eyes, made her gulp.

"I'm glad you enjoyed it so much. It was fun for me, too. Really. Really fun."

Although, plane rides and horse-drawn carriages and throwing money on wild things wasn't going to solve his real problem, which was how he was going to live day after day, year after year, without being true to himself. To who he was.

"You know, I think you're going to have to work a little romance into that *strictly business* marriage you keep talking about. It's in your makeup, you can't deny it."

His eyes shot to the middle distance, a bit of a sad pallor taking over his face.

She hated that she'd broken his smile. "I'm sorry, did I say the wrong thing?"

"No, no, it's fine," he said distractedly. "I'm just glad we have a couple of days more in Bermuda before the week is out."

"Yeah." Laney chewed her lip.

The mood in the private plane's small cabin had turned melancholy. Could he have been thinking what she was? That maybe making love was a mistake. Making heart-pounding, all-encompassing, heavenly love put them in jeopardy. Because in Bermuda at the resort, they were pretending to be a couple. Alone at the pond, they'd had no such obligation. Or in New York at the café. Or at the penthouse. Where they were merely Laney and Ian. They didn't have to convince anyone they were together. There was no reason what happened had to happen. Except that it had.

"What would you like to do when we get back to the island?"

She could tell he was making small talk. That was fine. She'd welcome getting out of her own head, worrying about what she was going to miss that wasn't real in the first place.

"Maybe not on a rowboat, but being in the water as much as possible. I'm not in the water much in Boston. Are you?"

"Not in town. But my family meets out at the vine-

yard fairly often. We have a compound there." A compound at Martha's Vineyard. Of course, the Luss family
has a *compound*.

She could only imagine, an enormous piece of property
with both developed and undeveloped portions. A mansion
with a swimming pool and tennis courts, maybe a private
beach or dock. Outbuildings, guest houses and dedicated
entertaining spaces, a band shell, gardens, animals.

Soon, he'd be returning to a life she could hardly con-
ceive of. She wouldn't see him again unless they were
invited to something by Melissa and Clayton. There was
nothing between them except this week of fantasy and
pretending. And not pretending.

What lay ahead for her when the week was over was
quite something else. She had to get a job as soon as possible and find an apartment she could afford so that she
didn't overstay her welcome at Shanice's. She had to build
up again. That was okay. Her mission was clear. Once
she found a job, starting as a barista or in lower management, she'd begin jockeying for a higher position. Maybe
a night job, too, so she could start saving money for the
big dream of ownership. On her own. As it should be.
None of that was the problem.

She looked over to the problem. The cut of his jaw was
tight, maybe even forced. His upright body was filled
with tension. All muscle strength and posture. Fighting
to not be the Ian who danced with her at sun up while
the violinist played their song. *Their* song.

She choked back tears. Because in the time they'd
shared together so far this week, there had been many
shards of sunshine when he'd let her see not Ian Luss the

billionaire who would find that serviceable marriage. No, in the wisps between dusk and twilight, between sips of morning coffee, between rowboats and New York and dancing foibles, he'd let her see who he really was. And she'd done the same. And now that she had, it wasn't something she ever wanted to stop doing.

This one man had the power to dissolve all the hurt she thought she'd carry with her for the rest of her life. Even if he could, would she let him? Would she take the chance? It was never to be, so the questions didn't need answering.

With seemingly nothing to provoke it, they exchanged a heartfelt smile as Hamilton came into view, neither saying any of what was going through their minds. Because, in a way, there was nothing to say. They both knew the laws. And to stop breaking them. Better that they just kept smiling and creating memories to hold on to. Why not continue to enjoy the grand masquerade when they got back to the resort? They held hands as the plane touched ground. She could do this.

The Bermuda day was glorious with sultry breezes. As soon as they got to the villa, they put on swimsuits and ran down those stairs that led straight into the water.

"I've got you," Ian growled as he grabbed her once they reached the bottom.

Picking her up, he flung her around until she could straddle his back and wrap her arms around his neck and her legs across his waist, piggyback style. He carried her farther into the water until he could swing her back again, this time cradling her in his arms. She sighed up at him as he held her, the sun behind his handsome face while he gazed down on her.

As long as she didn't let those thoughts of permanence blur the beautiful picture she was staring up at, of him looking down at her in warmth and approval and joy, there was no problem. She was just going to enjoy these last couple of days in paradise with him and then get on with her life. No problem. None at all.

"Good evening, Mr. and Mrs. Luss." Concierge Adalson waved to them as he passed by on a golf cart. "You're leaving us tomorrow?"

"Sadly, we are." Ian nodded.

"I hope you had a wonderful honeymoon."

"We did." Laney's voice was a little wobbly, but the concierge wouldn't have caught it.

They strolled the palm path near their villa, breathing in the early evening cool, admiring a flower here and there. It was their last night in Bermuda.

A housekeeper they'd seen a few times called out as she wheeled her cart, "Is there anything special I can leave in your villa for your final night with us?"

"We're fine, thank you," Laney answered.

Fittingly, they also saw the older couple they'd first seen on the plane from Boston. The two putted golf balls on a small green, and both waved as the Lusses went by.

Yes, they had become quite comfortable at Pink Shores. They were friendly and polite and were clearly in love. The staff had done everything they could to make sure their honeymoon was memorable and pitch perfect. Ian was certainly going to miss being here when they went home to Boston tomorrow.

He put his arm around his bride's shoulder, and she

followed suit by wrapping her arm around his waist, motions they both performed automatically now. She wore a long and loose floral print dress that they'd picked up at one of the resort shops, her hair wild and free, her skin clean. Ian had on a simple blue T-shirt and jeans. His brain and central nervous system were still swooning from the encounter in the water a couple of hours ago, although showering and dressing for the evening helped him balance out. He was planning to appreciate every minute of their last evening together.

Besides, what had happened on the steps leading from the villa to the water didn't mean anything. When they'd first arrived almost a week ago, a wicked fantasy had overtaken him of laying Laney down on the bottom of the staircase and making love to her in a way that half of their bodies were submerged in water and half above it. With the private beach, the greenery and tall hedges giving them complete privacy, it was practically possible.

But at the beginning of the trip, he never could have imagined that they would have joined their bodies in rapture and rhapsody the way they had in New York. They'd agreed not to do it again, that it was an extra complication that they didn't need as the week came to an end. The resolve lasted for a couple of days and nights despite all the time spent romping in the water.

Then, earlier today, before he'd made a conscious decision to fulfill that specific fantasy, he was doing it, lifting her up again in his arms and laying her down at the bottom of the stairs, making short work of removing the black triangles of fabric covering the few inches of her body.

Hovering over her, he kissed every inch he could get

his hands and mouth on before sliding into her and wrapping her legs around him. The cool waves that reached the stairs lapped over them, crashing gently onto their legs and across his back. Soon, they found the ocean's rhythm and joined it, moving along with the ebb and flow of each wave. He thrust into her as the sea crashed atop them and then he retreated, back arched, as the water receded. They repeated with the tide about a hundred times, because it felt that glorious. His lovely Laney, the Bermuda waters, all under the setting sun. For the last time.

The bartender put two cocktail napkins printed with the resort's logo in front of them as they entered the outdoor cocktail lounge. "What can I get you?"

"The other day we tasted the Rum Swizzle, the bartender mentioned another cocktail famous in Bermuda."

"Yes, the Dark 'n' Stormy."

"Two of those, please."

"Coming right up. This drink mixes ginger beer with dark rum. We pour it over ice and garnish with a slice of lime."

"It sounds wonderful," Laney said, approving.

"Ian Luss, we meet again." Connery charged toward them, the rail-thin Christie in tow. Oddly, a photographer trailed behind, a gangly young man with three cameras around his neck.

"Connery." Ian saluted with two fingers to his forehead, then pivoted back to the bar, hoping the bothersome man would go away.

No such luck in getting rid of him, of course. "I'm having some honeymoon shots done and figured it'd be cute to pose with a couple of the local cocktails. Bartender, fix us up something with lots of straws and umbrellas."

The bartender nodded and tried to conceal the speck of annoyance that washed over his face.

Ian had no choice but to rotate toward Connery again. "Nice idea." Maybe if he just responded to questions with short answers and didn't attempt to get a conversation going, Connery would move on.

The bartender presented the two drinks to Connery.

He grabbed them without any acknowledgment and handed one to his bride with such haste that a bit of it spilled over onto the ground, which he took no notice of. "Ian, let's get a couple of shots of the four of us."

"Oh, no, thanks, Connery. We're commemorating in our own way."

Ian didn't like Connery in general. In the few dealings he had with him, Ian found him too aggressive and un-willing to compromise. But what he really hadn't liked was when they'd run into each other a few days ago, he'd made some comment about assuming Ian would marry a *beauty queen type*. It was a slight at Laney that was in bad taste. Who would make a negative comment about a man's wife? On his honeymoon, no less!

What constituted a beauty queen wife, anyway? Purely beauty. And how was beauty defined, how was it not sub-jective? It was truly in the eyes of the beholder. From his view, Laney was absolutely lovely in her naturalness. Not to mention, it was her inner beauty that attracted him to her. It was a revolting thought that Laney's ex thought she should go under a surgeon's knife to add a *lilt* to her nose, to change an act of Mother Nature, who never made mistakes.

The way the sunshine reflected in Laney's eyes. Was there a measurement for that? And her kisses that took him to a jubilation he never wanted to return from. Did that have a numeric value? Not to mention the utter splendor of making love with her, feeling himself inside of her unimaginable lushness. Would that win a contest? To him, she was both a *beauty* and a *queen*.

In any case, Connery was so tactless that Ian couldn't wait to get away from him.

"Come on, Ian, what's the harm? Take a couple of shots with us," Connery insisted. He didn't wait for an answer as he grabbed Laney by the arm and asked, "What was your name again?"

"Laney." She forced a smile.

Ian was one move away from physically separating him from her. Meanwhile, Connery used his other arm to yank his wife over, which left Ian no choice but to join the foursome for the photo. He'd take a quick snap and then be done with it. At Connery's lead, they all held up their drinks and smiled.

"To happy marriages. Of course, mine is my third, but maybe three's a charm." He guffawed with a belly laugh. He turned to Laney and asked, "What was your name again?"

"We did it," Ian said as he held Laney's naked body against his own. "Our week as Mr. and Mrs. Luss comes to an end."

"In our marital bed." She laughed lightly against his chest. "I think we were quite convincing."

"Think of where we started."

"With the pillow fortress between us. Followed by you on the sofa."

"I was gentleman enough to not tell you how uncomfortable that was."

As Ian's fingertips traced Laney's breasts, she hoped he wouldn't stop the motion anytime soon. It was like he was painting her with the pads of his fingers, and she wanted to be covered by his color.

"Did the separation work for you?" Laney asked.

"No. I was thinking about what you were, or weren't, wearing," he said.

"Nothing."

"That's what I was afraid of."

"Yay for us, though."

"Yes, we were able to get to this," he said. "We explored what we wanted to together, and now we can part without wondering what might have been."

"And I would have, you know." She splayed her hand on his sturdy chest, letting the muscles underneath his skin imprint into her hand, solidifying another memory.

"I would have, too."

"Now we know."

"We took our masquerade to its ultimate conclusion."

"I came to relax and pull myself together after the fire and the creep."

"Did you?"

"I feel rejuvenated."

"Mission accomplished, then."

"And you? Are you ready to go find that proper wife?" Even though she was trying to be casual and cavalier, it hurt Laney to even say those words out loud. Because, in her heart—and she believed in his, too—the right partner for him had already been found.

He said only, "Now we'll part ways and get on with our lives."

"Exactly."

"Although, I bet we'll see each other again."

"Of course. Through Melissa and Clayton," Laney said.

"We'll be friendly at holiday parties," said Ian.

"Give each other a polite kiss on the cheek."

"After all, we were best man and maid of honor. That always makes a special bond."

"Everyone will laugh about the bride and groom and the bad oysters that launched the Great Bermuda Charade," said Laney.

"Maybe Melissa and Clayton will ask us to be godparents to their children someday."

"It could happen."

"But this will never happen again," Ian said.

"Neither of us would want it to," said Laney.

"It doesn't fit with our schemes."

"We knew that from the start."

"We are pointed in different directions," said Ian.

"Couldn't be more different."

"Couldn't."

And with that, Ian rolled on top of her, his magnificent weight bearing onto her, enclosing her. Sparking her yet again, *yet again*, with want.

Her arms circled his neck, hands feeling for his upper back, bringing him in closer to her, never close enough, sealing them together making sure they became one. Until…

"No more," she blurted suddenly.

He immediately moved off, not making her struggle.

"I can't do it anymore. I can't pretend this week didn't mean anything," said Laney.

His Adam's apple bounced as he resigned his back against the pillows beside her. "It meant everything."

"You've given me back the possibility of love. You've given me myself. You…" She couldn't say what came next. That part would have to stay in Pretend Land, a place that could never be.

They both knew that. Because he'd done more than just show her that love would be worth fighting for. Something that she'd wanted and had recently convinced herself she wouldn't have.

She still wouldn't. Because the lucky woman who would get to spend her lifetime with him would never get to see what Laney had this week. He was determined that no one would see what he was capable of.

"This week will be inside of me for the rest of my life," Ian said.

She blew out her cheeks and then let out a slow exhale. "So where does this leave us?"

"Nowhere." His answer felt like a blow.

The rowboat on the pond and the carriage ride in New York. Scenes from movies or his imagination come to life. Bursting from the black-and-white screen in his mind into the here and now. Will that be how he'll remember her, as an actress in the play he wrote? Making her wonder if he'd really been with *her* this week, or would any willing woman have been able to assume the role? That was an unbearable possibility.

Instead, she'd remember the special rapport they had with each other. How precious he made her feel.

She'd mentally thank him every day of her life for helping her choose the right path out of the crossroads she found herself in. She could have fallen into a pit, let events of the past trap her and hold her down. He gave her the confidence and the hope to pull herself back up. She'd make him proud, tell him of her gratitude every morning when she woke up and every night when she went to bed. She suspected he wouldn't be far from her thoughts anyway.

Yet his march toward the future was clear. It couldn't include her. He'd remain loyal to his family and she respected him for it. It made him the noble and trustworthy man he was. Even if he was her destiny, she was not his. What a cruel twist of fate that was.

Still, she wouldn't have traded this week for anything in the world. Because she'd always have it. It would affect everything she did, said, thought and felt until her dying day.

CHAPTER ELEVEN

MULTIPLE SPARKS OF emotion were fighting each other for Ian's attention after the plane's wheels lifted up to fly him and Laney off Bermuda and back to Boston. The obvious one was that he didn't want to leave that pink sand and the sunrises and sunsets that touched him with their magnificent display of colors. Another was that he'd grown quite used to spending almost every moment with Laney, who stared absently out the window while holding the cup of coffee she'd been handed but had yet to bring to her lips.

They'd supposedly said all that needed saying to each other. That in an uncomplicated world, they might try to be together. She might be able to trust again. Ian might fulfill his heart's desire to truly be in love with someone and to display it in every way possible. Not just with anyone. With her. Those were all *mights*. That was talk; it wasn't what was going to be. Instead, they agreed to part smiling and cherish this unforgettable interlude forever.

Except that Ian wanted to toss all of that *should do* crap and smash it against a wall until it shattered into a thousand pieces!

And once the pilot made the plane's Wi-Fi available, things got infinitely worse. Numbly scrolling through a Boston news site, his thumbs froze when he saw the photo. He and Laney and Connery Whitaker and his wife Christie. From when they ran into each other last night and that buffoon Connery insisted they take a jolly photo together. He told Ian he was documenting their trip. In fact, he made a production of ordering tropical drinks and posing with them. A click-through button on the screen said Read More.

"Laney." Ian summoned her attention, as they might as well bite the bullet together. He hit the button. "Look at this."

"What is it?" She put her cup down on the tray and leaned in to him so they could both see the phone at the same time.

"Is Ian Luss, one of the city's most eligible bachelors, off the market?" he read aloud.

"Ick."

He continued: "It seems it won't be a daughter of society that will join the Luss empire. Apparently, Ian's independent woman eschews high heels in favor of wearing an apron and pulling espresso. Records identify her as last co-owning a small café in the Berkshires. Laney Sullivan isn't a name known in the upper circles, which has left readers dumbfounded as to how this seemingly odd couple got together."

"Oh my gosh."

"That's infuriating." Ian put his hand over his chest as his rib cage collapsed. "It's sick that people want to read trash like that."

He wanted to scream. Because gossip about him wasn't embarrassing enough. No, they had to drag Laney into it.

With all she'd been through and that idiot Enrique making her feel less than. This perpetuated that exact same message. Who was worthy enough to marry. Who was acceptable to love. As if that was for someone else to decide. One of Boston's most eligible bachelors. Nauseating.

"Do you think…" Laney's spoke slowly because she was in shock, too "…Connery sent the photos to the site himself?"

"I wouldn't put it past him."

"It could have been some other onlooker who recognized you."

"Spilled milk at this point."

"I suppose."

The flight attendant returned, rightly oblivious to the shake-up he and Laney were reckoning with. She laid down a tray that had several compartments, all filled with snacks for the short flight. The dried fruits had a glisten, the nuts looked nicely roasted and seasoned, the grapes big and juicy.

Ian had no interest in eating. Laney looked the tray over with ambivalence as well. They sat in silence until it became unbearable.

"I'm so sorry, Laney. I failed to protect you."

"Was that your job?"

"It might have been."

Yes, he wanted to shield her from harm, both physically and emotionally. He wanted her surrounded only by people who supported her, who saw how smart and decent she was. How true to herself. He could still kick himself remembering when he'd suggested she might want to fix her hair at the wedding after it had gotten mussed. Not that she wouldn't have wanted to look her best, but why would anyone want to change someone as glorious as her? Her honesty shone in her face. He loved everything about her.

Wait...loved? Was this what being in love really felt like? Pain and agony? He didn't know exactly how love informed the carrier. Was it the buzz he felt when he was near her? Or was it the burning, distracting longing when he wasn't? Was it the overwhelming impulse to defend her against any foe, including his family's and society's expectations? Was it in looking forward to the next day, sharing an adventure and discoveries made together?

Poets and painters had their ways of interpreting romantic love, of declaring it. Ian didn't know how to label it. Because all he'd ever known was that he was supposed to avoid it. Had it defied him, found him in the crowd anyway? Had it crept into the cracks of the cement wall holding him back?

He wasn't sure whether to lament or rejoice.

A limo met Laney and Ian at the airport in Boston. They slid into the back seat, the usual champagne and chocolates at the ready. She thought *the usual* because, remarkably, that's what the week had brought. Every single luxury imaginable at the resort, a private plane, the finest everything. She didn't know whether she could ever get used to so much opulence. At the moment, it didn't really matter. The driver was speeding them toward goodbye, and that would be that.

She kept her eyes looking out the window because she was at the point where being with Ian was stinging like a wound. They'd already expressed they wished that things could be different, that they could continue to explore the compatibility and bliss they felt toward each other. They couldn't. Period. She would be grateful to Ian for the rest of her life for showing her that a good man wasn't like Enrique. A good man wanted the best for his woman, accepted and nurtured her, didn't try to bring her down to inflate his own ego.

"I can't apologize enough for that ridiculous Connery and those photos and captions."

"Yeah." She pulled out her phone to torment herself with them again.

Just look at your face! she wanted to scream at Ian. He was so alive in those photos, with the most genuine grin as he held an arm around her. They were the perfect newlyweds, giddy in each other's company, the promise of a lifetime together in their eyes. In a second photo, Ian looked at her with such awe, like she was the most heaven-sent thing he'd ever laid eyes upon. Didn't he see it, too, that by letting her go he was giving up on the very essence of who he was? How could duty make up for that? What his family was asking of him was too extreme, too unjust.

As requested, the driver brought her to Shanice's apartment building with the overflowing trash cans in front and the graffiti on the building next door. Three young men walking down the street stopped to gawk, as a limo was rarely seen in these parts.

"This is where you're staying?" Ian had obviously never lived in a neighborhood like this.

"I grew up a couple of blocks from here. This is me."

The driver pulled over to the curb and retrieved her luggage. It wasn't much, the small bag that she'd taken straight from the wedding onto the plane to Bermuda and the second containing what she'd acquired during the trip. The bathing suits. The navy evening dress. The heartbreak.

"Can I carry these up for you?" Ian pointed to them.

"No, I'm fine. It's only three flights of stairs." Her eyes pooled, and she battled not to let any drops out.

"I'm so sorry about…everything."

"Not your fault." Again, she wanted to yell at him, wanted to shake his shoulders. He was completely missing the point. She didn't care about the photos and being described with unflattering words by his colleague and the press. The way Ian made her feel was far more important than what some gossip website thought. He'd shown her that it was worth it to trust. That not only could she open her heart again, that she wanted to. She said softly, "I'll see you around sometime."

Even though she said she didn't need help, he swooped up the bags and headed toward the five-step stoop that led to the front door of the building.

Laney followed and used her key to open the door.

He elbowed it wide. "Sure you don't want me to come up?"

"No. I'll be fine." She took the bags from him.

"Laney, it was a time…" He couldn't finish.

"Yeah." She cracked a wry half smile. "It was a time."

She headed up the stairs and didn't hear the front door click shut until she got to the third floor.

As soon as she let herself in, she rushed to the window to see him climb into the limo's back seat.

Come back! Follow your heart! Choose me! she pleaded, although she didn't really. She only silently mouthed the words.

Watching the limo drive away, she finally let the tears that had been waiting spill down her cheeks. She was hurt and she was furious. That he couldn't do it. He couldn't choose her. He couldn't choose love.

She spent the next week traipsing all over Boston. Streets she'd known her whole life looked unfamiliar now. Dismal. Lonely.

She walked in Boston Common, the oldest park in America, and thought about the garden groves of the Pink Shores Resort with Ian. She ambled through the Freedom Trail, the path tourists always visited with its sights that tell the history of the United States. The harbor where Americans dumped hundreds of chests of tea into the water as a political protest.

She strolled on the Charles River Esplanade, thinking of when she and Ian fell into that pond and kissed for the first time. One day, she lingered in front of the Fletcher Club, where Melissa and Clayton's wedding took place, looking up to the windows as if there were something to see.

She spoke to Melissa on the phone and tried not to be too obvious in her probing to learn if she or Clayton had heard from Ian. Neither had.

Fortunately, after only a week, she was able to find a job as an assistant manager at a café a few blocks away from Shanice's apartment. It was a funky independent like she preferred, not part of a big chain that had a uniform way of doing everything. It was owned by a nice family.

Because she wasn't going to be making enough money to get a place of her own, Shanice agreed to let her share the rent for a couple of months. They reconfigured the living room with a standing divider so that Laney had a space that was her own. It would do for the moment. It was all fine.

Except that it wasn't. She missed Ian with every fiber of her being. Long nights were spent staring at the ceiling, wondering where he was, what he was thinking, what he was feeling. The truth was, it was never going to be fine without him. It was like she'd had hold of the best thing in the world. For a week. Until it slipped between her fingers.

Dutifully, Ian spent the next couple of weeks going on dates with unmarried granddaughters of his grandfather's world. Hugo accelerated the process to get Ian seen around town with other women in order to diminish interest in the gossip photos with Laney. They were women in the upper echelon, each and every one from wealthy families who were looking to make fortuitous matches that would increase their already high standings and statuses.

Abigail's lineage dated back to one of the original founding families of Boston. She had curly blond hair, an advanced degree and was fluent in five languages. Ian couldn't find words in any of the five to talk to her about. She devoted most of her time to charities that rescued kittens in need. Ian could tell from the get-go that she wanted children and would probably make a fine mother. It was also evident that she wanted to be in love above all else, which Ian couldn't offer.

With Jordana, he tried—he really did—to be interested in what type of granite countertops they'd want in the kitchen of the suburban estate they'd build, as she thought the *only way* to raise children was out of the city. Although she showed him stone samples on her phone, on the small screen, he could barely discern the difference between Caledonia and Santa Cecilia, let alone choose one. Yes, his kind of marriage would be about planning and organization. But he couldn't bear the shrewdness of picking out kitchen materials on a first date.

Morgan was the beauty queen that obnoxious Connery spoke of in Bermuda. On a scale of one to ten, she was a definite eleven. Groomed and poised. In her tiny red dress, she wrapped her arm in his as she tottered on high heels into the restaurant. Where she inserted a bit of salad from her fork between her teeth so as to not muss her lipstick. While Ian certainly appreciated a woman with a pleasant appearance, Morgan's lacquered lips made him think of Laney.

It was Laney who he thought was beautiful. Her and only her. Beauty wasn't a stationary thing that someone's outer shell was adorned with. Beauty was an energy that radiated from Laney and onto him, and it was with her that he felt normal, complete. Beauty was a way of living.

After every woman his grandfather chose for him proved to be an intolerable match, he simply couldn't stand any more wife *shopping*.

He loved Laney.

What he felt for her was necessary, like oxygen. It was not something he could do without. He was going to marry, all right. Even if it meant falling out of favor with his family. He hoped it wouldn't come to that, but it was a measure of his love that he'd do anything to have her. He would start by talking to his grandfather.

"Grandson," Hugo said from his padded chair behind the enormous mahogany desk that had been his throne and office for as long as Ian could remember.

Ian sat in one of the leather chairs opposite him. He finished explaining that he had fallen in love with the woman in those leaked photos, a woman who had no pedigree, and he could let nothing stand in his way.

Hugo steepled his two index fingers on the desk. "You know I don't make arbitrary decisions, Ian. Everything I do, I do for a reason."

"Yes, and I have the utmost respect for you, what you've done for the company and, in turn, for our family. But I can't live without her. That is to say, I won't." He'd never spoken so demonstratively to his grandfather. Had never needed to.

"Then I'll have to be the wise one, as my own grandfather was."

Ian remembered the story of his great, great uncle being swindled by a dishonest woman. "And look at what happened to your uncle Harley, and that was with a baroness! Love cost Luss Global tens of millions of dollars in bad decisions because Harley was too distracted by matters of the heart to do his job."

"That's not the same situation, Grandfather. Harley and Nicole were wild. They drank brandy for breakfast. He never cared about Luss Global. She left him before they could have children, and now he's gallivanting around South America not doing a thing."

"That's all true. Which is why it's dangerous to make changes. When we don't deviate, our policies work, and have for generations. I'm trusting the future of the company to you, Ian. I need you to trust me back."

"I also need you to trust that I'm not one of my uncles. I will watch over and protect the company, just as you did. With Laney by my side, I'll be even stronger and lead Luss Global to even greater heights. I've seen how you and my father run your lives. You do it with singleness of purpose, and that has paid you back. But I'm different. I've always had a hunch that there was something else out there that I needed. Something that would not only inspire but would sustain me and allow me to reach my potential. And now that I've found it, I can't let it go. I'd be an empty shell without it."

His grandfather's face changed. He softened, making some of the deep wrinkles disappear. In an instant, he looked like a younger man. "I'd hoped to take this to my grave, Ian, but I'm going to tell you something."

So, his grandfather held a secret. And Ian had one of his grandmother's, one he'd never told a soul just as she'd asked.

"You think you're so different than I am? That I don't know what you're talking about? About emotion? About romance? I do."

Ian looked to him in question. "What do you mean?"

Hugo rubbed his chin. "I abided by the rules of my grandfather, your great-great-grandfather. My father chose my bride, your grandmother, the daughter of a financier from Philadelphia. We met only a couple of times before the wedding was arranged. Within a year, she gave birth to your father and then two years later to your uncle Harley. Two male heirs, plus managing the mansion we lived in with full-time staff, and my wife's work was done."

He paused for a moment and looked over to the photo of Rosalie he kept on his desk.

"You miss her, don't you?"

"Every day of my life." Hugo ran a finger back and forth along the top of the frame, almost like a caress. "As I was saying, within a couple of years, Rosalie's jobs as wife and mother were smoothly running operations, other than her worries about Harley always finding his way into mischief. I was ensconced here at the firm, to my father and grandfather's liking."

"Implementing your visions for what the company would become."

"One Sunday afternoon, after we'd been married for about six years, we were taking a walk in the formal garden. The sun was shining just so, creating what looked like copper flecks in your grandmother's hair. We were laughing about a comic drawing we'd seen in the newspaper. We laughed so hard and riotously, I took her hand and kissed the top of it. And…all at once… I realized that I was in love with her."

Ian's stomach jumped. He could hardly fathom what he was hearing! "You did?" That surely put a spin on his grandmother's secret.

"The conclusion almost knocked me off my feet. I

suddenly saw my wife through the lens of someone who could never love anyone more, who could never obtain anything that made him feel as fulfilled as she did."

"Why didn't you tell her?" That was part of why his grandmother held her own secret, because she didn't know how Hugo felt.

"If she admitted to feeling the same, I was afraid I would get carried away spending time with her and not do my best for our company, just as my grandfather had feared. Or if she didn't love me that way in return, I would be heartbroken and unable to continue raising a family with her. It seemed the simplest and best decision to follow the Luss code of conduct, and conceal my true feelings. So, you see, I do know something about matters of the heart."

Ian balked at how difficult it must have been for his grandfather, if he felt like Ian did about Laney, to hold that truth inside of him. Especially not knowing the whole of it. Would his grandmother want Ian to act on her behalf and tell her husband what she'd buried all those years? Just so that he would know. And selfishly, might it help persuade him to let Ian and Laney pursue the future in open love? He silently asked his grandmother's spirit if he should reveal it now? Her answer was yes.

"She did."

"What?"

"Grandmother Rosalie did love you in return. Was in love with you."

Hugo's eyes became wet and milky, and a blush took over his usually pale cheeks. "How do you know?"

"Because she told me. Growing up, she was the only

one who understood the person I was. She knew that going along with the family plan was going to be a hard path for me. So she told me because she thought it would help me not feel so apart from the rest of the family. That she was madly in love with you. But she didn't know if you were in love with her in return or if it would be acceptable to tell you how she felt, so she didn't. She also told me she'd meet you in heaven, although she didn't want you to rush to get there."

Hugo took an old-fashioned handkerchief out of his vest pocket and dabbed at his eyes. He touched the framed photo again, staring at it as if the smile on her face had new meaning. Ian got up from his chair and went around to his grandfather's side of the desk, where they had a long, tight, love-filled hug.

"Ian, you've confirmed what her actions always said to me. Still, it's beautiful to hear it out loud. Your grandmother and I were fools to keep those words from each other. I don't want you to miss out on what we did." Hugo patted him briskly on the back. "You and your Laney go forth in love. I'll trust you."

CHAPTER TWELVE

EMANCIPATED BY THE conversation with his grandfather and the admissions that love had played more of a role in the Luss empire than was commonly thought, Ian was ready to reclaim his lifeblood. The agreement was made that Laney's humble beginnings shouldn't prohibit their union. Only he didn't know where to find her. A call to Clayton led to a call to Melissa. They were making plans for their belated honeymoon, which they'd changed to the Florida Keys.

Melissa was surprised that he was calling to find Laney. He hadn't told either of them about what happened in Bermuda and New York, and if he had to guess, Laney wouldn't have let on, either, especially given how things seemed to end with such finality.

Melissa answered, "She's working at a café in Dorchester. Do you want me to call her?"

"No. Can you text me the info? I'll just stop by." Dorchester. Where Shanice lived and Laney had grown up.

Arriving at the café, he went through its wooden front door with the scratched-up etched windows. Inside, the furniture was rickety, with tables and chairs anywhere they could fit. The old place needed some work, but he knew Laney liked character.

At the counter, a young woman with blue hair was ready to take his order. Looking left and right, he didn't see Laney, so he asked if she was there.

"She's off today."

Disappointment deflated him. He should have called first. "Is she in tomorrow?"

"Yeah, at eleven. Do you want anything?"

Yes, he thought. He'd rather sit at a table for a while and try to feel Laney's presence than go home to his big empty bachelor pad. "Cappuccino, please."

He took a small table and sat with his back to the wall so he could people-watch the entire space. He surveyed the staff. They looked like a friendly bunch who worked well together. A very thin man whose arms were covered with tattoos looked like he might be the one in charge.

After Ian sipped his drink for a few minutes, the tattooed man passed by and asked him, "How's it going?"

"Is this your café?"

"No, I'm the manager, Theo. Is there a problem?"

"No, not at all. I was just curious who owns it."

"That's Mr. and Mrs. Giordano. But now the place is up for sale. They're retiring."

Ian's ears perked up. "Really. Would you happen to know which real estate agent is handling the listing?"

"I can find out for you. Give me a minute."

The smile that crossed Ian's lips had enough wattage to light up the city.

"Someone was in looking for you yesterday," blue-haired Cora blurted as soon as Laney came around the counter to put her bag away.

That was strange. Who would be looking for her? No one even knew that she worked here. It had only been a few days. "Who was it?"

"It was a he. He didn't leave his name, but if you have no use for him, you send him my way, okay?"

Laney chuckled. So an attractive man was looking for her. As mysterious as that sounded, she couldn't imagine who it was. Maybe it was a mistake. Or maybe it was a customer. It wasn't Enrique; he was back in Spain.

There's no way it was… No, she stopped that thought before it could go any further. Impossible. She shrugged her shoulders.

Her first task of the day was to inventory the paper goods and see what needed to be ordered. As she did, her eyes wandered around. This would be a nice enough place to work. For a while. She needed to make the best of it. In addition to the failure of the café in Pittsfield and the disaster that was Enrique, now she had yet another piece of emotional baggage to learn how to carry around. Ian. For the rest of her life, it would be Ian. Her one true love.

What was he doing right now, she wondered as she completed her task? Probably having a grand date with a refined woman from a prestigious family. Maybe he was taking her on a horse-drawn carriage ride in New York's Central Park.

No! That was only for her. She couldn't bear the idea of him doing that with someone else. That was hers. She swiped a couple of tears away with the backs of her fingers, then quickly washed her hands at the sink. There was no crying at work. No matter how much she missed the man she loved.

"Laney."

She heard a voice behind her so familiar she was sure she was hallucinating. Wow, the mind was strong. Had she just been thinking so hard about him that now she was hearing his voice? What was next, having a memory of his arms around her? And as soon as she thought that, she did have the sense that his long and strong limbs were encircling her, pulling them into the private world that was each other's salvation.

"Laney."

She turned around. It hadn't been her imagination. Ian was standing right there, just like when they surprised each other by being on the plane to Bermuda. Here, the metal counter was the only thing separating them. Words came out of her mouth that didn't even sound like hers.

"What are you doing here?"

"What do you think? I came to find you."

"Why?"

"Because I love you."

Laney's heart thumped in her chest. Both of them knew they had fallen in love at Pink Shores but had never said the taboo words to each other. Now he was here saying them.

"And we're going to be together for the rest of our lives."

"I thought that wasn't possible."

"It's the only thing that's possible."

"What about your family?"

"It's time for a reevaluation. My grandfather and I are working it out."

"What do you mean?"

"I'll tell you all about it later. Meanwhile, I have a present for you."

He came bearing gifts. Laney was overwhelmed. This was so abrupt and so unlikely. Yet she wasn't going to deny that she wanted to be with him just as much as he was claiming to want to be with her. Could it be real? That love was in her cards of fortune, after all.

"What's the gift?"

Ian swept his arm from left to right across the café. "This."

"What?"

"The café."

"What about it?"

"I bought it for you."

"You what?" Now she really thought she was hallucinating. "How did you even know it was for sale?"

"Theo told me." He pointed to the manager, who gave them a thumbs-up signal. "I was here yesterday."

"Okay."

"Okay?" Ian read the displeased expression on her face. "What's wrong?"

"I want to own my own café!" she exclaimed. "I mean, it's beyond beautiful of you to offer, but I don't want to be in business with someone again. This is something I want to do for myself."

Ian's eyes became drawn and his face drooped into sadness.

Oh. She hadn't meant to shut him down like that, but he shouldn't have taken such a drastic action without talking to her about it first. She didn't want to be responsible to someone else if she failed, couldn't go through that again.

She watched inside his eyes as something bubbled. He swiped open his phone and did some furious tapping. Coming up for air, he announced, "Okay, Laney Sullivan. You are now the owner. You will make payments of—" he said and showed her a number on his phone's screen "—every month for five years, at which point you will own it outright. Do we have a deal?"

Laney's breath became fast and heavy. This was terrifying. "Ian, I…"

"There are two conditions of the sale."

Oh, here it comes. Everything always had a hitch. "What are those?"

"The first one is that you come around from that counter."

She slipped by Cora, who didn't even try to seem like she wasn't watching all of this take place. Same with Theo and a couple of other staff members.

"What's the other condition?"

"That no matter what happens with the café or Luss Global or any other business we might be in, that you'll be mine forever."

She threw her arms around his neck, and he wrapped his around her waist and spun her until her feet left the ground.

"You drive a hard bargain, Ian Luss. I accept."

She gave him a kiss to seal the deal.

* * * * *

THE BABY SWAP THAT BOUND THEM

HANA SHEIK

MILLS & BOON

For Kaysim.
The cutest little nephew
an aunt could be so lucky to snuggle!
Love you forever and more, habo.

PROLOGUE

"HE'S SO TINY."

Yusra brushed her fingertips over the back of her son's small curling fist, the peach fuzz soft, his skin warm and flushed red. He mewled in his sleep, shifting toward her at one point. One look and she was smitten. Now she understood what her mother meant when she'd told her that it took only a glance sometimes to fall in love. She'd thought and feared that after her difficult pregnancy and tumultuous, touch-and-go birth she would feel none of the maternal feelings she was meant to experience.

Thankfully all she felt were pure relief and love for the unknowing child in the bassinet.

"Would you like to hold him?" The nurse who'd been tending her guided Yusra to a padded rocking chair by a small picture window. A window that she shared with the two other mothers in the cramped, too warm hospital room. She forgot how stuffy the room could be when the sun angled in through the window and slanted shafts of white light over her hospital bed. Soon as her son was placed in her arms, the sweat beading at the back of her neck, under her armpits and tracking down her spine ceased to be a concern. Because she had everything she needed pressed to her chest and her drumming heart.

"Support his head this way, and make sure his hat doesn't slip off. We don't want him getting too cold."

Yusra smothered the laugh. She didn't think that could happen quickly. Maybe in one of the fancy, private rooms with the temperature control would such a problem exist. Not here. Not in the heated but cozy corner of theirs.

She cuddled her son, instinct driving her to bring him closer to her breast. This was her first time holding him since he'd spent his first two days in the NICU. The short separation made their reunion so much sweeter.

"I didn't think anyone could be so small."

"It might seem that way now, but they grow fast. Faster than you might be prepared for."

Yusra looked up from the small scrunched face of her son, her hand stroking his scalp, fingers lingering on his baby-soft black tufts of hair. He had a headful of the wispy curls, so unlike her own, but reminding her of his father.

Before her throat could get too thick to ask, she wondered, "You have children?"

"Three. The youngest is off to primary school, but it feels like yesterday when I was sitting in the same position that you are." The nurse looked down at the newborn son Yusra had to care for now all on her own. "Did you pick a name?"

"No, not yet. I'm still deciding." Yusra stared down at her son's closed eyes and pursing wet mouth. She caressed his cheek with a finger and marveled at his natural rooting instinct to turn in the direction and seek her breasts. She wasn't nursing fully yet, but she was trying. She didn't want to miss the chance to connect with him on that level if she could.

"Whatever you pick I'm sure will be the perfect choice." Then the nurse moved away to do her rounds. She returned ten minutes later to collect Yusra's son and place him in his bassinet again.

"I'll check your blood sugar and bring dinner over soon."

Being diabetic had erased her fear of needles a long time

ago. But she didn't anticipate her heart racing faster when her diabetes was mentioned. She imagined that the trauma she'd suffered only a few days earlier had further repercussions than she believed it would.

"Everything looks good," the nurse reported with a smile. "I know you like the coconut potato soup. I will sneak the one with the most avocado in it for you. And maybe the—"

A long, drawn-out, frightening wail pierced the air and cut off whatever else her assigned nurse was going to say.

The nurse rushed away, leaving Yusra to be grateful that the scream hadn't woken her son. Moving on her own and fast was still a challenge. She lingered sitting on her bed, a hand clasped around the clear-sided bassinet holding her baby boy.

What had happened out there?

She remembered her own perilous birth story. The vivid memories of the sharp uterine pains, the fetal position she'd been in when help arrived in the form of paramedics that a kindly neighbor in her apartment building had called, and the blood, the agonizing, awful pushing and her cries echoing off the walls of her hospital room. She'd thought she would die. She thought she would never see her baby, and no one would care for him the way she did now.

It had been concurrently the worst and best experience of her life.

But the cry she'd heard triggered anxiety in her. It hadn't sounded like a mother giving birth at all. It sounded…

Brushing a kiss on her son's forehead, she wrapped a shawl over her head and followed her gut. It lured her out of bed and her room. She met no resistance in the dimly lit hospital corridor, the nurses too busy attending to the new and expectant mothers on the obstetrics floor to notice her ambling slowly in the direction of the bloodcurdling scream.

She slowed at double doors, but pushed on undeterred.

She didn't know why she cared so much. Only that something resonated with her about the pitiful scream. It wasn't long before she noticed this new hospital area was brighter, cleaner and quieter. Also, the bustle she'd left behind was notably missing.

What am I doing? The thought came swiftly and rooted her feet.

She'd left her son to go snoop on another patient, like it was any of her business. Blaming her heightened maternal emotions, she turned to walk away, but stopped when she caught movement in her peripherals.

A shockingly tall, hulking man stepped out of one of the rooms. In his dark business suit, he didn't look like he belonged. And yet he pressed a big hand to the closed door in front of him, his broad shoulders caving in, and his head hanging low. Sorrow or defeat, she didn't know which had crushed him, but her sympathy went out to him. Surviving her own near death and becoming a mother had changed her into this self-reflective being.

Before she could leave him to his private display of emotion, she heard her name.

"Ms. Amin, you shouldn't be here."

It was her duty nurse. She appeared by her side and, gently gripping her arm, swung her back the way she'd come. Though not fast enough. The man looked up and over their way, his eyes and scowl as dark as his suit, long thick beard and short curly hair. With only one glance he communicated what she figured a man like him—a man who probably had the world clutched in his large hand and determined his own fate—would when someone like her tried to infiltrate his controlled bubble. *You're intruding here*, was what she felt his eyes accused her of doing.

And she really was.

Giving in, she allowed herself to be led away, and with no more backward glances.

Once she was in her room, the nurse tucked her in and gently reminded her of the hospital's rules. Listening with half a mind, she focused the other half on her final image of the man grieving outside the hospital room.

"Who was he?" she asked, realizing too late she'd spoken aloud.

She hadn't thought the nurse saw him, but she was proven wrong. "I think I know who you're talking about. I don't know his name, but he's just lost a family member to a terrible car accident."

"No wonder he looked so sad." That didn't explain why he was on this floor though. "Shouldn't he be on the emergency floor?"

The nurse whispered, "I really shouldn't say more." She looked pointedly at Yusra's son, her face softened by sadness. "It's not something a new mother should hear anyways."

"That might be true… Still, I'd like to know. Did someone else get hurt?"

She had an out-of-body sensation, prickling over her arms and legs, and cooling her despite the heat circulating the small hospital room.

Somehow, she knew the answer to that question even before the nurse nodded sadly. "There was also a female victim in the accident. Another family member. She survived the crash but was lost to childbirth. The whole family is grieving together right this moment."

"The baby?" Yusra's mouth dried, her puttylike heart sticking in her throat, chilly desolation seeping into her fast. "Is the baby alive?"

"Yes," the nurse said with a smile.

Releasing a loud, quick breath, relief chased off the emotional cold that had prepared her body for the worst news. At least the child had lived. She'd always hated sad, unpredictable story endings for that reason. She didn't want to cry. Didn't want to wonder why the world was unfair sometimes.

It made her think how close she'd come to that. Leaving her child behind. Losing the life she had dreamed up for the two of them.

That could have been her, the woman who died in childbirth.

When the nurse left to fetch her dinner, Yusra stroked and kissed the hands, cheeks and head of her tiny son. "I swear I'll always fight to stay with you," she vowed.

The heartbreaking story of loss and mourning only several doors away persisted to haunt her until she considered a name for her baby instead. A name that would represent the strong, sunny future she hoped to build for him so that he never felt something was amiss in his life. And while she did that, she almost, *almost* forgot about the scowling, dark-bearded man who suffered levels of untold pain where she had experienced immeasurable joy.

CHAPTER ONE

Two years and nine months later

A SMALL MOTORBOAT sliced across the still ocean, casting a frothing line of water in its wake and disrupting the calm horizon and illusory peace. Nothing about this morning was like any morning Bashir Warsame had experienced since committing to his unorthodox lifestyle. Living on board his seventy-meter superyacht for close to three years, and occasionally anchoring, had dulled his patience for company. Most people who worked for him or with him knew he didn't like face-to-face meetings. He managed his vast international hotel chain from the comfort of his private cabin, and he hadn't found himself missing any part of his existence on land.

And yet someone had missed the memo and was heading full steam ahead toward his ship.

Bashir waited until the boat was close before he walked away. As he made his way aft, he was met by his ship's senior master Nadim and Nadim's ever-present tablet computer. The man didn't go anywhere without it.

"I've briefed your team and ours on the security protocol." Nadim looked up from the screen of his palm-sized tablet, his data and figures and facts meticulously logged and tracked in the portable device. Bashir never questioned Nadim's reliance on it. Whatever he was doing, it was what had kept the crew and ship running smoothly and efficiently, and as far as Bashir was concerned, that was the only thing that mattered.

"Have they made contact yet?"

Nadim repeated the question into his earpiece, shaking his head. "They're boarding now. Security will hold them."

"Handle it. I'll be in the lounge." Nadim had his full trust. He didn't see a reason to interfere in the other man's duties. And he didn't give his confidence to others very easily. But his senior master had more than earned it, in time and service.

Wordlessly, Nadim dipped his chin and at the next junction they parted ways. Nadim toward where security would greet their unwelcome guest, whoever they were, and Bashir to his second most favorite place on his ship: the underwater observation lounge.

He took a deeply satisfying breath before entering the expansive room and again when he claimed the central spot on the smooth leather sofa facing the panoramic ocean view. As always, he let it sink in that very little stood between him and the yawning, hungry maw of the dark blue waters he was observing quietly. Nothing but glass panels. If he were the type to seek thrill from death-defying activities, he'd have thought himself to be entirely safe from the threat that the ocean always posed. He wasn't that naive. Though sometimes...sometimes he wished that he were.

Then he'd be able to close his eyes and finally rid himself of this constant alertness he lived with day in and day out. His vigilance a byproduct of having to fight for where he was today. Because of that, he had more at stake. Naturally, losing everything and everyone he cared for was a perennial thought. And if he wasn't always on guard, then that was when he was most susceptible to losing it all.

Bashir shut his eyes, breathed through his nose and almost attained a semblance of peace—when he snapped his eyes open and turned to the ruckus barging into the lounge.

It happened fast.

The polished oak doors into the room burst open and his toddler son Zaire came rushing in with a mildly harassed albino rabbit gripped in his small pudgy arms. Behind him, hot on his trail and looking more than hot under the collar, was Zaire's overpaid and equally overworked nanny. Bashir grimaced at both the intrusion and out of sympathy for the woman who had to mind his rambunctious son all day. Middle-aged Alcina might not have been the best choice for a toddler who hadn't yet grasped the concept of slowing down, but she'd been Bashir's only choice from the beginning. She'd started out as his housekeeper, back when he had roots on land, and when he had anchored away from his palatial island villa in Greece, Alcina had asked to come along and help him in any way.

Her loyalty was touching, but he supposed she possibly regretted it a bit now.

Alcina stopped fanning her flushed high-boned cheeks, and she stooped to catch his son when he all but launched himself *and* his ruffled pet rabbit into his nanny's open arms. Alcina dropped a kiss on his head and squeezed him to her.

Bashir amended his earlier thought. Clearly, Alcina was a perfect caregiver for his son in more ways than not.

He would've thought that disruption enough. Yet Nadim arriving in the lounge reminded him that there were more distractions ahead of him. Especially when his senior master gave him an uncharacteristic frown.

With puckered brows and a growing scowl, Nadim requested, "May I speak to you?" His eyes passed over Alcina and Zaire. The meaning in them clear as mud. He didn't want an audience for whatever he had to report.

Bashir understood. A final glance at the glass caging the ocean, and he stood to address whatever issue had now fallen onto his lap.

Nadim joined him in his office, a floor directly above the observation deck.

"What is it, man?" he asked soon as he was seated behind his executive desk. It was large and ostentatious, and he hardly ever used the whole space, but it communicated the kind of front his money could afford. Just like the glass in his underwater lounge separating him from the dangers of the waters surrounding them, he kept the world at bay in the same way, one hand always thrust out to discourage anyone getting closer to him.

Nadim and Alcina were the handful in his trusted circle of company.

He didn't make friends easily. And he hadn't had family in a long time.

Shaking off the tendrils of trauma that resurfaced whenever he thought of his long-gone family, he considered the power he now possessed to prevent Zaire from ever experiencing what he'd had to. It was why he appreciated Nadim for his forethought in suggesting their meeting be held elsewhere. His son might be a few months from his third birthday, but Zaire could be uncannily perceptive for a young child who was only beginning to learn his alphabet. There had been the possibility that his son would have sensed something was amiss if Nadim had chosen to deliver his news in the observation lounge. The risk of upsetting Zaire was abolished now that they'd swapped venues.

His senior master passed his ever-handy tablet over. "Do you recognize this woman? She's the one who hired a boat to ferry her to our ship."

The image on the tablet was of an older woman, her skin

a fair brown and the bags under her eyes darkly pronounced. She had the lower half of her face, from the nose down, covered by her shawl. Only those haunting eyes gazed out at him. Even through the photo he sensed her desperation. It clawed out at him, grasping at air, and right before it choked him, he flipped the tablet facedown over his desk.

"Who is she?" Rather than admitting he didn't know her and hadn't the faintest clue what connection she had to him, or why and how she'd come to be on his ship.

"A former nurse from the Kampala City International Hospital. She wishes to speak with you and says it has to do with Zaire."

About his son? What could she possibly have to tell him about Zaire?

"Did she say anything more?"

Nadim shook his head, his expression softly speculative. "Only that she won't speak to anyone but you."

Scowling, Bashir furiously sifted his brain on what to do next. Not that he had to think for very long. His options dwindled, soon as he heard his son was involved somehow.

He was sensitive when it came to his child.

Zaire's birth story was tragic. Bashir didn't like ruminating about his family as a rule, mostly as his mind always seemed to veer to its darkest, most depressing corners. But he couldn't stop the memories of the day he'd gotten the call that his cousin Imran had died in a car accident in Kampala, Uganda. Imran's pregnant wife, Tara, had been a victim too. Unlike Imran, she hadn't died at the scene. She'd gone into premature labor and, despite her grievous wounds, she had miraculously delivered a healthy baby boy. As Bashir understood it, Tara had gotten to hold her newborn son for all of a few minutes before she went into hemorrhagic shock, slipped into a coma and never woke up again.

By the time he'd arrived, Tara and Imran were both gone. Zaire was left alone.

Bashir knew what that loneliness was like. Twenty-eight years ago he'd lost his whole family—grandparents, parents, brothers, and sisters—to a flash flood that had swept through their Somali village. He had been the sole survivor of the tragedy, a confused and frightened seven year old.

Orphaned and homeless all of a sudden Bashir had moved to live with his aunt and uncle, Imran's parents. He hadn't met his cousin or that part of the family before, but he had been raised to respect all family members he encountered, and anticipated a good life with his aunt and uncle and many cousins.

And that was what he'd gotten. His extended family embraced him as if he were one of their own. In spite of their struggles, his uncle's farm bringing only so much food—and seasonal famines to contend with—Bashir never went hungry and was hardly ever exposed to any troubles. His cousins were all around his age, with Imran being the oldest and three years older than Bashir was. And yet their age gap didn't stop them from connecting instantly. Before long, Bashir could almost call Imran a brother. They did everything together. Imran allowed him to tag along to play with his older friends. They studied together. Ate all their meals as a family from one communal plate. Shared a bed, one of three cramped into a small room of the family home. For seven long years, almost as much time as he had with his deceased family members, Bashir existed in a state of bliss. He was happy with Imran's family. As happy as he'd been with his own family. And he didn't see anything changing his mind.

He never saw the anxiety coming until it struck him. The rabid concern that he would lose everything and everyone was a bolt out of the blue. And he couldn't rid himself of it. All through the day it taunted him. He'd envision losing his new family to another freak accident. Each day that passed him, he kept watch for the calamity that would snatch his newfound happiness away. Never knowing what exactly would change his fortune to misfortune again, but he was certain the other shoe would drop eventually.

Only Imran had noticed the change in him. But no matter how he tried to get Bashir to open up, it didn't work. Finally, Bashir had done the only thing that had seemed sensible to him. He'd run away from the happiness first, before it got taken away from him. Literally.

Stowing away on an inflatable dinghy—one of many smugglers were using—Bashir squeezed in with dozens of scared but hopeful asylum seekers who were also looking to flee their lives in Somalia. The journey to Greece had been arduous and dangerous. It ended months later in an isolated and awful refugee camp on a rocky, forsaken Cretan islet. It wasn't the place for a runaway fourteen-year-old boy. Yet it had become his home for years. In a way his salvation too. He no longer had to worry about losing those he loved. After all, he'd walked away first. And without his risky travel and the camp he wouldn't be where he was now, blessed with richness and successes. He also might not even have gotten the chance to be Zaire's dad.

But Bashir *was* his father. And it was his single driving reason to make Zaire's life the antithesis of what his upbringing had been. Zaire deserved the childhood Bashir was robbed of when he lost his family. He would fight to his dying breath to give his son every joy and opportunity life could afford him. Just as he would ensure nothing harmed or distressed him. He owed that much and more to Imran. Bashir couldn't save his cousin, but he would do whatever he could for Zaire.

Which was why, if this was a prank or ploy, Bashir hoped his uninvited guest knew who she was up against.

And if it isn't?

If this woman had a message of import about his Zaire, he needed to hear it.

"Shall I see her delivered to the coast guard?"

Nadim mistook his ponderous silence for displeasure, and he was offering a reasonable solution. Just not the one he was leaning toward.

Bashir drummed his fingers atop the tablet and then flipped it back over again. He willed himself to stare deep into those fearsome eyes of this mysterious caller of his. No memory slotted into place. Her face was an enigma—literally shrouded by her shawl. The only connection was that she had been a nurse at the hospital where Zaire had been delivered. "Is she still on board?"

"She is."

Bashir tightened his fingers around the tablet, glowering at the image that would haunt him if he allowed it. And there were enough phantoms from his past to contend with. He didn't need to add one more ghost.

"Bring her to me."

It was the only way he'd solve the mystery and perhaps salvage the peace he'd almost achieved.

CHAPTER TWO

"NOT AGAIN…"

Yusra grumbled under her breath as she ripped the late rent notice off her apartment door. She heard a door unlatch down the hall and quickly stuffed the piece of offending paper in her floppy, well-worn purse before her neighbor stepped out into the hallway.

"Yusra, how are you?" Dembe paused in front of her, his smile as infectiously happy as always. He was a few years younger than her twenty-seven years, but that hadn't stopped her from noticing how finely built he was. Lean arms and toned legs squeezed into a polo shirt, tweed vest and jeans. She knew he hit the gym regularly between his long working hours at an international bank. He pushed his glasses up his nose and peered at her through them before flicking a look at her closed apartment door. Exactly where the notice had been affixed seconds ago. "Is AJ inside, or were you headed out?"

Dembe meant her son, Abdul Jabir.

"He's at day care today." She didn't add that she'd had to beg the day care owner again to overlook the late monthly payment Yusra owed her. It wouldn't be long before she'd have to find another arrangement for her son while she was working. But for today, she had a safe place for him to be cared for, and she'd have to be thankful for that.

One battle at a time.

Dembe beamed. "Oh, that's good. Let him know I'm happy to do that rematch later if he isn't too tired when he comes home." Dembe had been teaching her son to play football on weekends and whenever he had free time during the workweek. Yusra thought it was sweet of him, but she didn't want to monopolize his time.

"You don't have to—"

"I know, but I want to," he emphasized with a shrug and smile. "See, the little man has real moves on the field. A future Bwalya or Okocha."

The names meant nothing to her, but then she wasn't a super football fan like Dembe and her son.

"That's why I would hate him wasting that talent sitting around at home. So, I'll see you and AJ later." He waved to her and squeezed past, the narrow corridor forcing them closer together so that when he brushed her arm with his, he smiled and winked.

Yusra pressed cool hands to her inflamed cheeks after he turned the corner toward the stairwell.

Her little crush on him was amusing. Nothing she sought to pursue, mostly because she was busy making ends meet, but also as she didn't want to ruin the friendship Dembe had fostered with her young son. Yusra's heart pattered at his thoughtfulness. Dembe didn't have to entertain a two-year-old—three in a few months—and yet he did, and he never seemed to heed her protests to the contrary.

If she had wanted to date anyone, Dembe would be a serious contender.

But she didn't.

And she owed it to the bad breakup with AJ's father, Guled. Though she didn't feel anything for him anymore, there had been a point in her life where Yusra had felt like she'd needed her ex-husband more than she needed air to breathe. She had loved Guled immensely and sacrificed plenty to keep him happy with her. He hadn't liked her working as an artist, so she'd packed up her tools and easel and sold them. Then when she'd switched to a career in graphic design and secured a job at a leading international marketing firm, Guled hadn't been satisfied with her commitment to long office hours and going on work-related trips with co-workers he didn't preapprove. Eventually he had told her to quit, and she'd caved and listened to him, letting go of a job she had liked. He hadn't wanted anyone else to get close to her. Nothing and no one else could matter but him. Not that those same rules applied to him.

No, he could go out and party all night long with his friends, while I sat home alone.

In all their years together, he hadn't ever bothered to invite her along for a night out. Almost as though he was embarrassed of her. Funny how it still stung to think about it. That was probably the worst part of their relationship for Yusra. Even after he'd pressured her into giving up on her art and then her job at the marketing firm, isolated her in their small apartment, gotten her pregnant, made promises that he would do right by her...she'd still wanted to see the good in him. The good in her love for him.

Of course he had then divorced her when he thought it too much of a bother to control her anymore. And it wasn't enough that he was leaving her, he hadn't wanted anything to do with their baby either. He'd refused to pay any child support or play any caregiving role, and he had told her parents as much once Yusra had called to inform them of the divorce.

It was perfectly normal that the implosion of her marriage to Guled had soured her on the idea of romance, except what she found in books, film and television.

At least between the pages of a book and on-screen she was safe from heartache.

The smile on her face vanished when she recalled the paper in her purse, the one she'd hidden away in panic. After pulling it out, she skimmed the short but succinct note from her landlord and sighed. It warned that she had all but a week to produce both last month and the current month's rents. Seven days and a few hundred American dollars to satisfy her landlord. What was she supposed to do in that short amount of time?

The panic started up again.

It coalesced into a fiery ball and fixed itself in her throat. She swallowed around the bilious heat ineffectually. As long as her bank account remained nearly drained, she wouldn't rid herself of the heartburn-inducing anxiety of providing a roof and shelter for her family. Her son was counting on her.

Yusra breathed deeply and whispered, "Calm down."

Packing the notice demanding rent and threatening eviction back in her purse, she then made sure to lock up and set off toward her office, praying that she would have more luck with her clients today. Her graphic design business might be operating out of the back room of a laundromat, but it was still serious work and she hoped luck was on her side and a steady source of revenue would flow in her direction. She needed it desperately.

As desperately as she needed shade when she stepped outdoors and the dry early summer heat clung to her like plastic wrap.

She waded through both the summery climate and the crowds, squeezed into an overcrowded bus and was dropped off onto the winding streets that led to her business. The laundromat was as busy as it could get during the day. Several mothers were juggling minding their young children and folding laundry, but there were also bored-looking students scrolling through their phones while waiting on their full cycle to finish. The laundromat owner monitored everything from behind the service desk with a phone pressed to her ear.

Yusra raised a hand in greeting and had hoped to pass through to the back unnoticed.

No such luck. The owner crooked a finger at her and briefly paused her lively chat to whoever was on the other end of the phone.

"Where's my rent?"

"I…" Yusra grappled for an excuse. She did a mental run of the ones she'd used before. "I'll have it soon," she finally said, settling on the vague truth.

The owner sucked her teeth and looked ready to tell her to pack up her office and clear out. She wouldn't blame her if she did. She'd skipped out on two months' rent. The backlog of payments was beginning to overwhelm her almost as much as her business toeing the red in her books and her bank account dwindling faster than her nearly empty fridge. She had a growing child and she was awake all night from constant worry that one day she wouldn't be able to feed him. And what kind of mother would she be then?

The kind who shouldn't be a mom, she thought disparagingly of herself, almost as much as she denigrated the situation she didn't have full control of. It wasn't her fault entirely that her design services weren't in demand. But she knew she could hunt for other jobs. Plenty of unsavory ones that would still add some money to her pocket. They wouldn't make her happy the way designing on her computer did, but they would keep her son's belly full and give him a warm bed and a fluffy pillow to lay his head on at night.

The stress brought familiar pricks of tears to her eyes. Frustration sparked and crackled in her. She sucked in a deep, clarifying breath and was just about to stand her ground and plead her case when she watched the owner flick her eyes away to a point behind Yusra.

She turned and confronted a shocking sight.

Five well-dressed men stood behind her, four of them with briefcases and one in a doctor's white coat over his fancy business suit.

The doctor one smiled directly at her. "Are you Ms. Yusra Amin?"

She frowned but nodded slowly, too tongue-tied to ask how he knew who she was and what he wanted.

"It's good we found you." The doctor held out his hand. "I'm the chief medical officer of Kampala City International Hospital."

Her eyebrows sprang up with her surprise. She hadn't visited the hospital since AJ's birth, but she knew they had her file, which *still* didn't explain how they had come to track her to her office out of the laundromat.

"How did you know to find me here?"

"We stopped by your apartment, and your landlord told us you conducted business in this building."

Yusra bit the inside of her cheek before she snapped that the landlord should have consulted her first. But she knew that the man had a grievance with her about her late rent payments and the eviction he persisted on threatening her with every time he saw her.

Nothing she could do about that now. She narrowed her eyes at all the men, memorizing their features and anything unique about them that stood out, in case they meant her harm. Not that she had a clue why she deserved it. Aside from late payments, she hadn't broken any laws or hung around any shady, suspect figures. Just Dembe, and he was her cute, generous-hearted neighbor.

Still, she gulped.

"May we speak with you in private?" The doctor smiled but the emotion felt forced rather than genuine.

"Sure," she said, possibly against her better judgement, and pointed out her office. "My office is over this way, if you'll follow me."

Only the doctor and one of the briefcase-carrying suits followed her. Good decision. Her tiny office wouldn't be able to hold more guests than that. She even had two seats for them across the small desk she'd wedged into the space. Squeezing around the scarred desk, she dropped into her chair and fanned out both her hands after they had gotten as comfortable as possible on the old spindly-legged wooden chairs.

"Now, what is this all about? And do I require a lawyer?" She laughed nervously at her joke. When they didn't join in, her heart sank into her stomach. Very weakly, and after a few thick swallows, she managed to say, "*Do* I need a lawyer present?"

Before either dour-faced man said anything, the closed door to her office boomed so loudly, the hinges heaved and squawked from the force.

What now? she fretted.

The pounding came again and both men looked at her expectantly. It was her office, and she ought to answer the door. Yusra slowly rose on her quaking legs and weakly called out permission for entry.

She hadn't finished speaking when the door opened in answer and a giant of a man revealed himself. Yusra couldn't believe her eyes. She was ashamed when she did a double take at first. He was just so...*big*. Tall. At least six-feet-nine or even taller. And he was thickly muscled too. His expensive-looking dress suit strained at his biceps and around trunk-like thighs. He had a wild long bushy beard to match those fierce eyebrows, and his black-as-night hair was on the longish side too and slicked back from his sculpted, hard-planed face. He was dark-skinned, yellowish brown, and that only made his dark eyes and dark facial hair that much more appealing.

But he was dressed finely in a three-piece blue-gray suit—arguably finer than the men sitting in her office.

Whoever this big man was, he took up space in more ways than just his physical presence. There was an unspoken authority that oozed off him and demanded all attention to him in a flash. He filled her doorway and had to stoop to get his head past the doorframe safely.

Soon as he entered, he passed a glance over the men before his sights zeroed on her.

She flinched...but not out of fear. Her body was responding to the electric current that inexplicably charged through her when their eyes collided.

"Yusra Amin." His voice was as mesmerizingly deep as he was large all over.

Also, unlike the other men, this newcomer spoke with confidence. And with that same confidence, he never took his eyes off her and addressed the men gruffly, "Nothing more will be said until Ms. Amin's lawyer joins this meeting."

Nothing had gone according to plan from the minute Bashir had discovered he'd arrived too late to intercept the bureaucratic goons from the hospital. Even if he had thought quickly on his feet and cleared them out of the cramped little room, it didn't change the fact that Yusra Amin looked ready to flee from him at any moment.

Her naturally round eyes narrowed at him from across the room. A tiny desk he could easily brush aside was the only thing separating him from her. But he didn't budge, studying her as warily as she was him.

Though she had more of a reason to suspect him. *He* had barged into her office, and not the other way around.

No matter. He expected some resistance on her part. What Bashir hadn't readied himself for was to be slightly frazzled when he saw her. This woman wasn't who he was expecting. She was attractive. Pretty in an understated way that could be polished into a quiet but powerful elegance. For that she'd have to be dressed in something other than a softly worn long-sleeved shirt and faded jeans. He would also have swapped the coarse dark blue shawl of her hijab for a material and color that complemented her rich brown skin better. And her long, graceful neck would look lovely adorned in the kind of gold that would make a sheikh's wife jealous.

Flickering his eyes up to her face, he frustratingly noted his attraction to her. But he wouldn't be deterred by any spontaneous feelings.

"We don't have much time."

"Who are you?"

Grateful that she spoke up, he realigned his thinking and answered her. "Introductions can happen later. What matters is that those men who were sitting here will be back soon." Once the hospital officials realized who he was and what was happening, they'd come knocking the way he had done. "It isn't long before we lose this window of opportunity to clear the air."

Yusra crossed her arms. "I would prefer the introductions happen now rather than later."

Bashir saw from her defensive posturing that he wouldn't get anywhere by pushing back against her. Time was a problem. She just didn't see that yet, as she wasn't working with the whole picture the way he was. And even though he had hoped to delay it by a little bit longer, he had no other option.

He pulled a sharp breath in through his nose. Then with a

courage he hadn't yet fully subscribed to, he gave her what she'd asked for.

"My name is Bashir Warsame, and our sons were swapped at birth."

CHAPTER THREE

"DID YOU HEAR ME?" Because it looked like Yusra hadn't from Bashir's vantage point.

She stood eerily still, her arms still folded over her chest, her shirt's stretchy material curving tighter around her breasts—

He pulled a mental wall down between himself and where the rest of that thought had been leading him. Especially right then. Inopportune didn't begin to describe the sudden spike in his libido.

Growling low from an overwhelming sense of frustration, he snapped, "It's imperative that you listen to me."

"Why?" she whispered, but it carried loudly in the silence blanketing the shoebox of an office. "So you can spout off some more nonsense."

He scoffed in disbelief. "Nonsense?" Had she really just said that to him? He got that the whole switched-baby angle was ripped off the script of a melodrama, but he wasn't trying to fool her. This was his life now. And hers—whether she perceived him to be a liar or not.

But he supposed he could try to convince her again. He gnashed his teeth, frustrated with himself for noting the sweet scent of her perfume when she shifted closer to him.

"You should leave, before you wear out my patience."

"Ya Allah," he growled under his breath, *his* patience

wearing out rapidly. With a quick calming breath sawing in and out of his flaring nostrils, he tried to reason with her one last time. "I understand it comes as a shock." He would know. Two days had hardly let his new reality sink in. He was still fighting against the riptide of doubt and hope that the baby-swap nightmare was just that, a nightmare that he left behind when he arose from bed. Only it wasn't.

From the moment the former nurse had walked into his office aboard his yacht, his life had changed irrevocably. Now all he could do was move forward and cope with it.

And he'd been doing just fine for a while. Bashir had bought the costly service of a private investigator and had finally tracked an address to Yusra. Sadly, the information had come to him an hour too late. Now he had the hospital breathing down his neck, vying to get to Yusra first, and possibly poisoning the waters for him to persuade her away from filing a lawsuit. At least one in the public court. He didn't want to imagine what that would do to Zaire to have their private world infiltrated by dangerously curious gossip-mongers. Even though he was confident that no family court would simply sign off on Yusra taking his son from him, he was still cautious—smartly so.

"A couple of days ago, I had a visit from a former hospital employee. A nurse. She alleges that our sons were switched shortly after birth."

Shaking her head, her suspicion written all across her pretty face, Yusra said, "I don't know who you are, but that's a sick thing to say to anyone, let alone a mother."

"A sick thing, yes, but it's also the *truth*. If you give me a moment to explain, I would happily do so." He regarded his blue steel, blue-strapped watch and clenched his jaw until the pain there superseded the headache marching through his skull. "I never repeat myself, but I will stress once again that we are pressed for time."

"For someone who is trying to convince me, you're being awfully rude." She lowered her arms, began rummaging through her purse, and whipped out her phone. "It doesn't matter though. Whatever you're attempting to accomplish won't work. I won't call the police if you leave now and never show your face again."

"I've given you my name, you have seen my face and," he waved an arm out to gesture to the closed door at his back, "all those people out there have seen me come in here too. If I really wanted to do you any harm, wouldn't I have tried something already?"

What could he do to open her eyes to that fact?

Bashir recalled the conversation he'd had with Nadim before he had left his senior master to care for his yacht, staff, and Zaire.

"Why tell this Yusra anything at all?" Nadim had asked him. *"Simply if she tries to sue, we'll counter with a lawsuit of our own."*

He hadn't answered Nadim. Normally he wouldn't have thought twice and taken that very action against Yusra and whatever harm she could pose him. But this involved his son. His family. He had to tread carefully.

Admittedly, he'd been curious too. The son that Yusra had raised was his cousin, Imran's son. He wouldn't rest easy until he knew that the boy was being raised by a suitable caregiver. And he also had to know that Yusra wouldn't try to battle him for custodial rights to the child who was biologically hers. Zaire.

So he hadn't come spoiling for a fight with her.

That, and he knew any of this leaking to the press and public would stymie his business dealings and upend his private life. When he'd told her they didn't have much time, he hadn't only been concerned about the hospital board looking out for themselves.

This baby-swap fiasco had caught him at a bad time. Though the world might think him an idle billionaire, Bashir was far from free of scheduling burdens and the sleepless nights that came with shouldering the livelihoods of his expansive staff. He had a multinational company to run. Thousands employed at his many hotel locations. People with families and financial obligations who relied on his business to bring home the bread and butter. If he stopped, they suffered. On top of overseeing that his business endeavors ran smoothly from the comfort of his ocean-faring home, there was the matter of his nonprofit refugee organization, Project Halcyone.

The ground breaking for the organization's headquarters was well underway. Having funded most of it out of his own pocket, Bashir had expedited construction and expected it to wrap up in the coming few months. Just in time for the end of summer. Then he had plans to garner more funds from generous donors. Donors he anticipated wooing at a charity gala on the opening of Project Halcyone's main office.

Being a migrant himself once, he understood the momentous change this nonprofit could bring to fellow asylum seekers and runaways. He didn't like speaking about his origins. It always left his chest with a terrible pressure, yet he'd had to set those feelings of discomfort aside when an overzealous reporter at a leading European business journal came knocking. Declining the phone interview had been a thought he'd indulged but couldn't afford. Halcyone needed funding to keep its doors open. What better way to do that than by the free publicity a reputable journal could bring? Of course he had known to choose his words carefully. Not all free advertising was good marketing. Some unpalatable parts of his past as an undocumented immigrant teen would surely do more harm to his image and that of Project Halcyone.

It should have helped that he had interviewed with the reporter before. Only instead of the regular questions he'd expected to be asked, the interview had swerved into his past and remained there for most of the half-hour appointment. No matter what he'd tried, no excuse had been enough to end the interview. His family was brought up. As were his years in the refugee camp—though gratefully no mention about his brush with local Greek police when he'd been an angry, sullen teenager. Answering vaguely hadn't satisfied the over-enthusiastic reporter. But he'd done his best, and still he had gotten off the call concerned that who he once was wasn't the only thing in danger of being revealed… Were the reporter to discover Yusra and the switched-at-birth drama with their sons, Bashir would have more trouble on his hands.

Trouble he didn't need.

For Project Halcyone to stand a chance, he required positive press and zero scandal around him as its founder. Bashir wouldn't allow anyone, not even a well-meaning mother like Yusra, to block him from making Halcyone a reality.

In a flash of inspiration, he grabbed one of the chairs that the hospital officials had vacated. Under his crushing bulk, the wobbly-legged old chair creaked and he might have blushed, but it was a scenario he was accustomed to experiencing—undersized furniture that could barely hold him in a world and environment that hadn't considered his comfort. But sacrifices had to be made in the face of extraordinary trouble.

Sacrifices that included balancing precariously on the thin legs of a too-small chair…

And looking Yusra Amin dead in the eyes before delivering the blow he prayed would have her see reason.

"Inshallah, my son will celebrate his third birthday on the first of September. And, if I'm not wrong, I believe he shares that in common with your son."

Quiet as a mouse now, Yusra's eyes widened and her alluring rosy-brown lips parted softly.

"Am I wrong?" he challenged.

She slowly shook her head and her grip on her phone trembled lightly. That was the instant he knew he had her.

My son. Your son.

The two phrases ran through her head in concentric circles. Like two suns in a binary system. Dancing around each other, until one tipped out of axis and collided into the other in a stellar explosion. An explosion that rocked her world, perhaps literally as the room began to tilt, spin and swim from her perspective.

Yusra squeezed her eyes shut.

A moment later she startled and opened her eyes at the touch on her shoulder. Big, warm and shockingly gentle given his impressive size and the gruffness with which he'd spoken to her.

Now, oddly, concern gleamed back at her in those starless dark pupils of his.

He'd called himself Bashir.

He bowed his head closer, astoundingly graceful even when he had to contort down to her level.

"If you're feeling dizzy, it helps to put your head between your legs."

She opened her mouth to tell him that it was his fault she suddenly felt sick to her stomach. But instead, she pushed away from him, turned her head and groped for the metal trash can under her desk. She clung to it until the immediate danger of sickness wore off and left her head feeling fuzzy and her mouth feeling absurdly dry.

"Water," she croaked.

As soon as she spoke, he left her in the office alone. She'd thought he abandoned her and almost laughed, wondering why she hadn't considered embarrassing herself earlier by retching out her breakfast to get him to leave her alone. If she weren't so weak, she'd have celebrated her victory over him. But she conserved her strength. Wiping her mouth, she set down the trash bin, and laid her forehead down on her arms atop her desk.

It wasn't long before she raised her head at the sound of the door clicking open once more.

"Water," said her hulking interrogator, his tone as gravelly as ever.

Annoyed that he helped her, Yusra accepted the water bottle and drank greedily from it. The fog around her mind cleared a bit, but the dryness remained in her mouth, and the weakness anchoring her bones and muscles still persisted as well.

"Food?" he said, reading her thoughts.

She flitted through her purse, this time determined to be her own hero, and unwrapped the straw of an orange juice box. It was a quick-fire way of knowing she wouldn't be knocked out by low blood sugar. As it was, she was reeling from what he had told her.

What she now tried and failed to pretend wasn't happening—which was impossible because it *had* happened.

My son. Your son.

Your son. My son.

She gave her head a jerk to clear her mind; little help it did. The words were seared in her brain. The truth almost too hard to bear.

"I was shocked too at first."

She sucked hard at her straw and flashed a quick, narrowed gaze at him, not ready to trust him enough with her feelings. She barely wrapped her mind around what he had said, but somehow, despite the clanging alarm for her to remain suspicious and cautious and argumentative—she *knew* that he was telling the truth. How else would he know her son's birthday?

It didn't stop her from blurting, "How do I know you're not some stalker who did your research?" Her voice was soft but accusatory. Anger laced her question too. Because she had nowhere else to direct the toxic and burdensome emotion. Unfortunately for him, he was the only suitable target in the room.

Though he didn't appear ruffled by it. He sat across from her again. Sitting up as tall and confidently as he was on his feet, he cocked his head and interlocked his hands between his legs.

"I could be a stalker, yes. But if I wanted to hunt you, Yusra, you *would* know."

"Oh, would I?" She rolled her eyes but froze when she saw his bushy black eyebrows snap down. When his lips moved, his smooth, deep voice pushed frantically at a primal button in her. She locked her legs together against the responsive heat from her feminine core.

"Yes, you would," he rasped darkly.

Under the weight of her hijab, her scalp prickled more, sweat lining her brow where her headscarf concealed her hairline. Even with the extra layers, there was this unsettling sense of exposure being around him brought out in her. More now that she noticed he was startlingly good-looking in a certain light. His face was all angles, brutally sharp cheekbones, a jawline that was strongly square, and a nose that hooked at the bridge before widening at the base. Dark brown lips were wide and pillowy and took up enough attention without his long, curly beard circling them. Funny thing being that his mouth was the only part of him that appeared soft, *and* he hadn't stopped frowning since he entered her office the first time.

Yusra blushed the more she took in of him. Her cheeks toasty hot by the time her eyes zipped up to meet his gaze.

The instant she did, her feverish skin began to cool. It happened suddenly. Ice-cold water poured over her head and froze the swift heated response to Bashir.

What am I thinking?

He had given her life-changing news, and instead of worrying about the safety of her family—about *protecting* her son, she was drooling over a man. Disgust rose up through her, curdling hot and nauseating. What kind of mother was she?

"What did you mean earlier?" she asked, hearing the fear in her voice and unable to do anything to plug its source. "How were our children... How could that even happen?"

"Our sons were accidentally swapped by an overworked, underpaid NICU nurse. The mistake was overlooked for years, and she'd sought to fix the problem on her own. She lost her job because of the error."

"That's awful." Yusra forgot she had the juice box in her hands until she squeezed the carton so hard that the juice oozed out onto her hands. She tugged napkins out of her purse, ignoring the fist crushing her heart when she had to move aside a pack of her son's favorite snack bars to get to the tissues.

But according to Bashir, AJ wasn't really hers. For nearly three years she'd raised him thinking he was her flesh and blood. The only good that had come out of his hopeless, heartless father.

No! It didn't matter what anyone had done in the past. AJ *was* hers!

"Let's say all of this is true, and our children were swapped, what are you planning to do?"

"Right now, those men out there are hoping to sweep this mess under the rug. They'll offer you money. Buy your silence."

"And you? Will you do the same?" Her belly quivered from the overload of nerves. There was a real possibility she'd heave the orange juice she'd drunk.

Big shoulders rising and falling subtly with the softest of sighs, he told her, "I won't lie to you and say I wasn't curious about the child."

He meant her son.

Her stomach hollowed. Weakly, she protested, "You can't take him. He's mine."

"And my son is mine." He scowled. "Do you think that's what I want? To steal your child? I won't delude myself to thinking that you trust me. I'd be a hypocrite if I expected that."

His meaning was clear. He didn't trust her either.

Bashir stared hard at her. "The truth is, my curiosity doesn't overpower my desire to protect my own child."

It struck her right then that he probably wanted to make this go away just as much as she did.

Yusra knew what it meant. She'd have to relinquish her biological tie to his son. She didn't even know the other child's name, but she worried if she heard it, she wouldn't be able to walk away. If she wanted this to go away, she had to turn her back on what could have been and recall that her present life had been perfectly happy before this bombshell went off in her office.

Okay! Truthfully, she could do with a bit more money. But that was because she was constantly anxious that she wouldn't be able to keep a roof over their heads or give her son everything in life that he deserved.

"We could walk away from this, right here and now," he intoned. "No costly legal battle needed."

Could she do it? Could she walk away knowing that she had another child out there?

Her heart fluttered and her insides swooped.

There must have been some sign of indecisiveness on her face that prompted Bashir into saying, "I have a suggestion."

She tensed but didn't stop him from continuing.

"Think on it."

"And then what?" Yusra challenged with a frown, her heart thudding and her leg bouncing from her nerves. She didn't think there was a chance that he'd just leave and never bother her again. She wasn't even *certain* she wanted him walking away like this, given everything that had happened. Because she still had questions she wanted answered.

Bashir rose to his feet, his tall, heavily built frame pulling up gracefully from the small chair he somehow managed not to break. He glanced cursorily at the walls of her office, presumably at the sketches and paintings she'd framed and hung. She had used a variety of mediums. Charcoal, watercolors, oil and even newsprint to create her art. These pieces were the only ones she hadn't gotten rid of and managed to hide from her controlling ex-husband. She had hung them to remember what she had gotten through. How she had survived a disastrous divorce and thrived as a single mother. But also to recall she'd had a passion once.

"You're an artist?"

"Graphic designer, actually." Small talk wasn't what she wanted though. Thankfully he was of the same mindset.

"You don't have to decide at the moment."

She raised a brow, arguing, "What happened to having little time?" She slung his words back at him.

Perfectly timed, a rapping sounded at the door to her office. It had to be the hospital personnel that Bashir had ushered out earlier.

Unheeding of the noise behind him, he pulled his analyzing gaze from her art and on to her. "Being pressed for time is always a factor in big, life-altering decisions."

The impatient knocking started up again. *Rat-tat-tat.*

"However, I *would* suggest calling a lawyer," Bashir continued calmly. "It'll help keep the hospital from imposing what's best for them on to you. And here's my card." She allowed him to place it on her desk without protest even though she wasn't sure she would contact him.

"Once you've processed this, call or email me."

"What if I don't?" Yusra kept him from leaving. A minute ago, she would have been relieved to see him exit her office. But now she was confused about everything. Including what she wanted, or what the best recourse was for her.

He looked back at her over his broad shoulder, his face expressionless but his eyes overly compelling and a danger to her rabbiting heart.

"You will," he impressed on her. He said it so self-assuredly that it bordered on smug confidence.

And yet, she didn't have the words to knock his ego down a peg or hold him back from walking out of her office and leaving her to process everything that had gone down.

CHAPTER FOUR

DESPITE HER RESERVATIONS about Bashir, Yusra still took his advice and refused to speak to the hospital personnel who wanted to buy her silence. And she called a lawyer. Her neighbor Dembe assisted her there. Luckily his older brother worked in the legal field and got in touch with a colleague who specialized in family law.

Everything happened so fast.

Within a few hours of learning from Bashir that their sons had been swapped at birth, Yusra heard back from the lawyer, who had then advised her to sit on the nondisclosure agreement the hospital had left with her and agreed to legally represent her pro bono.

She hadn't spoken to Bashir again, but their lawyers were doing the talking for them. From what she understood, after four days of deliberation, Bashir and his legal team had returned with an astoundingly generous offer. So generous, she questioned its veracity until she read the details for herself and had her lawyer break down any legalese. Bashir was offering monetary compensation in the form of a trust fund for her son, AJ. The extra zeroes were what had her eyes bugging. She'd have to sign a nondisclosure, of course. It would bar her from ever speaking of the baby-swap incident. Which meant she would be giving up any chance at meeting her biological son—the child who Bashir was raising.

I still don't even know the child's name...

This wasn't a decision she could make lightly. There were repercussions and lifelong regrets to consider. Could she truly walk away now that she knew she had another child connected to her out there?

Maybe that was why she had asked to see Bashir. Speak to him once more.

He agreed to meet with her on his yacht, requesting that they leave their lawyers behind.

She reluctantly accepted, but secretly worried whether he had the upper hand. They would be on his turf, not hers. It was hardly fair, yet she didn't see what choice she had, and especially when she felt this conversation would help her determine what choice was best.

Yusra didn't know what to expect after assenting to both of his stipulations on their meeting grounds.

But it wasn't a luxury sedan picking her up from her shabby apartment in her equally grungy neighborhood. The car ferried them through the congested traffic of Kampala to Entebbe International Airport where a private plane in a well-guarded hangar awaited their arrival. By that point she questioned her decision, but it was too late to back out, as her son reminded her.

Bringing AJ along had been instinctual. She hadn't wanted to leave him behind. Needed the comfort of his presence. Lately more than ever. Deep down she couldn't shake this unease that he could be taken from her. Irrational, perhaps. But considering the baby swap, was it such a stretch for her to be overly protective? So long as he was in her sight, she couldn't lose him.

And unlike her, AJ liked the idea of them boarding a plane. She'd already promised him a tour of Bashir's boat—not that she'd asked Bashir himself. That was the least of her problems though.

The flight lasted a little less than two hours before the pilot announced they'd reached the international airport in Mombasa, Kenya. Another sleek sedan whisked them from the airport to what Yusra hoped was their final destination. Bashir's ship.

They were traveling alongside the ocean. Deep blue waters endlessly rippling into the sun-blurred horizon. She rested her forehead on the cool glass of the car window and gazed at the large body of water, nostalgia flooding into her instantly. It reminded her of home and just how close she was to Somalia since she'd left her country to study and work in Uganda. When she'd lived with her parents and siblings, the beach and ocean were a short walking distance from her family home. She had spent many an evening with family members and friends just lounging in the sands and playing in the water. She hadn't realized just how much she missed it…

Until now, she thought sadly.

Her sadness faded when her ocean view was cut off by a large ship. She knew, straightaway, that it belonged to Bashir. Nothing that big could be cheap. Only a billionaire could afford the gleaming white monstrosity floating in the ocean. She'd met one such billionaire recently.

And she wasn't the only one who noticed the change in scenery. Beside her, AJ wriggled against his seat belt and gripped her hand tighter. "Look, Mama! Boat!"

"I see it, sweetheart," she said, her heart pumping faster.

Her son's excitement was contagious. It had to be. This giddy anticipation bubbling in her was a typical reaction to new experiences. The journey via a luxury car and private jet. Seeing the Indian Ocean again after so many years. Was it any wonder that her and AJ were overwhelmed? Visiting a boat was a first for them both—and Bashir's ship was massive.

The superyacht awaiting them seemed twice as large when she stepped out of the car with AJ balanced on her hip.

"Big boat!" AJ chirped at her and pointed to it. As though she could miss it.

She saw the big boat perfectly. But it was the big man waiting at the base of the walkway onto the giant yacht that had her body going rigid, her mouth dry and her belly all atwitter. That butterflies-in-her-tummy reaction that no man had elicited from her since her divorce was alive and well and flapping innumerable tiny wings all through her, and for Bashir of all people. Not even her crush on her cute and sweet neighbor Dembe had gotten that kind of biochemical fireworks. Yusra didn't know what it meant that Bashir had provoked the response in her. Only that she shouldn't follow the dangerous lure of the attraction.

Bashir wasn't alone. Though flanked by two other men, both males impressively towering in height and brawny in muscle, he still stood out as the largest and strongest among them.

"Yusra." He acknowledged her with a curt nod and an intense gaze.

"Bashir," she replied.

Feeling the press of eyes all around them, and the tight grip of AJ's fingers digging into her arm, she was reminded that they weren't here for a pleasure trip. She climbed the walkway, acutely aware of Bashir following her onto his ship. AJ wiggled in her arms, quietly asking to be let down. After gently setting him onto the teak flooring of the deck, she clutched his tiny hand and looked around at the unbelievable view from atop Bashir's tall and expansive yacht.

She didn't have much time to take in her fill of the sights and sounds before he engaged her in conversation.

"Is this…?" It was strange to see hesitance flit across his stern face. The first time she believed he'd shown an expression that wasn't powerfully confident in the short while she'd known him.

"My son," she told him and completed his thought.

He made a two-finger motion to one of the men behind him. "It appears we had the same idea," he said with a snort, his message enigmatic until she saw what he meant.

A slightly older woman walked up to them. She had her dark brown hair scraped back into an austere braid and wore a plain long-sleeved white shirt and blue jeans. And she wasn't alone. She carried a young boy in her arms. A boy who had Yusra's dark reddish-brown coloring and curly black hair.

Without needing to confirm it, her eyes watered and she knew who he was.

Bashir's son.

Now she understood what he had said about their thinking alike.

She'd brought AJ along on the fly, convinced she was worried to let him out of her sight in case she lost him. But now she knew that wasn't the full truth. Because now she suspected it was for the same reason that Bashir had sent for his son. He wanted her to meet the boy.

And it seemed she wanted the same for him and AJ.

Bashir saw surprise blossom over Yusra's face. It started with her dark brown eyes rounding and her breath audibly catching. He suddenly and fiercely, to the marrow of his bones, wished she were gazing at him. But he wasn't the reason she was so taken aback.

Her eyes glued on to his son, she breathily asked, "What's his name?"

"Zaire." He'd chosen the name for his son as Tara and Imran had both died before doing the honor. Given how his beginning was tragic, Bashir had picked an empowering name that was indicative of Zaire's more fortunate future. "It means river that swallows all rivers." He didn't know why he was telling her that. Just like he didn't know why it mattered when she didn't laugh him off.

Rather than laugh, she blinked suspiciously several times and murmured, "It's a good name."

Without Bashir needing to ask, she stroked the wispy curls of the boy stuck fast to her leg and introduced him.

"This is Abdul Jabir. AJ for short."

"A strong name too," he told her.

The boy gaped up at him, the toy boat clutched in one small fist and holding his mother with the other hand. Meanwhile Zaire clung shyly to Alcina when she attempted to approach them more closely. Neither child seemed ready to meet new faces.

Bashir had anticipated this reaction. Prepared for it. The children weren't the only ones who seemed uncomfortable. He read a similar hesitance from Yusra. There was a rigidity to her posture. Her shoulders were drawn up and her eyes warily flitted over his face, the meaning in her actions clear to him. She wasn't sure whether she could trust him. And she had every right to her suspicions. He ticked off all the reasons. She was on his ship. She knew he had more money than she did. Certainly more legal power and sway. From her perspective, it wasn't a leap for her to be wondering if she was at his mercy.

The truth? She had something he wanted that weighed far more than all his wealth and the power that came with it. Something he couldn't force from her. Glancing down at her son, and watching the boy shy away from him behind his mother again, Bashir felt his heart give a short, sharp lurch. A forlornness settled over him. This was Imran's son. To think that he might not ever have met him if that former nurse hadn't told him about the accidental baby swap. Not that he regretted having Zaire. Not for one second. He would trade anything to keep his son, but a new sensation muscled its way to the front of his mind.

Greed.

He wanted both boys. But he also wasn't willing to rob AJ from his mother. And Yusra didn't deserve that. From what he learned of his private investigation on her, she was poor, not a bad caregiver. In fact, she was the opposite. Worked hard to provide for herself and her child even when her business was slow and her income was scarce. It was obvious she'd do anything for AJ. He wouldn't break up their family just to satisfy this need to have the best of both worlds.

Grinding his teeth together at the conundrum facing him, he turned his thoughts to a problem he could solve. The awkward silence that had descended on them.

"I'll take him from here." Thanking Alcina and dismissing her, he plucked Zaire from his nanny's arms. His son gripped him tightly but snuck peeks at their visitors. Fear clashing with curiosity. Neither one winning yet. It was a good enough cue for them to move on.

"I know we're meeting under serious circumstances, but I hoped I could interest you in a tour of the ship first. If that's all right with you?" He would give her every chance to back out. Prove to her that she wasn't as powerless as she might believe herself to be.

Yusra pulled her son up into her arms. Then with a jut of her chin, she informed him, "AJ wanted a tour anyways."

He couldn't have asked for a better response. "I'll have to aim to please then."

"But we will talk after, yes?"

"Of course, that's a given," he promised before leading the way through his ship.

As they traversed from stern to starboard to bow and port, he pointed out the amenities. Because that was what a person did on a tour of their home, flex all that his wealth could afford him. A sports court and golf tee, an infinity pool with a rock waterfall, the top-class wellness center he rarely used but probably should, one of two private cinemas—this one outdoors, an indoor garden and the helicopter deck. He had merely scratched the surface, but Zaire was growing restless in his arms, and it appeared that Yusra wasn't having it better than him with AJ. Fidgety toddlers spelled trouble, so he changed tack and ended their tour abruptly by heading to their final stop. Zaire's playroom.

Yusra's first reaction was a breathy gasp. Then she asked, "How is this even possible?" Awe pulsed through her voice.

Bashir tried to see it the way she would. A whole playground on a ship. His money was seriously talking now.

AJ wriggled down from Yusra, and though he clutched his mother's hand, he toddled forward with her. Equally eager to explore, Zaire jabbed a finger at the swings and whined until Bashir carried him to one of two full bucket seats on the swing set of the sprawling play area.

Whatever shyness and fear had plagued both boys thawed now that the prospect of play was in front of them. Within minutes, AJ and Zaire were squealing with laughter. Yusra was helping AJ navigate the climbing structure, and Bashir pulled Zaire from the swings when he'd gotten bored and took him over to the remarkably colorful playhouse. Before long that turned into him waiting on his son to climb out of a crawl tube and trailing after him to where Yusra and AJ had been playing on the climbing structure. Bashir didn't know when he'd shed his suit jacket and tie, or when he had rolled up his sleeves and unbuttoned his collar. But it was less restrictive chasing after his son without them on.

Zaire squeezed onto his lap and they slid down the spiral slide together. But after a couple of times doing this, his son stopped and sat on one of the steps of the climbing structure to watch Yusra rock AJ on a boat-shaped spring rider. AJ rocked faster with her help and smiled toothily up at his mother.

Zaire slowly moved from the climbing structure over to where they were, and he stooped to pick up the toy boat that AJ had set aside temporarily in lieu of playing. By this point Yusra noticed him and stopped what she was doing.

Intrigued, Bashir watched the interaction close by. If Zaire needed him, he'd step in, but right now his son seemed comfortable approaching the newcomers.

Zaire held the toy up to Yusra.

She crouched smilingly to his level and accepted it on AJ's behalf. "Thank you, Zaire." Casting a quick look back at her son, she asked, "Would you like a turn to ride too?"

His son nodded timidly.

"What do we say when we ask for something nicely?" Bashir asked his son.

Looking between them, Zaire then said, "Please." Although it came out more like *puh-weeze*, it was still enough for Yusra to smile so fully and with this glowing radiance that even his heart quickened at the sight of it.

Zaire was totally won over once Yusra pulled AJ off the spring rider and placed his son on the toy.

AJ didn't cry. Overly mature for his age, he stepped back with his toy boat grasped in his small hands. Bashir still hadn't acclimated to seeing him as Imran and Tara's son.

"I like your ship, little man."

"Boat," he said.

Bashir smirked at the correction, but agreed, "Boat."

Looking at the portrait they made, almost like they were one big happy and *normal* family, he realized this would be difficult.

It's going to be harder than I imagined or hoped it would be.

As though hearing his thought, Yusra flicked a look back at him. Her open expression echoed what he felt, and he sensed she'd agree that no part of this decision they'd have to make would be easy or painless.

Getting Yusra to himself took far longer than Bashir believed it would.

Eventually though both AJ and Zaire had gone down for their naps following an afternoon of play. They hadn't fussed either. Just exhausted themselves asleep soon as they were in bed. Bashir walked quietly for the exit, sensing Yusra behind him. He paused when she lingered at the door into the bedroom. Bashir knew what she had to be feeling because he felt it too. Looking over her head at their boys tugged at his heartstrings fiercely. They had bonded quickly enough, as though it was all second nature to them.

He wished it could be as easy between him and Yusra. Particularly with the direction his thoughts had angled after watching their sons interact positively.

Leaving the boys to nap, he guided his special guest to a salon, the largest of three on the yacht. The living space garnered the same reaction from her as Zaire's playroom had.

Her breath hitched and she stood still upon entering the room. "I don't know why I'm surprised it's so beautiful."

Bashir hid his smile with the excuse to hydrate them.

Pulling out two crystal-encrusted bottles from his mini fridge, he then pried the lids off with a bottle opener and walked over to where she was standing before one of many windows offering a postcard-perfect view of the ocean. She accepted the bottle with a tentative expression touching her brows, and her fingertips tracing the sparkling crystals lining the top and bottom of the bottle label.

"It's water," he explained, realizing he probably should have led with that.

"Should I bother asking why your water's pretty too?"

He did laugh now. A short-lived chuckle that grated at his throat and reminded him of how long it had been since he'd laughed. Long enough to feel embarrassed at the abrupt show of emotion.

Yusra seemed to recognize his faltering too. Her eyes rounder, dark pupils contracting as streams of sunlight brightened the salon. But what arrested him most was her bottom lip caught between her teeth. The smooth pink flesh tortured by her unease. Or maybe it was worry? He wouldn't know. Just as he didn't understand why she had such an effect on him. Only that she did, and it should concern him. Yet it didn't.

Staring at her for longer than could be deemed polite, he sipped his ice-cool water as an excuse to quench his sudden thirst and a chance to recenter his composure. Because what Bashir had to tell her next would take all of his focus and power of persuasion.

She drank slowly from the bottle too, licking her lips of any stray droplets and murmuring, "It tastes expensive."

Smiling tensely, he nodded, his mind already a few paces ahead.

"The boys seemed to love playing together," Bashir observed. "Zaire isn't used to having playmates, so I'll confess

I was worried about how well he would share. But AJ seemed like he was used to it."

"He attends day care. Sometimes." Her voice pitched at the end, hinting that there was more to her statement. She didn't hold him in suspense for too long. "Childcare can be costly."

"I imagine it is. Especially when you want the best care for your little one."

She clasped the bottle with both her hands, her gaze avoidant now. "We aren't here to discuss that though, are we?"

"No, we aren't," he agreed, sensing that she needed truth more than anything, but also establishing as much rapport as he could squeeze into this moment. He needed her trusting him when he asked her what he had in mind. "Before we get to that, may I ask why you wanted to meet again?"

When he'd visited her in her office, he had given her his business card with little expectation. Especially once he'd had his lawyers send the offer of monetary compensation to her along with a nondisclosure to stop her from ever speaking publicly about the baby swap. Since Bashir clarified that the money would be held in trust for AJ until he came of age, he didn't think he'd hear back from Yusra. It had been a generous amount. But to him, it was a paltry fraction of what he owed Imran. Remorse throttled him whenever he thought of his cousin. Of the years he'd wasted not keeping in more regular touch with him. Now he was doing the same thing to his remaining family members. Imran's parents and siblings had tried reaching out before and after Imran's death, and Bashir had frozen them all out. If anything, losing Imran had reminded him that loss and death were unavoidable, and that caring and loving would only intensify the sense of loss and power of death that much more.

If he were being brutally honest with himself, he had wanted Yusra to take the money and vanish. It would have been easier on him. Instead, she'd called. Asked to meet. And he hadn't been able to deny her.

"I wanted to thank you. I wasn't expecting money." She bit her lip, walked to the glass sled coffee table and set down her bottle of water. "But I have to say, I won't accept the money if it's to pay me off."

"It isn't. Although I can appreciate why you might think it is." He couldn't tell her about Imran, and why he felt duty-bound to provide anything he could to AJ. Not yet. Maybe not ever, depending on how their conversation panned out. "To be clear, the money is exclusive of the nondisclosure."

He placed his bottle of water next to hers on the coffee table before dropping onto the leather sofa facing the incred-ible vista of the ocean. Shadowing him, Yusra grabbed the armchair diagonal to his position. This way they could face each other more comfortably.

Comfortable is a stretch...

Apprehension sucked the air out of the room.

Bashir believed taking this slowly would ease the pressure off him and give Yusra time to adjust, but the longer he held out, the worse his nerves jangled. He'd done enough tiptoe-ing around her. The more this continued, the less control he would have by the end.

"You could have thanked me over the phone," he remarked. "And why bring AJ?"

"I didn't want to leave him alone." The wrinkle between her fine eyebrows became more pronounced. "Besides, I could ask you the same thing. I hadn't expected to meet Zaire."

"I wanted to give him the chance to meet his birth mother. In case he never had the opportunity again."

Yusra shifted in her armchair, signaling her rising dis-comfort, and her hands closed into small fists atop her knees as though she was fighting her restlessness. Her lost hope. Bashir grazed his eyes over her. She had dressed modestly again, but her beauty wasn't muted. Disarmed by his attraction to her, he lowered his defenses.

"Recall that back in your office I asked you whether you could walk away. Now that you've had time to think on it, could you?"

"It would be harder now that I've met Zaire," she said.

"I feel the same about AJ."

She dipped her chin and smiled morosely. Even if he hadn't just heard her hesitation to part ways forever, he'd have seen enough by looking at her. She didn't want to walk away. But she was accepting the fact that she'd have to leave soon, and for good, once she signed off on the NDA to bury the baby swap. And naturally she mourned it.

As he should too. And he might have if he weren't clinging on to one last shred of hope.

"What if this visit didn't end?" he asked.

"What do you mean?"

He'd been thinking this over ever since he had seen AJ and Zaire together, in one room, playing carefree and cooperatively. Also whenever Zaire had approached Yusra and asked her to help push him on a swing or rock him on the spring rider toy. She hadn't treated his son any differently from her own. Except he'd caught a few longing glances from her toward Zaire, her maternal love unhidden and shining in her eyes. And why shouldn't she feel that way? He was her son.

Just as AJ was his family.

Seeing her apprehension staring back at him, he told her the plan he'd been ruminating on for the past hour. The plan he now believed truly had legs.

"What if AJ and Zaire could be in both our lives?"

"How?" she blurted. And just like that, her agitation wiped clear once he presented a solution to their shared problem.

"Fair warning, it's unorthodox. But it will relieve us from having to choose to walk away."

"Tell me." An unspoken resolve caught fire in her coal-dark eyes, added a richer red to her deep brown skin and straightened her backbone. And before she opened her mouth, he knew she was willing to hear his wild idea.

Only it sounded even more outrageous when he spoke it.

"Marriage. If we were to marry, then the children could stay with us both, and having to walk away would no longer be a problem."

CHAPTER FIVE

"MARRIAGE?" YUSRA HEARD herself repeating slowly, enunciating the few syllables, and all while feeling foolish. Because surely, she'd heard him incorrectly.

Bashir couldn't have just asked to marry her.

It was more likely that she had allowed her hope to get the best of her. She didn't want to leave Zaire behind, and like her, Bashir hadn't wanted to let go of AJ. Naturally then, for one brilliant, buoyant second, she had thought he had found a way to fix this.

But Yusra's fleeting hope passed as quickly as it arose.

And she might have remained convinced she'd heard wrong if Bashir didn't speak up.

"Yusra. I'm very seriously proposing this."

"This can't be for real," she whispered as a wave of dizziness swamped her. She was glad she was seated when Bashir had turned her world upside down. Possibly as much as the baby swap had. Weakly, she protested, "It has to be a joke... Right?"

She would even be willing to forgive him if it was, as cruel as it would be.

"Marriage is serious. It's a lifelong commitment." Yusra felt like a hypocrite once she said it. Her marriage hadn't lasted. It also hadn't been full of love and support and reciprocity. And the experience soured the possibility of a second-chance romance for her. Still, it didn't mean she held any less value for the long-standing institution.

His frown was immediate and tinged with annoyance.

"I wouldn't joke about anything that required the level of trust a marriage demands. I've given this plenty of thought. I wouldn't have proposed it if I hadn't." He then set his jaw firmly, the veins along his temples more pronounced, his brows two furry lines of severity. "Marriage would allow us to live together with the children. It would also present a united front to the hospital. They want to fix their error, and they've already contacted me about having us swap our children and righting the wrong."

Yusra knew about the hospital's request, as they'd made it to her lawyer. It was why she'd been scared of losing AJ one way or another. That fear retriggered her anxiety, and she curled her hands into fists, her nails carving into the fleshy pads of her palms. "All right, but what made you decide this was the only way? We could co-parent without the ties of marriage."

"It might not seem like it, but I'm traditional," he countered.

"But marriage is complicated. There are things couples discuss and discover even before they consider such an important oath." Even as she spoke, Yusra knew not even a willingness to openly communicate could prevent a marriage from falling apart. She should be happy that Bashir wasn't asking love from her too.

"Then we'll talk and negotiate terms, and outline and sign off on them. I believe it's possible. However, if you're not on board…" He trailed off, with the clear intention that he didn't plan on forcing her into anything she didn't want a part of.

It lent her a modicum of comfort. Though not enough to win her over on to his idea yet.

"I'll have to think this through."

Bashir had given her time to muddle a decision once before, so she wasn't expecting him to nod albeit with a reluctant scowl.

"That's fine, but you'll have to think fast. This problem of ours is better solved sooner. One way or another."

Yusra sensed there was more to his urgency that had to do with motives outside just wanting to spend limitless time with both their boys. And yet she agreed with him that the baby swap had shaken their lives, and nothing would begin to feel right again until they were unified on a decision.

That had been two days ago. Once she'd left the yacht and been returned to her tiny apartment, she'd given his suggestion plenty of thought, and after a grueling forty-eight hours, had come to a decision.

She would agree to marriage.

Yusra had thought this over long and hard. Sleep hadn't come easily to her the last two days. Every time she closed her eyes, she pictured Bashir's hard gaze, dark beard and his unsmiling but tempting mouth.

And during the day she couldn't help looking at AJ and wondering what Zaire was doing. She had her son around her more often now that he'd been removed from day care due to her inability to maintain his tuition. Which meant that she'd had no choice but to work from home or bring him along to client meetings in her small office out of the laundromat. It hadn't been an ideal arrangement, and though it had worked for now, she was aware it couldn't last forever. Mostly because AJ missed his friends and teachers in day care, and when he wasn't talking about that, he pelted her with questions about Bashir and Zaire. When were they going back to visit Bashir's big boat? When could he play again with Zaire's adorable albino rabbit, Puzzles? When was Zaire going to come and visit their home like they had visited his?

Yusra hadn't factored in the two toddlers bonding as fast as they had. She'd only considered her and Bashir's feelings on the matter. But clearly the boys missed each other, and Bashir's proposal of marriage did ensure that they'd live together like a family. It was starting to look less and less like an absurd idea after all...

And she wasn't entirely ignoring the fact that he was still offering to help with money. Just before she'd left his yacht, he had assured her that AJ's trust fund would remain, regardless of her decision on the marriage proposal. Having that nest egg for AJ lightened a load she didn't even know she had been shouldering. Knowing that Bashir cared for AJ as much as he did Zaire warmed her more to his plan for them to be family.

During the day it all seemed so logical and clear...

But at night, when she was alone with her traitorous dreams about Bashir's handsome face and big, strong body drifting closer to her, she succumbed to doubts as quickly as she did to temptation. She always woke up in the sanctuary of her bed, far, far from Bashir, but it didn't shift her unease about what life would be like actually living with him. Being near him a lot more. Possibly even sharing a bed with him.

No, that doesn't have to happen. That's where I'll draw the line.

At least that was what she promised she would do when she saw him next. And now that the moment had come, she was nervous and nowhere near as confident in discussing the possibility of intimacy between them.

Bashir sat across from her, his legal team filling his half of the conference table, while her lone lawyer sat next to her. Just the two of them against a whole army, and the billionaire general who led the charge. They had barely been seated when she agreed to his marriage proposal. All eyes on her, she fought against the knee-weakening embarrassment scoring her cheeks and fluttering through her stomach.

"Did you hear me?" she asked after Bashir showed no outward reaction to what she'd said.

"Just fine," he replied.

Why was he acting so strangely? His tone flat, and his expression without affect—although she'd grown used to seeing him like that. Bashir didn't express too much emotion since she had met him. But it would have been nice to have some reaction from him. Wasn't he thrilled that she was consenting to his wild proposal? Some fanfare from him would have been encouraging.

Disappointed, Yusra felt a spike in her anxiety again as a new thought struck her.

What if he's changed his mind?

Considering it had taken working up all her nerve to do this, she wouldn't be happy with him. Her choice went against both her lawyer's and Dembe's advice to reconsider Bashir's unconventional solution to their swapped-babies issue. Her neighbor had been the only other person who had known, and that was because she felt she owed him, considering he'd helped secure her a lawyer in the first place.

It was for the best that the less people knew in her life, the better. *For now.* She'd only drag her family into this when she was certain.

And if Bashir had changed his mind after all, she didn't want one more person knowing that she'd been rejected.

Yusra quelled the instinct to fidget in her seat. The ticking of the wall clock wasn't helping calm her. It felt like a countdown to a timer.

Or a bomb, she thought grimly.

Flicking a glance at the clock, she wondered whether AJ was having fun with Dembe. Her kindly neighbor had volunteered for babysitting duty. She hadn't wanted to bring her son with her this time. Not even when she knew that Bashir might be grateful for it. Protecting AJ was her top priority. Though he was too young to comprehend what had changed, she wouldn't disrupt his life any more. And she wouldn't let anyone else do it either.

As she thought this, she glared at Bashir and raised her chin. A silent challenge for him to say what he'd come to say. She was a big girl. Capable of handling herself if he backtracked on his decision to marry her.

"Can we have the room?" Bashir spoke, his eyes on her, his command for the other occupants in the room. "If that's all right with you?" he addressed her.

Tight-lipped, she stiffly nodded at her lawyer, dismissing her counsel just as Bashir sent his entourage away as well. Now, with the spacious conference room all to themselves, she locked her hands atop the table and stared back at him. He had to have a reason to drive everyone away. She was intrigued to hear it.

But not patient enough to wait.

"Are you having second thoughts?" She'd rather know now and get it over with, avoid any gallant effort on his part to soften the blow of rejection. Not that she would be upset or devastated. They weren't close enough to incite those feelings. She *did* need to know what he planned to do next if he wasn't going forward with the marriage of convenience.

He leaned back in his chair, his legs crossed, one hand plucking at his thick beard hairs and the other drumming his fingers over the tabletop. Like an island, the dark rectangular solid wood sat between them. He was so near, but his expression and thoughts were entirely out of reach. Without them, she was groping sightless in the dark, unclear as to where this would lead.

"I just need to know," Yusra said.

And she only breathed easier when he replied, "Nothing's changed. I only felt what had to be said should stay between us. We are the ones getting married. Speaking of marriage, shall we discuss our terms and expectations now?"

"That would be a good idea." She hadn't planned to agree to this without guidelines and contingencies for their marriage. They were two strangers who knew nothing about each other, and most couples in love still put all cards on the table. That way no party was surprised or hoodwinked, and the decision was as consensual as possible.

"Do you want to start first?" He stopped tapping his fingers over the table and fanned his hand at her, inviting her to take the lead.

"I guess we should begin with finances." A leading cause of why relationships fell apart. It hadn't been entirely why she and her ex-husband had broken up, but money had been an issue. Particularly as he'd thought she was making too much and somehow destroying his masculinity because her paychecks had more zeroes in them. But she didn't want to think of that, not when she was in the middle of negotiating her way into another marriage.

Yet, informed by her previous disaster of a relationship, Yusra highlighted her thoughts, "I won't quit my job." She wouldn't make the mistake of pleasing anyone again. She liked her job and shouldn't have to leave it even if her life would be changed by Bashir and his billions.

"I'm fine with you working."

"You live aboard your yacht, don't you?" She hedged, wondering if he understood what she was saying.

He nodded. "I do own homes though, throughout the world."

Homes. As in plural. She shouldn't have anticipated anything less, considering his immense wealth.

"What I'm getting at is that my work is here, in Kampala." She wouldn't leave Uganda. It wouldn't be fair of her to overturn her life and her son's when everything else was changing. Perhaps with time she'd reconsider, but right then she couldn't be convinced otherwise.

One big life decision at a time.

"I'm all right with that too," Bashir said. "Though that does bring us to our living arrangement. Where will we reside together?"

A little answering shiver zipped down her back like a bolt of lightning as she recalled her dreams of him. Vividly intimate dreams that seemed to feel more real every time she slept. No thanks to those dreams, she'd been fretting over having this conversation. Blushingly, Yusra accepted her attraction to Bashir, but she barred it from scrambling her good judgement. She just wanted to have both AJ and Zaire in her life; Bashir desired the same thing. That was it.

Channeling a calm she wasn't fully feeling, she said, "I was thinking we could swap homes. Spend the weekdays in Kampala, and the weekends on your ship."

"All of us?" Bashir's frown unnerved her. She wouldn't compromise about living on his ship full-time, but in fairness she was willing to work out the scheduling with him.

"I'd be willing to do Fridays on your yacht as well." And if work arose, she could take her laptop along and complete what she could from his vast floating home.

Still, even with this suggestion, his frown remained unchanged.

"Will that be a problem?" she ventured softly.

His scowling features grew fiercer. "Actually, yes. Zaire hasn't lived anywhere else."

In disbelief, Yusra exclaimed, "*What?* Why?"

Bashir had hoped to evade this question. He hadn't been bothered by his choice of lifestyle before. Soon after Zaire had come into his world, he'd purchased the megayacht and incurred the annoyingly costly maintenance of it for his peace of mind. His reasons for his unconventional lifestyle were simple: He had more control of his environment. Isolation meant less of a chance at risking accidents and the disquieting emotions that usually followed. For nearly three years he'd succeeded in protecting Zaire.

And protecting myself from losing him.

Bashir clenched his teeth at the mere thought of harm coming to his son. Keeping Zaire safe was all he'd wanted. And he had believed in his method.

Until now.

Until he sat opposite Yusra and watched inquisitiveness overtake her expression. She hadn't even heard his explanation and already she was beginning to look at him differently. Or that was what it felt like to him. Bashir supposed he also could just be overly sensitive. Seeing what wasn't there because that was what he expected. Her confusion. Her judgment.

Her objection.

Whatever the reason, it made it harder to discuss.

"I own homes and hotels the world over for when I have to travel for work. However, when Zaire was born, I quickly realized it wouldn't be fair of me to uproot his life every time my work called for it. It took some adjusting, but I work from and live on the yacht, and that arrangement allows me to be close at hand in case my son needs me."

"So, Zaire has lived all his life on the ship?"

Bashir's jaws ached from the pressure he applied. He relaxed his muscles enough to grit between his teeth, "Yes."

"You know that's going to have to change. It'll be a tough adjustment, but one that has to happen if we're going to make this *marriage* work."

Nothing in her tone suggested she pitied him or even held a shred of judgment against his parenting style. She was simply stating a fact. Both of their lives would have to change to accommodate their marriage and their family.

"Weekends on the yacht are fine then." Bashir didn't know what else to say. He was relieved that she hadn't judged him. He didn't know what to make of that. What to think *of her*. Most of all, Bashir didn't know whether to relish his good luck that of all people he had to be caught up in a baby swap with, that it was Yusra, or if he should worry that she would demolish his ironclad defenses with her get-along-to-go-along personality.

Even now, when she smiled at him, he felt an inexplicable warmth all over. A heat that nestled most beneath his breastbone and around a certain vital organ.

Her smile only faltered when she spoke again. "My apartment's small though. It won't fit all of us."

"We'll look into a bigger apartment," he said breezily. Money wasn't an issue. He'd gotten over one of his biggest obstacles, telling her about his and Zaire's way of life, and trusting that she wouldn't scorn him. The rest was a cakewalk.

Or not.

Yusra's brows drew together in frustration. "Okay, but I'll help pay the bills. You're already providing AJ with a trust fund. I don't expect more money from you."

Ah. That was what this was about. Her financial independence.

To ease her mind, he said, "Zaire has a trust fund too. I don't want one of them to have what the other doesn't. And when both boys turn twenty, they'll have access to their money. It'll give them a safety net as they navigate new adulthood." And since they were on the topic… "What are your thoughts on a prenuptial?"

"Wouldn't that be a bad omen to the marriage?"

"A prenup would give you more power and choice ultimately. Although the other option is a postnuptial later on." He was fine with either alternative.

"Then let's wait. I don't want to doom this before it starts."

His heart pattered faster at that. She cared about this marriage, even though it was a means to an end for them both. And though it was important for him to solve their baby swap as bloodlessly as possible, it wasn't like him to open himself to possible legal problems. His lawyers wouldn't like him holding off on a premarital agreement. They would ask him to reconsider, and he'd remember this moment with Yusra and hesitate. Did he trust her enough to do what she asked and pause on the prenup?

Yes.

Decided on that, he moved past it before he questioned where his sudden strong trust in her had sprung from.

"There was something else I wanted to ask. Does AJ have a father figure in his life?" Bashir needed to know that he wouldn't be treading on another man's toes. Though he knew she'd been married before, he hadn't asked the private investigator to dig into Yusra's ex-husband who was also Zaire's biological father. It felt too personal.

Yusra shook her head. "He never met AJ, and he wanted it that way. He probably wouldn't even want Zaire."

"He's a fool."

Yusra smiled, but the ice in her gaze for the man who'd

abandoned her and her son didn't immediately thaw. "What about you?" she asked. "Who do I have to thank for AJ?"

Bashir had known this time would come. He had asked her a personal question; now it was her turn to grill him. He'd just avoid mentioning his late cousin. "I didn't know AJ's biological mother well. She passed away shortly after giving birth to him."

That was all he'd give her for now. If he thought too hard of Imran he'd buckle under the pressure and tell her about his cousin. And he wasn't prepared for that. Not yet.

First, they had this marriage to commit to. And he had the perfect way to start their journey.

Bashir palmed his trouser pocket and the square-shaped object nestled inside for safekeeping. Discreetly he pulled the item from his pocket and fisted its velvety-soft exterior. He didn't know if there was a better time to present it. They were alone. They were agreed on this marriage and they had gotten on the same page about most of the values that mattered.

Closing his fist around the small but significant box, he said, "That takes care of your job, our living situation, finances. Anything else?" He fully expected her to tell him nothing else.

So when she lowered her head in an act of unmistakable shyness, he couldn't quell his intrigue.

"There is one more thing," she said softly.

Bashir lifted his eyebrows, curiosity thickening. "Yes?" he prompted. What had they forgotten to discuss?

"It's about our living situation," she said, studiously avoiding his eyes. It took some serious dedication since he was sitting across from her and there wasn't anything of consequence in the room her lawyer had arranged their meeting in. Anything that could grip her attention more than he could.

"Yusra."

He hadn't meant to speak her name firmly and impatiently, but it had the intended result. She slowly met his eyes. Excruciatingly slow. Time could have stopped for centuries and he wouldn't have been able to tell when she enthralled him in her gaze.

"Intimacy," she squeaked.

"Intimacy," he growled.

"Are you expecting us to...um...*sleep together*?"

She meant sex.

He'd thought of it too. But physical intimacy was too chancy. Too much of an uncertain variable he couldn't risk taking. No matter how attracted he was to Yusra, and there was an attraction there—how could there not be? She was beautiful. And she would be his wife soon. Those two reasons alone were temptation enough.

"Would you like us to be physically intimate?"

"*No!*" she sputtered, right before she softened the blow to his ego with, "It would be too soon. Right? We're strangers."

"Agreed. Our marriage will be unique. I wouldn't expect for it to conform to the norm."

"But what if you change your mind? What if I do?" Her brows crumpled. "Unless there's an end date to this marriage."

"Not unless you'd like to end things. I don't intend to initiate a divorce."

"And you're perfectly fine with the possibility of no intimacy forever? Really?"

Bashir sobered and considered the gravity of what he was agreeing to do. A marriage—a tie that would bind him to her for the rest of his natural life unless she permitted otherwise—and with no promise of consummating the union. It would be a great sacrifice, knowing the pleasure sex could bring at the right time and with the right person. But he didn't know yet that this marriage would be right or that Yusra was that person for him.

But what if she is?

Bashir held back a groan as doubt assailed him. He couldn't do it. Couldn't close the door completely on their not being intimate ever.

"We can table it for discussion some other time," he said instead.

"All right," she relented quickly and with the barest hint of a warm smile. Almost as though she'd been thinking the same thing.

He hoped she had been because he'd feel less alone if she desired him too…

"Before we call the lawyers back in, there's something I have to show you." Loosening his nerveless fingers around the all-important box in his hand, he walked around to her side of the table and set the box down before her.

She goggled at it, giving a sharp intake of air when he snapped the lid open for her.

"A ring," she breathed.

Not just any ring. He'd had it customized in Greece by a reputable jeweler. A two-carat oval-cut central diamond encircled by smaller pavé diamonds and set on a white gold band. Cost hadn't been his problem. Rather he worried she might not like it and comforted himself that they'd search for a ring together if that was the case. But he wanted her to like it. Wanted to know that he hadn't messed this relationship up right from the start, as he had with his late cousin's family.

He'd lost them without realizing it. And then he had lost Imran. He wasn't raring to make the same mistake a third time.

This marriage had to work. It had to last. He couldn't lose AJ, and to have AJ, he had to have Yusra.

So it wasn't a good sign that she hesitated to accept his ring.

"If it's not to your specifications, I'll book an appointment with the jeweler for you. You can take my jet—"

"Your jet?" she asked, her face awash with surprise.

"The jeweler's located in Greece."

"Bashir, I'm not going to Greece. Not for a ring." She looked down at the ring again, the brilliance of the gem-stone gleaming in her eyes. "It is beautiful though, and it must have cost a fortune."

"Is that what's bothering you?"

She snorted indelicately. "You make that sound like it's not normal to worry about money. But no, it's not about the price."

"You don't like it," he said, trying not to take it personally.

"It's not that either."

"But there *is* a problem."

"There is, but I can guarantee it's not what you're thinking."

Bashir wouldn't know what to fix unless she told him. He studied her, searching for some hint as to how to repair the situation, but instead he was distracted by her loveliness. Again. Her hijab was a silky black that shimmered with her every movement. Her blouse and loose-fitted trousers sim-ple and airy, sensible for the curtain of dry heat cloaking the city outside.

Engrossed by her, he nearly forgot he'd been waiting on an answer.

She gave him one finally. "The ring is beautiful, maybe too much so. That and, truthfully, all of this is just happen-ing so fast—I know it has to, and I *want* to do this, but it doesn't make it easier."

"It's a big decision and a big change," he concurred.

Yusra smiled shakily, but still a smile was an improve-ment to her pleated brows and disheartened frown. She then flicked her glance from him to the sparkling diamond ring. Snagging her bottom lip with her teeth, she gave it a nibble, drawing this out, teasing him without intending to, before giving him what he desired.

"All right." Her smile more carefree, faint laugh lines emerging around the corners of her entrancing eyes. "How do we do this?"

Galvanized into action, he pulled the ring from its temporary resting place and tucked the empty box away. Taking her hand gently, Bashir showed her exactly how. The ring slid down with ease, coming to a rest on her finger perfectly, as if it knew that it had found its forever home.

Looking away from the shiny new addition on her left hand and up to her face, he thought of telling her that the ring was most exquisite when she wore it. But that confession would be too much to say to her right then when they were still getting to know each other.

So he said the simplest and truest thing. "You're right. The ring is beautiful, Yusra, but perfectly so."

CHAPTER SIX

ALL YUSRA COULD think on the day of her wedding was whether she'd been this queasy and light-headed before her first marriage. Had it been like this with her ex?

She angled her handheld fan over her face and closed her eyes with a sigh. The air-conditioning in the building couldn't cool her stress sweat, and she wouldn't allow her full face of makeup to go runny before the day had truly begun. Although the wedding wasn't for another hour, she'd woken up early to go through the motions and prepare for the big moment when she and Bashir faced the imam in the traditional Islamic ceremony of nikah.

We're really getting married.

Her stomach clenched and her heart rate picked up as reality set in.

Rather than fall prey to her anxiety though, she redirected her thinking to her mental checklist. She'd gotten through makeup, her dress was waiting in the wings and she looked down at the henna on her hands, admiring both the ornate body art and the new manicure and pedicure she'd treated herself to at the last minute. That was all. She didn't have to worry about catering, guest service or anything else. Bashir promised her it would all be handled by his people. Even Zaire and AJ were in his care. The two toddlers had tuxedo sets for the special occasion. Yusra had seen them in their adorable outfits, and she was anticipating reuniting with them soon. The wedding itself was comprised of the religious ceremony followed by a party with a small and *exclusive*, as Bashir phrased it, guest list.

All she knew was her parents and siblings would be attending virtually on a large projector screen. She didn't want to do this without her family by her side, and Bashir had recognized that and made it possible for them to be with her. Yusra could feel herself smiling at his thoughtfulness even now.

So far, it was going swimmingly with him. He hadn't given her any cause to distrust him or her decision to agree to marry him. True, they had a long way to go to familiarizing with each other, but Yusra was optimistic that they would eventually settle into their relationship comfortably and companionably.

"Are you ready for the dress?" The makeup and dress personnel that Bashir had booked on Yusra's behalf had returned from their short break to finish what they had started early this morning.

Yusra nodded bashfully at the two women.

She was as ready as she could ever be. Ready to be a mother to AJ and Zaire.

And ready to be Bashir's wife.

Bashir stole glances at her from the side, not having gotten his fill of Yusra since she'd joined him in the small but tastefully decorated reception hall. At first it was to prove to himself that she was there, and she hadn't run off as he'd imagined she might. And then once he was certain that she was committed to seeing this through, he looked astonished at his wife-to-be's transformation.

She had been dressing modestly this whole time, and even

though he had his suspicions that she'd glow up well, Bashir hadn't been sufficiently prepared to see her like this.

Yusra wore a *dirac*, a traditional ankle-length Somali dress. The outfit and its matching shawl were of a sparkling green-and-gold chiffon-and-satin silk. Her makeup was more noticeable, too, but only that her lashes were longer and darker, her cheeks rosier and her lips more tempting in that shade of rich cocoa brown. And her perfume—he inhaled as furtively as possible, drowning his lungs in the enrichingly sweet and peppery scent of her oud before stoppering it so that he could possess it. She smelled heavenly, and it was distracting him because the imam bored his eyes into him, clearly waiting for a reply to a question Bashir had missed.

"Could you repeat the question?" he grumbled with the annoyance that he'd been caught daydreaming.

The imam gave him an indulgent smile as if he knew why Bashir had been ensnared by his thoughts before asking him again to confirm the mahr or dowry.

If only he knew that this marriage was borne out of a selfish desire for him and Yusra to keep their children in their lives. And what he hadn't told her yet was that he also had the added pressure of bringing his nonprofit project to life without the media causing a field day with a scandalous baby swap. The only thing those vultures would love more would be discovering that his and Yusra's marriage was purely business. But nobody knew of this, not even Yusra's family.

From Yusra he knew that her neighbor and her lawyer were both aware of their circumstances, but he trusted her when she said that her neighbor wouldn't tell a soul, and her lawyer had an obligation to her client not to reveal sensitive information.

Like a marriage of convenience.

On his side, there were two other people who were aware

of the true nature of his relationship with Yusra. Zaire's nanny Alcina, and his reliable aide Nadim. And he respected them enough not to insult their intelligence with lies. He hadn't ever brought a woman aboard his yacht before, and even when Zaire hadn't been in his life, he'd had very few romantic entanglements. None of those had become serious enough to warrant more than a paragraph or a hastily captured photo in a gossip rag. He had always believed he'd die a bachelor. His career kept him satisfied professionally, and the care he had for Zaire—and now AJ—was enough. He hadn't been interested in exploring romance or chancing love.

And he didn't have to do either with Yusra as she didn't want either herself. On paper and in person they were a perfect match.

Bashir held that closely in mind when he signed the marriage certificate after Yusra.

Then as witnessed by her family virtually, who Bashir had the briefest chance to speak to right before the ceremony began, and their other wedding guests, he and Yusra were officially declared wedded.

She's my wife.

He'd expected that outcome. What he hadn't been ready for was the confusing delight that came with that realization.

After the *nikah* ceremony, the *walima*, or wedding banquet, moved over to an adjoining conference hall. The room was simply decorated with a backdrop of champagne-pink drapes, white-and-blush-pink roses and sprawling green ivy. Gleaming gold candelabra, charger plates and vases were their table decor. Bashir guided Yusra up the white floor runner to the head table. She had her hand secured from under his elbow with her fingers lightly gripping his forearm. If he weren't wearing a couple layers, she'd have felt him tense briefly at that first touch before relaxing into her, familiarizing himself with what this would be like from here on out.

We're actually married.

He didn't feel too different.

Except now he had more responsibility hanging over him. Because he wasn't caring for Zaire only, but for Yusra and AJ now as well. He had a whole family relying on him. As worrying as that was, Bashir took one look at his new wife's beaming expression and tabled the threat of panic lathering up in him. Once they were done celebrating with those who had come to witness their wedding, Bashir would have all the time to concern himself with how he'd have to conduct himself from that point onward.

Until death do us part.

They hadn't spoken those explicit vows, but they might as well have, as he'd already told her that he had no intention of divorcing her. Unless she asked him for it. But he wouldn't instigate it, no matter how bad it got. He hadn't arrived at this point in his life by making careless choices.

Marrying Yusra had been more than ideal.

Not that he needed a reminder, but if he did, all he had to do was peel his eyes off her beauty for a moment and look ahead of them at the head table. Waiting for them there were their sons. Alcina had managed to get the two hyperactive toddlers seated before congratulating the couple and leaving to snag her seat at the only other table set for their small wedding brunch.

Yusra fixed her smile on the children, her attention and love equally divided as they neared and the boys clamored to greet them. Bashir guided her around to her seat, pulling out her chair before grabbing the one beside her. AJ sat on her side, while Zaire sat on his. But that arrangement didn't last because his son kept looking around him, his eyes rounding with curiosity at Yusra. Without asking, Bashir hoisted Zaire onto his lap, and shifted so that Yusra could beam that sunshine-personified smile down onto her new stepson.

Zaire shyly interacted with her, his tiny hand reaching out to stroke his fingers over her cultural Somali dress. He did the same to her chandelier diamond-and-emerald earrings when she lowered her head closer to his level and he tapped at the dazzling jewelry. Her gold bangles were next, then he grew preoccupied with the red henna wreathing her hands. Finally, Zaire brushed a curious fingertip over her engagement and wedding bands.

Bashir's heart thudded faster. Not for the first—or he suspected last—time, he gazed at the rings in wonder too.

Three years ago, if asked whether he imagined himself ever marrying and having a family, he'd have guffawed with laughter. And why not? He had worked so hard to distance himself from any and all forms of love. Losing his family, and then the constant needling fear of losing the new family he'd discovered with Imran's parents and siblings and Imran himself, had left him scarred and irreversibly convinced that loving wholly and giving yourself to another would undeniably end in grief and heartache.

Some might call him lonely. Pathetic even. But at least his money was more of a likely constant. More so because he had been smart with investments, guaranteeing that he didn't put his eggs into one basket whenever he did make bold financial moves. And being in the hotel industry had assurances of its own. People always traveled and required accommodation. He had no worry about losing business.

Bashir had been happy being on his lonesome. Now he could only hope he'd be satisfied with this marriage.

"Are you happy?" he asked Yusra suddenly.

The press of her stare was heavy, contemplative. Then

she blinked and her smile was as bright and warm as it had been for their children. "Yes." She looked down at the two small faces gazing up at her adoringly, totally smitten with her, and repeated, "Yes, I'm happy, Bashir."

He knew her contentment was due to the boys rather than because of him. But he didn't think an answer could be so perfect. It reinforced his belief their union could last if they avoided overwrought emotions that could only lead to anguish and heartbreak.

Yes, it's possible, Bashir thought confidently, while watching the family that was now his.

Zaire had climbed onto Yusra's lap, and AJ curled into her side and snuggled his head against her breast. She didn't fuss that they could be messing up her beautiful clothing or complain that their added body heat chanced melting her lovely makeup. Unfazed by their crowding, she gazed down at her sons with pure love in her smiling eyes.

Satisfied once more that he'd made the right choice with this marriage, Bashir stood and graciously addressed their small group of guests. They had this one last step before he and Yusra and their two sons started their new lives together.

"Do you want me to take them off your hands?" Bashir's pleasantly resonant voice sounded from beside her.

Yusra hadn't forgotten he shared the town car with her. Lifting her head from watching over the slumbering boys cuddled on both sides of her, she regarded him, understanding that this was her new life. This man, now her husband.

He had divested himself of his black silk bow tie, the first two buttons of his pleated-front dress shirt opened, and the collar parted so that her eyes couldn't miss the darkly brown swath of skin with its teasing hint of curling chest hair. Unbidden, her fingers tingled with the instinctual ache to stretch out and test if those hairs were coarse or soft to the touch.

Two hours into this marriage and I'm already messing up.

She chided herself, but even as she resisted her attraction to him, desire pulsed through her like a second, fluttery heartbeat. And it wasn't being helped by the narrowing intensity of his eyes on her. Could he read her mortifying thoughts about wanting to stroke his chest?

"They must be heavy," he observed in that even-tempered manner of his.

No, then. He hadn't clued in to her gutter mind.

"Your arms have to be hurting by now," he said.

He was correct. She barely had feeling left in them. They still had another ten minutes or so before they reached their hotel, so she wasn't too confident she could hold on to their sons comfortably until then.

Quietly, Bashir leaned in to help displace the weight of AJ and Zaire. He didn't have to stretch far to reach her. His firmly muscled thigh was already pressed to her leg, and she couldn't avoid the rest of him entirely. Bashir wasn't a small man. And she sensed that he knew that and was even pained by the fact that the world hadn't considered a person of his build and stature. But his tall height and muscular build weren't points against him. If they were, she wouldn't be so receptive to him every time he came near her, forget the few times they'd come into direct contact. Even her dreams were hopelessly affected by him. She'd been confident that her attraction to him wouldn't be a problem in this relationship.

She wasn't so certain of that anymore.

"There. Better?" Bashir asked after he settled AJ against him and helped her rest Zaire's head onto her lap instead.

"Much better," she said gratefully and with soft laughter.

"Though I should get used to this. Raising one toddler's a handful—I'm guessing raising two will be a learning curve."

"You're not alone there."

She gave him a knowing smile, her insides feverish again the longer he gazed at her. Afraid that she'd reveal her attraction to him, and only after they had embarked on this loveless and highly convenient marriage, Yusra sought a new topic of focus.

And she found one.

"Who was that man who hugged you as we were leaving?" Considering Bashir had shown nothing but emotional reservation in the short time she'd known him, it had been shocking to witness him being embraced by one of their wedding guests. A short, rotund older gentleman who had been dressed snappily in a three-piece silver suit had approached Bashir, kissed him twice on the cheeks and bear-hugged and clapped him on the back. It had made her see her new husband in a different light.

"Otis Alexiou Doukas."

"That's not what I meant," she said, stifling a sigh.

Bashir stared back at her. "I know." She thought he even smiled, but it was hard to tell when he looked out his car window. "He was my business mentor back when I didn't have a business of my own. Otis gave me my first job. He took me under his wing and taught me the ins and outs of hotel management. And before that, he rescued me from rotting in a Greek prison when I was caught pickpocketing. I was young, not entirely bright, and angry at the world like most teenagers seem to be, yet Otis still lifted me up. Everything I have today, I owe in large part to him."

"You're fond of him," she surmised.

"He's been a big help to me, that's all. I appreciate what he's done."

"So, in other words, what you're *saying* is that you're *fond of him*." Yusra bit her lip to stop the laughter tickling her throat. Bashir gave her a brooding look, and it wasn't helping her losing battle to keep from laughing in his face. He just looked so worked up and confused and it was so dorky and adorable.

With a soft grumble, he said, "He insisted on coming to the wedding once I emailed him."

"He wanted to support you, just like my family did for me."

Bashir grumbled again. "I warned him it would be a quick ceremony and banquet. Nothing to clear his work schedule for and drop everything, family life included, to fly out from Athens."

"Bashir, just be happy he came. Clearly Otis cares about you."

She heard him mutter unintelligibly, but she smiled around his mock protest. In spite of the way he was acting, it was obvious that it had mattered to him to have his business mentor and friend present at their wedding. It was better than no one showing up to support him. Yusra had been intrigued when no family of his had been added to the guest list. So, she had done a little digging online. It hadn't taken too many search engine results to learn that Bashir lost his family. The details weren't clear in the articles she'd skimmed, only that they'd died in Somalia, and that he'd immigrated as a young teen to Greece after their deaths.

Yusra had stopped reading after that, her heart torn. She wanted to sob on his behalf, just as much as she wished to confess about snooping on him. Especially since she had a secret she hadn't shared with him. She still hadn't told him about being married before. Hiding her divorce wasn't ever a plan. It just happened. In the midst of everything else, she'd lapsed in telling him and now she didn't know how to disclose the secret she was holding. Feeling guilty again, she grew silent and pondering.

"Reconsidering the marriage already?" Bashir touched his wedding band. An austere solid white steel. Simplistic in design, but obvious in its symbolism. He was taken. Spoken for. Off the market. Smiling a rare smile, he said, "I was kidding."

"I know," she whispered.

It took a few bracing breaths to explain herself. "There's something I should have said to you earlier. I...was married before."

Oddly, he looked more uncomfortable than she did all of a sudden.

"Actually, I was already aware of that information," he said, voice noticeably gruffer. Careful not to jostle AJ, he shifted in the hot seat, and his discomfort only became more pronounced. "I hired a private investigator to look into you when I learned about the baby swap and AJ."

"What?" she hissed. She wouldn't wake up the boys, not even when Bashir floored her with his news.

Looking away from her, out of embarrassment or fear she didn't know, he divulged, "I had to know that AJ was being cared for properly."

"So you combed through my life? That's your excuse."

He grimaced and met her eyes. "I sincerely apologize. I know now it wasn't the most appropriate course of action, but it felt efficient to me at the time. And to be clear, I didn't look up your whole life. Just your finances, your business and your first marriage."

"So just most of it, great. I feel less violated. Thanks." After her sarcastic outburst, she stewed quietly to herself for a moment, and by the time she spoke again, she wasn't anywhere near as upset as she believed she'd be. And she knew why. "Since we're confessing, I looked you up too. I had to ensure you were a real billionaire."

He snorted.

Yusra grinned, but her good humor dampened when she remembered his family and his sad past. She chose not to mention his loss. She didn't think they were ready for that yet. Their relationship too new, their trust far too young.

"Guess that makes us even, but next time I think we should just ask and talk to each other whenever we want to know something," she advised with a sage nod.

"You mean like a married couple." Another precious smile from him.

Yusra rolled her eyes even as she laughed at his joke.

She didn't know what their future held precisely, but if they had more moments like this, they wouldn't do too badly.

We might even be happy together.

CHAPTER SEVEN

YUSRA HELD ON to her optimistic outlook as long as she could, but on the third morning of her marriage to Bashir, she accepted that something had to change or they'd be staring down the start of a long, depressive life together.

She would've spoken up to her new husband, but he was once again working the day away.

Which left her, AJ and Zaire stuck in their opulent suites at a well-known five-star luxury resort in Kampala. Not the worst place they could be trapped. Honestly, she wasn't even stuck in the hotel. Bashir hadn't locked her in their rooms or barred her from leaving. She could go visit her apartment. Go to work. Take the boys to enjoy some of the resort's amenities, like the pool or the butler service. Basically live life as normally as possible prior to their marriage. And she *wanted* to do all of that, but she couldn't help feeling as though Bashir hadn't yet embraced the significant change in his life.

We're married!

That had to have made him pause and think. Didn't he feel different? *She* felt changed. Since their nuptials, she'd woken up every day with a mixed bag of emotions. First the subtle realization whenever she felt the weight of her wedding rings on her finger, and then the quiet glow of satisfaction at having found a way to keep AJ and Zaire with her, which was closely trailed by the gnawing curiosity of what Bashir was up to *and* whether he was thinking of her in that moment too.

The curiosity always inspired distraction. And with distraction came frustration and the loss of concentration and patience for pretty much everything else in her life except for their sons.

"Good thing I'm on holiday from work then," she muttered to herself on that third, very early morning. While Zaire and AJ slept snugly and soundly, she'd risen for Fajr prayer, the earliest of Islamic prayers or salah. After praying, she started her day. There wasn't any point in returning to bed when she was fully awake and too alert for her own good. Even now, as she quietly padded from her bedroom to the living and kitchen areas of the hotel suite, Yusra's mind was stuck on Bashir.

So when she saw him, sitting in her usual chair at the long dining table, she did the only sensible thing. She froze every muscle. Blinked hard several times. And gawked at him openly until he noticed her.

"Good morning," he rumbled simply, his eyebrows lifting in question when she stood there unresponsive.

Had she summoned him with her thoughts?

She unrooted her feet, her fuzzy slippers silently carrying her over to him. For once he was forced to look up at her, though even then his imposing height nearly brought them to eye level. Yusra reached for him with a finger. She pushed that digit into the thick hardness of his shoulder. He didn't yield to her hard poke. When she jabbed at him again, he held aside the tablet he'd been poring over with one hand and trapped her wrist with his other big, warm hand.

"You're really here," she murmured.

He squeezed her arm, thumb flattening over the tender flesh of her inner wrist, against her jackhammering pulse.

"Where else would I be?"

"You're never here though," she retorted softly. "I've barely seen you since we arrived at the hotel."

At that accusation, Bashir released her. "It's been busier at work than usual. I hadn't anticipated it, otherwise I would have better accommodated for it prior to our marriage. But that's changed now. My schedule's clear for the next week." He stared at her for a clenching heartbeat, maybe more. She didn't know. Couldn't tell how long they gazed at each other in silence. Because though he wasn't touching her any longer, his eyes stroked over the whole of her as if he were, and wherever he looked, those parts of her body warmed. "You're not wearing your hijab."

She jerked her hand up to her head and, sure enough, no headscarf blocked her from running her hands over her veritable nest of 3C curls. Emphasis on the *nest*.

Oh, my God!

She backed away from him, flushed hot with embarrassment. Considering this was the first time he'd seen her hair, she must have made a disastrous impression.

Yusra cringed. Would it be too conspicuous of her to leave him and fix her hair?

"Your hair's shorter than I pictured," was all he said.

She touched her soft curls. "Is that bad?"

"No. It's cute."

Cute? She could live with cute. Before taking her seat and resisting the urgency to go fuss over her hair anyways, she made herself her typical breakfast. A bowl of maize porridge and two slices of toast. She noticed he'd helped himself to the coffee. But that was all.

There was a sumptuous breakfast spread of Western and Ugandan dishes before him and his attention remained glued to his tablet.

Would he notice if I walked away?

She bet he wouldn't. It stung that he could be in the same room and still ignore her. If she'd known he'd be like this she would've asked him not to stay. And she certainly wouldn't have wanted him to spend time with her.

"Did I do something wrong?" Bashir's piercing gaze commanded her.

She swallowed, her throat giving a hard pull as tension trickled through her. "No… Why?"

"Unless I was mistaken, you were glowering at me."

"I was not!"

After a brief stare down, he resumed whatever he was doing on his tablet with absolutely no fight. Not even a whimper of protest. She wasn't worth any of that apparently.

"No, you're right. I lied. I was definitely glaring at you." She lowered her toast and brushed the crumbs from her hands once she had his focus again. "I did it because I'm annoyed. I've been cooped up in this beautiful hotel for days. And I know I'm not *actually* stuck here, but it feels like it when I sit around waiting for you to get back and, I don't know, talk to me. Maybe acknowledge that I'm here? I get that this isn't a normal marriage by any measure, but we're partners in a way. Right now, it feels like I'm doing this alone, and I don't like it. If I'd known it would be like this, I might not have agreed to it."

Bashir placed his tablet facedown. "I'm sorry."

"It's fine," she said, her cheeks the hottest part of her body right then. She blushed terribly. Her only saving grace being that he couldn't see the shift in mood in her. Without her annoyance, she only felt the mortification of having been so open and up-front with him.

But it's for the best.

She couldn't have bottled it a second longer if she had tried.

"No, it's not fine. I should have explained the demands of my work schedule. It won't happen again. Next time, I'll keep you updated."

She didn't know what else to say to that but, "Thanks."

Bashir settled his hand over the tablet. "May I show you something?" After she bobbed her head shyly, he got up and walked over to her and angled the screen so she could see whatever it was he wanted her to see.

"What am I looking at?" Yusra didn't recognize the thickly lush forest or the slender strip of river.

"Hopefully where we'll be for the remainder of the week. Assuming you're not too upset to spend a holiday with me."

Understanding clicked into place. "Was that what you were looking at this whole time?" Her humiliation skyrocketed when he nodded. Here she was believing the worst and going off on him when all he'd been doing was securing a vacation for them.

She groaned and covered her face. "I can't look at you."

Bashir's chuckle rained down over her. The throaty and sinfully sexy noise tickled her curiosity and she braved a peek up at him. Her breath snagging when she saw he was far closer than he had been a moment earlier. A strong sense of déjà vu slammed into her. They'd been in similar positions before, back when she had first met him in her office, and she'd gotten vertigo from her diabetes.

She felt dizzy now too. Only this time it had nothing to do with her blood sugar level.

Her skin felt hot and itchy and far too tight to contain her bones and sloshing blood. Her ears grew dull with the steady drumming beat of her heart. And her mouth had gone unreasonably dry on her. She licked her lips and breathed shakily when Bashir's stare dropped down to her mouth almost hungrily.

She swore desire roughened his voice as he asked, "Are we good on the holiday?"

"We're peachy," she chirped with the little air she had left in her. She hadn't kissed or touched him, and it felt like she'd done both and more. It was a baffling reaction after harboring irritation for him.

Did she want him or want this marriage to work? Because instinct and her failed first marriage warned that she couldn't have both. The whole reason she believed her relationship with Bashir could survive was that they weren't in it for love. They were in this together for their sons, their family. So it was either she risked ruining it with her attraction to him, or she fought to make their marriage work for them.

She had an awful sinking sensation that only time would reveal what she would do.

Mosquito bites, a mild stomach bug and stepping into the steaming, fresh droppings of what could either have been a chimpanzee or a red-tailed monkey, according to their tour guide, had been all the things that had happened to Bashir on four out of five days of their holiday.

What hadn't happened was another romantic moment between him and Yusra.

Which he should have been thrilled about. And he was, but it also didn't stop him from mulling over witnessing her desire for him. There had been no hiding it. She'd wanted him that day he'd told her about the holiday in their hotel suite. If he hadn't refocused the moment, she might have kissed him.

Or I could have kissed her.

Bashir hadn't been immune to her, just more concerned that if they were to stroll down that path, they'd have a hard time returning from it.

So avoiding any romance on this arguably romantic holiday had been his second objective.

His prime goal had been fulfilled: Yusra and their sons were enjoying themselves immensely.

And with one full day left before they journeyed from Jinja, Uganda back to Kampala, Bashir had a good feeling that his second goal was within reach as well. Especially for what they had planned for their final day.

White water rafting in the Nile didn't inspire the excitement of romance. No one proposed on dangerous rapids, Nile or no Nile. They would be moving too fast to risk kissing without chipping a tooth or two. And they'd be too busy holding the grab ropes and gripping onto their paddles for any chance at embracing. The only thing that would make it truly perfect in his eyes was if they weren't at the mercy of choppy waters.

"Are you ready?" Yusra gushed beside him, her face aglow with unbridled exhilaration.

She actually squealed when their instructor and guide hyped them up as they pulled away from the safety of the shore.

Bashir groaned. What inner beast in her had he released? But he could do nothing but grin and bear it when she looked damn adorable wrapped up in her bubble of oblivious enthusiasm. He was doing this so she had a happy experience. Why? He had asked himself that multiple times over since they'd begun their holiday. Finally, he understood there remained a part of him that worried Yusra would wake up one morning and decide this marriage wasn't good for her anymore. And then she'd take AJ with her, and he'd be back where he started, only this time with no other recourse if their convenient relationship ended.

He wouldn't lose her. He'd worked too hard for too long and burdened himself with too many sacrifices to risk another loss in his life. Because it would be a loss in a way. And not being with her meant forfeiting AJ and that wasn't acceptable. He would even sign up for several more white water rafting excursions to avoid that displeasing possibility.

Of course Bashir wasn't racing to volunteer anytime soon.

As he'd expected, the journey down the volatile midgrade rapids was nauseating to say the least.

He hadn't held on to anything so tightly in his life, but the grab rope became more than a safety line, it grounded him as he tore through the most intense sections of the river. He paddled when the guide called for it, and he wedged his feet into the thwarts whenever their raft slammed into the tallest of the white waves or squeezed past gaps between hazardous rocks. It wasn't exactly a death trap, and yet he still envisioned scenarios where things could go wrong. They could tip over the raft and get trapped beneath it. Or slam hard into the rocks and injure themselves badly. And those were only some of the ways this could end on a horrible note.

Strangely, there were points where his tension ebbed and a surge of endorphins dulled the ache in his calves and arms from holding on to the raft's supports.

It happened first when Yusra called to him and pointed out a pair of white-breasted birds midflight. They flew past them ahead, giving him a hopeful sign that the endpoint wasn't too far off.

The second time he looked back at her, she wasn't paying him any attention. Her bottom lip was caught between her teeth and she was struggling to help steer them away from a tricky rock that even the guide had missed. She pushed hard, but it wasn't enough, and her side of the raft tipped up as it climbed the rock.

The other six guests in the raft and the guide all noticed.

Everyone scrambled to right them.

All except Bashir.

He watched Yusra's water shoes slide out of the raft's foot

cups and her hands tighten on her paddle to no avail. Her body jerked in the opposite direction of where the raft had climbed on the rocks, and she flailed an arm to right her balance.

Bashir sprang into action. He seized her arm and yanked her toward him, hard. She slammed into his chest, her forehead bumping his chin and his beard softening the impact of that blow. But she was safe. Jolted and possibly bruised, but no victim to the thrashing waters ferrying their raft farther downriver. The frenzy of the moment itself was packed into a handful of seconds, though it might as well have been hours for the burn consuming his lungs and the prickling fire scorching his muscles.

Bashir drew her onto his lap more, sitting back as comfortably as they could as the raft jostled free of the rock it had climbed and they crashed back into the river safely. And once again, they were moving along, the guests cheering around them for having overcome that challenge together. It didn't matter to him that he hadn't been of any help to them. Yusra had needed someone. And he'd been there for her. Prevented her from getting hurt…and him from having to deal with her injury or loss.

The thought of her in pain wrenched his heart.

Bashir clutched her closer since he couldn't palm his chest and ease the ache any other way.

He peeled her back from him once his heart rate steadied and she wasn't trembling. Wide eyes beheld him, her mouth parted slightly, and her chest rising and falling with her quickened breaths. He bet she had questions. And since he didn't have answers, at least any answers he felt comfortable sharing right then, Bashir welcomed any distractions.

"Is everyone all right?" The guide called, seeming to notice they weren't manning their areas of the raft.

Perfect, he thought.

Grasping their cue, Bashir released his gentle hold on her arms.

But it was Yusra who moved away first, her hands back on her paddle, and her eyes still searching his face, seeking an explanation he couldn't give her that moment.

And that he didn't know if he'd ever be able to give her.

As a reward for completing their white water rafting experience, their guide urged them to take an hour to relax in the shallower pools where they ended their expedition of the famed Nile.

Bashir was just glad it was over. He'd have remained on the shore and observed everyone else happily, but Yusra walked up the rocky riverbed and onto the sticky shoreside with an outstretched hand for him. Like the other travelers with them, she'd been swimming in the river, calling out to him to join her. She finally tired of waiting and came to fetch him.

"Come on. You can't stand there and watch the whole time."

He could, but he didn't say that to her. It wouldn't do him any good. Bashir might not have known her long, but he was quickly learning to accept her tenacity.

Compelled by the eager glint in her eyes as well, he took her smaller hand in his and marveled at the strength with which she pulled him along. Almost as if she was afraid he'd change his mind on her at the last moment and not wanting to take that chance she was instead risking ripping his arm out of its socket. She stopped tugging him along when the river waters hit her waist.

Waist-deep for her wasn't the same for him. He had more than a foot on her, so he was spared the difficulty of a wade. The warm water pooled around his upper thighs, his board shorts and black leggings soaked along with his rash vest, but that had happened long before they'd stopped as a group to soak in the calm parts of the Nile.

Like he had, Yusra had come prepared in bathing attire. She had on a long-sleeved swim top over a bodysuit and ankle-length swim leggings. Her pullover hijab had been a good choice, never having slipped off during their rocky ride downriver. And when it was all put together, she looked good.

Maybe a bit too good, he thought with a quickly drying mouth.

The modesty of her waterproof wear still conspired to undo him whenever his prying eyes tracked over her shapely curves and the generous swells of her breasts. He'd felt all of her when she had been pressed into him, shielded from the angry rapids of the river, but not protected from him. His hands flexed involuntarily at the memory of holding her enticingly soft warmth. If they'd been alone on the raft, things might have turned out differently. He could see himself crumbling to the temptation his wife embodied and stealing a kiss.

They'd been married for over a week, and they hadn't even kissed yet.

If they'd been a normal loved-up couple, he'd be worried. But his concern was unfounded. They hadn't married for love, or for kisses or any kind of intimacy for that matter. So he shouldn't be keeping score of how long he'd gone without testing his theory that her mouth was as soft and sweet as it appeared.

"I forget how tall you are sometimes," she said and, taking his wrist, pulled him along farther into the still river waters. "There. Much better." She beamed up at him once he was submerged at the waist, and with the water up to her chest now. "Let's swim together. You know how to swim, right? I can teach you. When I lived in Somalia, my home was next to Liido Beach. I used to swim there with my brothers and sister all the time."

"That's not it. I know how to swim." He stroked his beard and shifted his weight from foot to foot, the soles of his water shoes keeping him upright. "I'm not fond of water." Again, a flurry of questions brightened the dark, mesmerizing pools of her eyes. This time he had to give her something. When he'd held her on the raft and hesitated to let her go, he didn't know how to explain his actions. But this, *this* he could. It wouldn't be easy though, and it'd require trust in her. Trust not to belittle his feelings primarily.

Clearing his throat, he said, "When I immigrated to Greece, I journeyed over land…and by sea."

"You did *tahriib*." The word was spoken quietly, her tone tortured…for him?

Tahriib was the practice of bribed smugglers persuading unknowing migrants on a dangerous journey to Europe. For some, it delivered the intended result of reaching a promised land where opportunities for jobs and good money abounded, but for others, it ended in injury and at its worst even death.

He had been luckier than those who had lost their lives or found nothing but more pain in a new and strange land.

But if he stopped to think of them, he'd never get this story out fully. "During the journey itself, we stopped several times. The last leg was a long trip over the Aegean Sea from a coastal city in Turkey. It had been dark and stormy. We couldn't see anything as we were buffeted by high winds and tall waves." Bashir swallowed down the bile that rose with the memories. "Our raft's engine was torn off by the winds or waters—we didn't know, but we lost it, and we were left floating, helpless. Then the boat capsized."

Drowning had become no longer a terrifying possibility, but a reality.

"At that point in life, I couldn't swim. I'd never learned how to, and never imagined I'd require it. But once I fell in the sea, I lost consciousness quickly and blessedly. I wouldn't have wanted to remember the harrowing journey my body made from sea to land." Later, he'd been informed by a coast guard who had been on the rescue that there had been a dozen drowned souls scattered on the shore beside Bashir. He shuddered even now at the thought of being surrounded by death. Just like he'd been with his family. But he wasn't finished telling Yusra all of it. "Those of us who survived were cared for and then sent to await our fates in a refugee camp."

After that, he'd taught himself to swim the first chance he got.

"Learning to swim kept me occupied that first summer in the camp," he explained.

"Bashir, that's awful." She slid her hand in his, small, soft fingers squeezing support into him. "We don't have to swim. Let's skip rocks on the river's surface instead. Or we could take pictures of the birds if the rocks aren't a good idea." She pointed to the white-breasted birds that they'd seen earlier. The ones who'd outraced them to this tranquil location. A flock of them herded on the opposite shore. Against the backdrop of the dark green forest, the birds were like flecks of white flicked onto an opaque canvas.

Rocks. Birds. It was all the same to him though. An excuse to avoid a thing he didn't like—a thing he even feared, rightfully so. But he'd been scared to tell her what had been on his mind, and his trust in her hadn't steered him badly. Now his intuition promised that he wouldn't be wrong to trust her with this too.

"No, let's swim," Bashir said.

Her radiant smile was certainly worth braving a dip in the river.

* * *

"Were you waiting long?"

Yusra startled at the sound of Bashir's voice in the enclosed space.

She looked over her shoulder at the opening to the pop-up bubble tent. Golden fairy lights lined the tent's sturdy fiberglass frame and the transparent fabric shielding them from mosquitoes. He sealed the tent closed after him before one of the little bloodthirsty bugs snuck inside, but not before she felt the balmy kiss of summer's night air on her face and the soles of her bare feet. Having arrived earlier than he had with their sons, she'd kicked off her shoes, the floor of the tent covered by a handwoven, vividly dyed and patterned Persian rug. Before her was a low wooden table adorned with a colorful hand-sewn runner, although they could hardly see it under the crush of dinner plates. Two divans draped in the same decorative and delicate handmade tapestry as the table runner faced each other and provided more than enough room for their family of four. She shared one of those floor sofas with AJ and Zaire. Bashir grabbed the sofa opposite them.

"Sorry I'm late. I hadn't expected to be tied up for as long as I was, but construction is in progress, so I'm on alert more than I'd usually be." He had been right behind her on their way to dinner in this cozy, well-lit tent when his phone had rung and he'd taken a call from his aide Nadim. He'd sent her along with the boys with a promise to catch up. But it had been a while since then, and she hadn't wanted to eat without him, so she had asked the resort's staff to bring plate warmers for everything.

As they uncovered the plates now, and began to eat, Yusra ventured, "A new hotel?"

"No, a nonprofit organization for migrants and refugees. It's called Project Halcyone."

That warranted her washing down the tenderized and well-seasoned chicken in her luwombo dish with freshly made passion fruit juice to clear her mouth and congratulate him. Though she was confused. This was the first she was hearing about his altruistic project.

Reading her thoughts, he said, "I didn't tell you because construction started three weeks ago, and I'm still waiting for it to feel real. I've been envisioning this project for some time now. I can only hope it will help as many people who need its services as possible once it's up and running." His stare grew hard and distant, and she recognized it from earlier. When they'd been in the river and he had told her about his perilous *tahriib* and the deadly consequences for some of his other travel companions.

She hugged their sons, their warm, small bodies staving off the chill brought on by her darkening thoughts. Holding them always did the trick in righting her mood. And she'd missed them for much of the day. AJ and Zaire had spent the time apart from her and Bashir with nanny Alcina. They'd been too young to go white water rafting with them, and given how the day had gone, Yusra was relieved for their absence. By the end of it, Bashir had gotten real with her. And some of that realness had taken them to a darker, grittier point of his past.

"It seems ambitious, but it always helps if your heart is in the right place. And yours is." She sensed Bashir needed this almost as much as the people he would be helping with his generosity. Still, it didn't take the sting of surprise away at discovering he was undertaking such important work. And she wondered whether *this* was the real reason why he'd proposed marriage to her. It wouldn't be the first time she had married a man who hadn't been completely forthcoming with her. With her ex-husband, it had taken her years to discern his little barbed comments about her job and salary, her homemaking skills and even her modest outfits. Yusra hadn't been enough for him in so many ways, and instead of telling her he was discontented with her and their marriage, he'd strung her along and wasted her hope, efforts and time on him. She'd tried to save their marriage by satisfying him, and only made herself unhappy along the way. She wouldn't do it all over again with Bashir.

She'd been about to resign herself to quietly worrying when Bashir shocked her again—this time with an apology.

"I should have told you earlier. Truthfully, I was concerned about the problem with the hospital." He looked from her to their oblivious sons. AJ and Zaire were busy playing with their food, their fists caked in deep-fried bread. Yusra had showed them how to eat the *mandazi*, but to no avail. Almost as much of the fluffy crumbs ended up on their faces as on their hands. Giving up, she allowed them to explore, barely flinching when their sticky hands pressed onto her belted maxi dress and shimmery abaya.

A testament to how focused she was on Bashir. She didn't want to miss what he had to say.

"I didn't know you, and therefore I wasn't sure what kind of person you'd be. I couldn't expose the nonprofit to any scandal."

"I can't fault you for that." She masked her hurt behind a false serenity, censuring herself for being so weak. Everything he said made sense. If she, too, had a big project underway, she'd want to do anything to protect it. And to be fair, she hadn't trusted him all that much at first either.

I don't even have complete faith in him now.

She of all people understood trust was forged through incontestable actions, the louder the better. That was why she asked, "Do you view me as a threat now?"

Bashir rolled his shoulders, his large muscles flexing under his collared shirt and stylish seersucker blazer. The tension coming from him didn't inspire confidence that she'd like what was coming. "I'm not yet sure. For that I'd have to know you better. Before today, I didn't take you for the adventure-seeking type. White water rafting?" He shook his head with a pleasing tilt to those thickly rounded lips of his. "Should I be glad I didn't let you talk me into bungee jumping?"

She flung him a grin full of her relief and humor. "Then that's our problem. We still haven't gotten to know each other." And she knew one surefire way to remedy that. "When we head back to Kampala, we should go out, just the two of us."

"Are you suggesting we date?"

"No more than this holiday of ours can be construed as a honeymoon."

Bashir laughed briskly. "I can't argue with that logic."

Yusra's laughter came easily at that. This was a much better start to their marriage than those first few days she'd spent sequestered in their hotel suite, waiting, and wondering if marrying him had been an error of judgement on her part. It wouldn't have been her first mistake when it came to choosing a life partner. But now she felt less of that pressing concern for their still so new relationship. She told herself that it was for the good of Zaire and AJ for their parents to get along. This dating business was merely a sacrifice, one of countless she'd have made to safeguard their family. Meanwhile she pretended not to feel Bashir's smile and sparklingly dark eyes warming her from head to toe, and inside and out.

CHAPTER EIGHT

As far as first dates went, this was the most unusual one Bashir had been on, and for more reasons than how he'd come to find himself on the back of a motorbike, clinging to Yusra while she navigated her city's traffic like a pro.

But he was also dating his wife.

Most of what they'd done so far had been out of order. Their family existed before their marriage, thanks to the baby swap ordeal. And they had barely known each other before agreeing to marry. Why did this have to be any different?

At least the honeymoon came after the marriage.

Honeymoon? When had he begun to see their holiday the way Yusra had, as a honeymoon rather than a simple vacation?

Bashir had obviously underestimated her influence on him. It likely wasn't any help that they'd spent the last week together in close quarters. Recognizing that she was sensitive to him working late away from her and their sons and wanting her to remain happy with her decision of marrying him, he had set up a second office from their hotel suite. In a short time, Yusra's satisfaction became as vital as Project Halcyone was to him. He told himself that he needed her cooperation for their convenient relationship, and though he knew that was partly true, it wasn't the whole truth. But he was resisting exploring what that meant. It'd be a danger to court any emotion around her. Affection for Yusra was a thing he couldn't risk. Because then he would grow to care for her, and *that* he wouldn't chance for the entire world.

Squeezing his arms around her a little more, he concentrated on the sights zipping past them. He'd seen parts of Kampala already. But not like this. Not at the total mercy of Yusra when he'd chosen to climb on the bike behind her. She was in control, keeping them upright and alive, and that was something new to him. Considering he'd spent most of his life caring for himself, and in so doing using his wealth to build the kind of life and world he wanted to live in, Bashir understood that this was more than a ride for him. He trusted her with his well-being. And that was significant for him. It would be important to her too if she knew what he was thinking, but that would require him telling her, and he wasn't inclined to do that. It would create a bond between them. The kind that wasn't easily broken or given up. The sort that would develop into deeper feelings and manifest even stronger ties to her.

Would that be such a bad thing?

With a frustrated grunt, Bashir narrowed his eyes at their surroundings, blurring past sometimes, and slowing down when confronted with bumper-to-bumper traffic.

"Is something wrong?" Yusra asked with a glance over her shoulder at him.

She'd heard him. Just how loud had he grunted?

"Fine." He gritted the word out as she gave a little wiggle of her rear. She was merely adjusting in her seat, but it dealt a catastrophic reaction in him. He felt himself go hard quickly, and with every little brush of her, she melted his control.

Focus on the date. On the views.

Yes, that was what he needed to do. Appreciate what he

was experiencing. Starting with how he liked the city's live-liness.

More than the feeling of her in my arms?

No! He clenched his jaws fast and hard, biting back at that disruptive thought. But Allah help him, the fiendish vibra-tions of the bike were like oil deliberately poured over a fire and then onto him. Whenever he attempted to shuffle away from her, the bike engineered them back together. He couldn't escape the bike's teeth-chattering, full-body quake, just like he was forced to accept that he'd be pressed against Yusra until they stopped. He muffled his instinctive groan when she drove the bike a little faster and her softly rounded backside rubbed along his front. She molded there so damn perfectly that he questioned whether the universe was taunting him.

It's my fault!

Bashir had no one else to blame. He'd seen how small the motorbike was: that it would barely hold the both of them, with him taking up most of the space. He had warned her that it wouldn't be a comfortable ride, and that it might not be possible for them to do it together.

Yusra had dismissed his objection. "The bike can hold the two of us, and I'll even promise not to let you fall off," she'd said with a teasing wink. That had done it for him.

And now he was reaping the reward of his inability to see this far into the future.

That was how the remainder of his ride with her continued. With him striving to cut off all feeling to the lower half of his body, starving out his desire for her, and with her calling out different landmarks in that cheery voice of hers. There was the Uganda National Mosque, the largest masjid in not only Uganda but among those in East Africa. The palace of the Kabaka, a king, of the regal Baganda people of Uganda, along with the tombs of four previous kings in the Kasubi Royal Tombs.

She mentioned some other landmarks. None of which he remembered because he was preoccupied with slamming the brakes on his libido.

So when they finally came to a blessed stop, Bashir could have kissed the solid dry road beneath the soles of his shiny loafers.

He leaped off the bike as though the seat scalded him.

"Was that really your first time riding a *boda boda*?" Yusra unstrapped her helmet and hooked it over one of the bike's handlebars before straightening her two-piece hijab over her head.

"I avoid unnecessary danger." Where would Zaire be if Bashir were to have gotten into an accident on a motorbike? Even before his son had come into his life, he'd avoided thrill-seeking escapades, having had his fill of near-death experiences when he'd almost drowned at sea.

"Well, I just thought with you being a billionaire…"

"I'd be more reckless?"

She shrugged laughingly. "Is that terrible of me to think that way?"

"No, not terrible. More predictable than anything."

With another silvery laugh, she steered him away from the motorbike she'd rented for the day and toward the white stone building ahead of them. Its roof gleamed a deep-baked reddish brown in the afternoon sun; its expansive green grounds teemed with lounging people.

"My alma mater, Makerere University," Yusra told him when she noticed his focus shifted. "I studied arts here five years ago. Unless you know that already."

"Why would I know that?" He snapped his head down to her, puzzled before it dawned on him. "I didn't look into your educational background." It had only mattered to him that she could care for AJ, and he had felt guilty enough nosing into her life that he'd simply gleaned what he truly desired from the PI's report on her.

"Relax, I was just messing with you," she said with a smile.

He harrumphed, his face warmer all of a sudden and his chest tighter. Belatedly he understood he was blushing. Her harmless teasing had his mind reeling a bit more than it ought to have. Normally, people acted playful when they were comfortable with each other.

When they liked one another.

Did that mean she liked him?

And why did that insinuation perk up all his nerve endings?

Eager to redirect their conversation back to easier ground, he asked, "Why this school? Why Uganda for that matter? I know Somalia has a few higher education institutes."

"During university, I did a school exchange for two semesters while studying fine arts in Somalia, and I got the chance to come to this city. I fell in love with it pretty quickly after that and never left. It helped that I qualified for a full-ride scholarship to Makerere to complete my studies." A sadness marred her beautiful features. "It was also around that same time I met my ex-husband."

Bashir's interest was piqued, and a sudden passion to know her more took hold of him. Even if that meant he had to sit through hearing about the man who'd left her and AJ to fend for themselves.

They walked along the length of the campus grounds, the chatter from the students milling on the green drifting over to, but not penetrating, their heart-to-heart.

"Guled was different back then. He was kind instead of cruel. After, the love he'd once shown me changed into contempt and resentment. By the end of our relationship, I didn't recognize him as the man I'd fallen in love with. We met here at the university. He used to work as an administrative aide at the student counseling office, and he had been assigned my case when I was in the process of transferring to study in Kampala."

"He's Somali too?" Bashir still found it odd that of all the women who had to be tied to him through an accidental baby swap, that it was Yusra, and that she was Somali like him. And when she nodded, he murmured, "Small world." Because it really was a freakish case of fate.

"We clicked instantly, so when he asked to show me around the school and city, it was an easy choice. We dated for two years, and a month after I'd graduated, we got married and moved in together."

"So two loves kept you here. Your art, and him."

Yusra stopped him with a hand. "I'm not in love with him anymore, Bashir." Her fingers squeezed his arm lightly, impressing upon him that she had no lingering feelings for the man who'd come before him.

Deep down it shouldn't have made a difference to Bashir whether she still held a torch for her ex-husband or not. Because it wasn't like anything could happen between him and Yusra. They'd been open about that much. She wasn't seeking love from him, and he had thought that part was the sweetest end of their deal. He had enough on his plate. Zaire and AJ. His nonprofit. And how to live with a wife he shouldn't desire nor love.

That was plenty for him to handle without adding more.

And yet Bashir still gazed down at Yusra and, before her darkly long lashes, sunlit brown eyes and glossy lips bowled him over, said, "He really was a tremendous fool."

Though was he any less foolish for allowing his heart to thump faster when she beamed an approving smile up at him?

Showing Bashir her university should have been the highlight of the day. This place was where her life in Uganda had started, and in a way, it had brought her AJ. Well, Zaire technically, because that was who Guled and she had conceived. Though without Zaire, she wouldn't have been at the hospital giving birth to him, where AJ had been at the exact same time, and the baby swap wouldn't have eventually thrown her on a path to meeting the man who'd become her second husband.

But the truth was she had too many highlights from that day she planned to label as happy memories and squirrel away in her mind. From the ride through the city on a *boda boda*, to stalking her old campus grounds with him, and now strolling the city streets like a normal couple. They were even holding hands!

But that's only because it's crowded.

That was partly correct. She hadn't wanted to lose him. But just as strongly, she wanted to touch him again. And she hadn't been above using any excuse to do it.

Innocently unaware of her true motive, Bashir had accepted her hand and didn't speak up when she had interlocked their fingers, their palms connected, and she couldn't be happier in the moment. They were getting along. And he was being nice and thoughtful and everything she had once dreaded he wouldn't be. Sure, she hadn't felt as certain about them when he had been bounding off to work and ignoring her, but he'd changed since their holiday-cum-honeymoon. Relocating his office from his yacht to their hotel suite, carving out healthy time in his schedule to spend it with her and their sons.

They were two weeks into their marriage now and the forecast was looking rosier with each new day. Not that it made an impact on her decision to refrain from romanticizing their relationship. With her first marriage, she'd actually been in love, and it hadn't ended well for her. So taking that logic, this second marriage had more of a chance to succeed in the absence of love.

And maybe that was why it was working so well between them.

She knew he hadn't been interested in romance either. It should have been a solace to her to know she wouldn't be forced to be intimate with him. Bashir was perfect for her in that way.

So, why am I sad?

It didn't take her long to land on a plausible theory. By choosing this marriage, she had given up on love, and that was why melancholy visited her suddenly. She was sad because she was shutting the door to ever falling in love again. Not just temporarily, but for forever.

And as long as she remained married to Bashir it would stay that way.

She didn't know what unsettled her more, that she had no hope of loving and being loved again, or that her gut twisted painfully in response to her picturing leaving Bashir. If it hurt her to think of that scenario, what did it mean?

Rescuing Yusra from spiraling deeper into her thoughts, Bashir gave her hand a squeeze and a tug before he pulled her to a gentle halt.

"Where's that?" He squinted at the distance, his lips pressing together firm and grave.

Yusra followed his line of sight to the Katanga slum. She must have grimaced loudly because he regarded her sharply.

It wasn't the first place she'd have shown him. Even for

those who were braced for the poorest parts of the slum neighborhood, the poverty could be a hard experience to cope with. Even Bashir with his past as a refugee and the horrors of his *tahriib* might find it a difficult place to visit. And the last thing she wished to do was remind him of what he'd gone through.

Stretching for a mile, and bordered by the university and a sprawling hospital campus, the Katanga slum was a mixture of student hostels and impermanent mud-and-timber dwellings. A sea of rusted tin roofs covered narrow access roads and the poor drainage systems to those living in the area. There were already thousands of homes packed into the small parcel of land, and with many more people seeking shelter all the time, driven there by everything from poor choices in life to an inflated economy and unfeeling landowners and property developers.

"Katanga slum. It's a well-known settlement in the city."

"Is the government not doing anything to help them?"

"They try, but there are landowners involved. Figuring out who owns what part, and what they're owed is difficult to tell. At least that's what I understand." Yusra thought it so sad. She hadn't come from a rich background either, but she'd had what she had needed growing up. Even now, her parents and siblings tried to help in whatever way they could, with money, or small gifts. She could rely on them if she ever had the need to leave the home she'd built in Kampala, and she always remembered she was fortunate for that alone. Not everyone had someone in their corner.

Looking at Bashir, she recalled he'd lost his entire family.

She looked from him to the slum that she knew had to pain him to see. It wasn't what she wanted him to remember of this date, and not when everything had been going well.

"I thought we could visit the market next," she wheedled in the softest voice she could.

His hand tensed in hers. "It looks like the camp I lived in for four summers. Chaotic, crushed with people and tents and with no definitive lines as to what belonged to you. Stealing happened frequently. Food and drink and bedclothes were all fair game if you looked away and didn't protect what was yours. The security guarding the camp never did anything to help. And the weather? Unbearably scorching during the days. I can't tell you how many sunburns I'd accidentally peeled, tossing and turning in my sleep. The nights were the opposite. Cold even in the summer sometimes. Cold enough for my chattering teeth to keep me awake."

Yusra listened to it all, her stomach bunched in knots for him, a sickness swelling in her for what he'd gone through, and when he'd been so young. The article she had read claimed he'd been only fourteen. *Fourteen!* She couldn't imagine what terrors an adult must deal with seeing the things Bashir had, but he had been a child. He hadn't deserved any of it.

She should have remembered this path would take them by the slum. She'd been so excited about taking him on a tour of her home, like he had his yacht, that she hadn't thought out their every step beforehand. And now he was glum, and any joy they'd had disappeared.

At least she now understood why he was trying to build his nonprofit. Since he had the ability and wealth to do it, Bashir would help the people who were going through what he had suffered. Rather than allowing the cycle of tragedy to continue, he was putting a stop to it.

"The worst part was the helplessness. I didn't think I'd ever escape."

"But you did," she said, her throat raw with the tears she

forced back. She wanted to pull him away from there, but she knew that would do no good. His memories would go wherever he went, and she couldn't change that, but he was wrong; she could add a bit of hope to a bleak reality. Gently, she led him from where they stood, their link solidified by their hands.

When they stopped again it was down a narrow road with long timber-and-brick buildings flanking either side of them.

Before he asked, she said, "It's the market in Katanga." She hadn't turned her back and run from the slum but took him to the pulsating heart of it. "The people here aren't as helpless as you might think. Those who can, do. And so then we can do our part."

Yusra sniffed the air, a smile splitting her face when she recognized the tantalizing aroma. She left Bashir and approached the old man who owned the food stall. When she circled back to him, she handed him one of the two grease-stained newsprint wraps in her hands and was several shillings short, but it was worth what was coming.

"Careful, it's hot," she warned while peeling back the newsprint from her sandwich wrap.

"What is it?"

"A *rolex*." She laughed at the wrinkle in his brow. "It's not the fancy watch you're wearing, but a popular breakfast wrap. It's basically an omelet and vegetables wrapped in chapati bread. Don't worry—you'll like it just as much, if not more."

He took his first bite, blowing to cool the freshly made sandwich before he did.

Bashir's appreciative groan told her everything and restored her confidence that she'd done right in bringing him to Katanga, and that as first dates went, this one wasn't a spectacular failure in the end.

That was the best feeling of all.

* * *

They were holding hands again.

Bashir noticed it had happened after they finished eating their rolex wraps, the delicious midday meal perking him up, but Yusra was bringing his buzz to dangerous limits when she grabbed his hand and interlaced their fingers together once more. This time he didn't think it was because she believed they'd lose each other.

The Katanga settlement was a maze of tight corridors, with people squeezing up against each other in the narrowest of spaces, but it wasn't overly cramped. They had plenty of room between them. And he was far too tall and too broad to blend in anywhere. She could've spotted him several feet away, so he wouldn't fall for the excuse she had used earlier.

Given Bashir had been on pins and needles around Yusra since the start of their date, it wasn't the most intelligent idea for him to entertain the allure of her. He was treading dangerous waters...

Yet here he was, touching her and liking it all too mightily.

It might have helped if the date was bad. But not only had their day gone incredibly well, even the one moment that could have blemished it all was turned around because of her quick thinking. She'd lured him into different stores, giving him reasons to spend money and help out the store owners who were also slum residents. It did his soul good, and Bashir got the feeling that Yusra had known that, and it was why she'd brought him to Katanga after all he'd told her about his life in a refugee camp in Crete.

When they finally emerged from the neighborhood, they immediately backtracked to where they'd left their motorbike. On a high from how nicely their day had passed, Bashir wasn't as averse to riding the blasted vehicle. He didn't even mind the stares he was getting as they whizzed by on the freeway. A large man like him on the back of a bike rather than in the driver's seat. But he acknowledged Yusra was the far better driver. She'd get them home safely to their sons. He hadn't thought he'd miss Zaire and AJ for a few hours, but he did and more greatly than he expected.

Thinking along the same line, Yusra said over her shoulder, "I'd like to go by the market before we head to the hotel. I wanted to grab some things for the fridge, and the boys are running low on healthy snacks." She'd gotten tired of the hotel food and taken over the kitchen in their suite.

This market had a similar vibe to the one in Katanga except for the colorful tented stalls. Yusra called it Owino Market. She shopped for produce, stocking up on everything she needed, and he carried her shopping bags instinctively. More than simple instinct though, it felt natural to do those things for her.

"Let's stop here. AJ likes the oranges from this stall. I hope Zaire does as well." She touched his arm to grab hold of his attention.

Bashir tried not to lean into the sparking imprint her hand had left behind. But like all the other times they came into contact, he was weakened by a blow of lust for her. He was one big throbbing nerve ending. Vulnerable to every little sensory provocation from her.

Like when she turned to him with an orange closely hovering beneath her nose. She sniffed and sighed with a dreamy smile, her eyes fluttering shut. "Mmm! I love the smell of oranges. If I could bathe in their juices, I would."

He wished he didn't have that image in mind, specifically as the vendor of the stall sliced an orange into fours and handed a quarter to Yusra before holding another quarter out to Bashir. The older woman mimed an eating gesture while she did it, smiling broadly and speaking in Swahili to Yusra, no doubt knowing she could translate.

"It's rude to refuse. She'd take it as an offense, and I like the fruit she sells, so you have to taste some. Spare me the embarrassment the next time I come to visit and buy from her," she said in Somali, magnifying the intimacy of the moment. Enhancing it hundredfold when she accepted the quartered orange on his behalf and tiptoed to get it as close to his mouth as she could. She almost reached him too…

But she'll need a hand.

Body on autopilot, and his common sense on pause, Bashir kept his eyes steady and unblinking on her when he gently curled his fingers around her wrist and drew down to meet her. The orange angled just right for his mouth to close over it; he started with a teasing lash of his tongue. Tangy citrus juice shot straight along his tongue to the back of his throat. Nowhere enough of what he wanted though, he dived back in, eagerness egging him on. He wrapped his mouth around the orange itself, her fingers just touching his lips, but held frozen to do his bidding while he helped her feed him. Then he bit down, his gaze blacking out everything *and* everyone but her. Only Yusra existed in that time and space plane. They could be anywhere, and he wouldn't know it with her large, heated eyes locked on him.

She held on to that orange just as tightly as he had a hold of her.

And he wouldn't have stopped them if it weren't for Yusra moving away suddenly.

She blinked, and her eyes widened for a whole new reason. Before she turned her head, he read the embarrassment streaking over her pretty face. And it was that shyness that had her ignoring him while she pointed out the oranges she wanted bagged before she paid the vendor for the service.

Then with no other choice but to engage him, she looked up but right through him and said, "We should get back to the boys. Alcina, as great and experienced as she is, could use a break."

Bashir sucked the orange clean, its outer husk all that remained, and dumped it in a nearby bin. Leisurely licking his lips, and watching her eyes follow the movement before she hurriedly evaded his stare, he nodded. It was more information he slotted away.

Another thing he'd learned about her.

Yusra desired him, and it equaled the attraction he felt for her. But one look and he knew that she wouldn't act on her emotions, not like he had.

Because she's stronger than me.

Shame seeped into him and churned sour the sweet orange she'd given him. It wasn't the note he wanted their first date to end on, but it was the last thing he remembered at the end of the day.

CHAPTER NINE

BASHIR HAD HIT a wall in his marriage with Yusra.

He'd anticipated it would happen eventually.

Just not as soon as it had.

And now that it had occurred, he had no idea what to do or how to overcome it. Because if they didn't, their relationship could be jeopardized.

And what did he do instead? Pretend like nothing was wrong.

Like he wasn't constantly replaying the last time he'd been alone with Yusra over and over in his mind, pausing only when his head pulsed painfully from the strain of remembering each minute detail from their date.

Their one and only date.

Bashir had thought their outing had been going well, and he'd even hoped they would get to do it again and more frequently. But that was before he totally blew that chance out of the water. A muscle twitched near his eye at the memory. His jaws firming together, and a headache thundering closer.

Just thinking of where it had gone wrong for him was enough for him to relive the shamefully awkward moment at the end of their date. Even now he questioned his uncharacteristic actions. Why had he grabbed her when she'd offered him a sun-ripened slice of orange? The feel of her warmth beneath his fingers, of her pulse at her inner wrist under his thumb and his sharp recall of her hitched breath, widened eyes and quivering lips was eternally branded in him.

He didn't think he'd look at an orange the same way ever again.

He had been a man possessed. Obsessed with the need to touch her. Throughout their date the temptation intensified, and naturally he had reached a breaking point.

That's not an excuse.

Self-loathing laced the thought, bitter and hateful.

He shouldn't have done anything to make her uncomfortable. Now he had irrevocably ruined the harmony they'd found in their convenient relationship. And with every day that passed, Bashir felt more certain Yusra wouldn't be able to get over what he'd done to her.

Apologizing had been his first goal. But getting the words out of his mouth was far more of a challenge than he anticipated it would be. Where did he begin? What did he say to her that wouldn't cause her any more discomfort? Bashir had spent so much time mulling over these questions and more that a whole two weeks had passed since the incident. Which only amplified the charged silence between them and heaped on the hopelessness he'd begun to feel about their sensitive predicament.

Still, none of that fully severed this irresistible pull he had to her.

To prove his point, his world screeched to a halt when Yusra stepped into his field of vision.

She exited the masjid, her teal-blue abaya instantly noticeable, her shoes in hand until her bare feet crossed the threshold. Having cleared the mosque, she slipped back into her pyramid-studded sandals. She crouched down before Zaire and AJ, helping them with their shoes. The boys had chosen to go along with her to the women's section of the mosque rather than join him where the men were praying. He hadn't been hurt by their decision. Her strengthening bond with their sons made him all the more certain that Yusra was perfect for their children, which in turn underlined just how terribly he'd bungled things with her.

And how important it is for me to fix it.

Shielding her eyes, she searched for him among the crowded outdoors, spotting him quickly when he stepped out from behind a large family who had umbrellas to shade them from the blazing afternoon sun. Searing rays of light beat over their heads but gave them a pleasing cloudless blue sky to look up at.

In that clement weather, Yusra approached him with their sons. Once they saw him and were close enough within reach, she let AJ and Zaire go, and the toddlers launched themselves at his legs. He hauled them up easily into the air one after another, their peals of laughter no doubt heard throughout the grounds of the mosque. Bashir basked in the happy music of their joy. He hadn't known it could be like this. With Zaire alone he'd felt like the luckiest father—but now that he had AJ too, he wasn't only lucky, he was blessed.

Swinging them up above his head and having their gleeful chortles rain down over him was the height of happiness for him.

He could name only one other thing that was missing.

More like *who* was missing.

Breathless from playing with their sons, Bashir caught Yusra appraising him with a patient smile. She was gorgeous with sunshine showering her, her brown skin glittering and her cheeks rosy from the heat baking off the ground. The urge to embrace her clanged through him loudly.

Of course his second thought wasn't anywhere near as harmless as longing to hug her. His gaze roamed her figure.

Her abaya couldn't conceal her curves from him, not when he'd felt the swell of her breasts and hips against him before. He looked to her mouth, his own lips sparking in answer...

No, damn it!

Bashir jerked his head away from her. What was wrong with him?

Angry at himself, he would have stormed off and gotten distance from her, but this wasn't the time or place to do it.

They were in the courtyard or *sahn* of the Uganda National Mosque on a Friday afternoon. Not shockingly, the masjid buzzed with energy. People were filtering out of midday prayer, Jummah, on the holiest of days for Muslims, and so, much like a church-on-Sunday mass, the congregation had a larger turnout than on any other day of the week.

When Yusra had asked him to join her and the children for the afternoon service, Bashir couldn't refuse. It had been a long while since he'd prayed with family.

Nostalgia, sweet and bitter, came to him in waves. Emotions he had long buried and even forgotten, and not all entirely sad, ebbed and flowed like the ocean tides. His mother's long robes in one hand, his father's rough palm gripping his other and the cheerful chatter of his brothers and sisters and grandparents as they walked out of a Jummah prayer together.

Bashir slowly but surely saw the faces of his long-lost family members more clearly than he had before today, and he owed it to Yusra. Without her he wouldn't have considered bringing Zaire to this sacred place. And it was one more reason why he shouldn't act mindlessly around her.

Pushing her away was a risk he couldn't take.

She was good for the children. Good with him. Somehow, some way, he had to heal what he'd broken.

And soon.

Even if it meant they had to revisit the topic of intimacy in their marriage. After all, it was either that or...

I create more distance between us.

Bashir didn't know which was the right choice, only that he'd had enough distance from her already, and he was tired of it.

Talking Bashir into climbing the minaret's three-hundred-plus steps to the top wasn't as hard-won a battle as Yusra imagined it would be. He had simply nodded, assenting when she pointed up to the masjid's abutting tower and asked, "Could we stop to take a look at the view from there?" No argument or questions asked.

And she wouldn't have minded his automatic compliance, if he weren't acting like a zombie again.

It had started right after their first—and last—date.

Yusra flushed hot all over just thinking about it. She'd have sworn Bashir branded her wrist from when he'd grasped her and used her to feed himself the orange slice she had offered him. He'd certainly left a searing imprint of the moment in her mind for possibly the rest of her life.

And she still didn't know whether that was a bad thing or not.

She rubbed her wrist, catching herself in the midst of the absentminded action. Blushing anew, she refocused her sights on the unbeatable views of her adopted city, and hoped by the time she peeked Bashir's way he was no longer staring at her broodingly.

"Isn't it breathtaking?" she exclaimed. "They call it a sky-scraper mosque."

Bashir carried Zaire, while she had AJ in her arms. They walked the whole balcony, the three-sixty vista as shockingly high as she remembered, before she stopped and regarded him with what she hoped was less embarrassment written across her face.

"You know it's our one-month anniversary tomorrow."

"I didn't," he said in an unusually gruff tone, his eyes darting away from her down the steep drop to the masjid's courtyard below. The people looked like dots from up here. Not that she was paying anything else any mind, not with the way Bashir was acting.

Did he not care about that milestone?

Their relationship might not have been brought about by love, but it was still a marriage. And she could still celebrate having lasted together for a whole month.

"I thought we could do something to commemorate it tonight. Dinner maybe?"

"Maybe," he said, again his tone decidedly blasé. Like none of it mattered to him.

Like I don't matter.

She couldn't stop feeling the way she did. Though she didn't have a right to it. She was his wife, yes, but theirs was a convenient partnership. They equally benefited from having married each other.

But I still care.

She stiffened her lightly trembling lower lip and popped up her chin, fighting back the frustration that burned through her and rivaled the sun's heat. It wouldn't do her any good to allow Bashir to get under her skin. To permit him to be any closer to her. This was as far as they should go, as a couple on paper but never in practice.

"Before we go to your ship, I'll need to stop by the office." As per their agreement, and just as they'd done every week for the last month, they were moving to his colossal yacht for the weekend. "There's a couple things I have to grab for work."

Bashir jerked his head in the briefest of nods.

Skin flushed now and sweat misting her brow, she glared at him. Surely the heat of a thousand suns couldn't feel hotter, yet he remained annoyingly cool in the face of her glower, and even looked away from her with a stubborn wrinkle to his brow.

What was wrong with him? Was he just being deliberately cruel, or was it something she'd said or done to offend him?

She couldn't even laugh when Zaire reached a tiny hand out to Bashir's long, curly beard and brushed at his father hesitantly.

Her first clue that something was wrong was the sudden weakness in her limbs. She'd believed it had been fatigue from climbing the stairs and hauling AJ up as well, but her muscles quaked and her heartbeat sounded in her ears. Her stomach clenched incessantly, reminding her she'd skipped breakfast.

"What's the matter?" Bashir demanded.

So, he'd noticed something was wrong with her.

His turn in mood might have left her with whiplash if she weren't busy trying to fight to control the world from swimming out of focus. Yusra closed her eyes and leaned against him when his arm circled around her, lending her the support she hadn't asked for but needed in that moment.

"Juice box," she said weakly, opening her eyes and patting her purse.

Bashir swept AJ out of her arms, which gave her a chance to search her purse for the sugar boost. It took two boxes, and some time recuperating against the wall of the tower, to regain her senses.

The first thing she could see was Bashir's barely restrained irritation.

"Did you not have anything to eat this morning?" he asked sharply.

She smiled nervously, fatigued from the low blood sugar. "I didn't have as much time for breakfast before we left the hotel."

All she'd had was a granola bar and a banana after she had taken her insulin. She blamed sleeping in, which wouldn't have happened if she hadn't stayed up late to work after she'd tried and failed to go to sleep. And Bashir was partly culpable for that. Yusra had kept herself awake thinking about why he was being so strange around her.

Was it really only because of the incident with the orange? *Or is this who he really is? Distant. Detached. Unreachable.*

Everything she didn't want in a life partner again.

Swiping her tongue over dry lips, she said, "It's fine. *I'll* be fine."

"Still. You should have told me."

She didn't see how that would make a difference.

And why is this more important than our marriage?

Her face must have communicated that petulant thought if Bashir's downturned mouth was any indication.

"We'll stop by your office *after* we grab something to eat." His tone brooked no room for negotiation.

She wouldn't have argued anyway. Her traitorous stomach chose that moment to grumble loudly, revealing she didn't mind his suggestion at all.

Seeing no resistance from her, he asked, "Can you walk back down the stairs?"

Was that concern she heard in his voice? *For me?*

Feeling silly about getting happy over something as benign as Bashir checking in on her, Yusra said, "I think I can handle it."

"If you can't, you'll tell me."

That was definitely concern she heard. *Interesting.* For

someone who'd walked around for two weeks like she hadn't existed, barely acknowledging her unless there seemed no other way around it, he appeared to have suddenly reverted back to who he'd been on their holiday-slash-honeymoon and, more recently, their date.

Though it didn't explain why Bashir had been like a completely different person with her lately. Of course she could ask him directly. But for that Yusra would require a full stomach and all her wits about her.

CHAPTER TEN

"WE SHOULD TALK."

Yusra's mouth popped open when Bashir uttered the exact same words as her at the exact same time and with the exact same urgent inflection.

If she needed a sign that the universe was thrusting them in this direction, she had it.

"Not here. Follow me," he ordered once his shocked expression wore off.

"Okay," she said squeakily.

Bashir's tall, hulking figure stalked ahead of her through his yacht. She hurried to keep up with his long strides, not wanting to fall behind. Getting lost on his large mazelike ship was a strong probability for her. An embarrassing admission as she'd now stayed a few weekends with him and should have known one end of the yacht from the other.

Her legs ached and cramped slightly when they finally stopped.

Yusra marveled at the salon he'd brought her to. Her eyes immediately landing on the room's central feature.

"Is that the *ocean*?"

"It is," Bashir replied.

She gawked at the glass wall, her feet in their slippers itching to go closer to the bruised black-and-blue waters shimmering under an array of dimmed LED lights attached to the ship's outer hull. Yusra wouldn't have expected to see anything like it on Bashir's yacht. Not when she knew that he didn't have the warmest relationship with large bodies of water. And yet he'd managed to surprise her, and that in and of itself wasn't a shock.

Her husband had proven he was a man of many layers.

Almost as greatly as she wished to touch her hand to that glass wall and *feel* like she was grasping the whole of the ocean in her palm, she wanted to peel back Bashir's layers to find the heart of him.

And then maybe I'll feel like I truly know him. Truly trust him.

As it was, she was still hesitant around him, especially given how he'd been acting, and so she calmed herself by glancing around the lounge area he had shown her. Painted and furnished in muted tones of beige and gray, and with its darkly varnished hardwood flooring, the salon oozed untouchable wealth. Skylights brightened her path to where Bashir stood and watched her from the middle of the room, his arms stiffly hanging at his sides, his hands clenched into fists and his shoulders subtly raised higher.

Great.

His defensive stance wasn't easing her mind. Like a bottle of fizzy soda shaken up, her belly roiled with her bubbling anxiety. Maybe she'd have been better off not indulging in the princely dinner that Bashir had asked his chefs to prepare specially for their one-month wedding anniversary. As lip-smacking good as the meal had been, the food wasn't digesting nearly as well as it had tasted.

But she couldn't run away from this anymore. She had to talk to Bashir tonight and right then. And it felt fated now that she knew he'd been thinking the same as her.

I just have to speak my truth. Easy.

That encouraging thought in mind, Yusra placed her hands over her upset stomach, willed courage to her, and walked as close to him as she could without running into his big strong chest.

Staring down at her without flinching was impossible.

Bashir ground his teeth against the rise of cowardice. None of what he'd done as of late felt like him. His actions, like his words, were an antithesis to what he *actually* wished to do.

I want to hold her. Kiss her. Give her pleasure like she'll never know with any other man.

"Bashir? Did you want to speak first, or should I?"

He nodded briskly. As gracious as she might think the gesture, the truth was he couldn't get a word out right then, not with his teeth locked together as crushingly as they were. If this kept up, he'd need a crowbar to pry his steely jaws apart.

"I'll come out and say it then. You've been acting really weird, and I can't help thinking it's because of me."

Her knitted eyebrows, large, sad eyes and downturned mouth could have doubled as a dagger plunging into his heart. His fists balled so tightly that the tendons of his wrists sent flaring pain signals to his brain, all of which went ignored. All that his mind turned over was the discovery that he'd hurt her.

I didn't mean to...

Bashir hadn't even considered that she'd have flagged the change in him. But now it was so clear to him that she would. It hadn't been the first time Yusra had intuited his mood before. She'd done it in the waters of the Nile where they had swum together, and he had ended up sharing the story of his treacherous *tahriib* by sea.

And she had done it again now.

"Are you angry with me?"

"No." He spoke with more force than he intended, and he withered inside when Yusra startled back from him.

Bashir's hands moved on their own. Grasped her wrists and pulled her in as he stepped closer to catch her against him. She came willingly, no fight registering in her, even as she gawped up at him. Only this time none of the fear he'd seen spark through her eyes was present. Shocked confusion snuffed it all out. *Good.* This was far better of a sight. And what a sight she made in his arms, her softer, smaller figure flush against his taller, harder-cut body. He didn't know how it had come to this. All he'd been thinking was that he hated this distance that had come between them. And his body acted on his deeply seated emotion.

Bashir waited on the regret for touching her like this again to barge its way through and bring him to his knees. Counted the seconds until she was ripped from him by his own cowardly thoughts and feelings.

One. Two.

He didn't get to three because he heard himself rasp, "I'm far from upset with you."

Then as though he wasn't a split second away from beating his chest and proclaiming her as his woman, he pushed air out through his nose, channeled civility and continued.

"I'm angry with myself, and I'd understand if you were too. Back in the market, on our date, I shouldn't have touched you the way I did. The way I am now." He regarded where her hands were splayed on his chest, caged there by him. "It's why I propose we reopen discussion on the parameters of physical intimacy within our relationship."

"O-okay," she stammered up at him.

"I was aware before we married that you showed lack of interest in being intimate, and since marriage we haven't shared a bed. Can I safely presume then that you're still not interested?"

"I'm not ready to share a bed, no," she spoke quietly, her eyes zipping over his face.

He struggled to control the disappointment surging in him. But her decision had to be unaffected by how he felt. He wouldn't have her any other way. If Yusra wasn't interested, then he could learn to grow uninterested too. And it was why when she asked, "Do you feel differently?" Bashir said no, even though he did and to such an extent he no longer recognized himself.

He then gazed at her with the heated depth and breadth of yearning he'd sealed away over the past couple weeks.

One last time, he vowed silently, committing every detail of them together like this to last him through their marriage. *Forever.*

Before Bashir broke his contact with her and began what would surely be a tediously long path to celibacy, he caught Yusra's lips tilting up into a smile. Her laughter came precious seconds later.

Bewilderment shot through Bashir's face, his brows storming down over his narrowed eyes, his soft, full mouth pinched at the corners, lips pressed firmly together.

Yusra could understand why he was confused.

To him it had to have looked like she was laughing at him—she wasn't—but she could see how he might think that.

"I'm sorry!" she gasped at the end of the giggling fit. "It's just that *I* thought you were upset with me when *you* were thinking the same about me." Widening her eyes, she hastily said, "I swear I'm not laughing at you."

He gave a snort and a small chuckle.

She giggled again. "It's funny, isn't it? And all we had to

do to save us all this time and grief was talk to each other like we just did."

Bashir's brooding confusion thawed quickly after that. His gusty laughter rolled up into hers, their mirth making the most beautiful of symphonies. Yusra had a feeling she'd be a wealthy woman herself if she uncovered how to bottle and sell their happy sounds.

At the end of it, she pushed her hands against him, her laughter gone but her awareness of him stronger. There was the quiet power of his long thick fingers on her wrists, the hard unyielding heat of his body, and the reverent caress of his eyes on her.

"About the market that day, with the orange, I never told you how I felt."

At her words, the storm cloud that darkened his face returned. Full of crackling thunder and gloomy rain, it drowned their happiness.

As sad as her heart was, she held her ground, knowing they needed to leap over this hurdle before they could get back to where they had just been. She was doing this because she wished for the laughter and easy conversation with him again. There was still so much she didn't know about him, and they weren't going to get over this but *through* this, together.

"There's a reason I haven't said anything." She wet her lips, her heart in her throat and drumming wildly at her ears simultaneously. "Truthfully, I liked it. And knowing what we said about physical intimacy, I didn't want to upset the new balance we've found after the honeymoon…er…holiday."

"Honeymoon," he corrected roughly, his dark brown eyes brighter, his thumb gently massaging the inside of her wrist. His touch provoked a shiver up and out from her core and a wash of goose bumps over her skin.

She fought to clear her mind and continue what she had

to tell him. "After our *honeymoon*, I wanted everything to be as perfect as it was. I wouldn't have let an orange ruin it."

Stroking her, he said in a rough voice, "It was a damn good orange though. If anything would have ruined it, it might have been that."

"I told you that fruit stand sold the best oranges…" She trailed into a sigh when he freed one of her hands and gripped her hip instead. If only she wasn't thwarted by all the clothing she wore. A thermal long-sleeved shirt, drawstring joggers and a fleece robe kept her toasty when she had been wandering the yacht's chilly passageways in search of Bashir before he'd found her instead. Now her clothes were obstructing her. She quivered at the thought of having his lightly calloused fingers and big warm palm on her naked flesh.

Another shiver rocked through her when Bashir slowly lifted her hand to his mouth, her fingers treated to a delicate kiss from him. One by one, his mouth alighted on each of her digits. With her free hand she dragged her nails over him to form a fist.

A switch flipped in her mind and the last of her fight evaporated. Even her fear in placing complete faith in him faded and, for once, gave her peace of mind in its absence. And it was a peace she deserved because Bashir had yet to give her a plausible cause to distrust him. It was how she knew she wasn't going to pull away from him. *Not this time.*

"Stop me," he gruffly commanded.

"I won't." Yusra defied him. Nothing and no one would rob her of what she knew was coming.

Bashir's narrowed eyes roved her face, and like the kiss he slowly, methodically pressed to the center of her palm, she felt it all over her body. Her breasts were heavy from her need of him, her thighs crushing over the source of relentless, driving heat between her legs.

"If you don't stop this now..."

His warning trailed off sharply, his breath hitching when she sprung up on her toes and kissed him. Well, kissed his beard, because she couldn't climb higher on her own.

Bashir freed a mixture of a grunt and moan. "Yusra." He dragged her name out, his shoulders bunching and flexing, his hands tightening over the parts of her he touched and his eyes locked on her mouth. "Do you want me to kiss you?"

Yes!

But all she could do was nod and pant eagerly. Nothing she said anyway could encapsulate what she was feeling.

Nothing except when he hauled her up so suddenly against him, Yusra experienced weightlessness. She was suspended by a fusion of her desire for Bashir and her trust in him to care for and please her. And the only thing that eclipsed the feel-good head rush of being dipped back by him and lovingly held close to his body was his mouth inches from her own. His hot breath mingled with hers and then, blissfully, he was there, exactly where she'd envisioned him all along.

It was a kiss to end all the other kisses she'd had before.

With that kiss, she forgot her jerk of an ex-husband, forgot her anxieties around the institution of marriage, and thanks to Bashir, she didn't even recognize herself.

Like who had that wanton moan come from? Who was clinging on to his hard, broad shoulders, and arching her back to get him to follow her and deepen their kiss? Who nipped his full and very soft lower lip when he didn't give her what she wanted?

Finally, Bashir groaned and gave in. Tipping her backward, he upset the *shayla* off her head, the slinky shawl slipping down to her shoulders before sliding to the floor. He broke their kiss, murmured, "Sorry," and might have said more if she didn't lock lips with him again.

The kiss left her breathless and wanting, her thighs chafing each other in their quest to have Bashir wrapped around her legs. Wrapped in her. As if he heard her thoughts, he fulfilled her fantasy, lifted her up and pinned her to the cool glass wall framing the ocean he dreaded. And never once did he stop kissing her, stop delving into her mouth and stoking a fire in her body and soul that rose higher, *ever* higher, until she was certain she'd combust from the overload of pleasure.

Still, she wouldn't tire of this. Not ever.

It was a shame they required air, their pathetic lungs begging for a breather. But it didn't stop her from clinging on to him, her hands sliding to the back of his thick neck and holding him to her desperately. She didn't want to part from him. Not even when dizziness dimmed her vision and swooped over her limbs. Her legs quaked under her, and if Bashir weren't supporting her, she'd have gone limp on the floor. She closed her eyes as her husband pulled away from her, his breath cool against her wet, throbbing mouth, his husky voice akin to velvet on her sensitized skin as he asked, "Are you all right? Is it your blood sugar?"

Opening her eyes, Yusra gazed at him smilingly while panting. Even looking sexily rumpled and ready to kiss the life out of her again, he possessed a rarefied self-control. She didn't fault him for being able to compartmentalize his emotions. Because she had witnessed his passion, and it had been solely and intensely directed at her.

"It's your fault. Kissing me to death." She laughed, rested her head on his steady chest and sighed dreamily. "It wouldn't be a bad way to go though."

"You're not going anywhere," he said as he swooped her wobbling legs out from under her and carried her, "but here, on this sofa, where you'll rest until you can stand on your own two feet."

Ever the gentleman, Bashir went back to retrieve her *shayla* from where it had fallen. Then he sat with her on the sectional sofa and positioned her legs onto his lap. Those small actions from him warmed her almost as much as his sweet, sexy kisses had done.

For a while they simply stared at each other. The silence pleasant and interspersed with their labored breathing.

She could have said a million things to him when her breathing evened and she could speak clearly. And she settled on pointing to the salon's glass wall and asking, "So, why this view? I presumed you disliked large bodies of water."

"I fear the ocean, that's true, and yet I appreciate that it's a home for many creatures. Then there's its beauty and life-giving qualities."

Under Bashir's potent gaze, Yusra could have mistaken herself for the ocean he lovingly described.

It was a mistake she happily didn't correct in her mind.

CHAPTER ELEVEN

BASHIR'S KISSES HAD been the reset they needed.

And in the days that followed, Yusra felt a certainty in their marriage working out. It might have just been positive thinking on her part, but whatever it was, it reflected in other parts of her life too. Business had picked up for her, and she had graphic design projects scheduled an entire year ahead. And with that, her bank account wasn't looking so anemic anymore. She'd finally let her apartment go after giving the pushy landlord all of his back rent. Leaving her neighbor Dembe was difficult, but they hadn't been seeing much of each other since Bashir came into her life. She'd also paid off what she owed on her office space to the laundromat owner before packing up and setting up her new workspace in their hotel suite. With his tuition paid for, AJ was back in day care, and Zaire had joined him when the boys refused to be separated for even a few hours. And after all that, Yusra had enough left over for her copays on her insulin and diabetic supplies.

She had not one but several reasons to be optimistic.

The best part was she'd started her art again.

That was how Yusra found herself sitting across from her old college friend Samira in her friend's well-established art gallery.

"When I got the call from you, I couldn't believe it. I

haven't seen you in so long," Samira said, hugging her again before they walked through the substantial gallery and climbed the floating staircase to the offices on the second floor.

Where Yusra had married and ultimately walked away from the art they both loved, Samira had gone on to interning with a well-heeled auction house. From there she had worked her way up the ladder before branching off and opening her own gallery to showcase artists. Yusra would be lying if she denied her envy. But her happiness for her friend's success won over.

"I can't believe you really did it. Opened your own gallery." It was all Samira had talked about when they'd been starry-eyed art majors. "This place is *big*. I know you have to be reeling in artists left, right and center."

Her friend smirked, giving away that she was, indeed, flush with choices when it came to picking which artists to lift up into the limelight. But rather than give her the lowdown on her business, Samira pushed Yusra down into the club chair across from her in the warmly lit, stylishly furnished office and she gushed, "So, is that a ring I see on your finger?"

"It's a long story, but yes," Yusra said with a blush as she covered her brilliant wedding bands with a hand, her thoughts careening over to Bashir. Like she hadn't thought of him on and off every day already. The man claimed prime property in her mind, sometimes even pushing out the things that should've mattered like, now that they had kissed, what came next?

More kisses…

Or just *more*.

She didn't know. But seeing that Samira wouldn't listen without hearing this story first, Yusra gave her friend what she clearly wanted, all the juicy gossip without the kernel of truth that was her marriage of convenience with Bashir.

So it felt disingenuous when at the end Samira sighed happily for her.

"Good. You deserve a second chance after that no-good dirtbag of a first husband."

Samira had known Yusra's ex, Guled, and she hadn't liked him, not then and certainly not now. She had warned Yusra about him, and she'd been right, but that was the past. No point in tearing open old wounds.

"Tell me about this Bashir. Does he love you? Do *you* love him?"

Yusra was saved from having to respond by a doorbell chiming somewhere in the building.

"I thought the gallery was closed for the setup of the new exhibit," Yusra began to say. She had seen a glimpse of the exhibition coming together below, the theme of reclaimed African art captured perfectly in an assortment of mediums by Samira's chosen African artists.

Samira popped up off of her chair and smoothed her hands down her trendy burnished-yellow pantsuit. "It is formally, but that would be the back door. I have a delivery."

Left alone while her friend conducted her business, Yusra wrung her hands and recalled her morning with Bashir. She had confessed to her anxiety about visiting Samira and asking for a chance to showcase her art. It would be a big ask. Samira wasn't an up-and-coming novice gallery owner. She had trotted the continent and even gone as far as Europe to see the best that the art world had to offer.

"What if I'm not good enough?" Yusra had fretted. She'd pushed at her plate—her breakfast tasteless to her in the face of her fears. "I don't want her doing this because we're friends. I want it only if she believes I'm good at what I do."

He'd held up a hand. "Stop. See, right there. That's your problem. You're worried about what she'll think of your art."

Bashir had stood and walked to where she sat. Cupping her trembling chin, and then framing his big hand over her cheek, he'd said, "You do your art for you, always. Nothing will stop you then, not even your fears."

Yusra had smiled silly at his confidence in her. It was so alien and yet refreshing to her to have a partner who supported her. Thinking of Bashir again, she toyed with her wedding rings absentmindedly and drifted off. From somewhere nearby she heard the muffled sound of voices followed by heavy footfalls closing in on where she waited for her friend to return. Could Samira have come up with the delivery person?

Yusra didn't have time to prepare. She sat, eyes wide, caught twisting her rings when the door to Samira's office opened and Bashir walked in with Samira trailing behind him.

Before she could ask why he was there, he apologized and explained, "Sorry to intrude. I have time-sensitive news, and I thought it was better that I deliver it in person rather than over the phone."

"I guess one of us still has a delivery." Samira winked and prompted Yusra's face to heat with a blush. "I'll give you some privacy," her friend offered kindly and turned to make herself scarce.

But Bashir stopped her from leaving.

"Actually, Yusra and I will walk your gallery."

"Sure, I could stretch my legs," Yusra agreed, masking her apprehension at what her husband had to tell her. What news had brought him out to see her? Whatever it was, it had to be big. She knew he wouldn't have disrupted her meeting otherwise.

As he led her away from Samira and down to the gallery floor, Yusra prayed that whatever he had to say wouldn't add to her frayed nerves.

"Greece?"

Yusra grew still beside him and her head spun from the elephant sculpture of colorful flip-flops they had been admiring, to stare up at him.

Bashir handed her his phone, figuring he would articulate himself better with images. She looked through aerial black-and-white photos of his nonprofit's construction site.

"I have drones sending back photos daily." Since he couldn't be present in Crete where Project Halcyone was being built, he had used his plentiful resources to bring the project to wherever he was. And lately that had been by Yusra's side, either in her city or on his ship. He hadn't wanted that to change, but she had been adamant once not to leave Uganda, so he would respect her wishes whatever they were.

"But *Greece*?" She sounded unsold.

"Yes, Greece. It would be until construction on Halcyone is completed. Another six weeks are projected. And if you're amenable to the idea, we'd reside at my home in a small village on the island of Zákynthos."

She shook her head, murmuring, "I need to think this over," and walked around him. With him following her, they continued to weave through the art gallery her friend owned, the art itself a blur to him now that his focus was on her.

"Of course, since I'm dropping this on you suddenly, it would be understandable if you didn't agree. The other option would be that I go to Greece on my own and the children remain with you here in Uganda." It wasn't an option he even wished to consider. Being apart from Zaire and AJ would be torment enough. But gazing longingly at Yusra, Bashir accepted he'd also miss his vivacious wife. Things had changed for the better between them, and they had regained a harmonious balance and peace in their unconventional marriage.

And it's all because we kissed.

Bashir passed his hand over his smiling mouth. Unleashing his pent-up lust for her and receiving an enthusiastic response in return had been apparently just the cure they needed to mend the rift in their relationship. And that was why this was a difficult decision. He didn't want her to come along and be unhappy with him in Greece, and he hated to leave her and worry that he was jeopardizing their marriage once again.

He was damned in either scenario.

"You'd really leave Zaire with me?" she asked, bringing them to a halt before a mixed media artwork of a slumbering baby in a traditional kitenge swaddle, not unlike the ones he'd seen women using to carry their young children on their backs around the city. Though parts of the painting were rendered in oil, the child's swaddle appeared to be crafted with threads of silk, cotton and some other soft cloth. It homed in on the exhibition's theme.

Tearing his gaze from the painting to her, he nodded. "He won't like being separated from you and AJ, and I trust you'll care for him."

"That's sweet of you, but won't you miss the boys?"

"I'll adjust, and it won't be for long," he lied. Six weeks was a long while to be apart from them. But to ease her mind, and his own, he said, "I can also fly home for the weekends."

Home?

The strange sensation that came with that realization quickly passed and what remained was a surety that Yusra and their sons *were* his home. But that didn't help him commit to leaving them behind. Even knowing it would be a temporary separation, it felt like his heart would burst from the misery.

Yusra touched a hand to his chest, her eyes probing him, and she appeared to have found what she was looking for when a sadness alighted over her. "All of that sounds well-thought-out, but it's not what you want, is it?"

In the reflection of her dark eyes Bashir saw himself, the stress written on his face not as cleverly hidden as he'd have liked.

She pressed her other hand to him, her neck craned back for him, a kind smile pulling at her round rosy-brown cheeks.

"Don't sacrifice your happiness for ours."

"I'm…" He was about to tell her he wasn't, but that would be another lie. And she'd already seen through his first one. Sighing wearily, he said, "All right. I'm not happy."

"Do you want us to come with you?"

His brows rose higher. Was that a trick question? If it was, he didn't care, he honestly replied, "Yes."

Her bright smile told him he'd answered correctly even before she spoke.

"Then we'll go with you."

"Just like that?" he asked, tempering his excitement in case he misunderstood her.

But it was obvious he hadn't when she took his hands in hers. "This means a lot to you, and I want to be supportive like you were when I told you about revisiting the artist in me."

He had done that, but because he'd selfishly loved seeing the luminosity in her eyes amplify whenever she spoke of her precious art. So, naturally, it had become precious to him too.

"You won't regret coming with me?"

"I promise there will be no regrets." A grin shaped the mouth Bashir had been fantasizing about more since they'd kissed last—this morning, but that had been three hours ago, and he was overdue another taste of her.

"Six weeks might be too long," he argued half-heartedly, the other half of his heart dead set on her joining him.

"Bashir, stop. I want to come with you, and the boys will miss you too. We either all go, or none of us do."

Hearing those words put to bed the last of his doubts that she was doing this out of respect for him rather than truly desiring to remain by his side. And now that he wasn't tangled in his negativity, Bashir's elation broke free and soared. It compelled him to hug Yusra to him. Crush her close until he couldn't discern where she started and he ended. She laughed against his chest—happy, fluted notes that captured his feelings perfectly. If they could remain like that all day, he'd see to it, but the approach of clacking heels on the laminate flooring forewarned their private moment had reached its end.

Yusra's friend Samira beamed at them, a phone clutched in her hands.

"I don't mean to interrupt, but I was ordering lunch and I didn't know whether to order for two or three."

"I'm not staying," Bashir told her.

Samira nodded and walked a short distance away to complete the lunch order for her and Yusra.

"Have you proposed your idea to your friend yet?"

Yusra pressed her lips together and shook her head. She went from being relaxed in his arms to having tension thunder across her face. Her idea wasn't a bad one. Bashir had glimpsed her art in her office, and she possessed ample talent. She just needed a confidence boost.

"Repeat what you told me at the dining table. Show her that passion and you won't fail," he advised.

She nodded meekly.

"Then again, I could bribe your friend by buying art-work…"

That had the desired reaction. Any sign of her uneasiness disappeared as Yusra swatted his chest lightly and cackled in mock horror. "You wouldn't."

"I would if it was what you wanted or needed, and it's nei-ther of those because you're a born artist and this place is crying out to showcase your heart and soul. So, go. Do your friend a favor and don't deprive her of your calling."

Yusra sniffed and blinked fast. Her eyes shinier after what he said. She pressed her heated cheek back to his chest and hugged him quietly and far more fiercely. He read her grati-tude clearly. No words required.

"We'll talk more about Greece tonight, but I'll let you get back to your lunch date." He dropped a kiss on her forehead before he talked himself out of the tenderhearted gesture.

Letting her go was hard, but it had to happen. At least he had gotten to see her.

At first in an effort to not disturb her, Bashir had wanted to relay his news to her over the phone. But he was glad he hadn't. Seeing Yusra in person had been the brightest spot in his busy day.

And perhaps it was his ego running the show, but he won-dered if that was true for her too.

Was seeing me the best part of her day?

Bashir discovered he sincerely hoped so.

CHAPTER TWELVE

BEFORE HE'D EVER entertained the notion of having a family, Bashir had lived alone most of the year in his isolated Grecian villa.

Out of the eight homes he owned throughout the world, these sprawling acres of undulating green valley interspersed with golden beaches and unobstructed views of the blue-as-the-sky Ionian Sea was hands-down his favorite. And he didn't share that opinion alone.

On her third day of her temporary stay in Greece, Yusra jabbed her spoon teasingly at him over her bowl of Ugandan millet porridge and said, "You thought that six weeks was too long, but I think you'll have more trouble getting me to leave this place."

And that encompassed his mood exactly.

Never had he believed he'd have missed living there, particularly as his last memory of being in idyllic Zákynthos wasn't as rosy as its scenery. Getting the call from a hospital in Uganda and learning of his cousin's death had happened on this island paradise. That had been a dark day, and just one more to toss onto the pile he stored in his memory. Others included the day he'd lost his family to a flash flood, and then again when he had nearly died in the sea on his cross-continental journey to Europe.

Bashir had been fully expecting to experience some upsetting flashbacks when they'd first arrived in Zákynthos. And he had, but his memories were murky and soft-edged, the brushes of disquiet against his mind gentler than he remembered. Certain spots of the villa itself were packed with more memories than other areas. His bedroom for one had been where he had kicked out of his bedsheets upon receiving the distressing news that Imran had died. The entrance hall was where he had dropped his car keys twice in his hurry to drive himself to his private airstrip. And the pristine white gravel up the driveway would always remind him of the grinding sound of his tires as he raced from his home to fly to Uganda, where he would eventually meet and gain custody of Zaire.

No, coming home wasn't what he expected.

But that isn't a bad thing.

It helped that Yusra and their boys were enchanted by the island. Its varied sandy beaches, craggy cliffsides, turquoise sea and charming village life were all things his wife and children experienced and delighted in just the last few days alone. And despite his workload Bashir joined them on all their family outings. He hadn't wanted to miss the expressions on their faces for every little new thing they did.

Today was no different.

After playing with Zaire and AJ at the secluded beach connected to his vast property via a private trail, the boys fatigued themselves into longer than usual naps, and Bashir proposed he and Yusra take a stroll of their own through the village closest to their home.

Her enthusiasm doubled when she saw his preferred mode of transportation. A gleaming blue high-end sports convertible, the roof down promising swift, sea-laced breezes on their faces.

"It's not your *boda boda*, but it's all I have to offer."

"It's perfect, Bashir!"

He grinned widely and was as close to preening as he'd allow himself. "It's yours soon—your international driver's permit is in the mail." He had plenty of other luxury vehicles at his disposal. Besides, the delight on Yusra's face was worth every euro to his name. In the face of all the things he owned, his ability to make her and their sons happy was priceless. Bashir shut the door on the other emotions swirling in there, not ready to analyze what his growing affection for her meant for their future, and whether he should be concerned by any of it.

They were living in the present; that was all that mattered.

And right at that moment they had an impromptu second date to go on.

Perfectly timed, Yusra turned to him and said, "Let's make this a date to remember," right before they roared out of the villa's long drive, the car engine purring smoothly as they accelerated onto the serpentine road with its sublime views. The fertile valleys on one side and on the other end a plunging limestone cliff with no barrier and the spread of aquamarine sea. And yet even then, with everything else to look at, his eyes were always drawn back to her.

She eventually caught him in the act, a slow-forming sexy smirk playing over her sheer-glossed lips when she had him.

That, right there, already made this a date to remember for him.

For so long Yusra had looked forward to another outing with Bashir, and now that it was happening at last, she spent it walking on eggshells and keeping an eye out for warning signs that the date was taking a bad turn.

She didn't want a repeat of how things ended on their first date together.

Didn't wish for anything to go wrong when everything and everyone was being so achingly perfect.

Every person they met welcomed them warmly. Some even stopped to strike up a chat with Bashir, their conversation friendly enough for Yusra to glean that her husband had friends on the island he called home once.

Which added to the mystery of why he'd left picturesque Zákynthos.

What had taken him from this paradise on earth? It was true that she no longer viewed his ship as being a cold and colorless attempt at what a home should be. Rather than seeing it as a floating prison that her powerfully wealthy husband used to separate himself from the world and the hazards it sometimes possessed, Yusra saw it as a place of refuge for him in the eye of the storm.

And now it's mine too.

That ship connected them, just as much as their marriage did. It had been where Bashir had proposed to her the first time. And it was where their family lived whenever they weren't on dry land.

But her newfound appreciation for his superyacht didn't settle her curiosity of why he'd chosen anywhere else but this island to raise a family.

She had mulled it over quietly through their stroll of the village grounds, and then again over their authentic Grecian lunch of garlicky baked eggplant, or *skordostoumbi*. But she had her limits, and she reached a breaking point where she couldn't hold her nosiness in any longer.

"Why did you leave?"

Bashir didn't miss a stride, his gait easy and relaxed, deceptively so because he studiously kept his eyes from meeting hers.

"Would you believe me if I said the island life had grown to bore me?"

She gave a snort. "I've done my research, Bashir. This place is known to host some wild parties, and tons of tourists tend to flock to this locale during the summer. Between those two you'd have a hard time finding nothing to do, and no one to talk to."

His laughter, deep and gravelly, fired a blush from her and the sweetest relief. For a second there she believed she might have pushed his buttons a bit too far. As curious as she was, she still wanted their date to go smoothly. She could push him, but only so far.

"The truth of why I left is simple in a way, and complicated in others." Looking at her directly, he then asked on a foreboding note, "Do you still want to know?"

Beneath his heavy-lidded gaze, she nodded slowly, her anxiety compounding on itself. Was she opening a box of ills that was better left undisturbed? She didn't know, but it seemed too late to back out on her decision now.

"I left because I was home here on the island when I learned that Zaire's mother died and he needed me. As you might have guessed, it wasn't the best of situations, and it left an ineradicable memory of this place."

"I'm sorry. I shouldn't have asked."

"Don't be. I thought I'd feel that way for the rest of my life, but I was wrong. Coming back here feels different but... good. Better than I imagined it would anyway."

Even if he was just saying that to make her feel less awful than she did about her nosiness, it was considerate of him to say so. And maybe that was why she disregarded the nagging sensation that Bashir hadn't been entirely forthcoming with her and there was more to the story than he had let on.

That feeling persisted in her until they returned to his car and drove a short distance away from the village's center. The road he took was rougher and narrower, but it passed directly through rows of olive groves. During their lunch Bashir had explained that the olive oil used in their meal came directly from local olive farms. She licked her lips whenever remembering the oil's perfectly warmed, richly fruity taste.

Bashir drove as fast as the locals did on the country roads, the ease with which he knew this island's terrain speaking volumes. Again, Yusra found her mind wandering to why she sensed that he hadn't been completely truthful of his reasoning to abandon Zákynthos for almost three years.

But why would that be?

And what could he be hiding if he was lying?

This time it was more of a challenge to dispel her rising doubts.

Distraction came in the form of Bashir turning into a long gated drive. He shifted the gear of his car to climb the inclining road, and with time Yusra glimpsed where they were headed. Buildings dotted the landscape of the valley, and the stone-built structures formed a concentric circle around a taller, three-story white stone edifice.

Bashir parked at the entrance to this central building.

"'Imran Villas and Suites,'" she read from the gold-lettered sign once she stepped outside the car.

Bashir circled over to where she stood, his head tipped back like hers, his sunglasses shielding his eyes, but his tone clearly proud when he said, "This is the first resort that I've owned, managed and renovated from the ground up all by myself."

She'd almost forgotten that he was a successful hotelier. He didn't speak of his job often, but it was plain to her that he loved what he did, and that passion had made him a billionaire tycoon. And now that she knew what this place was,

Yusra marveled at what he'd created, pride ping-ponging through her a heartbeat later. "Can I see it?"

She didn't miss his quickly flashing grin.

"I've already booked us a tour of one of the villas. We'll even have time to stop by the closest olive farm. The family who owns it has been in business for over two hundred years, and they've promised us an experience and taste of their olives like no other."

More delicious olives? That sounded great to her.

Yusra packed away any apprehension over what Bashir wasn't telling her, and she slipped her arm around his. He looked down at where she held him abruptly. But he didn't shrug her off, and once his surprise melted, he curled his biceps around her arm in return.

They walked the grounds and entered one of the villas.

Yusra sucked in a brisk intake of air at the beauty of the indoor-outdoor space. The first thing she noticed was the long, moving wall of glass. Bashir pushed a button on a small remote and the walls began folding in on themselves silently and their absence let in cool, sea-scented air. She tipped her face to the breeze and sighed her pleasure.

Wandering deeper inside to get her fill of this one-of-a-kind space, she felt Bashir's presence near her. But he didn't hover. Or prohibit her from touching anything. Instead, giving her the space to poke around the cavernous part concrete, part stone villa, he lingered close enough if she needed him, but far enough to let her curiosity guide her.

It took her a while to tour the building's interior, but she did at last make it outside. Because that was where she had wanted to go right from the start. How could she resist the inviting waters of the infinity pool, stone-paved terrace with its alfresco dining space and the wooden sun lounger shaded beneath a canopy?

She walked around all of it; her awe must have been written all over her face because Bashir came up next to her.

"If you like it so much, we could spend the night. Alcina won't mind caring for the boys for a while longer." They'd left his trustworthy nanny with AJ and Zaire before leaving their home.

But as tempting as his suggestion was, more for the reason that she would have time alone and uninterrupted with him than taking a break from the endless energy of their toddlers, Yusra couldn't take him up on the offer.

Shaking her head, she said, "We shouldn't, at least not now."

"Rain check then."

"Definitely," she concurred.

Gazing out toward the sea, Yusra closed her eyes, and let out another pleasure-filled sigh when Bashir moved her back to his front. The embrace from behind in this romantic spot had her questioning whether she'd been hasty in declining to stay here with him. They had pushed the envelope a little more every day since having kissed, and as nice as that was, Yusra was tiring of their slow, teasing pace. Like foreplay with no end, it only ever had her burning up with this febrile longing to be fulfilled by him.

Though she worried if she pushed him too far, he would stop altogether.

And she couldn't have that happening.

Never.

The possessive thought slashed through her mind before her consciousness blanked when Bashir's hands moved on her. He explored her cautiously, his big hands sliding up from her waist over her softly rounded stomach beneath her flowing long-sleeved tunic, and across the buttons that kept her shirt in place.

Far slower than she liked, he brushed his fingertips over the buttons, one by one, rising higher until he reached her shirt's collar. He unfastened the topmost buttons, careful not to bare her completely except to his searching hand. Bashir's thick fingers reached inside her shirt and rubbed across her clavicle before he dipped his digits teasingly to the valley of her breasts. He did this beneath the cover of her tunic, but anyone who could have happened on them would know, just by the placement of his hand, and the way her head tossed back against his chest and she moaned breathily, that he caressed the top of her heaving chest.

Yusra gasped, "Lower," and arched up into his seeking hand when he listened and another of her buttons was freed. He cupped her breast with one of his large palms, his warmth seeping through her cotton bra to singe her flesh.

I just need him a bit closer...

And lower. Much, much lower.

Unexpectedly Bashir's hand stilled both under her shirt and against her hip. Then, after a torturous pause, he completely pulled back from her without explanation.

At least not at first. Because then she saw for herself what had compelled him to stop.

A familiar-looking older man stood waveringly on the threshold of the villa's interior and exterior areas.

Yusra didn't look closer immediately to figure out where she'd seen this man before. Rather she shielded herself until she had her appearance in order. And by then Bashir crossed over to the man and ushered him indoors, giving her additional time to fan her heated face and calm her jittery emotions.

When she felt as presentable as she could be, she walked over to where the two men were now chatting with ease. As she neared them, Yusra recognized where she'd seen the older man.

At our wedding!

He was Bashir's mentor and friend. The one who had hugged him so fiercely.

Otis. She recalled his name.

Now Otis beamed at her, his friendly smile easing her embarrassment of having been caught with Bashir where they had been seconds away from a more compromising position. But she tried not to think too much on that.

"*Kalimera.* Hello again. Yusra, is it? Enchanted to meet you!" His boisterous, happy voice rang through the villa. It made her smile more brightly.

Taking her hand, Otis gave it a kiss. "I'm sorry that I didn't get a chance to formally meet you at your lovely wedding."

"It's all right. We're meeting now."

Otis laughed gustily. "That's true! My wife and I are visiting the island, and we stopped by your home first, but we were told you both weren't home."

"Well, you found us easily enough," Bashir drawled.

Yusra snapped her head up to him, surprised to hear a gruffness in his voice. It was borderline rude.

She compensated for his shocking rudeness with a shining smile. "We're sorry you missed us. Bashir was just eager to show me his villas and hotel suites. And I was just as eager to see them."

"Ah, of course! Perfectly understandable! This one's a favorite among his other establishments."

"Is it?" Yusra swung her gaze to her dour-faced husband before she agreed, "But, yes, it really is a special place."

"As special as its namesake," Otis said.

Yusra's smile faded. "Its namesake?"

She didn't miss Bashir spearing a glare at his business mentor and saying something to him in Greek. She wouldn't have been able to understand anything, but unlike Bashir,

Otis's emotions flitted openly across his face, and she didn't need a translator to decipher that. First there was the shock rounding his eyes and drawing his mouth open, and then came the confusion as his bushy, frost-white eyebrows lowered.

Otis acted oddly after that, his jovial expression reading as less genuine to her, as if something was bothering him. She could only make an educated supposition that it had to do with whatever Bashir said to him in Greek. And whatever it was that transpired in that other language steered Otis toward the villa's exit. With a nervous-sounding laugh, the older man called back, "Bashir, I'll be waiting over at Reception in the main building. *Endáxi*." Then to her he waved awkwardly and said, "*Adio* for now, my dear."

Otis's departure introduced a weighty silence.

A silence Yusra ended when she asked, "For now?"

"Otis and his wife, Evgenia wish to stay with us while they vacation for a few days."

Yusra didn't see a problem with that. Their home was huge, and the chances of any of them feeling cramped were slim. So she was baffled by why he looked as though that living situation wouldn't be feasible.

"Bashir, they'll stay with us."

He grunted noncommittally, but his brooding frown said otherwise.

She could've asked him what was bothering him—because something clearly was, but instead she blurted, "What did he mean that this villa has a namesake?"

If Bashir had appeared perturbed before, there was no denying his blatant troubled expression at her question. Quickly though, he shuttered the emotions filtering onto his face. And she could have stamped her foot out of frustration in just the same way their toddler sons did whenever they were throwing a tantrum.

She felt cheated. Like Bashir was showing her the parts he approved rather than the whole messy palette that made up who he was. And she wanted all of him: not bits and pieces, but everything that was her broodingly beautiful husband.

Yusra opened her mouth to convey her riled-up thoughts and feelings into words, but Bashir slammed an iron door shut on the conversation.

"I should go to him. I'll call a cab to take you home."

She hurried after him, catching him at the door with a hand on his back and a gasped, "Wait!"

"What?" he sighed, his gruff exasperation wounding her already aching heart. He glanced down at her over his shoulder, as if giving her anything more might be too much for him right then.

But why?

Why is he acting like this?

Yusra's mind reeled. She didn't want to say the mean things that came to her through her pain. Later, she knew, she'd regret all of it. So, she did what he wanted. She withdrew her hand and silently gave him permission to leave.

Not that he needed it. Bashir stalked away from the villa's entrance without another look back. Watching her powerful husband retreating from her was not the way she'd pictured their day ending.

Yusra had hoped this date would be their do-over. But now…

Now I have to wonder if we aren't cursed.

Or maybe it wasn't that they were cursed at all, but plain old incompatible with each other.

And that caused her far more torment than if they were just unlucky.

CHAPTER THIRTEEN

HOSTING BASHIR'S SPECIAL guests might have been pleasant if Yusra weren't stuck in her own head. But she was, and it was ruining what could have been a lovely dinner with new houseguests. And as much as she wanted to place the fault on Bashir, she couldn't. He hadn't forced her to trust him. Nor was he to blame that she began to care for him so deeply that her despondency only magnified as the day went by and the silence between them stretched on.

When Bashir had finally arrived home, he had come with Otis and the two men headed straight for the darkly furnished study that Yusra viewed as the perfect man cave. Bashir hadn't even bothered to make eye contact with her. Meanwhile Otis had paused long enough to greet his wife, Evgenia with a hug and a kiss.

Yusra hadn't known jealousy as fierce as hers in that moment, and it greatly disturbed her.

It was right then that she knew she had to keep herself preoccupied. Bashir had a personal chef, but Yusra had relieved her in the kitchen and sent her home early. Slaving over the hot stove was all that kept her from crying over this impasse with Bashir.

Well, that and playing with Zaire and AJ when they awoke from their nap, which gratefully had been by the time she came home alone and sulking from her and Bashir's failed date. But eventually she left the boys with Alcina and Ev-genia while she prepared dinner. And while she was in the kitchen, she gained a semblance of power.

Cooking was like art to her, just with different ingredients than when she was working with her charcoals, oil paints and pencils. Yusra was in her element, so nothing should have gone wrong. But she wasn't wholly herself, and so after she heard robust laughter and Bashir's name called out, she swiv-eled her head in that direction as she was pouring hot water into a pot of caramelizing onions…and burned her hand.

She cried out and dropped the pot.

No one came in to check on her. She was cut off from ev-eryone else, so she came to her own aid, running her fingers through cold water. Yusra sniffled as she located the first aid kit, applied salve and wrapped her injured hand. She worked more cautiously after that, but the damage was done. Her fin-gers throbbed painfully. But compared to her crushed spir-its, it was nothing. Her hand would heal; she knew that. She wished she were as confident about her trust being restored.

Once knocked down by her ex-husband, and now shaken up by Bashir, that outlook wasn't so bright.

Dinner with their guests was full of lively conversation. None of which Yusra contributed to or paid any heed. By that point she had fully retreated into her mind, shut the door and waited for her duties as hostess to end.

For his part Bashir wasn't the most gracious of hosts either.

He grumbled plenty during dinner, glowered at his food for more than half of the time, and generally brooded his way through to dessert which was served in the family room. Yusra skipped on the crème caramel dessert she'd made for their dinner party. Usually, the dessert would remind her of home, her mother's baking and the wonderful warmth guests could bring with them, but all she felt was a coldness driving into her skin, through her bones and into her bloodstream. Her brain felt frozen; her heart along with it.

Together she and Bashir must have made for a miserable duo.

Lucky for them, his friends were good people. An affable couple, Otis and Evgenia carried the conversation all on their own at times, regaling them with tales of how they'd met through an arranged marriage by their powerfully wealthy families. They hadn't felt love for each other at first, but rather admiration for their passions—Otis in hotel management, and Evgenia as an interior designer.

It wasn't unlike her and Bashir.

A marriage of convenience arranged by them to solve the issue of the baby swap wasn't very different than an arranged marriage, was it?

And Otis and Evgenia grew to love each other.

Yusra stared at the older couple with hope whenever they looked to each other, their love glowing undoubtedly in their eyes.

But unlike Otis and Evgenia who had been open to love, she and Bashir never were.

It was why they'd ultimately married.

And it's why I'm unhappy. She startlingly accepted the epiphanic thought. *I love Bashir.*

What a foolish thing to do. Falling for a man who, although her husband, was the last person she should love. Now what was she going to do?

Knowing what he had to do and doing it were not only two very separate things, but one was harder than the other, and Bashir discovered that personally when he found himself pacing the length of his bedroom. He needed to see and speak with Yusra, but he couldn't bring himself to go to his wife.

His extremely lovely wife who he was realizing he wasn't treating right.

I don't deserve her.

But that wasn't his only problem.

He liked her. Immensely. So much, in fact, it struck him that somewhere between meeting her and kissing her he had fallen in love with Yusra. And no matter how good that love made him feel, it was transient. Like life, love was fleeting. He loved her today, but what if tomorrow stole that love from him? Even today didn't promise a guarantee.

Bashir regarded the old photos of his family strewn on his bed, some faded and yellowed and others as clear as the day the photos were taken. But they were all proof of his point that love wasn't everlasting.

He'd loved his cousin, Imran, and he had thought leaving him would stop him from caring. But then his cousin died, and the heartache he was running from only caught up with him in time.

Would it be like that if I lost Yusra?

If she left him one way or another, would he ever recover from that loss?

No, the answer came to him instantly. He wouldn't be the same. Losing her would wreck him, more now that he acknowledged that what he'd been feeling for her this whole time was love. Deep and true romantic love.

Bashir slowed to a standstill, hating that he had to do what came next. But he couldn't hide out in his room all night. After a tense dinner only saved by Otis and Evgenia's cheerful humor, he'd shown his old friends to their guest room before retiring to his own bedroom. Of course it was then he had recognized that he and Yusra shouldn't sleep apart for the short duration of their houseguests' stay. What would Otis and Evgenia think if they learned of their marriage of convenience? Knowing them as he did, they'd ask questions of him, and pry in that annoyingly loving way of theirs. And that wasn't something Bashir wished to handle on top of everything else on his to-do list.

But it was a good excuse to go to Yusra. From there he would nudge them toward what he needed to tell her.

Striding to his door, Bashir flung it open and stopped in his tracks.

Yusra stood in his path, her hand in the air, knuckles ready to rap on his door, and a warm-looking woolen blanket curled to her chest. She lowered her hand slowly, looking shy all of a sudden, almost queasily so as she shuffled her feet.

He stepped aside with a silent invitation.

Once she was in his bedroom, he closed the door.

"I thought I should be here with you. I didn't want your guests to wonder why we were sleeping in separate rooms." She turned to face him, her shyness still mingling with obvious discomfort. He didn't like to see her like that, hated that he was likely the cause. Bashir surmised he had to be after the way their day had gone.

Now that he *knew* he loved her, it was through that lens that he looked at her.

But he had to shatter that lens. That was his goal.

Because I can't love her.

The risk to him was too great.

"I was just about to go say the same thing to you," he said.

She hugged her blanket closer. "So, are we both taking the bed? I could sleep on the sofa." She pointed to the love seat across from the king-size four-poster bed and before an electric fireplace. Between the two of them, the sofa would be a better fit for her than him, but Bashir wouldn't have it.

"No, you have the bed."

"Are you sure?" She glanced cursorily at it. "It's big enough to fit us comfortably. I wouldn't mind..."

You will after what I have to say.

Bashir shook his head. "The bed is yours, Yusra. I'll be fine wherever I sleep." He could fix a makeshift mattress out of extra blankets if he needed to, but he wouldn't have her sleeping roughly on his watch.

Nodding, she quietly went to place her blanket atop his bed, and right after, she appeared distracted suddenly. He saw why when she picked up the photos he'd forgotten he had left out in the open.

"Is this your family?" she asked.

Too late to prevent her from seeing them, he supposed it was a smooth enough segue to what he had to tell her.

"Yes, that's them."

The photo she held was one he'd committed to memory. It was his only picture of his family. Everything else having been washed away with the flash flood that killed them. If it weren't for his aunt finding the photo in an album, he wouldn't have been able to recall the faces of his parents, grandparents and siblings.

"It's all that I have left of them. It was our last Eid together as a family."

"And this one?" She held up a photo of his aunt and uncle.

"My aunt and uncle. They took me in after my family died and I had no one else to care for me."

There was only one photo that remained after that. Bashir tensed his muscles in preparation for when Yusra lifted up that photo to him. He'd thought he was ready, but he wasn't, and so it showed in his gravelly voice.

"That's me...and my cousin Imran." In one of the last photos with Imran before Bashir had run away from the only other family he had. And he wasn't counting Yusra and their boys, even though he should because if this conversation went south, he might lose them too. Forcing that despairing thought away, he said, "Imran was my favorite of all my cousins. We were close. Almost like brothers."

"Imran. Is he the one the villas and suites you showed me today are named after?"

Clever of her to connect those dots. But he'd seen her working it out the instant Otis had let drop about the resort villas having a namesake.

"That's correct. I dedicated it to him." But that had been before Imran died. Now the name held even more significance to Bashir.

"You look happy," she said and stared at the photo of his smiling self. In that photo, he had his arm looped around his cousin, and even though Imran had been older by a few years, Bashir had been a few inches taller and so comically his cousin stretched to get his arm around Bashir's shoulders.

Like the other photos, he'd gazed at that picture of him and Imran so many times, he had every detail trapped in his mind.

"We were happy," he finally said, his fists at his sides, jaws clenched achingly tight. That was it. He couldn't put it off any longer. And he wouldn't find a better window of opportunity when she looked up and her eyebrows bunched together.

"What's the matter?" she whispered.

"There's a reason I was looking at those photos, and a reason I'm telling you about my cousin." An awful beat of silence, and then, he said, "He was AJ's father."

"AJ's father..." she murmured, shook her head in disbelief and looked at the photo in her hand before her eyes snapped up to him once more. "If he's AJ's father, that means... You lied."

"I never lied. I just didn't tell you about Imran."

"Why?" she cried, controlling her voice so that it never

rose above a harsh whisper. She dropped the photo and marched over to him. "Why not just trust me and tell the truth? What happened to us communicating openly?"

"I didn't think it was a big deal," he lied.

"How can you say that when he's AJ's father!"

"*I* am AJ's father."

"That's not what I meant and you know that, so don't twist my words, Bashir. Don't you dare," she hissed warningly, her finger stabbing the air between them, and though she didn't touch him, he felt her angry jab all the same. Right over his wildly thumping heart. Prompting him to rub his chest.

"You're making this a bigger deal than it truly is." It was an incendiary comment. He knew it, and that was why he said it.

And sure enough Yusra froze up and stared at him, openmouthed, her eyes full of confusion like she didn't even recognize who he was.

Bashir wanted this. Her fury and his.

For the majority of their relationship, everything had gone so perfectly, it always felt like the other shoe would drop at any moment. Now that it had with his omission of truth, reality could set in. And if he was extra lucky it would diminish his love for her.

But it wasn't meant to be.

Because right before him her anger eroded, and in a shocking twist, she asked with a tremble to her chin, "Why are you doing this?"

"Telling you the truth, you mean," he said gruffly.

"Being an ass, I mean."

Her colorful language was another surprise. And with each one, he was losing grip on his plan to kill his love for her.

"Okay, I get it," she said on a shaky sigh, her head bowing, but her brokenhearted voice rising up. "Maybe you didn't trust me enough to know how I would react. And I never said you weren't AJ's father. Both Zaire and AJ are lucky to have you in their lives. I see that. And I'm not negating what you mean to our children. But you continued to lie about your cousin. Which means you still don't trust me. You can't imagine how much that hurts—"

She broke off, sniffled loudly and spun away from him.

Though not quick enough for him to miss the wetness on her cheeks.

She's crying because of me.

At that Bashir bit the inside of his cheek so hard he tasted blood, and with it an incessant pain where he purposefully wounded himself to feel anything else besides a guilt so vast it could rival the span of the sea near their home. But it did him no good.

With each tremble of her shoulders and soft sob from her, Bashir felt the worst of the worst.

She hid her wet eyes, her back to him as she spoke tearfully. "I guess now's a poor time to tell you that I love you." Then she turned around and swiped at her face, what little good it did her.

More tears rained down, replacing what she wiped clear and dripping off the chin she proudly thrust higher. "Did you hear what I said?"

"Clearly," he gritted.

"And?" she challenged.

He knew what she was after. A reciprocation of love from him. And he would have given it to her if he wasn't who he was, and if his past had been any different than what it ended up being.

But it isn't.

"And I don't feel the same."

She dropped her head, her sniffles making a comeback.

"I can't love you, or anyone else for that matter. Yusra,

I didn't run away to Europe because I wanted a better life. I ran away from the only other family I'd known because I was scared to love them and lose them just like I had my first family. And I left Imran behind because I thought I was doing the best thing for me, but I lost him anyways, and it still hurt like hell. I won't do it all over again."

He hoped that was enough to open her eyes on choosing her love wisely when it came to him. He was no good for her.

But Yusra lifted her head and gazed so forlornly at him that it nearly had him buckling under the pressure of having hurt her. "My ex-husband never shared his thoughts or feelings, and he left me out of his life. I've lived like that once already. And like you, I won't do it all over again. Because right now I don't have faith in you, and that… That's just as important as love is to me.

"I love you, Bashir, and that's why I can't do this."

She turned then, walked to the en suite and locked herself inside.

Bashir chased her to the closed door, where he raised his hand to knock and call her back out. But he stopped himself and forced his feet to go the opposite direction. Away from the bathroom Yusra claimed as refuge from him, away from his bedroom where he prayed she slept well after their fight and away from his home with her and their sons.

If there was ever a time for him to return to his ship, now was it.

CHAPTER FOURTEEN

YUSRA COUNTED THOSE first days that passed by the growing collection of finished artworks piling up in her bedroom. She obsessively created art. Not stopping even when she ran out of space. Simply, she used spare rooms all over the villa to store her pieces.

By the end of that first week without her husband, she finally found a dedicated workspace in Bashir's study. And since the owner of this palatial villa wasn't home, she did what she pleased.

Serves him right.

Yusra painted a hard, bold stroke over the new canvas, her broken heart guiding this latest piece. She used darker colors and the overall mood was ghastlier when she completed it hours later. Black, red and green swirled together in a chilling eddy and best captured the three emotions that had been her default for a week now. Outrage, envy, and worst of all, a desolation that wouldn't quit.

She was angry because he'd left her when they should have been trying to work it out together.

Envious that he clearly wasn't as affected as she was. How else could he continue to work on his precious nonprofit like everything was normal?

But the sadness with no end was the worst of all three.

Even after she'd cried all the tears humanly possible, she

couldn't dislodge the lump in her throat or rub the itchiness from her eyes whenever she recalled her last moment with Bashir. She sobbed herself to sleep and stared off into space whenever she wasn't doing her art or caring for AJ and Zaire.

Without the boys she'd have probably curled up in bed all day, and with only her misery as her constant companion.

But they gave her a reason to get up and get on with her life. And if Bashir could act as though nothing transformative happened in their relationship, then so could she.

And he did eventually call, asking her how she and the boys were faring in that irritatingly calm, even tone of his: the very same tone he'd once used to tell her about the baby swap that had changed their lives. She let him speak with their children, but it was only ever that. She ripped a page out of his book and channeled a dispassionate version of herself.

That was how the next month passed. In this state of disconnect between her emotions and thoughts and her body. She cared for AJ and Zaire, worked on the several graphic design projects her clients expected from her by their deadlines and created the art she'd been yearning to make for years now.

Yusra didn't think she'd ever want to feel again.

Then at the end of the fifth week, she realized two things. One, Bashir's nonprofit, Project Halcyone, would be opening its door in a short while, and secondly, she had cut herself off from her emotions but her love for her husband hadn't gone anywhere.

She still loved him.

More than that…

I miss him.

And just as she was accepting that fact, a gift arrived with Bashir's aide Nadim.

After making his delivery in person, Nadim left, no doubt

returning to his employer who cowardly hid out on his ship, and Yusra carried Bashir's mystery gift box away from where their curious toddlers could tear into it and break whatever was inside. She opened the box a while later when she found the time to be alone.

She gasped as soon as she saw what it was.

Paintbrushes. And not just any paintbrushes, but an entire set of Winsor & Newton Series 7 Kolinksy Sable Brushes. The whole set had to have cost hundreds—*thousands* if she gave her best estimate. And, yes, it might be a drop in the bucket to Bashir, but it meant the world to her. These brushes were reserved for the serious-minded artist. And somehow, he'd thought she deserved them.

Yusra didn't realize she was crying until pattering footsteps discovered her in the study amidst her art. Zaire came first, closely followed by AJ who was clutching their pet rabbit to his chest. Three sets of eyes peered at her. Two tiny humans and a cute, fluffy bunny. All three equally mystified.

She pulled them in for a hug, squeezing them close and laughing when Zaire touched one wet cheek, and AJ the other.

Yusra kissed their small hands.

How could she tell them that she was thrilled with their father? That for the first time since their argument more than a month ago, she was in a buoyant mood. Seeing the brushes was the first step in a positive direction.

Just holding them between her thumb and index finger and posing a brush's tip in the air awakened a long-slumbering inspiration in her.

I should do something for him. To show him I'm not mad. That I still love him.

Because it was so clear to her now.

Bashir was scared. He didn't want to lose her; he said so

himself in as direct a way as possible. He'd lost his family before, twice over, and naturally he worried. That still made him a coward, yes. But he was *her* coward.

The father of her children.

Her husband.

Her love.

One of the last things she'd said to him was that trust and love were equally important to her. And she still stood by that, but now that she wasn't looking at the situation through an angrily sad filter, Yusra had faith in one thing: that they would lose each other and their family if she sat here and did nothing.

But what can I do to show him that I love him?

She looked down and found the answer was in her hands all along.

And she had the perfect muses in mind.

With that, Yusra gathered her boys—and their adorable rabbit—closer and she cheerfully asked, "Who wants to help Mommy make a painting?"

CHAPTER FIFTEEN

"EVERYTHING IS IN PLACE, including the extra event you added to the schedule, and we're almost ready to begin with the auction."

Bashir turned to acknowledge Nadim's report with a cursory glance, his eyes veering back from his trusty aide with his equally trusty tablet to the ballroom. They were up on the stage that was temporarily erected for the special night. From that vantage point he could see everyone filing into the grand space they had arranged for their esteemed guests. And that was perfect because he had no plan to miss her when she arrived.

Yusra.

He had called to confirm whether she was coming. And though she gave him a hopeful answer, he still erred on the side of disappointment. Lowering his expectation would protect him if she didn't show up. Of course, like the sucker that he was, Bashir still hoped she would.

He missed her terribly. So much in fact that he was starting to feel physical effects of it. Headaches being the worst of it.

"These should help," Nadim said as he passed over a bottle of painkillers discreetly.

Bashir headed for the back of the stage, hurriedly dry-swallowed the pill and walked back out to keep a watch for Yusra. He wouldn't miss her.

"Have you spoken to Alcina? Did she mention whether they're en route?"

"Not yet," Nadim told him. "But the reporter arrived a short while ago. Security let him pass and they're keeping an eye on him as you've requested."

Bashir scowled. It wasn't the news he wished to hear. The reporter from the business journal had interviewed him once already, and it had nearly been a train wreck when the man had gone off the preapproved list of questions and entered more sensitive territory with Bashir. He abhorred doing it again, but when the journal called and asked for a follow-up interview at his charity gala and auction, Bashir couldn't refuse. Not when he could see the sound mindedness of having a reporter on hand at such a pivotal event for Project Halcyone. As long as he kept the questioning period short and on topic, he'd fare better than he had last time. If the reporter wanted juicy details, he'd get them, but he would accept whatever Bashir willingly fed him. No more, and no less.

"The auction will begin shortly. I'll touch base when we're ready for it." Nadim walked away from him, leaving Bashir to be on the lookout for his wife on his own. He just hoped he wouldn't overlook her as the sizable hall grew more and more populated.

Guests streamed in steadily, the ballroom filling up quickly enough. Tomorrow, that same space would be repurposed to house temporary shelter facilities for refugees, asylum seekers and migrants alike. But for tonight, it would cater to the wealthy and powerful elite of all of Europe and not just Greece. Bashir had pulled every string he could and called in favors to promote the interest of the nonprofit. Without funding, Halcyone was nothing. Even with his billions, he could only do so much. So, he hoped his guests tonight were extra generous and opened their checkbooks to the auction he'd planned.

Everything was exactly as it should be. From the magnificent chandeliers hanging down from between blood-red velvet ceiling drapes, to the golden glow those chandeliers cast in the room, their fulgent lights reflecting off the smooth hardwood flooring. Floor-to-ceiling windows showcased a view of the Cretan Sea. A new moon turned the waters an inky black, but inside, the warming sound of string music and growing hum of voices from his guests blasted away the darkest that night could challenge him with.

He didn't have the luxury of standing around and moping over whether Yusra would show in support for him, or if he'd pushed her away too far. A small blessing in disguise. He climbed down from the stage to hobnob with his guests, ensure that he knew their names and that they believed he was the right man to trust their money with when it came time to donate.

An hour into circling the room and making necessary rounds to introduce himself to as many people as possible, Bashir finally had time to himself. He grabbed a *soumada* from one of the drink servers. The sweet, syrupy drink wasn't his favorite, but it was a staple in Crete, and he needed the sugary boost to lift his sunken spirits.

He just didn't get it.

I have my Halcyone finally.

He should have been happier that the dream he'd had all these months was now very much real.

I should be over the moon.

Instead, he might as well have been anchored deep in the Cretan Sea. Sipping at his tooth-achingly sweet drink, he recalled what he'd last said to Yusra. That he couldn't love her. That he was incapable of it. And then he had fled from her, his cowardice bringing him to his ship where for the past six weeks he hid from her and the love he had for her that stubbornly wouldn't leave him.

Now he wondered what she was doing. And whether she missed him at all.

Was she happy that he'd invited her to the celebration? Or was she girding herself to do battle and break his heart by asking for the divorce that hovered over them since their argument?

Gulping more of the *soumada* than he intended, Bashir pressed a hand to his forehead and squeezed his eyes shut against the spike in his blood sugar. He felt a presence and squinted to address whoever it was.

Alcina stood before him.

He looked around her, not smothering his eagerness and not caring that he was being obvious. "Where is she? Have the boys come with her?"

Alcina avoided his eyes. A clue that he wouldn't like what she had to report. "They're on their way, but Yusra sent me along first."

Well. That wasn't the worst bit of news.

At least he now knew she was coming. But before he could question Alcina about how Yusra's mood had seemed to her, he heard his name.

Otis and Evgenia made their way over to him, their smiles as warm as the hugs and kisses on the cheeks he received from both in a customary Greek greeting. The last time he'd seen either was after he left the villa on the night he had argued with Yusra. He'd skulked off like a thief in the night, and though he was sure Yusra had tried to save face the morning after, Otis and Evgenia knew him too well. They might not know what had transpired exactly, but shortly after, they had called to grill him on what happened.

And that was when the whole truth tumbled out of him. Bashir told them about the baby swap and the marriage of convenience. He even made it clear that though he loved Yusra more than his life, he was afraid to let her in and lose her.

Much like they had done when they had taken him away from the refugee camp and welcomed him into their home and family, Otis and Evgenia consoled him and passed no judgment. They lifted him up, and it was with their help, and that of Nadim and Alcina, that he was able to be standing where he was now.

"Remember, you have a lot of groveling to do, son. A happy wife guarantees a happy life," Otis warned and wagged a finger at him.

Evgenia hushed him laughingly. "Otis, stop. They know what's good for them, and so they'll figure it out together. Besides, we had the birds-and-bees talk already when he was a young man. He needs none of our coddling in that department. Do you, Bashir?"

Blushing, he passed a hand over his heated face and shook his head. Bashir was saved from further public embarrassment when Nadim found him.

"The auction is nearly ready to start, but I wanted to let you know that Yusra has arrived."

Bashir's heart juddered. "Where?"

Nadim looked uncomfortable, and he took a few seconds too long to say, "She's speaking with the reporter. Our security team tried to intervene—"

Bashir had heard enough.

He shot off to rescue his wife. Only to discover that she needed no shining knight in armor charging to save her.

Yusra looked glorious in a showstopping, modest gown. The sparkling black of the dress like stars had been plucked and sewn onto the bodice, full-length arms and skirt. She'd styled her black hijab to seamlessly tuck under the gown's high collar. And the alluringly bold black henna twining her fingers popped out to him where she held AJ's and Zaire's hands.

Like a professional, she answered the reporter's queries poignantly at times and more reservedly during others. She even wrenched a laugh out of the reporter at one point. Bashir watched from the sidelines with other guests who began to circle and swarm out of sheer curiosity. He could see why. A woman with two young children made for quite a sight when no one else had brought their children along. He had delivered an explicit rule against younger guests attending, mostly as he wanted the message focused on Halcyone and the funds required to do the good he hoped the organization would bring to the disenfranchised newcomers to this part of the world.

But his children and wife were an exception. Sue him for being a billionaire who broke rules.

All of the questions asked of Yusra revolved around her relationship with him. Where had she met him? How long had they dated? What was married life like with a billionaire?

He hadn't thought she'd noticed him in the crowd, but Yusra's eyes found him suddenly; her beautiful smile felt personal. She kept flicking looks at him throughout the interview, and soon enough the reporter noticed and picked him out of the throng of people. He waved Bashir over to join his lovely wife.

From there they talked about his plans for the nonprofit, and Bashir spoke eloquently and at comfortable length on his hopes for what Project Halcyone would come to mean to those who needed its services.

And this was where he gave those juicy details that he once was resistant to speak on.

"As you know, I was a refugee myself. I came to this country and continent from a distant land. When I arrived, I had no family, no friends, no prospects on what I planned to do for a living. Twenty years later, I have several resorts to my name, friends who stand by and support me, and a family," he looked down at Yusra, and she smiled and nodded her encouragement, "who love me and who I love very deeply."

Satisfied with that response, and the others he gave, the reporter positioned them for photographs.

While Bashir held Yusra to his side and their boys stood before them, wriggling under the flashing lights of the camera, he whispered, "I'm sorry."

And she said back, "I am too."

It was all they managed before Nadim interrupted just as the interview wrapped up.

"We need you on stage. The auction."

Yes, of course, the auction.

How had I possibly forgotten?

Bashir curbed the sarcastic thought when he felt Zaire and AJ hugging his legs. Just as much as he'd missed his wife, he'd missed his boys. Crouching down to them, he squeezed each of them back, and even let them stroke his longer beard as they liked to do.

Above him, he heard Yusra tell them, "Okay, boys, we have to let Daddy go. He's got work to do. We'll see him later."

Like the moon tempering the ocean's tides, his gaze was pulled up to her naturally. God, he wanted to kiss her. Take her in his arms and remind himself what she tasted like and how it had felt to hold her against him. But most of all he wanted to do as Otis advised: grovel until she took him back.

Until she understood that he loved her.

That he had already experienced what losing her felt like and he never wanted that feeling to return and haunt him ever again.

"I'll be back," he vowed to her. Pulling away felt like leaving a piece of him behind with her, to protect until he returned.

Up on the stage, Bashir found Yusra immediately. She was seated closer to the stage, their children, Alcina, Nadim, Otis and Evgenia at their table. He noticed the seat beside her was vacant, and his heart soared with the realization she'd left it open for him.

The auction consisted of various items from different suppliers. There were rare decorative vessels carbon-dating back to the time of ancient Greece. Artful mosaics from the time of Roman rule in Greece. And even a worn pair of leather sandals that purportedly belonged to the herald of the gods, Hermes himself. Laughable, but they sold well when they hit the auction block.

Yusra's friend Samira had also sent along some of her African artists' works to be auctioned to buyers tonight. And they were a surprise hit with the guests. The auction itself went by fast. The audience gave generously. One by one, each auctioned piece was sold to a new owner. Believing that they'd reached the end, Bashir was surprised when Nadim signaled from backstage that there was one more. An eleventh-hour entry according to the update he was given on the final auction item.

Explaining that the art piece was a portrait of hope from an artist who didn't know its subjects but knew that they had been a great part of the reason Halcyone was built, Bashir grew as mystified as the audience.

Hushed whispers of intrigue drifted up to him as the item was wheeled up.

With a nod from him, the attendants pulled off the covering to a collective gasp from everyone. Or at least that was what he heard, but he couldn't be certain with his ears ringing as much as they were.

He blinked several times and gawked at the familiarity of the scene. It was his family staring back at him from atop one of the many green cliff valleys of his home in Zákynthos. There were his mother and father, his grandparents, brothers and sisters. But others were with them. Imran and Tara. His cousin and cousin's wife stood very naturally in the portrait as if they had really posed for the artist.

Staring at Nadim's tablet, he could see there wasn't a note of who the artist was.

But he had one guess who it could be.

He needn't have searched for her; having memorized where she was seated, his eyes landed on her easily. Yusra. It had to be her. He had glimpsed her art, but he hadn't thought she could bring his long-gone family back to life for him. And he suspected she'd used the photos he had shown her as inspiration.

Coughing to clear his throat of the suspicious thickness of emotion that settled there, he adjusted his headset mic and addressed the audience.

"I'll open the bid with one million."

Now there was no denying the collective gasping in the room. It came at him from all angles. And why not? He'd just made the largest bid of the night, several thousand over estimate. At this rate, Halcyone was certain to open its doors to the public with tens of millions at its disposal.

"Going once. Going twice."

Bashir locked eyes with Yusra as he hit the gavel. "Sold."

The auction wrapped up, he thanked his guests for their generosity and walked offstage, and on his way to his seat, he noticed that Yusra had gotten up and disappeared just as dinner was being served.

"Outside," Otis and Evgenia said, knowing where Bashir wanted to be.

Yusra was sitting on a bench with a sea view.

"I don't know where to begin," he rasped, claiming the seat by her, and draping his arm over the back of the bench they shared.

Yusra's lips quirked into a teasing smile. "That was a staggering bid. Wasn't the whole point to get others to empty their pockets tonight, and not yours?"

"There was no way I would have let anyone walk away with that portrait."

"I'm sure that would make the artist happy to hear."

He stared at her, knowing he wasn't wrong when he said, "Then let me say this formally, so there's no misunderstanding—thank you. For the portrait. And for showing up and supporting this inaugural night."

Thank you for sticking by me.

Bashir didn't know if he stood a chance at having her around for longer, but he didn't want the sun rising on her not knowing that he loved her. It had been a love that had sneaked up on him. For so long, he had been cautious to give himself up to any emotion that could inflict harm on him. He had loved his family and Imran, and he lost all of them.

But I already lost Yusra these past few weeks.

And he would lose her forever if he allowed this reunion to slip him by.

Because he would rather have loved her than have lost her. Both were an inescapable fate, but only one could give him a lifetime of happiness to experience and fondly remember.

* * *

"Did I ever tell you the myth of Halcyone?"

"No, I don't believe so," Yusra replied and leaned into him once his arm pulled down from the back of the bench and over her shoulders. "I like stories though."

Bashir's smile glowed down on her.

"Halcyone and Ceyx were a vainglorious couple who believed their love was as strong and powerful as that of Hera and Zeus, the queen and king of the gods. Angering Zeus, they were both killed. Ceyx while he was fishing the sea where he drowned, and Halcyone in her grief at losing her husband tossed herself into the very same sea after him."

"That's so sad."

"The gods thought so too. So, they resurrected them as a pair of halcyon birds. I always liked the story because it inspired hope in the bleakest of times. It's why I felt it was a fitting name for the nonprofit." Bashir squeezed her closer, turning so her hand and face rested on his chest. "I missed you. I shouldn't have walked away from you. It's a mistake that haunts me."

Yusra's eyes pricked at his kind words. They echoed her sentiments, but she was fearful to trust them too quickly. What if she was wrong again? Then nothing would have changed, and their marriage would be doomed to unhappiness. She erred on the side of caution, guarded her heart instead and quietly said, "I got your gift. The brushes were very thoughtful of you."

"I'm glad you put them to good use." Bashir paused. A dreaded beat lapsed and then, "You brought my family back to life again. I didn't think it was possible. And yet you made it so."

For a moment, her big, brooding husband sat quietly, his gaze drifting from her to the night-darkened sea. Finally, he said, "I went into this marriage, fully committed to the fact that it would be purely practical for us to raise our sons together. I wasn't in it for romance and love. I won't lie. Right from the beginning I was attracted to you. But I thought that was all it could be. Then the more I got to know you, the more my admiration and affection for you grew.

"Frankly speaking, it scared me. For so long I'd sealed off that part of me that knew how to love that I wasn't sure what to do about it. Even with my experience raising Zaire and being his father, it didn't prepare me for a whole family. For AJ.

"For you, Yusra." He looked at her, and she felt her jaws slacken at the emotion playing on his features. She spotted fear, remorse, anticipation, and beneath all three, the admiration for her he spoke of.

"You could have walked away at any point. Yet you took my calls, and you let me speak to the boys and you're here now. I'm just wondering what I did to deserve you when I've been nothing but a coward lately."

"I was scared too," she admitted and sought his hand, entwining their fingers together. "For so long, I had learned to believe that love wasn't trustworthy or steadfast. But I was wrong. I trust you with our children, and I trust and like myself when I'm with you, Bashir. You've supported my art. You have been nothing but kind and giving since I met you." She laughed softly and rubbed his long, thick curly beard. "Okay, maybe I could do with a little less brooding, but even that's not enough to diminish my faith in you and our marriage."

"I don't want to lose you," he breathed, his usual composure crumbling and panic looking out at her.

"I'm not leaving," she whispered with a smile.

Bashir sagged back against the bench, relief stark on his face. He closed his eyes and murmured, "Give me a second. Hearing you say that after longing for it—I need time to process."

She couldn't help the giggle that slipped free.

He lazily opened his eyes and looked to her, a sexy smirk kicking up his mouth. His low laughter rumbled out slow and sweet. It fluttered over her skin, heating her from the outside in. And it lured her closer to him, enchanted by the way he was looking at her—like she meant the world to him.

Like I am his world.

That was all she needed to see to do what she wanted to from the beginning. Bashir had the same thought apparently as he leaned in and met her halfway.

Their kiss was an explosion of their combined need for each other. Pent-up frustration and yearning packed into thirty breathless seconds. Coming up for air was torture in its own way. She could have kissed him all night, and still not gotten enough.

Cradling her onto his lap, Bashir smoothed his hands down her back before wrapping his arms around her waist. He pecked her mouth. And in between kisses, he murmured, "I think I love you, Yusra Amin."

"You think?" She held him back with a hand to his chest; her eyebrows snapped up with an unspoken challenge, his lips kiss swollen and hers feeling equally and delightfully puffy from their display of affection. But she wouldn't be distracted. "Do you *think* or do you *know*?" Because there was a difference.

She *knew* she loved this man, to the living, healing, loving core of her.

Bashir laughed deeply. Closing his hand over hers on his chest, he spoke the words she wished to hear. "I love you, Yusra. I knew it when I ran away from you, and it might have taken me a while to admit it to myself, but I know now. Just as I know I won't ever stop loving you."

At that, her overjoyed laughter mingled with a sob or two, her cheeks home to a lot of happy tears. She hugged him tightly, her arms squeezing him closer, her heart impossibly full of the love she had for him. "I love you too," she laughed and cried at once. She drew back and covered him in kisses, moaning against his mouth, "You taste sweet," when he teased past her lips and explored her more intimately.

"It's *soumada*. I'll get you to taste some later."

She didn't want anything else but him right now. And she showed him with more affectionate caresses and kisses.

They might have stayed like that all night too—just as she wished, but a score of bright lights illuminated over the sea. She stared in shock as a swarm of multicolored lights spiraled in time with each other through the air. Squinting, she thought she saw...

"Drones?" she said in giddy wonder at the fireworks show without the pyrotechnics. Hundreds of the small, unmanned vehicles took to the air and began a coordinated synchronized show of kaleidoscopic lights.

"Ah, that would be my surprise. I found another use for the drones, now that Project Halcyone's construction is done." He regarded his expensive watch and hummed approvingly. "Good, they're perfectly timed."

And almost as perfectly, the sound of children's laughter floated over to where they were seated. "Is that...?"

A nod and grin from Bashir confirmed it. "The boys seem to have found us."

Yusra had all but a minute to scramble off Bashir's lap and straighten herself out. He smoothed his rumpled dress shirt and dinner jacket and straightened his crooked bow tie.

Alcina and Nadim carried the boys to them, leaving as soon as Yusra and Bashir had Zaire and AJ in their care.

Zaire hugged her, and AJ snuggled Bashir. Smiling over at each other, Bashir brushed her hand and she slid her palm into his. Together, they looked out over the sea where the unmanned drones created prismatic shapes and figures, their family complete and wondrously perfect.

And to think an accidental baby swap had brought them all of this.

EPILOGUE

A week later

"HAPPY BIRTHDAY!"

Amidst the congratulatory cheers, Yusra mimed blowing out the candles to show her newly minted three-year-old sons exactly how to do it. But even with their impressive attempts, AJ and Zaire couldn't blow out the flames on their jungle-themed chocolate cake. Bashir came to their rescue. He sneakily huffed at the cake, and *whoosh*, the candles were snuffed.

Everyone clapped and the birthday boys beamed at the attention they were getting.

Someone flicked the lights back on, and the cake was served. But not before Yusra and Bashir snapped family photos with their children.

"You're not smiling in this one," she said after seeing how the photo turned out. She tsked up at her husband. "We have to take it again."

Bashir waited until the first flash went off on the camera phone.

He then leaned down and kissed her on the cheek.

His hand slid discreetly from the small of her back to brush her backside. A flash went off just as her eyes widened and she snapped her head to him. She batted his hand away before he could weaken her knees any more than he already had. Ever since they had fully consummated their marriage, he had been even more insatiable than usual.

"I couldn't help myself," he said cheekily. But she couldn't take his apology seriously when his eyes twinkled mischievously. And before she could half-heartedly scold him, he scooped up Zaire and AJ and hurried away from her, back to their guests in a room festooned with yellow, green and brown balloons and streamers, potted palm trees and even an inflatable round pool filled with sand and beach toys. Bashir had wanted to bring in chimpanzees for the jungle-themed birthday party, but she'd talked him out of it. There would be enough to keep the boys occupied. They were only three, after all.

Despite anticipating leaving Greece once Bashir had successfully launched his nonprofit, Project Halcyone, they were still living at the villa in Zákynthos. After some discussion, she and Bashir decided to stay there for a little while longer. Their boys liked the tranquil island, and so did she. Eventually they would return to Uganda and finally look into purchasing a home together for their family. And she had one more reason to look forward to going back now: her art was being showcased in her friend Samira's gallery. Yusra had finally braved asking her friend to review her work, and it was like Bashir had said, Samira had immediately jumped on inviting her to join her upcoming, buzzy exhibition. Yusra would be one of many African artists showcased, and she couldn't think of a better way to celebrate her return to her art.

As the party wound down, Yusra began clearing up, but she paused to take a look around the room full of their friends and family. Otis and Evgenia, Nadim and Alcina, and others who had come to celebrate the day with her and Bashir and their family. She looked over to the projector screens, recalling them from her wedding day. This time they hadn't just been used to include her parents and siblings, but Bashir's aunt, uncle and many cousins in Somalia as well. Bashir had invited them virtually after finally reconnecting with the family he'd thought he had lost when he ran away from them.

She knew how hard it was for him to revisit the past, but he had done it for the sake of their children.

And he reminded her again when he found her alone in the kitchen after the gifts were unwrapped and the boys were left to play with their many new toys.

"Did you have a good time?" he asked and turned her to face him gently.

She pressed her hands to his taut abs. "I was just about to ask you the same thing."

"I did. The best part was having our families meet. I think my aunt and your mother will get along thick as thieves, and your father and my uncle will likely continue that spirited discussion of theirs on which is better—a coastal city or a country farm. Though I will say when we finally all are in one room together, they might be a bit too much to handle."

Yusra snorted laughter. And then she sighed blissfully and hugged him. "I love this for you."

"I love it for *us*. The boys should have all the family they can get. It's something I missed, but I don't want them to have the same past as me." He rubbed her back and embraced her closer. "I wouldn't have any of this without you."

"Me?" she squeaked up at him, shocked. "What did I do?"

Bashir gazed down at her, his eyes searching, probing. Then seemingly finding what he wanted in her, he huskily said, "I always thought I was happier alone. And then I met you. I forgot how good it felt to be loved, and now I also know what it means to be *in* love."

Yusra couldn't have agreed more.

* * * * *

COMING SOON!

We really hope you enjoyed reading this book. If you're looking for more romance be sure to head to the shops when new books are available on

Thursday 6th
July

To see which titles are coming soon, please visit

millsandboon.co.uk/nextmonth

MILLS & BOON

MILLS & BOON®

Coming next month

PREGNANT PRINCESS AT THE ALTAR
Karin Baine

"Your Majesty." He nodded to each in turn. "I know the circumstances are less than ideal and this morning's headlines haven't helped, but I don't think berating Gaia is going to fix things either. She needs our support."

"Do you comprehend the seriousness of impregnating my granddaughter out of wedlock, Mr Pernici?"

Neither of them had dared contradict the King's misunderstanding of the baby's parentage and Niccolo didn't think telling him there was another man involved would placate him in any way. If anything, it would further enrage him and Gaia didn't deserve any more of a pile-on.

"I understand that this is a very delicate matter—"

"Are you going to step up to your responsibilities and marry my granddaughter?"

"Pardon me?"

"Grandfather, no, Niccolo isn't—"

In that second Niccolo believed there was only one option available to both of them. A single deed which could save both of their reputations and save them from any more of the King's ire. It didn't matter what he did to try and distance himself from the whole scandal, as far as everyone was concerned he was involved.

"Yes, we're getting married," he announced, surprising himself as much as everyone else in the room. He put an arm around Gaia's shoulders and she leaned into him as if he were the only thing keeping her upright.

The only way he could see to salvage his reputation and his livelihood before they were ground into the dirt again was to act as though he *was* this baby's father. It wasn't a role he'd ever wanted, and he didn't know how he was going to fake his way through it. He would have to embrace the part completely. Having an emotionally distant parent was as damaging as losing one. Gaia's baby didn't deserve to feel as though it was a burden, so he would have to come to terms with accepting complete responsibility for this child and not simply be a token father figure. He had no intention of imitating his dad but it wasn't going to be easy raising someone else's child. Especially in these circumstances, where he'd been forced into a corner if he wanted to keep his career and the life he'd just got back.

Continue reading
PREGNANT PRINCESS AT THE ALTAR
Karin Baine

Available next month
www.millsandboon.co.uk

Copyright © 2023 Karin Baine

LET'S TALK

Romance

For exclusive extracts, competitions and special offers, find us online:

f MillsandBoon

🐦 @MillsandBoon

📷 @MillsandBoonUK

♪ @MillsandBoonUK

Get in touch on 01413 063 232

For all the latest titles coming soon, visit
millsandboon.co.uk/nextmonth

MILLS & BOON

THE HEART OF ROMANCE

A ROMANCE FOR EVERY READER

MODERN

Prepare to be swept off your feet by sophisticated, sexy and seductive heroes, in some of the world's most glamourous and romantic locations, where power and passion collide.

HISTORICAL

Escape with historical heroes from time gone by. Whether your passion is for wicked Regency Rakes, muscled Vikings or rugged Highlanders, awaken the romance of the past.

MEDICAL

Set your pulse racing with dedicated, delectable doctors in the high-pressure world of medicine, where emotions run high and passion, comfort and love are the best medicine.

True Love

Celebrate true love with tender stories of heartfelt romance, from the rush of falling in love to the joy a new baby can bring, and a focus on the emotional heart of a relationship.

Desire

Indulge in secrets and scandal, intense drama and sizzling hot action with heroes who have it all: wealth, status, good looks…everything but the right woman.

HEROES

The excitement of a gripping thriller, with intense romance at its heart. Resourceful, true-to-life women and strong, fearless men face danger and desire - a killer combination!

To see which titles are coming soon, please visit

millsandboon.co.uk/nextmonth

JOIN US ON SOCIAL MEDIA!

Stay up to date with our latest releases, author news and gossip, special offers and discounts, and all the behind-the-scenes action from Mills & Boon...

 @millsandboon

 @millsandboonuk

 facebook.com/millsandboon

 @millsandboonuk

It might just be true love...

MILLS & BOON
A ROMANCE FOR EVERY READER

- FREE delivery direct to your door
- EXCLUSIVE offers every month
- SAVE up to 30% on pre-paid subscritions

SUBSCRIBE AND SAVE

millsandboon.co.uk/Subscribe

MILLS & BOON

MODERN

Power and Passion

Prepare to be swept off your feet by sophisticated, sexy and seductive heroes, in some of the world's most glamourous and romantic locations, where power and passion collide.

Eight Modern stories published every month, find them all at:

millsandboon.co.uk